The Milky Way
{Bel Tra Chart Pack XVII}

☆ ?

Drenard

☆ Lok

Palan ☆

Glemot ☆   ☆ ?   ☆ Dakura

Darrin ☆

Canopus ☆ Menkar ☆
                  Sol ☆

|—— 20K LY ——|———— 100,000 Light Years ————|

molly fyde
and the parsona rescue

THE
BERN SAGA:
BOOK 1

by hugh howey

Molly Fyde
and the Parsona Rescue

Copyright © 2013 by Hugh Howey

All rights reserved. No part of this book may be reproduced in any form by any electronic or mechanical means including photocopying, recording, or information storage and retrieval without permission in writing from the author.

ISBN: 1481222880
ISBN-13: 9781481222884

www.hughhowey.com

Give feedback on the book at:
hughhowey@hotmail.com

Second Edition

Printed in the U.S.A.

To Amber

PART 1
THE TCHUNG AFFAIR

*"It started with a nightmare.
And the nightmare became a dream.
Then the dream became real..."*

~The Bern Seer~

1

Molly floated in the vacuum of space with no helmet on—with no protection at all. In the distance, a starship slowly drifted away. It was her parents' ship, and they were leaving her behind.

She swam in the nothingness, trying to keep them in view, but as always she spun around and faced the wrong direction. It was the only torment the old nightmare had left. After years of waking up—screaming, crying, soaked in her own sweat—she had whittled it down to this.

She gave up fighting for one last glimpse and tried to relax, to find some breath of peace. They were out there, even if she couldn't see them. And as long as she stayed asleep, suffocating and alone, her parents remained among the stars. *Alive.*

"Molly."

A voice pierced the dream. Molly cracked her eyes and blinked at her surroundings. Beyond the carboglass cockpit loomed a scene similar to her nightmare but filled with a fleet of Navy ships. The fire of their thrusters blended with the stars beyond, little twinkles of plasma across the stark black.

"Gimme a sec," she mumbled, rubbing her eyelids before snapping her visor shut. She scanned the constellation of lights and readouts across the dashboard and over her head. She could see at a glance that everything was in order. This spread of twinkling indicators and glowing dials was as familiar to her as any star chart, as recognizable as a loved one's face.

"Take your time. Your shift's not up for another ten."

She turned in her nav seat to face Cole Mendonça, her pilot for the last two years. Molly sat to his right in the Firehawk's "girlie" seat, a term meant to motivate the boys from flunking out of flight school and ending up as lowly navigators. All the insult did for Molly was infuriate her—she'd never even been given the *chance* to fail.

"Another ten? Drenards, Cole, then why'd you wake me?"

"I wanted you to see something. I just sent it over. Check the first tab."

Molly frowned at her pilot and pulled the reader out of its pouch. She resented not being able to fly, but she had a hard time taking it out on Cole. Partly because he had earned his position, but mostly because she considered him a friend. And in the male-dominated galaxy in which she lived and operated, these were as rare as habitable worlds.

She yawned and tried to stretch as much as the flight harness would allow. If only civilians knew how boring space flight truly was. All they ever saw were the buzzing battles on the Military Channel, the great swarms of spacecraft darting through torrents of laser fire. In reality, flying for the Navy mostly meant dull chores: astronavigation and chart plotting, taking turns on flight shifts while your partner grabbed precious few winks, and digital paperwork. *Lots* of digital paperwork.

"What exactly am I looking at?" she asked. She assumed Cole was going to have her perform some more clerical heroics.

"It's our system update log. Read it."

She turned to Cole, her fears confirmed. "You woke me up for an *update log*?"

"Read it," he insisted, facing her. With his mirrored visor down, only his lips were visible, pursed with worry. Molly heard the AC unit in her flightsuit whir to life, whisking away her excess body heat. She glanced up at the reflection in his visor. Both helmets repeated themselves over and over in a series of infinite regressions. She tried to follow herself as she receded into the indiscernibly diminutive.

"Firehawk GN-KPX to Molly Fyde, come in," Cole said mockingly. "Can you read me? Over."

Molly pulled her gaze away from the familiar illusion of reflections and focused on the reader.

"Well?" he asked.

"Gimme a sec, would you?"

She skimmed the report, not sure what to look for. It was standard stuff from the IT department: a software upload to their ship four days ago by Specialist Second Class Mitchell and signed off by Commander Hearst. A few bugs fixed, some navigational data updated. None of it warranted the worry in Cole's voice.

"I don't see the problem," she said.

"That's because I haven't shown it to you yet. I just wanted you to see *that* before I presented *this*." With an unnecessary flourish, Cole pulled up the Firehawk's diagnostic information on the main screen of the dash.

It took a second for Molly to see it. She gaped at him in disbelief and annoyance. "Are you serious? You're worked up over *this*?" She jabbed a finger at the time of their computer's most recent update. It said the fourteenth. Yesterday. Two days later than the maintenance report suggested. She groaned. "I'm sure it's just an input error, Cole." She flipped the tab shut on her reader and stuffed it away. "And I was having such a good dream, too."

"First of all, you don't have good dreams. I know because you mumble in your sleep. Secondly, the reason I tracked down the report was 'cause I was *already* suspicious. I saw someone tampering with our Firehawk this morning. You're looking at the *confirmation*, not the clue."

"And why would someone tamper with our ship?"

"Now *that's* the mystery," he agreed. "Hopefully just someone messing with us. Jakobs, maybe. Whoever it was had his build. Man, I should've suspected something and taken a closer look. Still, what in the galaxy would someone be doing updating our ship's programming? Who even knows how to do that outside of IT?"

Cole's voice lowered to a conspiratorial whisper. He was enjoying this entirely too much. "And what if it isn't a practical joke?" he asked. "What if it's something . . . *worse?*"

Molly nearly burst out laughing. Once Cole's brain concocted a good conspiracy theory, there was no stopping him. She'd seen it play out dozens of times, him always jumping to conclusions with the barest of facts. It used to bother her, but then she figured out that this habit of his—playing connect-the-dots without bothering to read the numbers—was better than any game of Drenards or Dare. When Cole drew what he *wanted* to see, rather than what was actually there, that's when Molly learned the most about him.

"Hey, it's my shift," she said, too tired to egg him on or argue. "Why don't you take a nap and try dreaming in your *sleep* for a change."

Cole opened his mouth to launch a witty comeback—but he never got the chance. Because that's when the long tedium of astronavigating from point A to point B came to an abrupt end.

And the part people see on the Military Channel finally began.

○ ○ ○ ○

Intelligence reports had projected an enemy force of a dozen, tops. The fleet had subsequently planned for two dozen, just to be safe. What winked out of hyperspace was several times this. So many that Molly didn't have time to count them visually. Even her SADAR unit had difficulty teasing the clusters into individual targets. Fifty fighters? Half a dozen heavy bombers?

Cole slammed the Firehawk to full throttle, and Molly felt her chest constrict as the flightsuit struggled to compensate. Millions of tiny pockets pushed anti-grav fluid wherever it was needed, offsetting the shift in acceleration. With the suits and their conditioning, Molly and Cole could tolerate forces that would normally tear the human body apart. Which was precisely how it felt at times.

"We have three fighters breaking off for a flanking maneuver," she noted. She kept her gaze locked on the targets while her gloved hand pressed buttons by her thigh. The representations of all three enemy ships blossomed with an orange glow for Cole to consider.

"I see 'em," he said, peeling off to intercept.

Riggs—their wingman in the neighboring Firehawk—locked in as well. The two ships coursed across the formation to head off the threat, even as the acting fleet commander barked orders for all craft to engage in a full-frontal attack.

Molly watched as Riggs's Firehawk wavered on SADAR, their wingman torn between two duties, two disparate layers of command. Cole's hand never twitched on the flight controls. He ignored the fleet commander in favor of Molly's threat assessment, and the two Firehawks continued to barrel after the trio of enemy fighters.

"We're gonna come in pretty hot," he warned, his voice calm and soothing considering what they were up against. Riggs answered back on their private channel, his choice made. Meanwhile, along the front line, streaks of plasma jolted across the gap between the two fleets. Fired by the jittery and eager, these premature tendrils lanced out with no chance of inflicting damage, not at such a vast range.

The three targets Molly had chosen were trying to get around the fleet. The combination of superior numbers and crossfire would end the fight before it ever truly began. Glancing at her SADAR, she saw two other enemy groups pulling the same maneuver on opposite sides of the fleet. None of the other Firehawks were responding. She broadcast a warning on the emergency channel, more concerned with the threat than she was with violating rank and protocol. A chorus of male voices shouted her down, all of them insisting the main fleet body remain in formation, some of them telling her to shut the hell up.

Molly ignored the insults. The threat of encirclement was there. It *had* to be taken seriously, even if this meant thinning the formation before the first casualties were suffered.

Cole and Riggs seemed to agree. They closed in on their targets, still out of effective laser and missile range, but the gap was rapidly decreasing. Thanks to the quick response, they had a great angle on their enemies' trajectory. They would easily cut them off.

The trio of enemy pilots realized this as well. The craft nearest them altered course, whirling around with incredible speed and precision. It darted for Cole and Riggs, one ship bearing down on two in a suicidal gambit designed to buy his partners some time.

"Lock missiles." Cole's voice hinted at the first sign of strain.

Molly's fingers danced across the targeting console; the orange triangle around the attacker turned red. "Firing," she said, pulling the trigger.

Nothing happened. Confused and flushed with heat, Molly looked at her controls and checked the safety overrides. Everything was green. It took a moment for her brain to go through the reasonable explanations. When it ran out of them, it considered Cole's silly conspiracy theory—and how it didn't seem quite so silly anymore.

"We've got a problem!" she yelled.

The first volley of enemy laser lashed out at Riggs on their starboard side. At this distance, it was easy to avoid. Cole rolled away to give his wingman more room, his foul language suggesting a similar problem with the lasers that Molly was having with the missiles. Without weapons, they'd be useless out there. Defanged. Flying nothing more than a scout ship in the biggest naval engagement of their young lives. Molly tried in vain to comprehend the nightmare they were in.

And then it got worse.

The fighter bearing down on them spun away from Riggs and launched a volley at Cole, and he was too distracted with the malfunctioning lasers to respond. Molly nearly got out a warning before the glancing blow struck the nose of their ship.

The cockpit flashed for a moment and then went dark. The Firehawk fell into a flat, lifeless spin, its nose slowly pointing back to the fleet. All three thrusters were knocked out and off-line. As the lights on the dash winked out, the other lights beyond the cockpit became vivid and bright. The stars and pink nebulae beyond the fighting glowed with intense beauty, while the laser blasts directed at their wingman bloomed something sinister.

The next volley flashed by their cockpit, illuminating the interior with a red pall of death before slamming into Riggs's Firehawk head-on. His ship blossomed silently into the glowing cloud of debris and flaming ash that Molly had come to associate with a Navy death.

So quick.

The enemy craft flew past the carnage it had created, whipping the fine particles in its thruster's wake. It seemed impossible, but Molly swore she could hear the ship screaming across the vacuum of space as it circled around—preparing for a run on her lifeless and useless ship.

○ ○ ○ ○

"Cole!" Molly shook his arm, but there was no response. She leaned forward and initiated a cold boot of every system, hoping some of their defenses would come back on-line. Anything.

To Molly's astonishment, the entire dash lit up. The laser blasts had locked up the computers and knocked out Cole, but the ship was coming back to life. Even the thruster control indicators winked from red to amber. In ten minutes she'd have propulsion again—if she could just hold out that long.

She took a deep breath and wrapped her left hand around the flight controls. Situated between her and Cole, the controls catered to the 82 percent of pilots who favored their right hand. Incredibly and unfortunately, this was one area in which Molly could be considered "normal." Despite hours of practice from the nav seat, she would never fly as well from that side of the cockpit as she could with her dominant hand.

The large propulsion thrusters at the rear of her Firehawk were still warming up, but she had control of the maneuvering jets. Molly used them to swing the Firehawk around, squeezing the trigger as she did so, hoping the reboot had fixed the weapons glitch.

Nothing. And now she *knew* this was no accident. Cole's conspiracy theory had grown legs—they kicked her for not listening.

Ahead, the enemy craft completed its victory lap around the dispersing nebula left by Riggs's Firehawk. The first bolts of red laser winked from the sleek fighter and raced her way. Molly used the maneuvering jets to shift sideways. Her right hand flinching as her left hand worked, the dominant side of her squirming to help, to take over for its feeble partner. Molly screamed Cole's name once more, hoping to rouse him, but he didn't respond.

The approaching ship released another burst from its cannon as it raced toward her on a vector straight as a taut string. Molly maneuvered the Firehawk to the side, dodging the attacks. The bolts of plasma slid by her canopy, missing her by a handful of meters. She glanced at them with envy. She was being toyed with. Chewed on and released like a wounded animal.

The oncoming ship released one last round of laser fire from close range; Molly barely had time to react. She spiraled the Firehawk in place, the violence of the maneuver yanking her against her flight harness, her head snapping around with the weight of her helmet. When she came to a rest, her attacker flew by so close she could see the glint of his visor through the windshield. She wanted to throw something, *anything*, at him.

The ship circled wide for another run while Molly rotated her Firehawk to follow. If she could survive one more pass, she'd have the main thrusters back. But she couldn't rely on her enemy's ineptitude; she needed to *act*.

The next round of enemy fire approached. Molly resumed the dangerous dance, stepping side to side as beams of potential death raced by. It made her feel like one of Cole's Portuguese cavaleiros trying to survive multiple passes by an enraged bull. The only difference: Molly was all cape and no sword.

This image gave her an idea. She pulled up the service modules and flight deck routines—they all seemed to be working. She might not be able to *arm* her missiles, but she wouldn't *need* to. Another round of deadly red ribbons reached out to her. She slipped expertly to one side. With her other hand, she brought up the docking interface and lowered her landing gear.

Molly performed some dirty calculations in her head. With the craft bearing down on her along a fixed vector, she was able to roughly determine where it would pass her. The landing gear extended fully, and the deck routines went from grayed-out to a selectable yellow. With the twist of a dial, Molly highlighted the missile unload commands. As far as the ship knew, they were in a hangar bay preparing to unload munitions—not moments away from being mauled by a raging bull.

Her enemy was a few thousand meters out, closing at a high but steady velocity. The laser fire became more intense, reaching toward her in a rapid volley. Molly twisted the Firehawk, trying to fit it inside the pattern of deadly plasma. One of the wings took a hit, a minor burn but a reminder that her time was running out. The bull prepared to roar past.

Molly darted across its path and thumbed a switch, releasing a single missile from the Firehawk's belly. She may have been a harmless cape swishing in space, but behind her, an unarmed and inert hunk of metal like a gleaming sword was left in the bull's path. A sword to impale itself on.

The enemy never saw what hit him. The missile impacted the cockpit right where the glint of visor had been, tore through the center of the ship, and ruptured the rear of the vessel, sending out large chunks of debris. Her Firehawk's tail was knocked to one side, slamming her into her harness, and Molly fought with the flight controls to keep out of a spin.

After a tense moment, she regained full control of the ship.

Her ship.

Molly elbowed Cole, whooping with delight, but the life support readouts showed her the awful truth: She was alone.

The thruster indicators went from amber to green.

Molly gave them a test, feeling the acceleration add more weight to an already heavy chest. Out of immediate danger, she took a moment to survey the flow of battle on SADAR. The blue and green dots were no longer approaching one another in separate spheres. They intermingled, swirling in pairs until one of them disappeared.

Her side was fighting nobly, but the three sets of flanking craft were closing in for what would soon be a massacre. And there wasn't much Molly could do to help.

She should run. She would score points with the higher-ups simply for surviving—for saving Navy hardware. But she couldn't help but wonder if there was something she could do for the fleet. Would an act of creative heroism prove what she already knew? That she more than belonged out here with the *boys*?

Molly's hand came off the throttle. She started spinning up the Firehawk's hyperdrive, instead. She wondered what "the boys" would make of this next idea.

They'd probably tell her she'd lost her mind. By every standard of common sense, jumping through hyperspace during a battle was the height of folly. To travel through hyperspace safely, you had to account for every object on *both* sides of the jump. Even a small gravitational disturbance could deflect you off course, or worse, suck you in.

Another danger was that objects in "real" space have dibs—they can't be dislodged by something else. Try to occupy the same coordinates as even a tiny object, like the millions of chunks of debris surrounding a space battle, and no one would even notice your attempt. You'd just vanish. To where, nobody knew.

These were the dangers. Navy instructors only had to go over them once. After that, everyone just *knew* not to try what she was contemplating.

But her fleet faced certain destruction, pops of orange violence burst in the distance as her wingmates succumbed to superior numbers. Cole and Riggs were gone. There was no one there to talk sense into her. And by the moment, she was growing convinced her Firehawk had been sabotaged, tampered with. She was living on borrowed time, which made suicidal risks suddenly worth calculating.

Checking her SADAR, Molly saw a pocket of space between the two remaining enemy craft flanking her fleet and made an approximate calculation. Crossing one set of fingers, she punched in the hyperspace commands with the other. It was her second game of chicken in less than a minute.

Once again, she didn't hesitate.

OOOO

The stress of entering hyperspace was topped only by the pain of *leaving* it. The nausea and panic attacks engendered by a successful jump were likened to a bombardment of loud bass sounds. Many pilots never developed an immunity to the discomfort, and Molly was one of them. She often fought to hide the severity of her reaction. This time, however, she reveled in it.

The pain meant she was *alive*.

But a glance at her surroundings didn't inspire much hope for remaining this way. She stood between the fleet and the two flanking ships, and they were closing in fast. Their lasers lanced out greetings at her unexpected arrival. Molly flinched, shoving the ship sideways and away from the attack. She powered up the glorious thrusters and raced parallel to her fleet, presenting a target that moved side to side.

The cape-and-sword gambit would never work with these guys. There were two sets of crossing laser fire to avoid. And surely they were aware of their fallen comrade by now, which meant she couldn't rely on them underestimating her. This was confirmed as each enemy craft spat out a missile keyed to her ship's signature.

Molly took the gesture as a compliment.

She keyed up her defense menus and scrolled to the missile chaff.

Four pods were stowed in the rear of her Firehawk, each capable of emulating her ship's signature. Dropping one at a time should negate this new threat, but the delay in dealing with the missiles would prevent her from protecting the fleet. Precisely what her enemy intended.

When the chaff menu came up, "drop" was selectable from the chaff menu, but not the "arm" command. The sabotage had been extremely sophisticated. The pods were useless.

Molly cursed and pulled on the flight stick, sending her Firehawk back on an arc toward the two ships.

Their incoming missiles altered course slightly to hone in on her. There was no way she could outmaneuver them.

But Molly had another crazy idea. She recognized the old Tchung ship designs they were up against. If the missiles were Tchung as well, they had a design flaw she could exploit: their homing software was slightly more advanced than their thrusters. They could *think* faster than they could *turn*. Normally, this wasn't a problem, as it required extreme velocities before the limitation became a factor, and most targets were wise enough to move *away* from missiles.

Molly came about as sharply as she could, forcing out puffs of air against the Gs. She pushed forward on the accelerator. Once again, she was prepared to stand in doom's path in an attempt to escape it. Cole's stillness made it easier—she was only gambling with her *own* life.

Molly shook her head and focused outside the cockpit's carboglass. Beyond the two incoming missiles, she watched her prey speed toward her fleet. They weren't wasting time following up the missiles with laser-fire. Their primary objective was reaching the Navy's unguarded rear.

She wished she had time to appreciate the skill behind the tactics, but the missiles were closing in too fast. Molly just hoped it was fast *enough*. She did more dirty math. Her suit could take around 40 Gs; her body could probably withstand a dozen more. At her current rate of acceleration, twenty degrees was as much as she could alter direction without crushing her brain against the inside of her skull. It wasn't a large vector change; she'd have to wait until the very last second—fraction of a second, even.

That sort of timing required as much luck as skill. The window was so small, the delay between *thinking* and *doing* could get her killed. Her left hand twitched slightly in awkward anticipation. Molly wished Cole were the one trying this.

The missiles were nearly upon her, or she was almost on them. Her danger-sense warned her prematurely—screaming at Molly to alter course *now*. She fought the urge, waiting until it felt too late. Only then did she issue the command to her left hand, feeling it move a millisecond later.

The nose of the Firehawk deflected up the programmed twenty degrees. The missiles vanished from view past the carboglass of her cockpit. Her body was pummeled by the radical shift in gravities.

Molly tensed up, partly to protect herself from the violent force of dozens of Gs, and partly in anticipation of a sudden death.

The corners of her vision turned black. The blood in her brain forced itself into her chest. The ring of darkness tightened until she was peering through a straw.

Molly Fyde passed out.

2

When she came to, Molly feared the battle was already over. But before she could shake the fog out of her brain, she realized she'd only been out a few seconds. The two missiles were still out there—seeking her ship's signature. SADAR confirmed this as a curving line that had zipped right past her and was now pulling around toward her new vector, the missiles so close to each other they may as well have been one.

Molly straightened her ship back up and raced off for the enemy craft. The precision of the missile attack had saved her. If either projectile had lagged behind the other, she would've dodged the first and eaten the second. For the second time, her enemy's accuracy had meant her salvation.

At full thrust, she chased down the two ships and took a moment to survey the flow of battle. Her side wasn't doing half-bad to be so outnumbered. The additional sets of flankers posed the biggest threat as they worked their way around the other sides of the fleet. Her squad mates finally moved to head them off, their slower response negating their functioning weapons systems. They would be too late to do anything about the encirclement, while Molly and Cole had been swift enough but *powerless*.

It appeared the Navy forces would be wiped out in a battle for the ages, but it might take longer than Molly had initially thought. It was enough to force a grim smile, as sick and sore as her body felt. The Navy geeks who enjoyed scoring these encounters would have a blast with this one.

She returned her focus to the ships ahead of her and the lovely, zooming gifts they'd left behind. She brought up the nav calculator, temporarily comforted by her usual duties. The thrill of playing "pilot" had been tempered somewhat by the pressure of being responsible. A small part of her missed the warm embrace of being a role player. *I'll do my simple tasks and let someone else risk failing*, she thought, and then pushed it to the back of her mind. She needed to concentrate on the numbers.

Three moving objects. It was a word problem flight instructors would adore. They'd be able to phrase it so no pilot would understand what in hyperspace was going on. Molly knew better than to make this more confusing than it needed to be. There were really two different problems here, and each could be solved individually.

First, she plotted the speed and direction of her ship and the two flankers. This gave her the coordinate in space at which they would meet if she kept gaining on them. Next, she did the same for her Firehawk and the missiles speeding toward her thrusters. This gave her another set of coordinates. She hoped the first point in space would be nearer than the second, giving her a chance to hurt *them* before they hurt *her*.

But the plots didn't show that. In fact, Molly thought she'd done something wrong. Only a single nav result showed up on her display. She started to run the calculations a second time when she recognized the improbable: both problems had the *same solution*. She would reach her enemy at the precise moment their missiles reached *her*. A ship overtaking two ships, being overtaken by their projectiles.

And maybe this wasn't a *bad* thing.

She only had half a minute to prepare for impact. She pulled the defense menus up one more time and drilled down to the useless chaff screen. She might not be able to arm them, but maybe she could give her ship a bit of a buffer. It helped that the flankers were now in firing range of the fleet. Distracted with laser-fire from the Navy, they weren't keeping a vigilant eye on their rears. Molly and the two missiles zipped down their wake, all three players set to meet at a single point.

Worst-case scenario: the missiles take her out just as she arrives between the other two ships. The blast would vaporize her, but it should also take her foes out of the fight. If she ended up with three dead bogeys after entering a battle with no offensive capabilities, Molly would consider it a victory of the highest order.

The best-case scenario was too much to wish for, but it had all four of her chaff canisters deploying and the missiles making impact, saving her cockpit from the blast and directing the force to the enemies on either side. It was yet another bold stunt with slim chances, but Molly decided to keep gambling while she was on a lucky streak.

As she entered the thruster-wash of the enemy, she placed her thumb over the release button. Time slowed to a silent crawl. The laser fire ahead of the flankers seemed to spurt forward like drips of red molasses. Everything moved so slowly that none of it appeared threatening, as if she could reach out and just pluck the hot plasma from outer space.

And then she was there, riding the wake of the two ships, buffeted in their thruster-wash. Her thumb twitched a command, releasing the useless chaff.

The missiles made impact, an orange glow wrapping its silent arms around her Firehawk.

And for the second time that day, Molly's world went black.

○ ○ ○ ○

"Molly."

It was Cole's voice.

Her vision returned, the black in front of her visor opening like a camera's iris to reveal the battle raging ahead. Their Firehawk was still partly intact, the protective shell of a cockpit drifting through space with twisted hunks of metal trailing behind. Her life support readout indicated that she was dead.

"Damnit!" Molly slammed a fist into the flight controls, hurting her hand more than she did the simulator.

Cole reached his gloved hand over and patted her thigh, trying to comfort her. "What're you so upset about? You did *good*, girl. Those other two ships caught most of the blast. They're goners."

Molly glanced at Cole. A smirk peeked out below his visor. She smiled back, a bit reluctantly. "Huh. I guess you're right. I was hoping I'd keep getting lucky. What the hell happened to you?"

Cole tried to shrug his shoulders in the flight harness. "I dunno. The simulator said I was dead, so I must've been. Didn't make sense from the damage we sustained, but *nothing* about this exercise makes sense. Oh, and by the way, my suit ignored the fact that I was lifeless and gave me the same Gs you took in that missile maneuver. Remind me to beat your ass later."

She pouted. "Yeah? Did Cole get a tummy ache?"

Cole laughed, and the joke lingered in the cockpit for a few minutes. On the screen, the remainder of their fleet tried in vain to stave off defeat. Gradually, the humor faded, and they started asking more questions. Serious questions. They went back to the conversation they were having before the exercise went hot, Molly more open this time to Cole's conspiracies.

When the last Navy ship tried to flee, there were still seven fully functional enemy craft left for the mop-up. The cadets wouldn't find out until the debriefing which race they were up against today, but Molly already suspected the Tchung. More tax dollars spent training against a non-enemy, a race no one had seen for generations.

The last Navy ship was surrounded, creating a traitorous feeling of anticipation. The end of this exercise would bring relief. Being dead and having to watch her fellow cadets struggle to extend the inevitable made Molly's entire body twitch. It was like her right hand trying to pilot from the nav side of the cockpit. Finally, with a puff of orange pixels, the battle was over. The panorama of carnage went black, and one horror replaced another: the summation screen showing the casualty and damage reports. It wasn't supposed to be a scoreboard, or taken as a game, but that's how the students saw it. All but one of them were boys. Comparing anything *measurable* was their favorite pastime.

Molly scanned the list from top to bottom. Jakobs/Dinks sat on top with 2.5 confirmed kills, which meant one of their enemy had taken damage from another crew. They also had a wingman assist and a tactical bonus for recognizing the flow of battle and reacting properly. Subtracting their eventual death left them with 550 points. Not too bad a score, considering.

Down at the very bottom was Cole/Fyde with zero kills, an unassisted wingman penalty, three tactical violations, and a self-kill. With a score of -2080 rendered in bright red, it made everyone else look as if they knew what in hyperspace they were doing.

Cole shook his head and patted Molly's gloved fist with his. Her AC revved up to whisk away her body heat, partly rising from the shame of the score and partly—from something else.

A window on the right side of the summation screen opened up, and Captain Saunders scowled back at the cadets, his round and oversized head resting on rolls of fat. "Not bad, boys."

Molly cringed at the masculine pronoun, a military staple.

"This exercise is meant to test your endurance and teamwork. Two days of sleeping in shifts before a battle is the real deal. This is what any of you who actually graduate and fly for us can expect. We've been putting senior flight crews through this exact maneuver for over thirty years. Those numbers look bad, some of them especially, but you'll be pleased to hear you've fared better than any other class since I've been here.

"Too bad you're all dead," he added sarcastically. "Not screwing up worse than previous generations of know-nothings means I don't want to hear you celebrating. If more of you had recognized the real danger was the flanking craft and not the main body, we could've seen this scenario defeated, a feat *real* Navy pilots pull off in their sleep. But it's hard to match their coordinated defense with twitchy trigger fingers on some of you and inoperable ones on others.

"The three bottom crews need to report to me immediately for a dressing down; the rest of you hit the showers then start writing up your failure reports. And I want to read what you did wrong, not excuses for *why you* did it wrong. The real winners today were the Tchung, so don't feel proud for getting lucky. Dismissed."

With that, the screens went translucent, and Molly stared out at the familiar wall of cinder blocks. Out her starboard side porthole a line of cramped simulator pods stretched out for a hundred meters. Their hatches popped open almost in unison, but she couldn't hear them—their hatch was still shut.

Molly snapped her helmet off and looked at Cole. He held his own helmet in his lap, his face serious.

"I don't care what they say, you did great."

"Thanks." Molly loaded the word with sarcasm and rolled her eyes. If she ever allowed herself to take a compliment from Cole, her face would betray the way she felt about him. It was the only thing she had in common with these boys: the need to be mean in order to keep her distance.

"I'm serious. Another thing: let's keep the sabotage business to ourselves for now. All they need to know is that the weapons systems were off-line. They should adjust our score for that. Get rid of that bogus wingman penalty, at least."

"Sure thing, *Captain*." The half-smile turned into a full one, even if it was forced.

"You know, it's not really a sign of respect when you say it like that." Cole grinned and popped the hatch, letting in the sound of soldier boots as they clanged down the metal platforms outside the musky, slept-in simulators.

Jakobs and Dinks loitered by the rear of their pod. Molly could guess why.

"Nice shooting out there," Jakobs said, smiling from ear to ear with the demented visage of the sleep-deprived. "Oh, I'm sorry, you never even got a shot *off*, didja?" He checked with Dinks, who validated his joke with a silent, breathy laugh.

Molly glared at Jakobs. "Your lapdog is panting," she said. "Does he need some water?" She tried to push past them, but Jakobs grabbed her arm, spinning her around.

They glared at one another while the other two boys sized up the situation. Jakobs was tall for a seventeen-year-old, and he had the sort of good looks that inspired poor behavior in boys. He'd been getting away with figurative murder his entire life—soon the Navy would pay him to do it for real.

"Go to hyperspace," she told him.

"Flank you," he said, his dark eyes sparkling with a glint of superiority. Molly knew better. He bullied for acceptance, scaring people into liking him. She focused on his Roman nose and dreamed about punching it.

"Go watch the replay, ass'troid." Cole spat the words and tugged Molly away from trouble. She wondered if he was sticking up for *her* or protecting Jakobs from a beating. And if he was defending her, was it simply as his navigator?

She turned and marched out of the simulator room with her eyes fixed straight ahead, the rims of her ears burning. The hyperspace nausea, induced with subsonic bass speakers, churned up her stomach acid. Or maybe that was just Jakobs and Dinks.

From behind, the duo kept hounding her during the long walk down the hallway. She couldn't hear them over the pounding of her own pulse, but she could see the effects of their taunting. Sneers of petty delight spread across the faces of every cadet they walked by. Everyone was ignoring Saunders's commands, reveling in how well they'd done.

All except for the Academy reject, of course.

oooo

Outside Captain Saunders's office, Molly and Cole joined Peters and Simons on a well-worn wooden bench. The four clustered together, shoulders touching, as muffled shouts wormed their way through the wall panels. It was somehow worse that they couldn't make out specific words. The Captain's tone was more torturous—raw and full of all kinds of nasty potential.

At the tirade's end, a moment of silence descended as excuses were likely made. Everyone on the bench could imagine the lame apologies; they were all busy rehearsing their own. The door opened with a slight click, and two despondent students shuffled out, not even pausing to wish their comrades luck.

As second-worst performers, Peters and Simons went in next. The muffled shouting resumed. The space between Molly and Cole felt more oppressive and stuffy than the crowded bench had seemed just moments ago. She wanted to talk, but she could tell Cole didn't. It was like being back in the cockpit—next to his corpse. She needed a partner, but he was unable to reciprocate thanks to some external command to do nothing—that pressure from the other boys in the Academy to see her as a girl in every way but the one that mattered.

Or was it an *internal* command Cole felt? Was it a complete lack of the type of feelings Molly had to force herself to keep in check?

There was a third and far worse possibility: Maybe he felt the same way and kept waiting for *her* to engage, while Molly's need to be a man amongst boys prevented her from finding out.

A period of silence jolted her back to her senses, and she and Cole sat up as straight as possible. After another round of muted apologies, the door clicked, and the two boys filed out of the office. Simons glanced over his shoulder at Molly. The beat look on his face made her want to rush to him—give him a hug and tell him everything was going to be okay. She didn't know him that well, but a few minutes on that bench together had been as much of a bond as she got out of most cadets in the Academy. She hoped her expression communicated her concern for him.

It probably just looked like fear.

Following protocol, Cole stepped into the office first. Molly took up a space to his right, her hands overlapped behind her back. She forced herself to meet Captain Saunders's gaze and saw how tired he looked.

He was a big man, but still not fat enough to fill his skin. It hung down around his face, sagging in leathery flaps, as if he'd spent most of his career on a large planet. His white uniform, so immaculate and crisp it seemed to glow, squeezed folds of flesh from his collar. A wall of small, rectangular medals stood bricked up over his left breast—accolades from a lifetime of service.

He didn't begin by yelling at them the way he had the others, which worried Molly even more.

"What in the hell am I going to do with you two?" he asked. He sounded sad. Confused. Molly wondered if he really wanted their input, but she wasn't going to say anything unless she was addressed. Cole stayed mum as well.

"There were enough targets up there that you could've fired blindly and hit something." He looked at

Cole. "Mendonça, I'm disappointed in how quickly you were knocked out of action. I blame *you* for that—but everything else falls on this young lady."

Saunders turned to Molly and looked her straight in the eye. His disappointment was worse than the anger she'd been expecting. She felt her mouth go dry and knew if she spoke, her voice would sound unnatural. Broken.

Saunders listed her offenses, referencing a report projected onto his desk. "You misfired a missile, you went into hyperspace during a battle—" At this, he glanced up to ensure his disgust registered. After a pause, he went on. "You pulled over 40 Gs in battle. You deployed your landing gear?" He shook his head. "But the worst is that it appears you released your full ration of chaff at once, which is a tactical mistake, you didn't even arm them first, which is inexcusable, and you did this with the worst timing possible—taking out the rear half of your bird in the explosion."

He looked up at Molly. "Navigators go through flight school for a *reason*, Cadet Fyde. The basics are expected out of you in the event your lesser talents are needed from the nav chair. I didn't expect you to shoot down any enemy, but you did everything you could today to get yourself killed and the Navy's equipment destroyed.

"I'm not certain this is a problem we can fix, to tell you the truth. You've had a hard time fitting in here, and

I'm sure you know I was against your enrollment from the beginning. I never cared that the Admiral and your old man were close. I have a lot of respect for both of them, but I will *not* be held responsible for graduating someone who might get my boys killed in a real battle."

Cole raised his hand. "Sir, I—"

"*Can* it, Mendonça!" Saunders pushed his bulk up from the chair and rose slowly. His jowls were still moving from the outburst, and he jabbed a meaty finger in Cole's direction. "If you spent less time sticking up for her and more time getting her up to speed, we wouldn't be *having* this discussion. I've had it with you putting her ahead of the rest of the fleet, son. You're dismissed. Now get out of my office."

At this, tears drizzled out of Molly's eyes and started rolling toward the corners of her mouth. She licked away the salt, ashamed her partner might see her like this.

Cole stepped forward to salute Saunders. He clicked his heels together and jerked his arm down to his side. As he spun around, his eyes met Molly's tear-filled ones, and she saw his cheeks twitch. Water had already formed a reflective barrier on his brown eyes. For a brief moment, they were looking into each other's visors again. Molly's lips trembled at the sight, and with the thought of being expelled and never seeing him again.

He brushed against her as he moved to the door, leaving her alone with Captain Saunders.

"Are you crying, now? My goodness, girl, what made you think to join the Navy? Did you really dream of being like your father one day? Did you think you could bring him back from the dead?" He stopped himself, but had already gone too far. He looked down at his desk.

"Dismissed," he said. It was like the last bit of air went out of him to say it. Molly forgot every bit of Navy protocol and flung herself out the door and after Cole.

But her pilot was already gone.

3

Molly wiped the wetness from her cheeks and set off for her bunk. If she skipped a shower, she might be asleep before the boys came back to rag on her. There was certainly no point in writing up her battle report if Captain Saunders's hints of expulsion were true.

For once in her life, she didn't care about the Academy or becoming a pilot. She didn't look forward to post-battle reports and tactical analyses. There'd be no fantasizing tonight about what she'd have done differently had *she* been at the stick. Instead, an overpowering sense of disgust and shame propelled her down the empty halls. She just wanted an escape from the abuse.

"Cadet Fyde?"

Molly turned to see Rear Admiral Lucin standing in the doorway of his office. His customary hat was off, his weathered head streaked with extra wrinkles of worry. Molly felt one weight come off her chest and a different one take its place. She longed to run and wrap her arms around the old man, but she hadn't done that for years. She wondered what it would feel like to be comforted like that again.

She snapped to attention instead. As much attention as her body could muster. "Sir."

"Could you step into my office, please?" Lucin vanished into the pool of light pouring out of his doorway.

Molly fought the constriction in her chest as she followed him inside. Lucin was the reason she was *in* the Academy. He had fought alongside her father against the Drenards. She knew it was a cliché—the military student doted on by the old general—but the stereotype existed for a reason. When children followed their fallen parents into battle, they were inevitably surrounded by the survivors who had promised to look after them. She wasn't even the only one in the Academy with ties, just the only *girl*.

After her father left, Lucin had taken her in and enrolled her in the Junior Academy. It gave her a place to live. More importantly, he let her spend as much time in the simulators as she wanted—which was a lot. As long as she kept her grades up—which was never a problem—she could sit in a full military-spec Firehawk simulator for hours.

Sometimes longer.

At first, Molly would just soar around the simulated vastness of space, pretending to search for her father. Or maybe just trying to recapture her memories of him. One of her earliest recollections was of sitting on his lap in *Parsona's* cockpit, her mother's smell—the only thing she ever knew of her—lingering off to one side. Perhaps it had happened when she was an infant, or maybe the scent of her mom was just infused in the navigator's seat. Maybe she'd made it all up.

She had clearer memories of flying with her father as she got older. How her eyes would flicker from the stars to the lights and glowing knobs on the dash. She could remember his hands on the flight controls.

During their last trip together, he'd let her do a lot of the steering. She remembered how frightening his trust had been. Instead of holding her hands steady, preventing mistakes, he just turned and peered out at the stars through the glass, talking to Molly in that deep and powerful voice of his. Usually about her mother.

They may have been running away from one life and into a new one, but she didn't remember either of them having a care in the world.

The first time she fell asleep in the simulator, it was Lucin who found her. She had startled awake, afraid she'd be in trouble. Instead, the old man—so much older than she remembered her father being—scooped her up in his lap and let her fall back asleep. The stars kept drifting by through her eyelids, a little more of the simulated galaxy foolishly searched.

Now they stood in his office, a Navy desk and so much more between them. As soon as she'd entered the Academy, Molly could no longer be his daughter. Favoritism had to be countered with rigidity; love with harshness. Despite this, everyone whispered she was only there because of his string-pulling. So every ounce of love she went without, the affection other cadets were showered with by their families, had been given up for nothing now that she'd never graduate.

"Care to sit?" Lucin gestured to the simple wooden chair across from his desk.

Molly shook her head. She didn't want to be too comfortable; it would make leaving his office impossible.

He nodded once, and Molly saw how tired he looked. Despite his age, Lucin had a very lithe frame—tall and thin. His youthful gait was a fixture at the Academy, his pride in its operation evident in the bounce of his step and his eternal smile. Perhaps this was why the cadets loved him so much. Captain Saunders could whip them into shape while old Lucin bounced in to tousle their hair or slap them on the back. But all of that was missing from Lucin's face right then. Molly could see the fatigue in his sad and wrinkled eyes. His undying devotion to the Academy—which was capable of filling his chest with unmatched joy—could also break his heart. It was doing so right then.

"Captain Saunders called."

Molly nodded.

"Hey, I'm sure when I go over the tapes I'm going to be impressed with whatever you did out there. You always amaze me with your tricks, maneuvers even this old dog never heard of, but Saunders is in charge of the personnel decisions, and he has it out for you."

Molly looked at her feet to hide the tears, but one of them plummeted to the blue carpet, sparkling like laser-fire in the harsh rays pouring through the window. Lucin fell silent as the tear winked out of existence in the worn sea at her feet.

"I'm talking to you as your friend now, not as the old geezer who runs this joint. Look at me."

Molly did.

"I love you."

A strange bark came out of Molly, something between a gasp and a cough. Her breathing grew rapid and shallow as she started crying in earnest, her shoulders quaking uncontrollably. She hugged her elbows and tried to hold it all in.

Lucin may have been crying as well, but she couldn't see anything. His voice may have just sounded funny because she was hyperventilating.

"I do, Molly. I love you like my own daughter. But you don't know what I've had to do to protect you from him. I know it isn't fair, but if you think life has a bad reputation for that, the military puts it to shame. There's a lot of politics involved. And look, I'm babbling here so don't repeat any of this, but Saunders and his wife couldn't have boys. They have three girls, and maybe he's taking that out on you as well."

Lucin sighed. "I just don't know what to do here. He says you're out. Do you have any idea how hard this is for me?"

Molly bobbed her head and dragged her hands down her cheeks. They came away slick. She wiped them on the front of her flight suit.

"Maybe this is for the best. You can still be a *pilot* somewhere else, but you've seen what it's like in the Navy. They just aren't ready for you yet. Listen, I know Commander Stallings, he runs the Orbit Guard Academy, I can get you in there. You'll have a great career flying planetary patrols. Atmospheric stuff. None of this navigation junk. Don't you think that would be better?"

Molly kept her head perfectly still. She would never admit that.

"I also have old friends in the commercial sector. With your simulator hours, you could have your hundred-gigaton license in no time. Run freight or ferry—hell, you could get a job driving those rich snobs around in their fancy space yachts." Lucin laughed.

It wasn't that funny, but Molly craved the levity. She peered up through her tears and forced a half-smile. She swiped away more tears, her entire face a chapped mess. "Arrgh," she said, slapping her thighs and bending over to breathe. "Who was I kidding, right? Just because I can fly doesn't mean I *can* fly, does it?"

"You can fly like nobody I've ever seen. It's the *system* that's screwed up, not you. Give the private sector or Orbit Guard a chance. As soon as they see what you can do, gender won't matter to them."

"You said the same thing when I joined the Academy."

"I was wrong," Lucin admitted, looking sad again. "But plenty of women make a career out of flying in other ways."

"Plenty?"

"Okay, some. And none of the ones who've made it have your talent. You'll see."

"I don't want to give up, live a boring life, and die young like my mother, Lucin."

The Admiral's face twitched, and Molly knew she'd slipped. She'd called him by his name. Her body and brain were just in a bad place, and bad things live in that bad place, and her mouth was right there—an easy escape.

Lucin's face twisted up in a scary mask of rage. Wrinkles bunched up into muscles that weren't supposed to be there.

Molly didn't think her slip-up was *that* bad. But then—she was concentrating on the wrong mistake.

"Don't you say *anything* like that about your mother ever again, do you hear me?" Lucin took a deep breath, tried to relax his face. "Listen, you didn't mean it. You don't know what your mother was like. She . . . she was a lot like you. She fought some of the same fights. So don't disrespect her memory, okay?"

Molly nodded.

"Okay. So go get showered up. I'm going to make some vid calls and see what options you have. You can stay in the barracks tonight, or you can bunk at my place. Think on it."

"I don't need to," Molly said. "Just put me in a regular school, Admiral. No more simulators. None of any of this." She turned without waiting for permission to go. "I mean it," she added over her shoulder. "A normal school."

And it was a good thing her back was turned. It kept her from enduring the new expression that spread across Admiral Lucin's face.

4

Molly's shower stall had been built under protest—hers and everyone else's. Her twelve-year-old body hadn't looked much different from a boy's when it was constructed, and she just wanted to be treated equally. Everyone else protested against her even being there at all.

She hated to admit it, but the stall had become her cubicle of solace. A place where she could be alone. She let the hot water cascade down her body, burning the tightness out of her sore muscles, and thought back to some of her private history studies. When she was ten and first broached the idea with Lucin of attending the

Academy, she did some research at the Naval library. What she discovered had shocked her.

Women used to fight alongside men. They used to fly ancient atmospheric ships and go into combat. It was hard to determine the numbers from the history books, but it was common enough that people didn't seem to notice.

Something happened to change all that. Somewhere along the way, it was decided that women could be Presidents and CEOs and Galactic Chairs and work in the support side of the military, but they could not fight.

What the history books *wouldn't* tell her was why this had changed. And anyone she approached with the question, including Lucin, brushed her off or reprimanded her for being "too inquisitive" or "naive." And she had been naive. Back then, the knowledge of what women used to do gave her the optimism needed to join the Navy. Now she saw it differently. The precedents set by history didn't mean something was *possible* in the future. No. The fact that they were able to go *away* from this progress meant something far more sinister. And final.

Molly relaxed the tension in her body, allowing her hopes to wash down the drain along with her physical pains. Somewhere, deep in a mechanical room below the campus, a filter would take this water and make it drinkable. Molly hoped the boys gagged on her disgust.

As soon as she returned to the barracks, Molly could tell something bad had happened. Her arrival in a towel invariably led to whistles and catcalls from the male cadets. These were usually followed with bouts of derisive laughter, assuring Molly the flattery was a joke. Five years ago, Molly saw these taunts as signs of fear. An androgynous eleven-year-old stick of a girl had entered their ranks and could outfly every single one of them. Later, as she grew into a young woman, she sensed they were hiding a different brand of fear. Despite the Navy's poor excuse for food, her thin body had filled out. Workouts and womanhood had wrapped long, lean curves over her tall frame. The narrow face that had once made her look like a gangly boy produced high cheeks, a straight nose, and a tapered chin. She was beautiful. She knew it. And she hated that everyone took her less seriously because of it.

She strode across the long room of double-bunks, and nobody whistled. Not a one of them even looked up at her. This made Molly even more self-conscious than the rude attention had. She'd briefly toyed with the idea of sleeping here one final night, but she knew that was impossible now. She couldn't bear being in this room any longer than it took to get dressed.

Her bunk was at the far end of the room, a sign of disrespect but a fortuitous position. Snapping off her towel, Molly tucked one edge of it under the top bunk, creating a temporary dressing room. The idea of donning Navy black sickened her, but she had no choice. She pulled a fresh set of casuals out of her clothing tube and slipped them over her damp skin.

Molly looked at herself in the small mirror on the wall. Her short brown hair stood off her head in wet clumps. She leaned closer, studying her brown eyes and the starburst of yellow around the pupil. She didn't recognize them. And she didn't look the way she felt. She looked powerful, not broken.

"I *am* powerful," she reminded herself, mouthing the words to the mirror.

Saunders didn't know it, Lucin probably didn't even fully appreciate it, but Molly knew. She was good at what she did. That she wasn't going to be allowed to do it anymore was *their* loss, not hers. Molly concentrated on this, on focusing the shapeless pain inside her into something that could be hardened and made useful. Something she could cling to and wield with power. She gathered her belongings, a few old-fashioned books, a change of Navy casuals, her toiletries, a towel, extra boots, and her reader, and stuffed them in a black duffel. She threw it over her shoulder and turned to march out of there.

While strolling back to the door, Molly thought about Cole. What he would think when he found out she was gone. He was probably the reason she'd considered spending one more night in the barracks. Another night they could spend whispering in their corner, sharing jokes and insults and making each other laugh. Childish stuff. She needed to get over that nonsense and forget about Cole. Lumping him in with the others would help; she could create distance with her anger.

The march out of the barracks took place between two walls of mannequins. Molly had no idea what prevented them from celebrating her departure. It was as if they were scared of something. Or someone. She didn't care. She suddenly felt older than they were. Her delusions and naiveté had been forged into something sharp and dangerous. Something the military wouldn't get to use in a career of killing. It was a deadly thing she would smuggle out of their blasted Academy and use for her own protection, like armor. Never hurting again.

It was a good idea. While it lasted.

oooo

Rounding the corner to the administrative hallway, Molly ran right into Cole. Literally. Her face crashed into his chest, and her bag slid across the hall. Both of Cole's hands went to her shoulders, steadying her.

"Whoa, tiger."

She looked up at him to say something rude, something that would let him know he was no better than the rest of them—she was gone and didn't care if they ever talked again.

And then she saw his face.

One eye was completely swollen shut—a black slit between two purple bulges. A bandage crossed his nose, his nostrils chapped with blood. The top lip of his perfect mouth had been split wide open, black stitches tied off in a rough knot, their ends cut too long. His left cheek was a band of hues Molly had never seen before; the colors rose up to mix with the blackness below his eye. And he was standing there, *smiling* at her, trying to wash her worries away.

She touched her own upper lip, speechless.

Cole jabbed one of his thumbs over his shoulder, pointing back the way he'd come. "Heh. You should see the other guys. Infirmary." His voice sounded funny, his nose stuffed and his lips avoiding each other.

Molly couldn't speak. She threw both of her arms under his and locked them behind his back. She wasn't sure how it was possible, but she started crying again, pressing her cheek into Cole's unwashed flight suit. It had the same musky smell of a simulator after a battle—and something else. The smell of a real fight.

"I'm gone. . ." she croaked.

"I know," he said softly. "Those bastards."

There was so much more to say, but for now, this was enough. Molly held Cole for as long as she could stand it, until his arms reciprocated just a little, and then she pulled herself free. She ducked around him without making eye contact, grabbed her forlorn black duffel, and disappeared around the corner.

Cole called something to her as she ran away, but she could hardly hear anything over her own sobs.

5

Molly leaned back in her desk, reading *Jim Eats Corn*. With five years in the Navy reading nothing but technical manuals and tactical treatises, the fiction offered a blessed change of pace. Not as good as the romantic space operas she'd read in Junior Academy, but a lot better than she thought it would be.

For as long as Molly could remember, she'd been an avid reader. Her father had taught her at an early age. On Lok, he'd collected ancient children's books for her, antiques with board backs and individual pages. She couldn't recall their titles, but she remembered the bright colors and the odd words. She'd been reading ever since, another hobby that made her different.

Since transferring to Avalon High, she'd started working her way through the recommended reading list, the "boring" books that were supposed to teach life lessons. Surprisingly, she found herself enjoying them, and they helped kill the excess time the other kids needed for the tests.

The pace of her new school had been a major transition. Everything was dreadfully slow; the other students got distracted by anything and everything. No one seemed to be here to actually learn—it was more like a daily prison sentence kids endured before they got to do the stuff they *wanted* to do.

The first week had been particularly torturous. Molly came into the school with the high expectations instilled by the Navy. It was a philosophy that clashed at Avalon, where tardiness and procrastination were the norm. Here, kids celebrated whoever got away with the worst behavior while shunning anyone attempting to do the right thing.

It was an attractive scheme, easy to be lured into if one was soft. Molly decided early on that she would not become like them. At the same time, she didn't want to ruffle feathers or hurt feelings, so she decided to view Avalon High as just another tactical dilemma. She saw herself surrounded by aliens, and she could either let them defeat her the way the last bunch had, or make the best of it.

She chose the latter, using the slow time to educate herself in the things the Navy had neglected to teach. Once her teachers saw the quality of her work, they stopped asking her to put away the pleasure reading, which was why she could read while her classmates bent over a math test. She watched them scribble furiously, testing the multiple-choice offerings to see which ones created the least ridiculous results. Five months ago, she had been solving integrals in her head while worrying a wrong answer might get her and Cole killed.

Cole.

The smallest things reminded her of him. She found herself constantly wondering what he was doing at that very moment. Last semester it had been an easy game to play, what with the rigidity of the Academy. She could look at the time and know he was sitting in the simulator, or working out in the gym, or falling asleep during Space Strategics 202.

After winter break, she had no sense of what his schedule might be. He was everywhere and nowhere, so the game wasn't as enjoyable anymore. Eventually Molly realized: she wasn't having fun with wondering where *Cole* was, she was just fantasizing about where *she* should be. As hard as she struggled to accept this new life, some part of her still longed to be back at the Academy. Even as a navigator and Saunders's "whipping boy," she still had those hours of performing well in the simulator. And Cole.

"Time's up, class." Mrs. Stintson rapped her desk with her moon-rock paperweight, creating a beat for the chorus of groans. Pencils slapped desktops in frustration. Somebody continued to scratch away.

"*TIME*, Jordan." One more pencil smacked down.

When the bell rang, the students filed up to the teacher's desk with their tests, transforming glum into good cheer. The weekend. And Spring Break was just a week away.

Molly programmed a bookmark in *Jim Eats Corn* and shoved the reader and her computer into her bag. As she stood and stretched, Mrs. Stintson caught her eye and waved her over.

"Yes, ma'am?"

"Someone here to see you. Check in with the office on your way out."

"Yes, ma'am. Have a nice weekend."

A visitor? Molly couldn't think of anyone who knew her outside of the school and the Academy. And nobody from the latter would be caught dead here. Vaguely intrigued, she ambled toward the door thinking of Jim's problems with the corn harvest, unaware of how profoundly her life was about to change.

Mrs. Stintson watched her prized student file out before sliding Molly's test out from the bottom of the pile, placing it on top.

oooo

As soon as Molly opened the door to the school office, she knew who her visitor was. She knew it before she even saw him. It was in the way that all of the women were holding themselves. Even the Vice Principal was attempting to stand at attention.

Admiral Lucin.

Molly dropped her bag and went over to hug him. It was one of the small joys of being out of the Academy. She didn't see him as often as she would like, but he was a friend again. The infrequent hugs always helped heal some of the pain that seeing his uniform caused.

"Hello, Wonderful." He held her tight.

"What are you doing here? I thought you had business this weekend."

"Well, this is part of my business. I'm here on official duty. They were going to send some flunky to break the news, but I told them they were out of their minds." He looked around the office and then out through the smudged windows. "Let's go outside so we can talk."

Now Molly was *really* confused. What official business could the Navy have with her? Once you were out of the Academy, there was no going back. Ever. If they made an exception, it wouldn't be for a *girl*. Would it?

She led Lucin out through two double doors and into the school courtyard. A handful of students were still hurrying off to their weekend, so the two friends sat on a bench off in one corner. A Japanese cherry tree provided some shade and left a carpet of pink blossoms to stir in the breeze.

Lucin took in a deep breath and admired the campus. "It's beautiful out here," he said.

"Yeah," Molly agreed. "I eat lunch over there in the grass. They give us an *hour*. Beats the old cafeteria with its two-meter ceilings and bare walls." She compared the two experiences in her mind. She knew this talk was probably not about going back to the Academy, but she still made the comparison. And part of her betrayed the rest in wanting to switch places. "Anyway, what's orbiting, Lucin?"

"*'What's orbiting'*? Is that the sort of English they're teaching you here?" He looked at her with mock disapproval.

"Yeah, it's *nebulous*." She said it with a grin, and Lucin returned it.

He reached over and tousled her brown hair. "It's getting long."

"I'm trying to be normal."

"And how's that working out for you, young lady?"

"It's unique. Being normal." Molly pursed her lips. She'd never known Lucin to avoid getting straight to the point. Then she understood why *he* would be the one coming here. Why he was having a hard time bringing it up. Why he would do this at the school. *This has nothing to do with the Academy*, Molly thought. *This is about my father.*

Her face must have betrayed it. Lucin's brows came down in recognition of whatever flashed across her own. He nodded slightly. "We've located his ship." His voice was small and tight.

"*Parsona?*"

"Yes, *Parsona*. A Navy operative working undercover on Palan came across it. It was discovered by one of the pirate gangs there and has been impounded. We're working on getting the paperwork together to get it out of there."

"On *Palan*? But that's on the other side of the galaxy from where Dad was last seen." Molly leaned back and looked up into the pink blossoms, doing some calculations.

"I'm glad your astralogy hasn't gone the way of your English," Lucin joked, a sign he was nervous, or keeping something from her.

"What're you gonna do with the ship when you get it?"

"That's why I'm here. Legally, it's yours. It was all your father had, and he left it to you in his will. The fact it's been lost for almost ten years doesn't change that. So eventually, you'll need to think about what you want to do with it. We'll need to look over it first, of course.

See if there's a clue in the logs about where he was, signs of struggle, all of that."

"My father's dead, Lucin. Don't give me any hope. I could feel something different in my bones the day he died. It's hard to explain."

"There's no need, I felt it too. Even before I knew he was gone. I'm not saying we'll be able to find him, or even give him a proper burial. But the Navy needs to know what happened."

"Why?" Molly felt herself getting a little angry. "He wasn't in the Navy anymore, remember? Why do you guys care?"

"I care." Lucin was solemn. "I care, Molly. I want to find out if someone was responsible, and if so, I want to hurt them." He looked down at the chips of pink color around his feet. "I mean I want to bring them to justice."

She nodded.

Then she felt that hardened thing inside her twist into a new shape. Another layer of the film that kept her from seeing the world pulled back and the sky and the courtyard came into a tighter level of focus and detail. She looked at Lucin, and she could see the valleys in his wrinkles and the individual pores in his face. Her mind was so keen she expected to see mitochondria swimming around in his skin cells.

"I'm going to go get *Parsona* and bring her back."

It wasn't a question. It wasn't even a decision. It was a statement of fact, as if she were reading about something she had done in a history book. It was as real as if it had already happened.

"We have spring break next week," she continued. "I'll go to Palan—it's only, what, three jumps from here? I can be there by Monday and grab the ship, and I'll be home before the weekend."

"Molly—"

"As long as the hyperspace drive is working, and even if it isn't, we can install a new one, maybe your guy can check that ahead of time. See if the astral charts are updated, clear the paperwork."

"Molly—"

"I can do it myself. This is basic stuff, Lucin. You know I can do this. I'm almost seventeen, and I've already tested out for my private captain's license."

"Listen, Molly—"

But she couldn't stop talking. Thinking. "I've flown that ship with my father from one side of the galaxy to the other. I know it like I know my old simulator. C'mon, didn't you say the ship was mine? I have my license. It's totally legal."

"It's suicidal, Molly. Stop it. Settle down for a second." He didn't seem angry. A smile snuck 'round his mouth, Molly's excitement rubbing off on him. "Palan's a bad place. The Navy has almost no presence there.

Also, you are *not* traveling alone. What am I saying? You aren't traveling at all."

"You know I am. You can help me, or you can see if I can do it on my own."

Lucin leaned away from her, blinking, as if he couldn't take all of her in. His brows eventually came down, throwing shadows over his eyes. "I haven't seen you like this since the day you talked yourself into the Academy."

"Except *this* will work," she insisted.

They were both silent for a while. Molly couldn't tell if Lucin was thinking back or planning forward. "There will be strict conditions, young lady."

She nodded vigorously. She would agree to all of them up front.

"First, my agent is going to accompany you back. I don't want any evidence on *Parsona* lost just because you didn't know what to look for."

Molly kept nodding.

"Second, you bring the ship straight back with minimal jumps, and she goes into my hangar for a few weeks. We need to make sure we haven't missed anything and perform a deeper safety inspection than you'll be able to do on Palan."

Her neck started to hurt.

"Finally, I want you to have someone you trust accompany you to Palan—I don't want anything to happen to you on the way there."

Molly froze. "Who?"

"Someone who can navigate, even help pilot if you end up needing to do shifts." He ticked requirements off his fingers, but Molly felt as if he was describing someone in particular. "Someone you know and trust who will stick his neck out for you if you get in a jam."

"Cole?" It escaped as a whisper.

Lucin nodded. "He graduated at the end of last year. Several of your classmates did. The war with the Drenards has gotten nasty. I'm sure you've been following it. Saunders felt another semester would be wasted on some of them. Cole, Dinks, Riggs, Jakobs, some of the others you knew."

"*Jakobs*? Jakobs is out there flying an actual ship with loaded weapons?" Molly was horrified. She knew that was what the Academy was for, but it had never seemed *real* until right then. They were all still kids in her mind.

"Most of them aren't doing front-line stuff. Support. Recon. Patrols. It's the final stage in the learning process. Hell, if things . . . if things had been a little different, you'd be out there right now."

"No, you're right. I wasn't thinking about ability. I was thinking about—never mind." Her thoughts returned to Cole. "Do you think he'd want to go? What about his duties?"

"We have one of our best agents dedicated to this mission. I think it'd be a good training exercise for Cole if he went and worked with the guy. A bit of escort duty—"

Molly bristled.

"Not that you need it, of course, just that Cole could use the experience."

"Better," she said, nodding once.

"If you're serious about this, I can make it work. It'll actually make the paperwork easier on both ends since you're the legal owner of the ship. And nobody's going to suspect you and Cole are working for the Navy's interests. That could help with the pirates on Palan."

Lucin scratched his chin. "I'll get detailed instructions to our agent, make sure he understands who you are and what needs to be done before you arrive. The Navy will pick up the tab for the flight out and the jumps back. All you'll have to worry about is being safe."

"No problem." Her head felt light. The idea of going on a trip with Cole made her stomach flutter. Even with a Navy chaperone.

"All right, then." Lucin placed his hand on Molly's knee and used it to press himself up. "Pack some clothes and your book reader and get ready for the longest week of school in your entire life."

Hyperspace! She'd forgotten about that. She didn't even want the *weekend* to get in the way. For once Molly wished Monday would hurry up and come.

6

From her meeting with Lucin to her arrival on Earth's Orbital Station, it felt more like a month than a week. Especially with all the lazy scheduling teachers did prior to spring break at Avalon. She tried to concoct busywork for herself, doing all the problems her teachers said to skip, but it barely dented her anticipation.

There was so much to look forward to, she couldn't decide which part of the trip tortured her the most. Was it seeing her father's old ship? She wondered if any of his stuff would still be aboard, the old tools scented with oil and the clothes smelling of his hard work.

Or was she giddy at the prospect of *owning* her own ship? Gods, that thing, even as old as it was, it must be worth a fortune. Molly could start a shuttle agency right out of school. Or be a freelance courier. The opportunities were endless.

To a small degree, it was both those things. But mainly—and it made her feel silly to admit it—she was ecstatic about seeing Cole. She would be sitting beside him on a twenty-hour pan-galactic flight to Palan. Hearing what he'd been up to. Joking with him without the other boys around.

Part of Molly's preparation for the trip had been to go through her reader and delete a lot of required reading material. Now it was loaded with more adventurous fare, most of it meant for boys. These books were typified by their shallow, male protagonists and the author's poor grasp of space tactics, but she'd also found a little gem. A series of books about a woman on a frontier planet forging a life for herself. It was the closest thing to a female's adventures away from Earth that Molly could find, and the setting sounded a lot like her birth planet: Lok.

She was tempted to pull her reader out and start one of the action books, but she knew she wouldn't be able to take her eyes off the arrival gate. She'd chosen a seat in the Orbital Station, facing the security entrance. Cole's shuttle should be docking at any minute. Once he arrived and they boarded the passenger ship, their adventure would officially begin.

Molly was glad she'd gotten there first and on a separate flight. Thrusting out of Earth's gravity well would have been nerve-wracking if Cole had been there. She would've been torn between acting cool and nonchalant and wanting to geek out over the experience. It also allowed her to be a tourist. She got to alien-watch a little without him berating her for being a gossip, and she was able to explore some of the shops with all their strange trinkets from various planets.

She'd chosen a foreign snack (the one that smelled least likely to ruin her breath) and eaten it in the observation bubble, gazing at Earth as it spun below. She felt impatient for Cole's arrival the entire time, but these were great experiences she probably wouldn't have thought to do if he'd been there. The alien watching and the shopping because he might think Avalon had changed her. The Earth gazing because she feared it would come across as too romantic.

So she sat, chewing minty gum and stalking Cole's arrival point. Was she being transparently desperate? She was overthinking everything.

There weren't any windows on the airlock side of the Station, so the first hint at his arrival was the stampede of passengers pouring out of security. A man with Cole's build was near the front—Molly perked up. Then she settled back, trying to look noncommittal. It wasn't him, anyway. Two young men in Navy blacks got her heart pounding, but she knew he'd be wearing civvies.

Molly double-checked her own garb. She had tried on several dresses at the mall before realizing how overtly stupid this would look. Cole probably wouldn't even like it. So she'd gotten a new pair of khaki pants with these great pockets running down both sides. They kept her legs from looking too skinny, and she fantasized about the things she could organize in them. If she'd actually owned any of those things, of course.

The top was a yellow, short-sleeved thing, blousy up top and puffy around the sleeves. It had a slight lace around the collar and hem, and pale blue flowers dotted across the yellow. It looked simple, but Molly liked the way it made the starburst in her eyes stand out. Casual and lovely. Practical and girly. Perfect.

She'd almost bought two of them. Instead, she'd packed some comfortable shorts, a few nice T-shirts and tops, plenty of underwear and socks, and a scarf to tie around her hair. Thinking of this made her reach up and tuck her brown locks behind her ears. Her hair was almost down to her shoulders, and she worried Cole would find it too "girly." She considered cutting it close to Navy regulations, but figured he'd find that too "boyish."

She was miserable with excitement.

Besides her clothes, Molly had packed her book reader, her portable computer, a new journal she swore she'd be faithful to this time, a flashlight, a small medical kit, and some toiletries. It was more than she figured she'd need, but the panicky sensation she'd forgotten something started washing over her again—then a familiar shape pulled out of the herd, and all her worries dissipated.

Cole.

She almost yelled out to him like the schoolgirl she was (but didn't want to be). Instead, she watched him scan the crowd for her and tried to deduce what emotions were on his face.

He just looked annoyed, she finally decided.

When his eyes finally found hers, she waved and widened her own, as if they'd just seen each other at the exact same moment. His white teeth stood out on his tan face in a friendly smile. He strolled up to her with long, relaxed strides.

"Hey, girl." He stopped a meter from where she'd risen from her seat. The last time they'd seen each other, it was in an embrace that felt wonderful, yet awkward.

Molly wasn't sure what to do.

"Hello." She waved a little, as if he were much farther away. "You packed light." She nodded at the backpack over his shoulder.

"Yeah, you too. Is that your only bag?"

"Yup. It's only a few days, right? I figure most of our time will be on the trip out and the trip back, stuck in one outfit forever. It saved me from thinking too much on what to wear."

"Well, you look great. You look like you're getting more sun."

She hoped enough to hide the blushing. "They let us go outside."

"No way!" And they both laughed. "I like the hair."

Molly instinctively put a hand up to brush some of it behind her ear. "Thanks."

"So," he said, "You wanna go ahead and get on the ship and get comfortable?"

"They aren't boarding for another half hour, I don't think."

Cole pulled a Navy badge from under his collar. "You sure?"

"Gods, Cole." Molly glanced around nervously. "Don't be such a Drenard, we're supposed to be undercover."

"Forget about it. We're stellar until we jump into Palan. C'mon, let's go check out our seats."

Molly grabbed her bag and hurried after him. It was amazing how natural this felt already. Five seconds of nervousness after a week of dread, and it already felt as if they'd grown up together in a civilian world. Acting normal. Just being friends.

Molly suspected her time at Avalon, training to be a regular kid, made this a stronger feeling for her than it was for Cole. But so far, he led the way. Maybe he was really good at this undercover thing after all.

The pass worked wonders on the gate security and boarding stewards. The scrutiny might have lasted a bit longer than for two adults, but the handheld scanners beeped their consent, and this seemed to be enough for their wielders.

Once they got onto the ship itself, they were treated like royalty. First-class tickets meant sleeper chairs with pillows, blankets, and divider screens. The flight attendants delivered juice and then busied themselves putting their bags away.

Molly had mixed feelings about the treatment. She was used to doing things for herself. And the way the pretty women were doting on Cole was probably no different from the way she was being treated, but it still made her feel possessive. She tried to wrestle this jealousy aside so she could enjoy some luxuries her parents would never have been able to afford her. Part of her inwardly resented the Navy for pulling strings and doing something *nice* for once.

Just as she was thinking this, Cole launched out of his seat and started for the nose of the ship. Molly guessed he was going to the restroom, but he passed the sign and continued toward the cockpit door. She couldn't believe his gall; she leaped up and set off after him. He was already smooth-talking the navigator by the time she got there.

". . . same instructor." Molly caught the end of what the navigator was saying. She poked her head into the cramped cockpit and was struck with how young the speaker looked. He couldn't be much older than twenty.

Cole squeezed himself into a smaller pocket of the room and let Molly in. "This is my girlfriend Molly." The navigator nodded his head and the pilot raised one hand, his back to Molly as he fiddled with a radio set.

There wasn't enough room in the cockpit for all of them and this new "girlfriend" term as well, so Molly tried to push the word back into coach.

"Jeremy here went to the Academy. He had Rogers for Basic Flight."

How had they already shared this information? Cole was in his element, and Molly had a sudden pang of doubt about whether or not his being nice to her had anything to do with how he felt or whether it was just a product of his ever-present charm.

"Is that a Grumin 4200?" She leaned into the space between their two chairs and pointed at the SADAR screen.

The navigator smiled. "Now I *know* they don't have those at the Academy. But, yeah, that's the latest and greatest. If we turned it on, we could see the shuttles attached to various gates of the Station."

The pilot quickly pressed a button near the SADAR, taking it off standby mode and down to a black screen. He made it quite clear to the little gathering that the devices on the dash were his and his alone. Molly took the hint and leaned back toward the door. Her arm pressed up against Cole's. It started feeling really hot in there.

"Well, gentlemen, thanks for letting us look around," Cole said. "We're going to go settle in before the stampede begins."

"Good thinking," said the navigator. "You kids enjoy the trip."

"Bye," Molly said with a little wave.

oooo

Back at their seats, Molly arranged her belongings as if she were in a simulator. Her computer went in front, creating a miniature dashboard. She tucked her document reader by her right leg. As she buckled herself in, she noticed Cole performing the same ritual. To her *left*, she noticed. In the *pilot's* position. They hadn't even checked their seat assignments, they'd automatically taken their usual positions. It made her wonder how hard it would be to assume command on the *Parsona*. Or if he was even expecting she *would*.

Cole dropped a tan folder in Molly's lap, interrupting her thoughts. "Reading material," he said.

It wasn't heavy, but it bulged slightly as creased paper tried to spring back into shape. She gave their depositor a sarcastic smirk. "I brought my own, thanks."

"Not as good as this, *girlfriend*." He drew out the last word, already sensing that their cover annoyed her. But Molly wasn't sure if he realized why that was. For now, it seemed to be playful banter.

"What is it, *sweetie*?" She opened the folder.

"Everything I have on the *sabotage*." He made quotation marks with his fingers as he said the word. "Did Lucin tell you why we were graduated early?"

"Yeah, he said some of you didn't need the extra semester."

Cole laughed at this. "Well, that's crap. You remember that last mission? The one with the Tchung having a few extra ships?"

"Hmmm. No." She gave him a withering look. "Doesn't ring any bells, sorry."

"You're hilarious. Now look, there's something serious going on here. We never did another full-scale mission after that one. And even though our class did better than some others, there wasn't anything particularly inspiring about individual performances that day. Well, except for yours, and you got *expelled* for it. But get this: our simulator was never used again. Ever. Right up to the day some of us were graduated. Check the maintenance log."

Molly thumbed through some reports and maintenance schedules.

"It's the green one, there." Cole tapped the edge of a piece of paper and then continued in a lowered voice. Other first-class passengers, mostly humans, were filing onto the shuttle now.

"I was teamed up with Riggs in his simulator, and his navigator got the boot down to Services."

Molly looked up from the folder. "You were a navigator for *Riggs*? Not that he isn't a good pilot, but why weren't you just given a new navigator?"

Cole looked startled for a second. "Didn't Lucin tell you? I was demoted after the Tchung simulation. I graduated with the navigators based on my scores from the previous year. I mean, I get to keep my simulator hours if I ever want to be one of *those* guys." Cole tossed his head up toward the nose of the plane, "But no Navy ships for me."

"Oh." Molly looked back to the folder's contents.

"Hey, I'm not upset, so don't get all pitiful on me. Hell, you always wanted to be a pilot more than I did. I love the math and the tactics. And training as a pilot made me one helluva navigator, so I have no problem with the decision. I'm more worried about this conspiracy. Our simulator was taken off-line almost before you were out of the building."

"That makes sense," said Molly, "the thing was screwed."

"No. It was screwed *with*."

"That's right, you thought you saw Jakobs by the control panel of our pod earlier that day."

Cole corrected her. "I never said it was Jakobs."

"You said it was someone who reminded you of Jakobs."

"Right. Same size, same swagger, but it could have been anyone in Navy black. Look at this page right here."

Molly pulled out the one he indicated. It was a library computer log. "How'd you get this?"

"I had two months left at the Academy to gather this stuff together. And you wanna know what they demoted Riggs's navigator down to?"

"What?"

"Cryptography."

They both giggled at this.

"He got me a lot of this stuff. The rest I got through Saunders's secretary." Cole's voice seemed to taper off at the end of this sentence.

"Do I even want to ask how?"

"Yeah, you obviously do. But I don't kiss and tell." Cole raised and lowered his eyebrows suggestively. He was obviously lying.

"Yeah, right," Molly said. "So what do the library records tell us? Oh." She traced Jakobs's name. "Lemme guess, this is the time when you thought you saw someone by the simulator?"

"Bingo. Wasn't him. Besides, he isn't smart enough to do something like this. And why would they shuffle me around, graduate us early, close down that simulator, any of the other stuff if it was a cadet prank?"

"No way. You're suggesting this was higher-up?" Molly started flipping through some more pages, wondering what Cole had uncovered.

"I'm not sure. But the people they graduated were *not* the best cadets. They were the few people close to you, the ones that really interacted with you on a daily basis. Whether it was the people that liked you, which would be me and. . ." Cole scratched his chin and made a point of looking up at the ceiling of the fuselage.

It took a few seconds for Molly to get the joke. "Ha. Ha," she said.

Cole beamed in triumph. "Thanks. So it was me and Riggs and the people bullying you all the time. Only six of us were graduated early. And what sense does it make to *demote* me and then say I'm obviously too capable for another semester?"

"Well, Lucin did confess something to me that day. But you have to promise not to tell."

He gestured to her lap. "You're holding crap that can get me thrown in the brig for a very long time. Try to think of those documents as a promise ring, okay?"

Molly smiled. She hoped she twisted her lips enough to make it *seem* sarcastic. "Saunders had it in for me," she confided. "Lucin said he and his wife had three daughters and no boys, so he didn't want me to succeed or something."

"That seems a bit backward, but it might be better than what I've been working on."

"Yeah? What's your big conspiracy?"

"I was starting to think it had something to do with your father."

The words punched her in the gut, the folder heavy in her lap. Molly chewed on Cole's suggestion. The idea was ludicrous yet seductive. She shook her head. It was tempting to have this be about something more significant than schoolyard pranks, but she knew that wasn't true. It was just a fantasy to want the Tchung simulation and her expulsion to have greater meaning, for the cruelty of life to have some larger purpose.

"That's ridiculous," she finally said. "I don't know the first thing about my father's disappearance. I haven't seen him or the ship since I was six years old. And besides, they didn't find it until *after* they booted me out."

"Yeah, but I was thinking your father was connected before I even heard of the *Parsona*."

"Why? How could you?"

Cole gestured to the folder. "Because this is too much effort for a bunch of cadets. It has to have something to do with your father. Nothing else makes any sense."

"Sure it does. Somebody screwed with our simulator because *I* was in it. Part of that sabotage included getting you killed from a minor scrape and leaving me in charge. The rest of this nonsense is someone cleaning up afterward." Cole frowned at her, clearly unhappy with her sound reasoning and its banal conclusions. "Look," Molly continued, "I agree that this had to be higher up, that it wasn't a simple prank, but no way does this have to do with my father. Somebody just wanted me out of the Academy. I mean who knows how to program those pods besides the geeks in IT? Saunders not only had access—"

"It wasn't Saunders, he's too fat and—"

"Don't interrupt. I know it wasn't Saunders you saw, but he could have had any of the IT guys do it. And we know his motive: he didn't want me in the Navy, and he had the power to pull off the early graduations, so it all fits."

"None of the IT guys were transferred."

"What?"

"That yellow slip is the personnel change summation for the end of the year. If they were trying to hush this up, they didn't move anybody who would've been able to do the most illegal part of the job."

Molly shuffled through the folder, looking for the slip. "What are these thick white bundles stapled together?"

"Heh. I brought those along for your enjoyment. They don't have anything to do with my theory, though."

Molly turned to Cole. There was a faint white line where his lip had been busted open. The scar remained invisible unless his full mouth thinned into a smile. "What are they?" she asked.

"Medical files for Jakobs and Dinks. From the day you got kicked out." He settled back into his chair. "There's a lot there," he added, a smirk on his face.

Molly thumbed through the stapled pages and looked back to Cole. The silence in the barracks that day finally made sense. She wasn't sure she approved, but it was nice to feel him beside her, even across the extra room provided by the first class tickets. She didn't really appreciate the space, but it was balanced out by their not having to wear their visors, reflecting back the world around them. It was just her and Cole. Their real faces. Scars and all.

7

The best thing about first class, as far as Molly was concerned, was getting to see nearly every single passenger of the ship file by. For an alien-watcher, it was a cross between a parade and a fashion show. Even the humans, who made up a majority of the crowd, were garbed in such splendid regalia that some of them looked stranger than the handful of aliens wearing simpler outfits.

Children bounced past excitedly, chased by nervous parents. There was an air of excitement in the crowd as vacations began, homes were returned to, and business deals still held the potential of not falling apart.

The only morose passengers Molly saw were the handful of Palans who must have been returning home from vacation. She assumed they didn't like their stay on Earth very much. She was dying to ask them why and find out more about their home planet. In fact, Molly wanted to set up a tollbooth in the middle of the aisle, stopping each passenger and demanding answers for passage:

Who are you? Where are you going? What are you going to do there?

She wanted to know everything about everyone. But part of her suspected this urge was only half the story. The other half was her desire to let every single one of them know that *she owned a starship*, and the cute guy beside her was pretending to be her boyfriend.

When a Delphian in coach had a hard time reaching the luggage bins and wouldn't accept offers of help, she nearly got her tollbooth. The meter-tall, stubborn little alien wrestled with his bag as the parade slowed to a crawl. Molly smiled and nodded at each person that passed her by, hoping they wouldn't think her a snob just because she was in first class.

When the procession came to a full stop, a young Palan girl, her eyes fixed on Molly, crashed into the back of her father. She quickly checked to see if Molly had noticed, and then her face flashed with embarrassment. Molly smiled at the child and waved her fingers, which sent the girl's face into the folds of her father's coat, hiding from the world. Molly was fascinated by the girl's skin, the color of dull steel. The ears on her stubbly head were very low, almost pointing downward. Molly wanted to try out the three or four words she knew in Palan, but she couldn't muster the courage. Neither could the Palan child, who remained hidden until the line lurched into motion. As her father moved away, she peeked out and smiled shyly at Molly, and then was carried off by her grip on his coat.

One of the last floats in the parade was a stunner: a Bel Tra couple. They sat in the very front of first class, which provided only a brief glimpse of their tall, thin frames and colorful attire. They both wore traditional Bel Tra lace, the dozens of layers of different transparent colors piling up to create an opaque hue unique to each individual. Molly felt goose bumps ripple up her arms; she nudged Cole to make sure he was looking.

"Huh?"

Molly turned in her seat to start talking his ear off, only to find Cole's head resting against the window.

"Are you asleep?" Molly asked.

Cole didn't even open his eyes. "I *was*," he complained.

"Do you have any idea what you're *missing*?" she hissed.

Cole cracked one lid and gazed at Molly for a second. "My nap?"

"*Bel Tra!*" Molly whispered.

"Seen 'em before." His eyelid returned to its state of rest, sealing him off from the sights.

Molly couldn't believe him. She thought they'd been watching the cultural display together. She leaned out and peered up and down the aisle, wondering if anyone would mind if she took some pictures with her reader.

Beside her, Cole emitted a strange snuffling sound. Molly turned back at the man of her dreams.

Just as he started snoring.

oooo

When the passenger ship reached Earth's primary Lagrange point—the spot in space where the gravity of the planet and its moon cancel each another out—it began its countdown for the jump to Menkar.

Molly leaned across Cole's sleeping form to gaze through the small porthole. Earlier, she'd been eager to wake him, but now she was glad he wasn't witness to her nervousness. She hadn't done this outside of a simulator since she and her father came to Earth. The thought of getting sick, or having her heart race uncontrollably, as it often did, had Molly squirming in her seat.

She glanced up at the numbers ticking down by their reading lights. When the counter reached "2," she looked back through the carboglass, tightening her stomach reflexively. The only visual cue anything had happened was each star shifting to a new place. It was indistinguishable from a simulator display.

But there was no nausea. *The hyperdrive in this monster must punch a big enough hole in space to prevent the sensation*, Molly thought. She settled back in her chair and slowly released her grip on the armrest. The blood returned to her knuckles, coloring them pink.

So far, the grand adventure was proving to be a dud. Molly hoped all that would change once she took possession of *Parsona*. As long as their chaperone didn't get in the way, she'd have Cole to herself and be able to keep him so busy with navigational duties that he couldn't sleep through the trip back.

The Navy had pulled some strings to make this flight nonstop to Palan, an oddity for a frontier planet, but a measure to reduce the number of things that could go wrong on this mission. As they passed through Canopus, Molly heard several first-class travelers express their dismay. Their final destination was Canopus, but they were having to return here via the Palan system?

Once more, the Navy's thoughtfulness irked Molly. She felt horrible that *she* was responsible for messing up flight schedules. Even the sole Palan couple in first class seemed upset at the itinerary. Molly couldn't understand this unless they, too, were eager for layovers on new and strange Orbital Stations.

What everyone got instead was a direct flight from Earth to Palan. It took almost a full day to make the trip, most of it in a dimly lit gloom of people trying to sleep half as well as Molly's companion. By the time they arrived at the Palan system, he must've had eighteen hours of uninterrupted rest. No bathroom breaks. No food. No flirting.

Molly couldn't understand how he contained himself. Even from the last.

Stressing about it prevented her from getting any sleep, herself. It even made it difficult to read or watch a holovid. Then she started worrying he would be a ball of energy on the trip back, while she would be a zombie. And this anxious line of reasoning made any chance of a nap impossible.

Cole finally woke when the Palan shuttle airlocked itself to their giant passenger ship. Palan's Orbital Station could handle a vessel this size, but with only a few travelers getting off here, a direct shuttle flight made more sense. Molly wondered if this wasn't just more of Lucin's protectiveness. What a wreck he would've been if she'd gone off to fight in the Navy.

The airlocks on the two ships pressed together, sending a faint vibration through the hull. Cole bolted upright, wide awake. "Where are we?" he asked, completely alert.

"Palan," she said, as grumpy as everyone else on the ship, but for a different reason.

"Already? Man, that went by fast. Why didn't you wake me?"

"You seemed pretty out of it. And when you started snoring really loud, I went and sat with some guys back in coach. They taught me this cool card game called Mossfoot. You start off with—"

"I don't snore that loud," Cole interrupted.

"Well, I just got back and people were complaining."

"Hmmm. Record it next time. I don't believe you."

Molly stood in the aisle with a few other passengers and reached up to collect her bag. "You're just jealous I had a great flight and all you did was sleep." She yawned and stretched, feeling exhausted. She really needed a nap.

And a shower.

PART 2
ESCAPE VELOCITY

*"The floods will come to wash away
the wicked. And I'll go gladly."*

~The Bern Seer~

8

Only a dozen or so passengers boarded the shuttle to Palan's surface. Molly and Cole were the only two humans, making *them* the aliens to gawk at. The young girl from earlier was just as shy the second time around, recoiling from Molly's wave, but with a timid smile. A Palan steward came down the aisle, checking that all the passengers had their harnesses secure before rushing to join the pilot in the cockpit. *Or had that been the pilot?* Molly wondered. There didn't seem to be many crew members on the shuttle.

Cole automatically sat to Molly's left again, beside the window. Molly assumed it was more so he'd have a place to rest his head than any attempt to pull rank. He nudged Molly, and she turned to see him pointing out the glass. There was nothing out there but stars.

"What am I looking at?" she asked.

"*That!*" he said, rubbing his finger on the glass with a squeaking sound.

Molly loosened her shoulder straps and leaned over Cole, focusing on his finger. There was a faint crack in the carboglass running the length of the window! Molly felt the airlocks decouple and the shuttle slide sideways in space, preparing for its descent.

"Should we tell somebody?" she asked, cinching her harness up tight.

Cole craned his neck to inspect the porthole one row back. "That one's even worse," he marveled. "There's no *way* this ship passed inspections."

Molly felt they should warn somebody, but the shuttle was already accelerating, pinning her to her seat.

"Wow. That's a few Gs," Cole said. "Somebody's in a hurry."

If he was trying to lighten the mood, it wasn't working. A few minutes later, the shuttle hit the atmosphere and started taking a beating. None of the passengers spoke; they just looked ahead or out to the steel wings, which seemed to be flapping up and down like a bird's. The sounds of grinding metal and bending trusses groaned throughout the ship, reverberating over the roar of air knocking against the hull.

After a few minutes, the heat inside the shuttle became intolerable. There was no air coming out of the vents overhead. Molly reached up, straining against the Gs, to twist the nozzle open. The plastic unit came off in her hand. She held the broken piece in her lap, beads of sweat streaking back from her forehead as the friction of reentry blasted the fuselage, heat radiating through the insulation and into the cabin. Molly sweated profusely, partly from the rise in temperature, but mostly out of fear.

She couldn't remember being this scared in all her life. She *needed* to be in control, or at least be up in the cockpit so she could see what was going on. As they stopped accelerating, switching to a glide against the atmosphere, Molly considered unbuckling her harness and going forward where she could at least know how they were going to die. All she could see through Cole's window was the glare of a bright sun and glowing-red steel.

They hit a pocket of turbulence and the shuttle lurched upward, pressing Molly violently into her seat. She decided to stay put and cope with someone else being in control but was not at all comfortable with it being anyone other than Cole. After a few minutes of frightful shuddering, the mad plummet ended, and the pilot smoothed out into another glide. The sun disappeared behind gathering clouds, revealing a vast ocean spread out below. A hiss filled the shuttle—the sound of air leaking in through cracks or maybe passengers heaving a sigh of relief.

Molly released Cole's arm; she couldn't even remember grabbing it. She looked down at his tan skin and saw small white frowns of indented flesh where her fingernails had been.

The landing felt like another bout of turbulence as the shuttle rebounded off the tarmac several times. When they came to a halt, Molly felt the urge to applaud the pilot. In fact, the murmurs of relief washing through the shuttle made her expect a standing ovation at any moment. Instead, the passengers collected their bundles and hurried toward the exit, the sense of urgency palpable, as if the shuttle still posed some sort of threat. Molly moved eagerly as well, but for a different reason. She was dying to get out and explore her first new planet in ten years.

The landing ramp descended, and the first thing Molly noted about Palan was the heat. It assaulted her before she even got to the exit. It felt like a wall of water flooding the aisle. Molly took a deep breath against it, but the humidity was so high, it felt as if she could drown. The wetness stuck to her, transferring heat straight to her bones and making her loose shirt cling to her stomach.

She and Cole swam with the others through the thick air, down the boarding ramp, and into a half-circle tunnel of corrugated steel. They were pressing toward a cacophony of clanging and yelling—poverty's soundtrack. This was a tune Molly recognized from her childhood on a frontier planet. It was a chorus of competitive complaining, a group having very little yet wanting much. The sounds were as thick as the atmosphere; Molly could feel it all driving her back like the force of acceleration, back into the shuttle and out of there.

As they exited the tunnel into the Shuttle Terminal, Molly's architectural tastes gagged. Even after a steady diet of what the Navy considered "spatially pleasing," she couldn't believe how rough this place was. Everything in the Terminal had the appearance of a temporary structure, something that could be packed up and moved when trouble arose. Palans conducted business in crowded clusters around rickety stalls and tents stretched with patchwork quilts. Molly noted they needed yet more patching—little of the original fabric remained. Frayed edges hung in long rows of tatters and thread.

No two things looked the same, preventing the collection of oddities from taking on a quaint, cultural aspect. Instead, it was just a noisy, hot, wet, crowded mess.

Cole studied the photograph of their contact one last time and seemed able to ignore it all. Molly wiped the back of her hand across her brow, and new sweat leaped out to replace the departed. She watched Cole tuck the printed picture inside his jacket pocket and wondered how he could possibly wear that thing in this heat.

Then she realized he probably had a stun gun or something Navy issue underneath. She preferred not to know, assuming this was going to go as smoothly as cutting butter would be in this heat. One night on Palan, max, while they sorted out customs and ownership, and she and Cole would be out among the stars in her very own spaceship.

Chaperoned, of course.

A man in a brown robe approached them. Large holes in the thick fabric were spanned by strips of colorful cloth, straining valiantly to hold everything together. The man's hood was up, shading a face the color of stainless steel. Copper-colored hair hung from the shadows above his bright eyes. He looked right at Molly. "Cole Mendonça?"

"Does she look like a Cole to you?"

The man with the metal-colored face seemed reluctant, but he finally pulled his gaze to Cole's. "Jusst becausse I wass looking at *her* doesn't mean I wassn't asskking *you*." He looked back at Molly, leering. "Better get ussed to it with *her* around." A purplish tongue came out and ran itself along the man's lips.

"Who in hyperspace *are* you?" Cole demanded. He moved between the stranger and Molly to steal his gaze back.

Molly looked away nervously. Several people were watching the exchange, but maybe they'd just never seen Humans before.

"Drummond ssent me. For my good Englissh. No? Come, I take you." He stared at Molly over Cole's shoulder. Cole glanced back at her, his eyes raised and looking for a consensus.

She shrugged. "Do we have a choice?"

"Fine," Cole told the stranger. "Lead the way."

○○○○

"Ssoon Palan be a firsst classs world, eh?" Their guide walked ahead of them, his arms spread out to indicate the activity on either side of what really couldn't be considered a terminal. Instead of organizing travelers into queues and providing them a place to rest, the building didn't have lines *or* chairs. The shuttle just deposited everyone right into some sort of disorganized market designed to remove any cash brought onto the planet—all legal tender recognized, and some that might be questionable.

Their nameless guide kept his arms stretched out, splaying his brown canvas robe open like a giant wing. Molly couldn't tell if it was a display of pride or sarcasm; the inflections were alien and accompanied with much hissing. She followed along, taking in the scene around her.

Being born on a frontier planet prepared her for much of what she saw. Various races clucked and hissed in an assortment of languages. Foods she'd never seen before—which meant they probably didn't merit exporting—added pungent odors to the thick air. Everyone bartered with everyone else, all exhibiting the agitation and nervous energy that accompanied this universal pastime. The figures not engaged in this activity milled about, doing a poor job of hiding the bad thoughts rattling around in their dull heads. Overhead, tangles of wires knotted together in a grand display of unplanned infrastructure. Each line went as directly as it could to where it was going, no routing or compromise for the sake of simplicity or safety.

Molly wondered what Cole's experiences were off-planet, and the question filled her with a shocking sense of how little they really knew about each other. In the Academy, you only concerned yourself with what had happened since you arrived and what you planned on doing once you graduated. Not that she hadn't attempted to pry into his childhood, she'd just never been able to create a crack. How much did she even know about the boy she was absolutely, positively, one-hundred percent falling in love with?

She chewed on this and slipped a hand inside his arm, grasping his bicep. The casual flexing of it comforted her as they walked along under the pull of a little more than one Earth gravity. Also comforting was the occasional bump against something hard hidden beneath his jacket. The chances that this would go smoothly seemed to be lessening the more she took in their surroundings. And her esteem of the planet wilted while their guide's question regarding its future hung in the nauseating air.

"Yeah, lovely planet here, guy," Cole answered for her. "Now where's Drummond?"

"Ssoon. Ssoon!" He waved them forward without looking back, as if they were lagging behind. "He iss in the Regal Hotel. We go there now. Jusst a few blockss. Come."

A few blocks? From a shuttle terminal? Molly couldn't imagine the racket they'd made landing there. It was like parking a space cruiser in downtown Chicago. Most planets are sensible enough to locate their space ports in the middle of nowhere.

Palan's problem in general appeared to be a complete lack of planning. The guiding principle here was chaos divided by large gutters. Molly had yet to see any sign of law enforcement or security; this was a planet with no obvious rules to follow—social, legal, or commercial. The results were just what one would expect.

They exited the terminal to find the parts of the market that wouldn't fit spilling out with them. Rutted and degrading roads radiated away at odd angles, a high crown in the center curving down into deep gutters. The sidewalks were lined with poles to prevent the cars from intruding, and traffic coordinated itself with an endless sequence of horn blasts and profanities. People seemed to move by bumping off one another, none of them willing to give, everyone resisting the barter.

They stayed in their guide's wake as he cleared a path to the hotel. The throng gradually thinned as they moved away from the market. It was as if Palan's population was densest around the hope of escape represented by the shuttle. They clustered around it in a mass of messy desperation.

Molly understood the urge to be near the exit. After walking two blocks through the bustle and feeling her damp clothes wrap themselves around her, she wanted out of there as well. At first, she'd been desperate to leave the terminal, getting out into fresh air and away from the crowds. But now she felt as if they were going the wrong direction. They should have arranged for *Parsona* to meet them on the tarmac so they could leave straightaway.

She felt relieved a block later when their guide signaled their arrival. "Here we are," he said. "The Regal Hotel." Their guide treated them to another flourish. Once again it was impossible to determine if this was sincere or a snide insult. He waved them into a structure that would leave a stain on the word "regal" for the rest of their lives.

The lobby, even more packed than the streets had been, contained almost no furniture. Loiterers leaned on the walls or squatted on the floor. Many were completely prone, resting on sheets of paper as if even the locals couldn't stand direct contact with their world. Nobody seemed to be waiting on anyone or preparing to go out for the day. This was it. For all Molly could tell, these were patrons paying a lesser fee to live in one large room.

With no clear path through the maze of bodies, the trio cheated by stepping over the labyrinth's walls where they were lowest. Molly quickly learned to pass over the sleepers so she didn't have to bother with an apology. She fought the urge to cover her mouth and nose with her hand. The air in the lobby was pungent and thick.

Their guide was all smiles. "Come, come. Up to a room. Drummond hass a room."

This confirmed Molly's suspicions about the lobby's renting arrangements. It also increased her fear that they were being led into a trap by a complete stranger.

"Why don't you have Drummond come down here and meet us?" Cole asked their guide, seemingly in sync with Molly. "We've shown you quite a bit of trust by following this far. The least he can do is meet us halfway, shake hands, and then we'll conduct our business. Yeah?"

The guide's face said No, but he hissed a Yess. "Wait here," he said. "Wait."

So Molly and Cole both looked around for some place to get comfortable. And decided this was pretty much it.

oooo

Drummond came down the steps peering in every direction, back and forth, but never quite at Cole and Molly. He looked horrible. His clothes, rumpled and stained with sweat, matched the disarray of his matted hair, which was smeared against his forehead in wet clumps. He resembled the guy in the Navy photo, but as a long-lost cousin might. Drummond was either the Navy's top special agent at going undercover, or his time on Palan had not been kind to him.

When he reached the bottom of the staircase, he seemed reluctant to descend down from the last step, choosing instead to lean against the shadowed wall of the tight stairwell. He finally made eye contact with his visitors and waved them over, the signal full of desperate frenzy.

Molly and Cole moved as quickly as they could without hurting anyone. With his longer legs, Cole reached the stairs first. He held out a hand, and Molly heard him introduce himself. Drummond looked at the limb as if it were an alien life form. He whispered loudly, "Come upstairs. We can't talk here. Can't be seen together." He leaned farther back in the shadows and jerked his head at the figure behind him. The guide from the spaceport descended the stairs and lurched out into the sea of bodies.

Cole looked back at Molly, and she shrugged her shoulders again, renewing her grasp on her luggage. Cole nodded and followed Drummond up the stairs. Molly hurried after, noticing the man went *up* much faster than he had come *down*.

They exited the stairwell on the third floor. Drummond hurried down the hall to one of the rooms and held the door open a crack, barely far enough for them to squeeze their bodies through. His paranoia was odd considering the complete dearth of other people around.

Molly shoved her bag through the gap and pressed in after it. The inside of the hotel room reminded her of the rest of Palan: disorganized, humid, and reeking. At least they had it to themselves. She no longer felt assuaged by the idea that they would only spend a single night on Palan. She wanted to get aboard *Parsona* and get the hell out of there. Pronto.

"I'm Molly Fyde," she told Drummond. "I'm here to collect my ship, the *Parsona*."

The agent looked at her with the same lack of comprehension Cole's hand had warranted. "Yes. Of course," he finally said. "But . . . there's a bit of a problem here."

"What sort of problem?" demanded Cole. "We were told you had this handled on your end."

"I did. I mean, I do." Drummond walked to the window and stood as if he were looking out, but the shades were drawn tight. "The paperwork and bribes went through customs without a hitch. The Smiths were given the bounty the Navy wired through. So the government and the pirates are both cleared up."

"The Smiths?" Molly wondered aloud.

"Yeah, the pirate gang that found the ship. It was drifting around Palan's smallest moon. They claim the thing was spiraling down, so they wanted a fifty percent salvage bounty." Drummond looked up at the ceiling. "Surprisingly, the Navy didn't even barter."

"I guessed who they were," Molly said. "I was just expecting a more menacing gang name."

"Are you kidding?" Drummond locked eyes with Molly. "That's an unusual name around here. And the locals can't stand saying it." He leaned toward both of them a little. "Mum's the word, but my real name is Simmons. Can you *imagine* the reaction?"

Cole shook his head politely, but Molly was getting annoyed with the cultural lessons. She wanted action. "What's the holdup?" she asked. "What do we need to do?"

"I don't know," admitted Drummond. "Some other party is interested. Or the Smiths are no longer in charge. I got permission to move some supplies onboard the ship. I was checking the astral charts to make sure they were up-to-date, running ship's diagnostics, all the usual stuff. Then some locals barged into the cargo bay like they owned the damn thing. Never seen 'em before in my life.

"So I tell them I'm a lawyer and I'm serving a client's last will and testament, and they tell me I'm full of it. This is their ship and I get off now or I'm a dead man. They didn't even let me grab the supplies I'd already loaded.

"I went to the Smiths, and they played dumb. Said they'd no clue who these guys were and they weren't interested in getting involved. So I went to Customs, and those guys pretended not to know me. I showed them the paperwork from the day before, showed it to *the same guy* who signed and stamped it. You know what he said?"

Cole looked as if he wanted to tear his hair out. "How could we?"

"Forgery. That's what he said. No problem, I thought. These backwoods hicks want to play around with me? I'm the flankin' Navy! So I went to my stash, a hidden place where I keep my radio, my Navy credentials, my second gun, everything. You know what I found?"

Molly saved Cole the trouble. "What?"

"Nothing. It was gone. All of it. There's no way anyone stumbled on this, and I've *never* been followed. You'd have to think a damned spy satellite was tracking me for anyone to know where that stuff was. But no problem, right? I was just progressing down the list, right? So my next step, I mean I had to blow cover, so my next step was to go to the Naval offices and request the use of their long-range. I had to get through to Lucin's aide."

"You're working directly through Lucin?" Molly asked.

"No, Lucin's *aide*, in Saunders's office. This operation's being run by the Academy. Anyway, the guys in the Naval Office tell me it's no big deal, private interests and personal matters, is what they say. But it doesn't matter 'cause the Naval secretary couldn't confirm me. Said I wasn't in the system."

Cole and Molly glanced at each other, eyes wide. "What do you mean, you weren't in the system?" Cole asked.

"What I just said, man! They were patient with me at first, I mean . . . I must've seemed real sincere, you know? Because I was being sincere. I *am* being sincere. I told 'em I was working for a Rear Admiral, on special assignment, scan my prints and see. So they do the retinal scan and the palm prints and they get *nothing*. I didn't believe them, so they let me see the screen. Nothing, man. I don't exist. Now they're looking at me like I'm crazy, so I get the hell out of there.

"Navy people have been following me around ever since. Probably have Palan's only spy satellite devoted to me, right? That doesn't sound crazy, does it? I mean, how do you explain all this?"

That's when it dawned on Molly: *this* was their chaperone. This paranoid wreck was supposed to be looking after *them*. Instead they were being talked to like adults and having to cajole him along like a younger brother. Their safety net had been pulled away. Molly took a side step toward Cole and reached a hand into his arm, finding her comfort place. But all of Palan was pressing in around her, the smell getting stronger, the heat rising. Their ride off this planet had been hijacked, and their official contact was completely useless.

Cole must have been thinking some of the same thoughts. "Okay, the first thing we need to do is go to the Navy Office ourselves. I have my credentials with me, and Molly should be in the system as well. We'll get them to loan us some Marines, we'll go clear out the *Parsona*, and then we'll get out of here."

A wild look of agitation shivered across Drummond's face.

"Don't worry," Molly said, raising her hand, palm down. "We're gonna take you with us."

"Our cover is busted," Cole added, "so the pirate gangs will realize they're dealing with Navy. That means we'll have to get out quick. If they realize the bounty came from Naval personnel, with no bartering at all, they may think they have something priceless. We'll never see that ship again."

He looked to Drummond. "We're gonna need you to round some stuff up so we can make a quick escape. Tell me which systems you checked out on the ship and what condition she's in."

"Yes, of course. I can help. Oh, thank gods you guys are here. You have credentials, which is good—"

"The ship's *condition*, Drummond."

"Yeah, sorry. She looks great on the outside—I mean, for an older ship. No big dents, could use some paint. A few micro-meteor burns, but what ship doesn't, right? Um, the inside is a bit rough, but the important bits seemed shiny. And uh, diagnostics didn't turn up anything, but I did a quick scan, you know? Before I was interrupted."

"Okay." Cole turned to Molly. "Are you fine with this? We go to the Navy, show them the ownership papers, storm in with Marines and all that? It's your call."

"No. I mean, yeah, Cole, that sounds like the best course." She was glad he was here, that someone was making decisions. There were times when she flashed back to the Tchung scenario and felt as if she were the one playing dead while he took the helm. If they could keep doing this for each other, taking control when the other was out, everything should be all right. As long as both of them were never out of commission at once, or separated, this hiccup might not turn out to be a big deal after all.

9

Picking her way across the sad mounds of prostrate bodies, Molly found herself looking forward to the lesser stench that awaited them outside. Her left foot came down between two forms and slid a little on something wet. She regained her balance but nearly dropped her black duffel.

"And *why* didn't we leave the bags in the room?" she hissed back at Cole, who lagged behind this time. The lobby had become more crowded; it favored small feet rather than long legs.

"Did you see that place? If Drummond didn't run off with our stuff, one of the rodents would have. Besides, if all goes well, we'll be sleeping in the ship tonight. I don't care if it doesn't have overnight bunks, I'll spread out on the diamond-plate steel in the engine room and work on my cute snore there."

Molly nearly retched as she passed through a small pocket of foulness that stood above the rest. It smelled like death. Like the time a bat got trapped in the ceiling above the cadet dormitory and died. It smelled like that, but times a hundred.

"Some of these people might be dead," she whispered above the moans and shuffling of those who clearly weren't. Yet.

"Not funny."

"I'm serious. Who would check them for a pulse, and how often? Look at all the luggage and bundles scattered between them. Some of it looks like it hasn't been disturbed in ages." She considered this.

"Hey, that gives me an idea." She veered to the side, picking her way toward one of the lobby walls. "This way," she called back to Cole.

○ ○ ○ ○

He swerved to follow, and one of his large boots pinched an arm. He pulled his weight off that foot, collapsing forward as the limb sucked in like a startled snake. No yelp. No complaint. Cole turned back, leaning down to apologize. . .

"Ssorry." It was barely a whisper, a mere hiss leaking out of the prone, bundled form.

Cole teetered on the edge of apologizing back, confused. Then it occurred to him that the lobby guest may actually consider the fault *theirs*. They weren't leaving enough of a clear path for the room's intended purpose. Inconsiderately spread out. Unconscionably *too comfortable*.

He rose, shaking his head as he carefully picked his way to Molly; she'd come to a halt in a small pocket of floor space along the far wall of the lobby.

"We're leaving our bags here." She stooped to nestle her duffel between two other mounds. Cole watched, bemused, while she rounded up a few bits of trash and sprinkled them on top, as if garnishing a meal.

"Uh, why?" His backpack didn't budge.

"'Cause my bag is heavy, for one thing," she told him. "I'm sick of carrying it. And also, 'cause there's a slight chance crazy boy upstairs isn't all that crazy. I can't see Lucin trusting my life with a deranged lunatic. Which means he either ate some bad fruit here, a possibility I rank pretty high, or the Navy is up to something, an idea you've been lodging ever deeper into my head.

"So we leave the bags here, a spot where you could hide a dead body in plain sight. We'll grab them on our way back to collect Drummond and his supplies.

Trust me, nobody's gonna touch something that people here are sleeping beside."

"Great plan. For *your* bag." Cole gave her a grin and hitched his pack further up his shoulder in protest.

"I'm serious. If you have anything important in there, it'll be safer here. I've got my ID and a copy of the will and transfer papers, but everything else is staying, just in case."

"And I'm taking my bag, *just in case*. Think of it as having our eggs in two baskets."

"Whatever," grunted Molly, leaving him behind again as she picked her way toward fresher air.

Cole made careful note of where she left her duffel and hurried after her.

oooo

Outside, the slightest sense of a breeze brought a little relief. They hadn't been on Palan for two hours, and already Molly could see how a traveler could get used to pretty much anything. She wasn't there yet, and probably wouldn't be on such a short stay, but her imagination could piece together a sequence of events that led from disembarking the shuttle to sleeping on that lobby floor. She shivered at the thought, picturing how quickly it could happen, even to her. A simple series of bad decisions could lead to a life of prone depression in the Regal.

Cole hurried past her, waving at the first taxi in a line of four. Each was a small, completely enclosed vehicle balanced on three wheels. The driver didn't respond to Cole's gestures. In fact, he appeared to be fast asleep.

The gutter between the sidewalk and the parked vehicles was too wide to step over, and the small bridges arching across the gap were too eroded to trust. They looked more like sculptures than pathways, curves of cobblestones erected to protest gravity. Molly watched Cole vault over the gap and did the same, landing neatly as he turned to help her across.

"Thanks anyway," she smiled.

Cole looked a little flushed. "No problem."

Molly beat him to the taxi and rapped on the windshield. "Hello?" she called through the glass.

The driver slowly brought his head to a full vertical. No startle reflex, as if this happened to him dozens of times a day.

He cracked his door open. "Where to?" he asked.

"The Naval Offices. How much?" Drummond had insisted they get a price before entering a cab.

"Earth credits," Cole added from behind her.

The driver lit up at this—almost literally. The metallic sheen of his face seemed to glow as though a dull light shone upon it. He looked past Molly. "Twenty," he said.

Cole grasped her arm and gently pulled her away from the driver, heading back to the next taxi in line.

The driver opened his door wide. "Fifteen!" he yelled after them.

"C'mon," Molly pleaded. The next driver was waking up from the ruckus, and she didn't want to waste time bartering them down few more bucks.

They turned back to the first cabbie, who held the door open as Molly slipped into the tiny rear seat. Cole squeezed in beside her. Their driver stepped to the back of the vehicle, and Molly heard the sound of chains rattling. She tried to see if threats were being made between the two taxis, but it was too cramped to shift even slightly. The driver returned in a flash, muttering to himself and rocking the car as he pulled the door shut.

"Firsst time on Palan?" he asked as he pulled out into the light, yet frantic, traffic.

Molly looked up to meet his eyes in the rearview mirror, but there wasn't one there. In fact, there weren't *any* safety devices or indicators anywhere in the buggy. It was just a smooth shell perched on thin wheels, two narrow benches comprising the seating arrangements. The driver took up most of the front one, and Molly and Cole were pressed together in the back.

There weren't even any windows to roll down, just solid carboglass on the sides. As bad as the smell of Palan was, Molly longed for a breeze.

"First time," confirmed Cole.

"Firsst day?"

"First day," parroted Molly, giving Cole a smile.

"Where you gonna watch the rainss?" The driver asked, looking up at the sky through the windshield as if they were due to begin at any moment. Distracted, he almost ran into another rolling egg. He leaned on the horn and yelled through the window at the other driver, obviously not concerned with the answer, just making small talk.

Something triggered in Molly's memory at the mention of the rains. Something she'd learned in an old Planetary Astralogy course in Junior Academy. And then the filling lobby started to make sense, the wide gutters, the locals setting up their market in the shuttle concourse. It occurred to her why this rickety taxi seemed to have only gotten one thing right: being watertight.

Even some of the Palan smells started to register in her olfactory nerves as various types of mildew and mold and rot.

The driver performed a post-yell grumble routine in his own language, gripping the steering wheel with residual anger. Molly tilted her head toward Cole's to explain what she could remember about the torrential downpours and regular floods.

Cole absorbed the PA lesson, his eyes flashing a hint of memory as well. "Drummond, you *fool*," he muttered. "We're gonna have to be quick in the Naval Office to get back to the Regal in time."

Molly nodded. She leaned forward and interrupted the angry grumbling. "How far away are we?"

"One more than five minutess," answered the driver.

Molly settled back in her seat, wondering if that was their way of saying "six." *Such an odd place, Palan.* Outside the glass she saw two silver-faced people wrestling with a package. It looked as if things might get violent. As they passed, she craned her neck to follow, but there wasn't enough room to turn her shoulders.

She felt Cole twisting to survey the same scene. "Not much law here, huh?" he asked quietly.

"Too far from the war, I guess." She looked straight ahead. "The fight with the Drenards means fewer security forces on the frontier. Lok was the same way when I was young. I think my dad took me away from that place 'cause of the violence. Crazy how the Drenards can affect us without being able to push the war beyond their arm of the Milky Way." Molly laughed at herself. "Listen to me. A few months exposure to opinion reporting at Avalon, and I don't talk tactics anymore, I just moan about the toll the war is taking on innocent civilians."

Cole grunted. "No one mentions it at the Academy, but everyone must see it when they look at the charts. We can't win this bloody war. The Drenards have an entire arm of our spiral galaxy well defended. They never push the fight into our space, and we seem hell-bent on breaking through. It's become an imaginary wall in space that we throw money and lives at."

"Well, don't get me wrong," Molly said, "I want to beat the snot out of them just like the rest of the galaxy. What they did at Turin—what my father and Lucin fought through—that was the worst sort of crime. Unforgivable. But the way the stars are laid out in this galaxy, with those damn spiraling arms, there's just too much empty space to stretch supply lines across, even with hyperdrives. It's like Major Clarke taught us in Philo-History, how the Revolutionary War was immoral 'cause independence was assured by the Atlantic."

"Clarke was a loon," Cole jerked his head toward the world beyond the carboglass. "Try telling these people to wait patiently while progress meanders forward. No thanks."

The taxi fell silent, and Molly sucked in a deep lungful of it. She missed these conversations with Cole. Not so much the philosophy, but the history and the tactical ruminations. They used to stay up late in their bunks whispering bold plans that would turn the tide of war one way or the other, always with bold gambits the generals missed simply from being at it too long. Some of those ideas seemed ridiculous to her now, but then she remembered the stunts they pulled off in the simulators that no AI routine had ever been ready for.

The nostalgia made her chest swell and feel heavy. She'd put that behind her at Avalon. Eventually. She thought back to those big plans and her dreams of being a great Navy pilot, ending the war with the Drenards. She could almost feel the confetti sticking in her hair. . .

But those old dreams made her sad now. Especially as she looked out at this miserable world sliding by. It wasn't just her ambitions that had taken a hit, so had this planet and its people. She knew from her Materiel Analysis class what each missile and bomb cost. She imagined what a few munitions could mean here if they were converted to Earth Credits. It drained the last of her giddiness away. The excitement of retrieving *Parsona* and traveling with Cole back to Earth was being replaced with the ugliness of Palan, the problems detailed by Drummond, and the fear of not knowing what to expect from the looming rains.

Cole had fallen silent, gazing out of the carboglass. Maybe he was thinking along the same lines as she, or was it something else? Here they were, two pilots with tons of potential, crammed together in a dinky cab on this miserable planet and stuck with a worthless guide while a war was being lost. *What kind of sense does that make?* Molly wondered.

"Do we have to take Drummond with us?" she asked aloud, breaking the silence.

"Who?"

"Drummond. Do we really have to take him with us? Once we get *Parsona* back, I just want to fly her home ourselves. Spend more time talking like this."

Cole leaned close to her. "You mean *Sssimonsssss*," he whispered with a hiss.

They both laughed. And for a few moments, their lives returned to normal.

oooo

Their little bubble of metal and glass lurched to a stop. "Naval!" announced the cabbie, not even attempting the word "offices."

Cole handed him a wad of Navy funds and exited the cramped cab mostly by falling out of it. Molly spilled out the same door as Cole vaulted over another massive gutter. He turned, and this time she accepted his outstretched offer, his hand wrapping around hers. It felt smooth and warm, unlike the stiff flight gloves they normally bumped together. It reminded her that she and Cole had been around each other as civilians for less than two days, and most of that time he'd been asleep.

It always amazed her to feel the rapid bonds foreign situations could weld. It reminded her of a math camp Lucin sent her to one summer. She was only there for a week, but some of the friendships she formed felt unbreakable at the time. Something about being with a person night and day, never leaving their side, made hours feel like months.

As Cole released her hand, Molly thought about how equally fast those undying bonds faded as soon as she and her new friends went their separate ways. She wondered if the same would happen between her and Cole when they got back to Earth.

She snapped away from the depressing thought as Cole held open the door for her. She passed under the GN Creed, Latin for "Expanding Freedom," and into the foyer of the Naval Offices. There was the faintest impression of an old official seal in the marble tile, but a million shuffling steps had worn it down to a sad smear. A waft of air-conditioning leaked through the next set of doors, beckoning them inside.

The room beyond was much smaller than seemed possible from the block building's façade. Unless the walls were as thick as the foyer, there was some sort of optical illusion at play. Molly suddenly realized they were in a bunker *disguised* as an office. A room meant to take the worst kind of pounding and survive. For some reason, walls so thick made her feel *less* safe. As if she had moved to the center of a bull's-eye.

A man in Naval black stood behind a low greeting desk, peering down at a mess of papers. Both of his hands were spread out and pressed flat on its surface, as if removing them would send the documents fluttering off to safety. He looked up at the squeak of the door. "No refuge from the rains—" He paused. A glimmer of recognition flashed across his face, or perhaps it was the obvious conclusion that this young couple was out of place on Palan. "Can I help you?"

Cole held out his credentials. "Ensign Mendonça, Cole, Naval Special Assignments, sir."

The man behind the desk frowned and took Cole's badge from him. "Didn't know they had Ensigns in Special Assignments, Mendonça." He looked at Molly with a sly smile. "You must be the Admiral?"

One of the men stationed at another desk snickered.

Sarcasm was not what Molly had hoped to find here, but she could understand someone posted to Palan having a bad attitude about it. This must be where the absolute worst were sent to rot their way to retirement.

"Sir. We're here under the direction of Rear Admiral Lucin," Cole explained. "We've been sent to retrieve a Gordon-Class spaceship salvaged by the Smiths. My partner here, Molly Fyde, is the legal owner of that ship."

The Officer seemed to be waiting for something else.

"There are people claiming ownership of the ship right now, and we need some Marines—"

"*Marines?*" It came out high-pitched and sudden. "You come in here asking for *Marines?* To do what, go storm this ship and shoot it out with some thieves? Are you right out of the Academy, or what?"

Cole's cheeks reddened; Molly could tell he was getting agitated. "Very well," he said, leaning forward to study the man's badge, "Officer *Jons*. I humbly request the use of your Bell radio so I can report back to Admiral Lucin myself."

The officer seemed amused at the request. The other few Navy men in the office had stopped what they were doing to follow the exchange. "Radio's out, son. Containment tower washed away in last month's rain. Hasn't been fixed yet." He glanced at Cole's badge before swiping it through his scanner; his hand rested on the edge of his monitor guardedly while he waited for the information to pop up.

His eyes widened, then narrowed. He looked up at Cole and Molly for a moment before turning to wiggle a finger at several of the staff. Two large officers stood, their chairs squeaking with relief at the removal of their bulk. They headed toward the front desk while Jons addressed Molly and Cole, a grave look on his face. "It'll be just a moment," he assured them.

Molly saw movement to her left and snapped her head around; a skinny man in Navy casuals was working his way along the wall, trying to get between them and the exit. Molly put her hand on Cole's elbow, trying to break him away from a glaring contest that had broken out between him and Jons.

"Cole." Her voice was soft and steady.

"*Cole.*" More insistent. She tugged at his elbow, but his boy-brain was locked with another boy-brain. This wasn't good.

"*COLE.*"

He looked down at her.

"We need to *go.*"

His head whipped around at the movement of the black uniforms in the room. Molly was relieved to see that he finally recognized them for what they were: enemy ships. Two heavy bombers there, a scout trying to flank them here, and a battle line drawn right through the center of a cluttered desk.

○ ○ ○ ○

It was another Tchung scenario, Cole realized. Except here, the unfair properties of hyperspace travel weren't intervening. There was an option they didn't have in the simulator.

Retreat.

Molly was already pulling him toward the double doors. Cole pushed off the edge of the desk with his foot, propelling him after Molly while shoving the heavy wood of the furniture into Jons's thighs. Immediately, the two bombers lurched into motion, reaching for the batons strapped to their thighs. Cole's brain wrestled with how sarcasm had made its way to assault in such short order. He stumbled toward the exit, his badge, the radio, the marines, all forgotten.

Molly had a head start and would get to the doors before their flanking scout. Cole wouldn't. He fumbled inside his jacket for the stunner Saunders had issued him and flicked it to what he hoped was a low setting. The small man lunged to tackle Cole as Molly held the door open. He could see her straining for the next set of doors leading outside.

Cole zapped the scout with the stunner. Too early. The electricity arced across the air and spread out across the man's hands, most of the charge dissipating in the thick atmosphere. He kept coming. Cole was almost through the door when his pursuer secured a grip on his backpack, nearly pulling Cole off his feet.

Molly yelled something and rushed to his aid, kicking past Cole at the man attached to his back. Cole slipped one arm out of his pack's strap and spun around, punching his pursuer in the face. He considered using the stunner again, this time with full contact, but the man had released him to cover his nose. Molly pulled him out into the street; the last thing he saw before the door shut was the two bombers catching up to the scout.

10

"RUN!" Molly insisted. She was already heading up the street in the direction from which they'd come.

Cole cursed his stupidity. He'd assumed someone from the Naval Office would take them back to the Regal. He should've asked the cab to stay put. He should've left the backpack at the hotel. And he should've paid more attention to how they had gotten here.

He put the other strap of his pack on and started after Molly. The stunner stayed out. Molly looked back to make sure he was catching up—her eyes flashed at something behind him. Cole checked over his shoulder and saw the doors to the Naval Offices exploding open, disgorging a small fleet of pursuers. He sprinted to catch up; surely both of them were in far better shape than these office workers.

The sound of a gunshot and the zing of an old-fashioned metal bullet careening off the brick ahead of him ended that tactical assessment. The noise from an old siren wailing to life decreased their options to almost none.

Cole came up alongside Molly and tugged one of her arms. "This way!" he said, darting into an alley. Molly nearly stumbled, her head dipping as another shot rang out and whizzed by overhead. Cole pulled her around the corner, and they picked up their pace.

oooo

The Palan sunlight was fading quickly, and the narrow alley was already full of shadow. They dodged the piles of debris and garbage the locals had set out by the gutters. The sound of distant thunder melded with the wail of an approaching siren. The skies ahead promised to take out one set of trash while the men in black promised to handle another. Molly felt fear coursing up with adrenaline and concentrated on pumping her legs.

At the end of the alley, Cole cut back to the right and ran across the street. Molly followed, and they weren't the only people running. The sound of the first roll of thunder and the darkening sky flipped a light switch on a room full of roaches. Palans scurried every direction, looking for shelter. Many pleaded at doors, all of them shut tight. Molly dreamed of the safety of the Regal Lobby, not to mention the privacy of a room upstairs.

Another shot. The zing of a ricochet sang out for an incredibly long time. Molly was in the middle of the street, completely exposed. She dipped her head from the sound of danger while another rumble of thunder descended, closer now. Her brain seized up, unable to flip from one threat to another. Cole headed into an alley across the street; he turned and beckoned. She ran, the sound of heavy boots drawing nearer.

Little traffic remained, and the few drivers caught out in the thunder seemed to be pulling over, doing something at the rear of their cars. Were they anchoring the vehicles to the street?

Molly panted as she tried to catch up to Cole. "I don't know how long before the rain," she yelled ahead to him.

"I know!" His voice sounded urgent. She followed him into the alley.

Even though they were running almost as fast as the taxi and traffic had been moving, they had to be at least ten minutes from the Regal. Molly wasn't sure exactly where the hotel was, but she caught a glimpse of the shuttle's massive nose sticking over rooftops in the distance. They'd already raised the thing for lift-off, eager to get out of there. It was the Palan beacon of hope, a lighthouse flashing now and then through gaps in the low buildings, giving Molly a general idea of where they were.

Cole sprinted ahead as if he knew precisely where he was going. He bolted across another lane and into their third alley. Molly saw red flashing lights and heard the siren turn down the street they'd just left. Someone yelled something behind them, but it could've been one of the locals seeking shelter. Several doors faced the alley, but it was pointless to stop and check them. The Navy was on their heels, and plenty of evidence suggested this town was locked up *tight*. Molly heard the slap of boots on pavement getting closer. She wondered how much time before the rains came and what their pursuers had in mind for their own shelter.

She popped out of the alley and into a little more light; Cole snagged her arm, yanking her around the corner. They both flattened themselves against the brick wall, completely exposed to the few Palans still running along the street. They were perfectly hidden, however, from the stomping boots echoing through the alley.

At the corner, Cole held the stunner upright. His other hand rested on Molly's stomach, pressing her back against the rough brick. She took deep breaths and laid one of her own hands on the back of Cole's, holding it there. The world slowed back down, but her head continued to spin. She looked at Cole, wondering what he had planned. The muscles on his neck were twisted around in lean ropes, one cheek flattened against the building. The boots were as loud as the thunder now; both sounds mingled, making each seem nearer. And then black shapes flew past, out into the open.

Cole let the first one go by. The Navy man stopped a few meters out of the alley, looking up and down the street. The second one came out gasping for air.

Molly covered her mouth with both hands, focusing on the gun held by the lead man in black. Their lives could end at any moment. Terror held her in place as Cole darted out to the winded man's back, his stunner crackling like lightening. The man crumpled to the sidewalk with a huffed "Oh!"

The lead man spun around with the gun. Molly tried to call out to Cole, but he was already bringing up his forearm up to meet the man's elbow, stopping the spin. The gun went off with a bright flash and a spit of smoke; the wall beside Molly's head exploded into sand. She ducked reflexively, if a bit late.

The two men struggled for control of the weapon as the car with the wailing siren rounded the corner, red flashes painting the world around them. Molly ran to the stunned Navy man, his body still twitching slightly, and pulled the metal baton from his hand. She spun around the gunman, swinging the stick with both hands like a galaxy baller, striking him on the base of his skull.

The crack was like another report from the gun. Molly's elbow went numb from the vibrations in the stick, and she lost control of the baton. Cole grabbed her wrist and began pulling her across the street and away from the red lights, but all she could think about was collecting those weapons.

"*Wait!*" she yelled, yanking her arm out of his grip.

She spun away from Cole and dashed back to the scene of the fight, the headlights from the Navy car bearing down on her. A flash of light lit up the entire street for a moment, followed by a roll of thunder that Molly could feel in her chest. The first drops of rain started pattering down as she threw herself on top of the two black shapes. The car screeched to a halt between her and Cole, the doors popping open.

"FREEZE!" someone yelled.

A shot rang out. Both doors flew open and the two bombers spilled out, their bulk seeking shelter by the small vehicle. The man closer to Molly clutched his shoulder with a grimace; she held the gun straight out, trembling.

"Drop it!" she commanded, and two objects clattered to the pavement. The men looked at each other over the red flashing lights before glancing up to the sky. Molly seemed to have their attention, but recognized that it was divided between her and a larger worry.

Cole ran to her and took the gun, keeping it trained on the wounded man. "This is your plan?" he asked, gesturing to the small hole in the open driver's door.

"Yeah, we need to get in that car." The rain started coming down in a heavy drizzle, punctuating the tension in her voice.

oooo

The men in black seemed to realize what was going on. One of them made a move to get back in the vehicle. Cole didn't hesitate. He fired a shot over their heads.

"Shut that door," he commanded.

The large Navy officer did so.

"If you have a place you can get to, you'd better start running."

The two Navy men locked eyes, visibly frightened; the rain pummeled them in steady sheets. They seemed to arrive at some silent agreement, and both of them took off down the alley—back toward the Naval Office.

Cole watched them go and then turned to check on Molly. She was gone! He looked up and down the street and inside the Navy car. Nothing. A wave of panic rose up in him.

"I need help back here!" he heard her yell through the pounding of the rain against the metal car. He ran to the rear of the vehicle and found her crouching in the street, fumbling with something.

"What're you doing?" Cole hollered.

The hatch she was wrestling with finally wrenched open; a length of metal chain cascaded onto the wet pavement.

"The taxi we ran past was doing something with this."

Cole blinked the rain away; he looked up and down the street and saw the metal posts sticking up along the road like parking meters. He'd assumed they were for keeping the cars from flying into the gutters, but now he understood what they were really for.

They had not been taking this rain as seriously as they should have.

He grabbed the end of the chain from Molly and told her to get in the car. She nodded and disappeared into the veil of falling water. Cole dragged the chain toward the nearest post.

It wouldn't reach. The Navy guys had stopped in the middle of the street. Cole heard something like thunder, but different, roaring down a distant road. "Molly!" he yelled as he ran back to the car. "We need to push!"

She nodded and jumped out, back into the torrent of rain. They both shouldered the doorjamb of the vehicle and pressed back toward the nearest post. The car was still in gear, but it was incredibly light and the road was already submerged beneath a thick layer of water. They fought for traction, new boots on rough stone, and were able to budge it a little.

"Good!" Cole shouted. He ran back for the chain as Molly disappeared into the driver's seat and out of the deluge.

Cole figured out how the hook at the end of the chain fit snugly into the links, so he wrapped it through the hole halfway up the post and secured it. He hoped he had done it right because he could hardly stand in the rain now. It threatened to push him down into the rising puddles and drown him.

He fought his way back to the car, fell in, and pulled the door shut. Molly had crawled into the back to give him room.

"Oh my gods," she said. "I shot that guy in the arm. I was just aiming for the *car*."

"It's okay, you did good. Real good." Cole fingered the hole in the glass; water dripped through it in a steady trickle. "I'm not sure what to expect here, partner." He reached into the backseat to squeeze her hand. Hers was cold and trembling.

Cole pulled off his backpack and searched inside for dry clothes. The assault of water on the roof was impossibly loud. It made it hard to hear the first wave of water that came down the street and caught their car, sliding it back. And now Cole realized why the chain was so short. You were supposed to park close to the post on the downhill side. They were in the wrong place. The chain wasn't going to hold them until *after* the floods pushed them to the other side of the anchor.

The second wave of rushing water hit. The narrow tires and egg-shaped body shed most of the wave's energy, but the vehicle shuddered once more and slid another meter. Cole could *feel* the slack in the chain. He could imagine the danger if a large wave hit them right now. Molly leaned forward and held onto his shoulders, pressing her wet cheek against his arm. Her teeth chattered through his jacket like distant thunder.

He heard the next wave before it hit, even over the pounding on the roof. The wall of water roared like the ocean on a paved beach. This time, all three tires came off the pavement. Their little haven swung around like a child's toy, back in the direction it should have been parked. One of the rear tires touched down first, flipping the bubble on its side and sending it on a dangerous slide toward the sidewalk. The roof of the car slammed into the next anchor post down the street.

Molly tumbled forward, across the back of his seat and onto Cole. They landed with a combined grunt on the driver's side door. The shape of the anchor post showed clear through the dented metal roof. The car lurched again as the wave slid by, the glass with the bullet hole scraping across the pavement.

"Are you *kidding* me?" Molly asked.

"Bad parking job," Cole grunted, holding her on top of him.

Neither of them laughed. They held their breath in the din of rushing water and pounding rain, straining to hear the sound of the next wave, if indeed there was going to be one.

oooo

There was.

The next rumble started advancing, even louder this time. The windshield provided an amazing view down the street: the glass spanned sideways from cement to sky. They were still facing the wrong direction; the car's momentum had bounced them across the wide gutter and onto the sidewalk. Now they looked back toward the two entangled Navy men, their black-garbed forms washed several meters closer from the waves. The standing water already halfway covered their nauseating stillness.

Except one of them wasn't perfectly still. The smaller one—Molly thought he may have been the scout in the office—shook his head. It was hard to see through the rain, but he seemed to be rising from the pavement.

Molly was lying on top of Cole, the driver's bench vertical and useless. She tapped his chest and pointed.

"I see it," he said.

The skinny man, bathed in the pulsing of the red lights from the roof, stood upright and looked around at them. The wind blew water off him in sheets. He leaned back into it and staggered forward. Something shiny materialized in his hand.

Molly screamed and Cole wrapped his arms around her, trying to rotate his body between her and the gunman.

The Navy man raised his arm and pointed it at the windshield. Then he paused. He looked back over his shoulder. An avalanche of water rose up behind him. Even over the maelstrom, Molly could hear his high-pitched shriek of terror.

The large body on the ground was lifted up first, and then the man with the gun was hit by the foaming wave. His knees buckled, and both men disappeared in the churning wall of white. A wall that headed toward Molly, Cole, and their thin glass barrier.

The smaller guy hit the car first, his body materializing out of the shuddering sea of confusion. His face pressed against the wet glass in a comical grimace as the car was pinned to the sidewalk by the breaking wave. The man was flattened to the vehicle, underwater, bubbles leaking from his nose and mouth. He looked right at Molly, his yellow teeth clinched tight as his lips split open in a sneer. The hand with the gun pulled back, twisting the barrel around to face her, determined to not be swept away alone.

Then another large wave hit the car with astounding fury, spinning the entire vehicle around in the proper direction. There was a shriek of grinding metal and glass followed by a metallic shot as the chain finally snapped taut; the car came to a rest, straddling the wide gutter. Detritus and debris from the alleys and streets of Palan thudded off the car as it passed underneath.

Wherever it went to, the garbage clinging to the windshield was going with it.

11

Parsona. Molly could read the word clearly on the starboard wing, the faded black stencil spread across the wide metal surface. She hovered above the "O," the letter bigger than her outstretched arms.

Before she could even walk, Molly had spent time out here; she would crawl around while her father worked on the surface controls. Now and then he'd scoop her up when she got too close to the edge, then hold her in his lap and look out across the prairies of Lok. It was up here that she'd learned to read her first word, spelling out her mom's name one letter at a time.

Now she floated just above it, weightless. Her old nightmare had returned, but it was different. She was closer, and there was something to push against.

Molly reached down and touched the cold metal with her bare hands; she hooked her fingernails on the edge of a line of rivets and pulled herself toward the gleaming hull. She floated, pulling herself along, working toward the glow emanating from the cockpit.

Someone was inside. She wanted to see who. Her father? Her mother? Was she dead, here to join them?

She approached the navigator's porthole, so close to finding out, when she felt the first vibrations—the thrum of the main thrusters reverberating through the hull. She screamed for them to wait as the ship lurched into motion, but her wails would not carry in the vacuum. Her anguish reached no farther than her own ears, transmitted through her tear-streaked jaws. Molly pounded the hull with her fists, struggling to alert someone to her presence, but the violent act just pushed her away. Off into the vacuum. Through which *Parsona* moved easily. . .

Molly startled awake, a shiver from the nightmare traveling into the real world with her. Or was it the cold? Last night's events washed over her, filling her with a hollow dread. Her head rested on her hand, which was palm-down on Cole's chest. She could hear his heart thumping, like the thrum of an idling engine.

A warm and mostly dry shirt was draped over the back of her soggy blouse, the hem pulled up to her neck. She rolled her eyes up Cole's chest and neck and found him wanly smiling back at her.

"Good morning," he said.

But it was still dark outside. The rain pattered softly on the passenger side door; various leaks had allowed rain to seep in, collecting at the bottom of the damaged shell. Molly felt sore and cold, but happy to be alive.

"How long have I been asleep?" She pushed up from his chest and searched for a way to brace herself in the awkward confines of the upturned car.

"Not long," he said, sitting up and wincing, rubbing his neck as if it were stiff. "I think the worst is over, but we'd better get out of here before the authorities come looking. I figured out how to shut off the lights, but I'm sure we still stick out like a sore thumb."

Molly agreed. She thought about their next moves and realized they didn't have many available: back to the Regal, and now they were relying on Drummond for help. The thought absolutely mortified her.

Cole made some room, and Molly stood on one door while trying to operate the other. The impact had jammed the seam a bit, but it opened with a creak of warped metal. She tried pushing it up and out, but the feeling in her arms hadn't fully returned from the nightmare.

"Little help."

Cole wiggled his way up beside her and shoved the door out into the early morning air. It flopped back into the darkness, and a drizzling rain invaded their temporary shelter. Cole boosted Molly up to the side of the car, and she slid down with a splash into the street.

"It's deep," she warned him.

She heard him grunting as he forced himself up and out. He landed beside her with his backpack held over his head.

"Not *that* deep, silly."

Cole shot her a look. "Thanks. You know, I take you out for the night, hold the door for you and everything, and all you can do is make fun."

Molly laughed and waded in the direction of the Regal. The water was up to her shins, the wide street flowing like a lazy river. The slight crown in the pavement kept most of the flood in the deep, wide gutters, but Molly saw that they could stand to be even bigger.

"This is ridiculous," she said, looking around. "Why not build the city underground? Why build here at all?"

"Are you kidding?" Cole sucked in a deep breath and blew it out. "And not enjoy this fresh air?"

Actually the air did smell quite a bit fresher. And the water was moving, carrying the last of the detritus with it, rather than standing and festering. As they splashed down the dimly lit street in the general direction of the hotel, Molly could see that the alleys were clean, the bags of refuse gone. The city was clean again. For now.

"Do you remember if these rains happen every month, twice a month, or what?"

Cole shrugged. "Nope. You seem to recall more than I do. I'd say it can't be daily. I mean, people will build in some silly places, but like you said, this is just ridiculous."

"I wonder if people ever get used to it."

"Did those Navy guys seem used to it?"

"No, but I only saw a handful of locals dashing around after that first thunder. It looked like off-worlders and tourists."

"I think we're the only tourists here."

They sloshed down several blocks in silence as the sky slowly brightened. Either the days here were extremely short, or Cole had lied and had allowed her to sleep for quite some time.

"It's freezing," she said, wringing water out of the bottom of her new blouse. Several of the pockets along her thighs bulged with rain. Molly slapped at them, sending out a spray. At least her boots seemed to have been a solid choice. The strap across the top had kept the water out, just as advertised.

Cole caught up to her and put his arm across her shoulder, trapping their heat together. Side-by-side, they kicked through the water, splashing downstream through an ankle-deep flow.

"What're we going to do now?" she asked.

"I don't know. I just wanna get out of here, to be frank. We might not even see this ship of yours. I spent all night trying to figure this out, but nothing makes sense. The Navy seems to be pushing us *toward* the ship while also keeping us *away* from it. It doesn't add up."

"I think we killed two Navy Officers last night. Maybe four, if those other two didn't get back in time." Molly felt sick just saying it. Being trained to kill aliens from a distance hadn't prepared her for this.

"I know," he said. "I spent a lot of time thinking about that as well. I don't know when the next shuttle leaves, or if there's another ship down here besides yours that can scoot us off-planet, but we need to get to Drummond and tell him he isn't crazy."

Molly nodded. "Yeah, this *world* is."

oooo

The sight of the Regal Hotel, so recently hideous, filled Molly with cheer and hope. She felt the urge to skip through the puddles toward the lobby, but the sight of crowds milling nearby forced her to restrain herself. They were going to draw quite enough attention as soaked off-worlders.

Pushing against the flow of the crowd, Molly and Cole swam upstream and into the emptying room. There were still plenty of people lying about, and the smell was awful, but it wasn't quite as bad as it'd been the day before. Molly rushed over and claimed her bag, shooting Cole an exaggerated smile.

"Yeah, you think you're so clever," he said. "But we coulda used that last night."

"Funny. As a weapon, you mean?"

"As an anchor!"

"Har. Har." Molly hoisted the bag over one shoulder, tempted to paw through it right then and change into one of the fresh outfits inside. But the room, with its safety and privacy, was just up the stairs. She followed Cole up there and down the hall, and nearly bumped into him as he came to a sudden stop.

"What's up?"

Cole brought a finger to his lips and pointed to Drummond's door. It was open. *Wide* open. Something was wrong. The day before, Drummond hadn't been comfortable cracking the door enough to let them inside, no way would he leave it like this. Molly felt her empty stomach grumble and twist into knots. She followed Cole as they crept forward. The gun from last night materializing in his right hand.

He reached out and used the barrel to press the door inward the rest of the way. It squeaked on worn hinges. Somewhere above them a kid thumped down a hallway, laughing. "Drummond?" Cole called out. "Be easy, we're comin' in."

Cole peeked around the corner, and Molly peered around Cole. The room was a wreck. Even more of a wreck than earlier. The dresser was on its face, the mattress from the bed leaned against the window, and the blinds were up, allowing a pool of light to gather in the room.

In the center of that pool lay Special Agent "Drummond" Simmons. She could tell at once that he wasn't alive; his limbs had an unnatural shape, as if he had gone down flailing. Crimson fluid spread out from his head, a pool-within-a-pool. Drummond's face pointed toward the door, staring at them with a frozen expression of shock, as if he couldn't believe he was dead.

"Don't move!" someone yelled.

But they didn't give them a chance. Boots thundered down the hallway and several men tackled Molly and Cole, pinning them to the ground.

"He'ss got a gun," someone hissed. Molly heard Cole grunt from a silent blow. The world went black as something was pulled over her head.

She tried to struggle, but she was suddenly too tired. Her body had gone limp, her brain emptied of any thoughts. It was just too many bad events over too short a period of time. She was entering what Corporal Joss, the man who had first pushed her hard in the simulators, used to call "battle fatigue." She could recall his face so clearly, could remember the training—something stirred inside of her. It fought back the black cloud that was attempting to make her envious of Drummond, jealous of the long nap and the pleasure of having this end. Her training pushed these dark thoughts into the primal lair of her brain, the old cave in which they lived.

She was not going to be consumed with hopelessness, she decided. She stayed limp, conserving her energy. But she wasn't done fighting.

12

Molly jostled between two other figures. It had already been a long, dark journey to wherever they were going. The only thing said between her and Cole was his advice to keep quiet as they were dragged down the hotel stairs.

"No talking!" one of their captors had yelled, smacking each of them through burlap sacks.

There had been quite a commotion in the lobby, orders barked in an alien tongue, and the sounds of people scampering. Molly had a clear look at the arm that pulled the hood over her head. It'd been clad in red, and it felt strange to be relieved that these weren't Navy people. For all she knew, they just wanted them for Drummond's death, a rap they could clear—but only with an alibi that was even worse!

Another bump in the road was accompanied by the splash of a puddle and the rough canvas itching her nose. Her world reeked of mildew and rattled with an alien language. Unlike the English that Palans hissed through their teeth at off-worlders, their native tongue popped and gurgled inside their mouths. It would have been a pleasant sound if Molly weren't so worried about what they were saying.

The vehicle came to a sudden stop, sending her head forward into something hard. Molly filed the gurgling huffs that ensued away in her mind as laughter. The doors popped open, and one of the men hauled her out roughly. More mirth spread as she tripped and fell to her knees. Her reward for amusing them was another slap to the back of her head.

Molly concentrated beyond their grunts of pleasure, attempting to gauge her surroundings. A strong wind howled nearby even though she felt but the slightest breeze against her damp shirt. There was a steady musical tone resonating from the wind. It sounded like a child puffing air across the lip of a bottle. She also heard water rushing to get someplace—but before she could deduce any more, she was dragged into a building.

"Downstairss," someone commanded.

There was the clink and rattle of keys and the heavy groan of tired hinges. A voice told Molly to watch her step as she was led down uneven treads. The darkness inside the hood became even blacker. Molly heard Cole call out her name.

"I'm here, Cole. I'm all right."

Another smack to the back of her head. A more serious one. "Sshut it!"

Molly was practically carried by two strong arms on either side of her. She touched her feet down cautiously, waiting for them to drop her but wary of being tripped up. Their muscles, their strength against her, had the opposite effect Cole's did. The part of her intent on surviving became worried again.

At the bottom of several twisting flights of stairs, they hauled her through what must have been half a dozen metal gates. She could hear the keys jangle and the hinges peal. The precaution seemed silly until Molly thought back to how many bodies she and Cole had already left in their wake. She wanted to feel awful for their deaths, but all she could sense was fear for her own safety. She dwelled on what she would tell her captors about last night's events.

Hopefully it wouldn't be as complicated as her nervous brain was making it. It seemed as if everyone had gone mad with conspiracy theories, but there might be a simple and rational explanation for all of this. She had to remind herself: *the galaxy was not out to get them*. All they would have to do was explain who they were and what they were doing here. Maybe show them some paperwork. And then they'd hand over her ship.

She really wanted to believe this.

Another set of hinges sang out loudly, off-key. Molly was pulled to a halt, the hood roughly tugged off her head, and she was shoved her into a cell. Metal clanged behind her; somewhere in the distance she heard Cole yelling her name. The cry was cut off with an *oomph*.

Molly was alone. In a stone cubicle. A mesh of thick steel bars covered the side through which she'd been pushed. The opposite wall was solid rock with a square window cut out of it, spanned with two bars.

Beyond, she could see the far side of what appeared to be a massive canyon. The wind moaned as it tore across the small opening before her. She leaned close to the bars, focusing on a series of vertical streaks of white on the other canyon wall. They waved slightly, like strings hanging in a breeze. Waterfalls. Hundreds, maybe thousands of them plummeting into the void.

The window was too cramped to see to the bottom of the canyon, but she thought she could hear the rush of a river below. So *this* was one of the Palan canyons. The new context jarred more memories of the Palan rains. Facts memorized for a test percolated into her long-term memory. She could visualize the planet, its sole continent a high plateau carved with deep ruts. The water rushed across it from the rains and into an ocean more vast than her Pacific. Molly cursed herself for concentrating on star charts for this trip, neglecting to study any of the planets between. That oversight was costing her.

She gripped the bars and allowed the cool wind from the canyon to punish her shivering body. The steel was unnecessary, she realized. Unless her captors were simply trying to block an *easy* way out. How fitting: a world of notorious criminals and pirates had concocted a method of containment so simple, so effective, and so hopeless. They'd just carved it into the side of a canyon and provided prisoners with an open window through which they could chuck any hope of escape.

Molly sat down on a stone ledge carved out of one wall. She rested elbows on knees, then noticed the hole in the cell floor for the first time. Scurrying over to investigate, she wished she hadn't. The hole was a funnel carved out of solid stone, leading down to an opening about a decimeter across. The mess caked on the edges marked its purpose clearly.

She recoiled away from the discovery and sat back on the rock cot. For just a moment, she was glad she'd had nothing to eat or drink in half a day.

There was a rattle at her door.

"Sstay back, prissoner." A large Palan with hairy arms and a broad, metallic face worked the lock. As he opened the door, a smaller man stepped around him, his hands behind his back.

"Molly Fyde?" the thinner man asked.

"Yes!" she nearly leaped up to clasp the man, thrilled that someone would know her, for whatever reason.

The Palan brought his hands in front of him; he was holding a stack of papers pressed flat on top of her leather reader case. Molly settled back down on the ledge, the excitement drained from her.

"A nursse?" He thumbed through the medical records, pages from Cole's conspiracy file.

"What? No, no. Those were—it's nothing. I'm just a student. I'm here for a ship called the *Parsona*. My father left it to me. It's all in there."

"Yesss. Much paper in here. Not all of it real, though." He smiled up at her. "But at leasst your name iss real. Your reaction told me." His smile broadened at his own cleverness. "Now, prissoner Fyde, why are you trying to rob me of my sship?"

"Your ship?" Anger welled up. "Who are you? The Navy paid you fair and square!"

She'd said too much; she saw it in his reaction, the way his head tilted to the side and his eyes widened.

"No matter, prisoner Fyde. You'll not be tried for a theft you never got around to. Drummond'ss death and the messs you made on the avenue last night will be *enough*." He sorted the paper back into the pouch.

"Enough for *what*? Who are you?"

"Enough for your death, prissoner Fyde; you will be tried in court. To answsswer your query: we are the Hommul. We are in charge of Palan Ssecurity now. The Ssmitthss. . ." her captor seethed with effort, ". . .are no more. And neither iss whatever deal you had with them."

With that, he turned and left. The brute of a Palan standing in the hallway sealed her door with a loud clack. Both silvery men shuffled off in the direction she thought Cole had been taken.

A trial? From *these* guys? She couldn't imagine what their concept of justice would be like. Certainly bribes had a lot to do with it—bribes and bartering seemed to rule the Palan economy—but Molly had no money. She knew Cole had some funds from the Navy, but surely the pirates would've taken that, along with everything else they owned.

Molly fought back the black cloud swirling inside her and recalled last night: how lucky she was just to be alive. She went to the window, pulled in large gulps of fresh air tinged with the scent of water and vegetation, and tried to remain positive.

A scuffling sound behind her interrupted her meditation. She turned to find a Palan boy smaller than herself standing outside the bars. "Food and water," he said, holding something out to her.

Molly approached the gate cautiously, looking into the silver eyes of a boy her own age, maybe younger. His coppery hair was trimmed back short, his clothes baggy, but not stylishly so. More like hand-me-downs he'd been forced to wear.

"Thank you." She reached through the bars and took the two metal tins. One sloshed with a yellowish fluid, the other rattled with large brown pebbles of what she assumed, by the process of elimination, must be food.

The boy turned to go.

"Wait!" she said. "What's your name?"

He turned back to her and smiled. "Walter," he said.

"Hi, Walter. I'm Molly."

"I know. Molly Fyde. I heard. And don't worry, the trial will be very quick."

"Quick? How quick?"

"Today," he said. And Molly couldn't tell if it was a smile now, or a sneer. The boy returned to his cart and was about to move on.

"I have lots of money," she lied.

Walter turned and approached the bars. "Palan people can ssmell a lie," he informed her. "Even the day before the rainss we can ssmell a lie. You have nothing."

"I have a ship."

Walter sniffed. "Maybe you *had* a sship. But my uncle hass it now. One day *I* will have it." He turned to go; Molly pressed on.

"Only if your uncle is still in power long enough. Look, let's barter, okay? I can't give you the ship, but I can get you a reward for getting me out of here. Help me and my friend escape, and I'll take you off this planet to more money than you can dream of."

"*Leave* Palan?" He snorted. "Why would I want to go? What iss there for me beyond Palan?" It was definitely a sneer.

"Whatever you want. No more working for your uncle. The Navy'll reward you for helping us. Richly." There was a ripple across his metallic-looking visage. He looked Molly up and down, and she suddenly became aware of the way her soaked shirt clung to her chest and wondered whether the boy would be more likely to help her or *hurt* her.

"I'm the daughter of an Admiral in the Earth Navy," she told him. "You could have more riches than your uncle ever dreamed of. I *promise*." Even if the boy betrayed her to his uncles, this information might make her freedom worth bartering for. Lucin would be outraged at how this had turned out, but Molly didn't see any other path to take. Besides, she wouldn't *be* in this mess if Navy personnel had cooperated.

Walter sniffed the air, his nose creeping up toward the rock ceiling. "You do not lie. Interesssting."

Molly tried to think of more to say as Walter pushed his cart of food and water cans further down the aisle of cells. Over the rattling of the tins and the noise of metal wheels scraping on rock, she could hear the strange boy mumbling to himself in a different language, one devoid of anything that hissed—like the sounds of flooding water.

○ ○ ○ ○

Hours went by on the stone ledge. Molly's stomach grumbled louder at the Palan jail food than it had when she was starving. Several hunks of the meal were still in the tin, but the precious calories—if indeed the chalky stuff had any—didn't seem worth the foul taste.

The can of yellowish water, still half-full, sat beside the food. For a planet renowned for its fresh rain, this stuff must have required quite a bit of preparation.

The colors outside her window dulled with the rising sun, and still no word from her jailers. The one time she worked up enough courage to call for Cole, it returned nothing but jeers from some distant prisoners. The waiting and the unknown took turns torturing her.

It was past midday when she heard the squeaking of Walter's cart heading her way. He had never returned from the other direction, and now he came as before. Molly figured there were multiple ways up, or a second hallway around. None of this info likely mattered, but the tactical training would likely remain with her forever. She'd been soaking in it ever since she was born.

"Food and water." It was the same greeting. Molly got up, felt a little weak and dizzy, and clung to the bars. It was the same fare.

"Walter, I need some clean water. Some different food."

"No. I'm ssorry." He shook his head sadly. "Your trial iss not going very well. They will not wasste food on someone who may be guilty."

"My trial is underway now?" Molly felt as if she was going to be sick.

"Yeah. There iss not much defensse. You have killed more people at your age than my uncle had. It iss the only thing they like about you."

"Have you thought about my offer? Surely you don't want to be an errand boy for your uncles, do you? Think about the freedoms you could have off this planet. There'll be a reward, I promise." Molly considered the items she could barter with and then added: "We could be friends."

This elicited a smile; he sniffed and nodded. "Ssome of that iss true. Hard to ssay which." He rubbed his hand back and forth over the stubble on his head, peering at the ground.

"Yeah, I thought about your offer, and I could get you out, but not the boy. They have him passt my cart and my key. He isss down where there iss only one room. And, anyway, hiss trial iss already over. He'll be dead by morning."

as well have reached through the bars
.. .lly in the gut. She sank to her knees, her hands gripping the bars for support. *By morning?* This had to be a nightmare. A stupid bad dream. She'd had these silly fantasies of traveling across the stars and doing odd jobs and being with Cole forever. She had gone into this as if it were a vacation instead of a serious mission, and at every step things had gone horribly wrong.

She started to cry, her hands still up on the bars, her back moving up and down with her quiet sobs as tears rolled down her cheeks. She could sense Walter kneeling down across from her.

"Don't cry," he told her, touching his own face, his eyes narrowing. "I'll help you out. We'll esscape tonight, okay? Forget about the boy."

Molly pulled up the hem of her ruined T-shirt, still moist from her last horror and clinging to her chest; she wiped away snot and tears.

"Forget about the boy," Walter said again. There was a clanging of a gate down the hallway. He stood quickly and hissed a final "Tonight" before turning to go.

But Molly could only think about the morning.

oooo

There was no chance of sleeping as night fell, and no dinner had been served. Molly cried as much as her body was able and felt sore and cold from the effort. The breeze reaching through the cell chilled her to the bone, even after wringing most of the wetness from her shirt.

There was no telling when or if Walter might try to spring her, but she'd been thinking of as many crazy ideas as she could to keep her mind off it. Some of these plans relied on her jailers coming in and making mistakes. Some assumed Walter would be bringing weapons. Some pretended her hand-to-hand courses in the Navy had somehow worked miracles.

One of them toyed with the laws of physics.

This mixture of daydreaming and waking nightmare made the hours feel like days. She had no idea what time it was when she noted the soft padding of bare feet followed by Walter whispering her name.

She grabbed her boots, tied together by their laces, and draped them over her neck; she slid silently to the door. Walter was fiddling with a can of oil and a key. "The hingess," he said quietly, passing her the bottle after he worked some into the lock.

Molly carefully squirted some oil on the three large hinges and watched Walter work the key into the mechanism.

It opened with a small click.

"Come," he whispered.

"Wait here," Molly said. She rushed off to the left on silent feet, concealed by the sounds of alien snores.

Fifty meters down the hallway she came to a gate with a massive lock. She could see more gates beyond.

Several of her plans ground instantly to dust.

She rushed back to Walter, who seemed agitated by the delay.

"Forget him," he said. "Come."

Molly followed him back through the same gates she'd been dragged through earlier that day; they left them open as they hurried along. When they got to a flight of steps, Walter continued straight ahead and Molly hesitated. This *had* to be the way she'd been brought down.

"Come," he said.

She did, following him down another dark corridor and through several more gates. Then, without warning, Walter darted to the side and disappeared into a solid wall. When Molly caught up, she saw there was a nook in the stone. A rusty ladder was fastened to the back side of the indention, leading through holes above and below.

Walter's bare, grey feet disappeared through the passage above. Molly remembered what he'd said about the "room below" where Cole was kept. She wanted to go down and explore, but this place was full of gates and she had no key. All she had was a guide who didn't seem to care whether Cole lived or died.

Her heart sank. Grudgingly, she ascended the ladder after Walter as more of her rescue plans melted away.

At several holes, the rusted iron ladder went through small round gates. Each of them hung open, smelling of Walter's oil. After a few minutes of climbing, Molly emerged into the fresh air of a cool evening, but she couldn't feel good about being free while Cole awaited execution. She crouched next to Walter, who was peering into the black. Only one plan really remained.

"Where's the ship?" she asked.

"Near," he said. "They moved it after Drummond tried to ssteal it. There iss a docking platform at the bottom of the canyon. It iss there. I checked it today, full of energy. Not much food." He turned to look at her, and she spotted the dull glow in his eyes. "You can fly?"

She nodded. *Oh, yes . . . I can fly*, she thought.

He dipped his head once and sneered. Then he stole across the packed ground toward the sound of wind and water. Molly stayed in a low crouch and tried to keep up.

When Walter came to a sudden stop at the end of the path, Molly bumped into him, and they both leaned forward, regaining their balance.

"Watch it!" he hissed, and she could see why. They were poised at the edge of a canyon that moonlight could not fully penetrate nor cross. It was even bigger in the dark, with her imagination filling the void. It would take them forever to work their way down.

"Put it on." Walter held something out to her. It looked like the flight harnesses sewn on top of Academy jumpsuits. It had the same sort of D-rings and layout. It was hard to figure out exactly what went where, but Walter seemed eager to assist her. His touch made her shiver as they worked the leggings up over her pant legs. She returned his sneer with a half-hearted smile.

Once they were both in and before she could ask what they were doing, Walter clipped something onto her back with a loud *snick*. He contorted his body to do the same to himself. Then he gave her one last wicked grin before shoving her over the edge.

Molly couldn't help it—she screamed. As loud as she could.

She dropped three meters straight down before the harness yanked at her chest and sent her zipping away from the ledge. The webbing around her thighs pinched her viciously, but before she could register the pain, she was hurtling forward into a stiff breeze, flying toward the far side of the canyon. Something mechanical screamed above her, steadily increasing its pitch. A wheel on a wire, spinning.

It was impossible to see in the wan moonlight. Even so, Molly could sense the bulk of the other side approaching, as if a different sort of blackness loomed ahead. She braced for impact, pulling her hands above her exposed head, but none came. She continued to fly at near-terminal velocity as the large wall of dark hardly got closer. It was *huge*.

She flew farther, the bitter wind stinging her eyes and chill bumps popping out on exposed skin. A gust of wind tore through the canyon, whipping the slack wire sideways and eliciting another wild scream of pure terror. Molly tucked her knees to her chest and wrapped her hands around them, shivering and terrified.

She wanted it to stop.

Gently.

She could barely hear the whine of the wheel above her over the deafening wind, but she noticed a shift in its pitch, a blessed lowering. Her stomach dropped as she started gaining altitude, having reached the bottom of the drooping wire that stretched across the canyon. As she slid up toward the other side, her speed slowed to something only moderately insane. She urged it to reduce even further when a new danger occurred to her: not *enough* speed and she'd drift back to the center of the canyon. Toward Walter, if he'd been crazy enough to follow.

She blinked the tears out of her eyes and squinted into the darkness, straining to see what was ahead, to see if that wall of black was getting any nearer.

Without warning, something appeared below her: a rock ledge of some sort. She pulled into an even tighter ball, scared of hitting something, but the platform was several meters below. She glided above it, still moving dangerously fast, when two vertical nets of webbing began slanting in from both sides. She was flying into a wedge of some sort, still rising up and losing speed. As soon as they squeezed in close enough, Molly reached out and grabbed at them. Her right elbow snagged itself in one of the loops, twisting her violently to the side as the crazy ride came to an end.

Then Walter slammed into her back, forcing the air out of both of them with a combination of grunt and hiss.

Walter won his breath back first. "Fun, no?" He laughed. It was the sound of air escaping a balloon.

Molly would have slapped him if it wouldn't mean letting go of the webbing. "Maybe if you told me first, you jerk."

Her complaint just increased the air pressure of the balloon. "People pay good money to do thisss."

Molly climbed up the netting to take the slack out of her tether. It was awkward, but she was able to reach around to unhook herself. She climbed down until she reached the bottom of the netting and to the walkway below. Above her, Walter made noises as he struggled to free himself.

She reached out and tested the platform before letting go of the webbing. Solid rock, probably carved out of the cliff. She didn't need directions from Walter—one way led out to emptiness—so she hurried toward the face of the canyon, the sounds of a descending waterfall working through the ringing in her ears.

Walter caught up to her and ran past, huffing for breath. When they got to the end of the walk, he led her over a turnstile and pushed through a flimsy door leading into the canyon wall. The hallway beyond was wider than the ones in the prison. The soft glow of electric lights illuminated their passage through a room full of harnesses and a waiting area with benches. No rusty gates barred their way as they wound down a flight of steps. Molly followed Walter through a large room with lots of tables and chairs and a small stage, and then into some mechanical spaces. A loud humming emanated from somewhere nearby.

"Generatorss," Walter explained, as if he could smell her confusion.

Hydroelectric, she figured, remembering the ribbons of water cascading down. She followed along through more mechanical rooms and toward the dull roaring. Every piece of machinery they passed had the look of obsolescence. It all seemed cobbled together and poorly maintained, with wires snaking from one point to another along the ground rather than properly routed through ductwork or the ceiling. Tools lay scattered by one large electrical cabinet, probably left there until something else broke. *Won't be long,* she surmised. Tape seemed to hold much of the equipment together. It was as if things were fixed just enough to get them running and no more. Why do preventive maintenance and help out whichever clan took over next?

As they snaked through several more industrial-looking passages full of wheezing equipment and squeaking bearings, Molly thought about how closely Palan society resembled its weather. They let everything get out of control here, not a care in the world. Meanwhile, they waited for the next violent wave to sweep through and start things over again. To Molly, it seemed like a process that celebrated erosion—and all *that* was good for was digging large ditches.

The depressing sight of so much ruin and the long jaunt through repetitive scenery had her mind wandering away from what she was running toward. This made the shock so much more intense when she burst through another door, no different from the rest, and staggered—fighting for her breath—into the large cavern on the other side.

Molly couldn't believe what she was seeing: *Parsona.*

GN-290 PARSONA

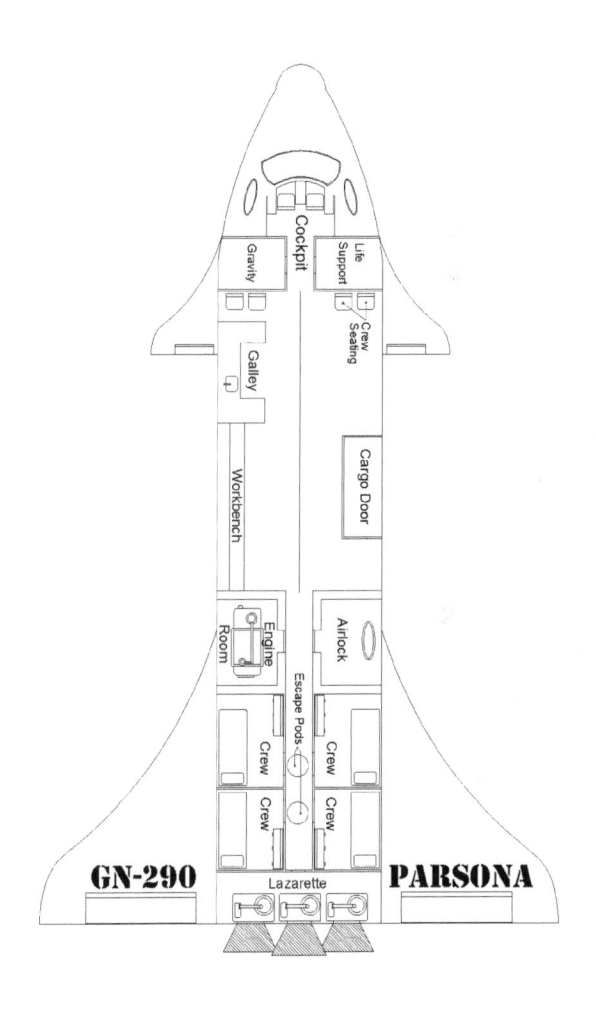

- Cockpit
- Gravity
- Life Support
- Crew Seating
- Galley
- Workbench
- Cargo Door
- Engine Room
- Airlock
- Escape Pods
- Crew
- Crew
- Crew
- Crew
- Lazarette

13

She could've picked that shape out of a used shipyard full of a thousand hulls. It was the profile of a family member: a large window spanning the cockpit, rounded nose below, wide-swept wings that made her as good a craft in atmosphere as she was in a vacuum.

It was a classic design, inspired by the first ships to soar in space and float to the ground.

She was beautiful.

Along her back were the ridges for flight control and the jutting vertical fins many of the modern starships went without. Two small wings, identical to the larger ones at the rear, stood out below the cockpit windows. The hump behind one window marked the life-support systems, a vulnerability that partly explained the GN-290's discontinuation.

Despite her age and the limited run of the model, she looked swift, even at rest. Flecks of paint were missing here and there, and lots of micrometeor burns streaked down the hull, but overall the ship looked to be in fine condition. And aside from being lazily parked nose-in, a habit typical of jittery pilots, *Parsona* looked ready to fly.

Frozen in the doorway, Molly absorbed the sight. She wanted to shout for joy, but thoughts of Cole locked up in a rock cell tempered her enthusiasm. She needed to get to work.

Walter seemed to agree. He clapped his hands to break her spell and asked about getting the hangar doors open. Molly nodded and watched him scamper over to a rusty console. She left him to it and rushed around the other side of the ship, where the cargo ramp stood wide open. Her feet hit the old metal, the sound and spring of it taking her back to her childhood. Inside, familiar scents greeted her, bringing back more memories. She paused, feeling closer to her family than she had in ten years.

Then the enormity of their predicament hit her, making her feel alone and overwhelmed. This was a massive piece of machinery. *Real* machinery. She'd learned to fly in a simulator. In classrooms, she'd learned basic maintenance and mechanical duties. Now she stood in the cargo bay of a starship over fifty meters long. When she fired it up, actual mechanical bits would be roaring into motion, not the simulated vibration of a glorified computer. The thought of taking off in this thing without someone here to help her made her stomach flip; she had a sudden urge to use the bathroom.

She fought these self-doubts and nervously made her way toward the cockpit as the sound of metal scraping on metal filtered in from beyond the ship. Molly heard the hiss of a powerful wind and glanced through one of the portholes. Walter had the hangar doors opening up.

He joined Molly inside the ship, anxious to get underway. "Take off," he told her.

"It's not that easy," she explained. "I have to do some things first."

"No time. Daylight ssoon."

"Walter, we can't get out of here until I fix the hyperspace drive. Arrange those boxes or load some more supplies. I need at least an hour."

"An hour?" Walter frowned, then sniffed the air. "An hour it iss." He ticked off fingers with his thumb. "Four tripss to the ssupply room," he muttered to himself before hurrying down the cargo ramp.

"I was kinda hoping you'd help out *here*," Molly called after him, but the boy was already gone. "Okay then." She turned to the workbench and charged up her father's old welding torch. *This is going to work*, she told herself.

She lost herself in each task: cutting lengths of metal tubing from one of the bunks, welding them into a single rod six meters long, running wires from the engine room. The distraction forced her worries away from Cole and the upcoming challenge of flying the old ship.

It also freed her subconscious to secretly fiddle with a puzzle of its own: if Walter didn't have keys for the gates leading to Cole, how had he disappeared that direction yesterday without passing back in front of her cell?

oooo

Cole lay prone on the freezing floor. He had no choice; his cell was a meter wide and just as tall—a stone coffin. Yesterday, his new friends had to drag him into the hallway to have enough room to beat on him properly. One of his ribs felt cracked from their hospitality, and he'd been spitting up blood all night.

The window at the end of the cell, however, was the primary source of his misery. A steady flow of cold evening air poured in, and he had no way of escaping it. He tried blocking it off with his feet, but even through his boots he could feel the chill damaging his toes. His teeth chattered violently as he rubbed his arms to keep the blood circulating through his chest. The uncontrollable shivering was a relentless assault on his tender ribs.

The only food he'd been given looked like something you'd feed a dog—one you didn't particularly care for. A hissing Palan had tossed the pellets in by Cole's head. A tin of water thrown in after spilled across the stone and soaked through Cole's shirt. He couldn't turn around to see who tormented him, but the mysterious figure promised he'd be executed in the morning.

Cole wasn't sure he could hang around long enough to make the appointment.

What hurt the most, the thing that kept digging into him, was having failed to protect Molly. No telling what their captors were doing to her. Would they give Molly and him a trial? Would Molly have to watch him be executed? Would Lucin and the Navy ever be able to piece together what had happened here?

Cole's neck cramped up from the shivering of his head and shoulders, and his jaw felt numb from the continuous muscle spasms clattering his teeth together. Minutes dragged out into hours as he suffered the longest night of his life.

It seemed a lifetime later when the faintest glow of a new day began filtering past his boots. Cole parted them, allowing the chilled air to travel up his stomach and chest. It was worth the pain to watch the distant canyon wall color itself in a welcome dawn. The sunlight signaled his promised execution, but also an end to the biting cold and the strange mixture of numbness and agony.

I may just live long enough to be killed, he thought. It made him want to laugh out loud, this private joke. Laugh and scream.

Delirium must be setting in.

And now he was hearing things. Over the rush of the wind and the staccato of his crashing teeth, Cole imagined he could hear starship thrusters roaring outside: the high pitch of jet turbines mixing with the loud air nozzles used for maneuvering. It seemed awfully detailed for an auditory hallucination.

Pulling his boots completely out of the window, Cole raised his sore chin and looked down the length of his beaten body.

Through the small square of light, he gaped disbelievingly at the mirage rising into view.

If *that* wasn't real, Cole knew he'd really lost it.

oooo

Walter tested the webbing harness, yanking the tether that secured him to the cargo bay. He couldn't believe he was going along with this. He'd nearly mutinied when he learned what Molly had planned. Not that he understood how this would work, but nobody *broke out* of Palan Max. He'd tried it himself. It was impossible. The only two ways out were bribery and death. And most Palans only had coin for the latter.

Then again, he'd gone and helped her escape for nothing but a promise and the mere hope for reward. What had he been thinking? Or *had* he been thinking? This girl—floods take him—she was strange and incredible and intoxicating, making him do stupid stuff. And he was *not* stupid.

Walter watched the canyon wall slide by beyond the porthole, wondering how he'd gotten himself in this mess. *Doesn't matter now*, he decided. There was no turning back. Someone would be waking his uncle soon, blabbering about an empty cell and a lot of oiled hinges. He just needed to stall the escape and hope the guards had already gotten to the boy. What choice did he have? He couldn't fly this contraption, and now he *really* needed to get off-planet. He'd return for the other spoils later. Much later. When someone *else* was in charge.

He shifted the strange contraption in his hand. It was nice and light; he couldn't see how this thing was going to free the human. At one end of the pole the girl had welded a wide cross, about six feet between the tips. The other end, about twenty feet away, had a chain attached, which snaked back to the workbench.

Four wires trailed from the tips of the cross and disappeared around the corner into some sort of mechanical room.

Walter supposed they could be blasting wires. He'd seen explosives that worked like this. Was the plan to blow through three feet of Palan stone? If so, she was going to be pretty upset when she saw how small the boy's cell was. And what will be left of him inside?

The loading ramp opened a crack, letting in a sliver of morning light and a loud hiss of wind. He leaned against the tether and tightened his grip on the cold metal.

He'd help rescue her friend, Walter decided, or at least make it appear he'd tried. Besides, he'd have plenty of opportunities to get the human boy out of the way.

Later.

oooo

Molly lowered the cargo ramp from the cockpit and turned on the floodlights to illuminate the side of the canyon. Once the ramp extended fully, she pulled the ship up, pivoting it around until the open bay lined up with the solitary, barred window. She shot a brief glance over her shoulder and saw Walter extending the long boom through the opening.

She performed more calculations in her head, thinking about the thickness of the wall in her own cell and how much mass was likely in the rock. She kept dialing the hyperdrive down, far past its lower limits. Safety overrides flashed red and chimed at her relentlessly as the howling wind coursed through the ship. Molly's hair had grown long enough for the ends to flick into her eyes, but she couldn't take her hands off the flight controls and the maneuvering jets to do anything about it.

This was her *least* sane plan. The one that toyed with the laws of physics.

She could get only within five meters or so of the canyon wall, even with *Parsona's* wings retracted in their zero-G position. Harsh gusts swirled and buffeted the ship from every direction. Holding her steady while simultaneously performing rough hyperdrive calculations was a challenge of dexterity and clear thinking unlike anything the Navy had ever thrown at her. Deep in the recesses of her female ego, Molly wondered how many men would be able to pull this off, much less dream it up.

Then again, it was precisely this sort of stunt that had won her demerits at the Academy and eventually got her expelled.

She had the cargo security cam pulled up on the dash's vid screen. It was one more thing demanding her attention. On it, she could see Walter struggling with the long aluminum frame, yelling at her over the howling wind, complaining that the contraption was too heavy.

It shouldn't be, she thought.

"OKAY!" he hollered. "Ready!"

Molly silently urged Cole to the other side of his cell. She reached over quickly to turn down the hyperdrive a little more, just in case, and then checked the security cam again.

The device wasn't in place. Walter was holding one of the tips in the center of the cell window.

Damn. She'd explained it a dozen times. No way was she going to pull away and go over it again; they were running out of time. She kept her eyes on the video screen and fought to hold the ship steady in the howling wind. Both of her hands twitched with every gust, counteracting each blast of air with an opposite one from the maneuvering jets. Flying while looking at the screen felt like combing her hair in the mirror for the first time. She moved the wrong way, corrected, tried to get the hang of it.

They only had one shot. Molly boosted the ship up a meter or so to compensate for Walter. She also brought the ship closer to the cliff wall, pressing the device in place herself.

The jump coordinates were already plugged in—she'd chosen to move the mass thirty meters straight up. She let go of the maneuvering jets and punched the hyperdrive as fast as she could.

With a loud ZAP and a yelp from Walter, the drive fired, trying to move the ship through hyperspace and up thirty meters. But instead of sending these instructions to the four anchor points throughout the ship, they travelled down the less-resistant wire Molly had added. What they found at the tips was solid rock, and not knowing any different—mass was mass—they moved the specified amount to the programmed coordinates.

The window and one side of Cole's cell vanished, entering hyperspace. Thirty meters up, the material would find no place to return and disappear forever.

On the vid screen, Molly checked the hole she'd made. The size was right and had punched all the way through. She held her breath and moved the searchlight over. Something moved.

Cole.

A mix of dread and relief swelled up inside. He was alive, but what kind of hole had they been keeping him in? The cell was much smaller than the chunk of rock she'd removed. She watched him scoot forward and lower himself to the ledge formed by the evacuated square of stone. She could also see something else on the camera screen: something moving beyond him.

She shut down the hyperdrive to transform the magic wand into a lifeline. "Walter!" she yelled over her shoulder. "Get the pole back up there!" He had let it sag after the zap. Cole stood in the square hole, the incredible thickness of the gaping wall creating a nice perch. He looked over his shoulder at whoever was crawling in after him, then turned to look back at the ship.

"Grab the cross!" Molly yelled at the screen, as if Cole could hear her over the roar of the thrusters. She focused on Walter as he wrestled with the wind for control of the aluminum pole. Molly urged both of them along, wishing she could do more as Walter turned to the security camera and yelled something, shaking his head. His metallic face contorted into a mad grimace from the effort—a sneer of sorts.

Molly felt powerless. The autopilot would never be able to hold them in this wind. She tried to pull up a little to again position the long rod herself, but it sagged too much and hung too far away. She watched the screen in frustration. Beyond Cole, she could see someone squeezing into the hole after him—large hands reaching out.

Cole threw a fist into the darkness and then spun back toward the ship. He was arching his back, trying to keep out of someone's clutches. He teetered forward, his eyes peering through the cargo bay. It seemed as if he was looking through the security camera and right at Molly as he leaned forward, falling.

And then he jumped.

Molly gasped as Cole vanished beneath *Parsona*. Her hands twitched, her concentration broken. The tip of one wing made contact with the rock, sending a shudder through the ship. Molly pulled away and heard another loud bang of metal.

It was the chain welded to the workbench pulling tight. Walter jumped away from the lifeline, his hands up in the air, the aluminum pole gone. Molly pulled farther away from the cliff, freeing up a hand to switch to the belly cam. There he was, swinging across the vid screen and out of sight, his arms locked around the aluminum cross.

You crazy jerk, she thought.

Molly pulled across the canyon, back to the landing platform outside the hangar bay. The original plan had been to reload at the lip of the cliff, but that seemed too far away. She needed to get him inside the ship before her chest burst open.

It wasn't until she brought Cole over the landing platform that she could breathe again. She lowered him slowly, saw him drop from a meter up, and waited for him to stagger out of the way. She set *Parsona* down gently, but the landing gear didn't even have time to compress fully before she heard him stomping up the loading ramp. She looked over her shoulder to confirm everyone was onboard; Cole staggered into the cargo bay, nearly collapsing.

Fighting the urge to rush to him, Molly concentrated instead on getting off that cursed planet; there was no telling what kind of pursuit they could expect from pirates or the Navy. She keyed the cargo door shut and nosed back into the dawn-streaked canyon.

Below *Parsona,* four wires dangled, shorted together as the forgotten aluminum frame was crushed by the cargo door. The wires sparked to life, leaving a bright trail in the wake of their flight.

As the starship *Parsona* rose up and out of the Palan atmosphere, her unique hyperdrive kept humming on an unusually low setting. Instructions continued to stream down to the fused wires, but all they encountered was the fabric of the cosmos.

So they ripped it open—creating a tear in space.

PART 3
THE MECHANICAL BEAR

*"Many undiscovered things . . .
are best left that way."*

~The Bern Seer~

14

Nothing rose in the atmosphere to challenge their flight. Molly wasn't sure if it was the recent changing of the guard or the general disorganization below. She didn't care. Physically and emotionally, Palan was proving to be an easy planet to run from.

She wanted to rush back and tend to Cole, but he made his own way into the cockpit. She could see his reflection in the carboglass, one hand pressed to his ribs, the other one reaching forward to tousle her hair.

"Miss me?"

Molly wanted desperately to turn and reach out to him, to verify he was safe. But just the feeling of his cold hand on her scalp made flying difficult. She had too many emotions racing through her, mixing with the adrenaline. She pulled her head away and reached for the radio, dialing it to full scan mode. Her hand shook visibly; she left Cole's question unanswered.

He stood beside her, peering at the vid screen. She glanced at it as well and saw Walter glaring toward the cockpit.

"I guess not," he said. "So. You've been out making friends while they tried beating me to death, is that it?"

Molly tried to laugh, but thanks to her nerves, it came out more like a cough. "You're *welcome*," she managed, her voice quaking.

Cole slid his hand down the back of Molly's neck, supporting himself on her shoulder as he leaned over the flight console. He peered through the windshield then scanned the dash, checking out its SADAR unit and nav charts. "She's a beaut," he said.

Molly nodded. Cole's hand no longer felt cold. Or maybe it was just her neck flushing with heat. The adrenaline shakes went away in an instant, replaced with a feeling of paralysis. She didn't want to move and hoped Cole wouldn't either.

But he did.

Leaning down, Cole kissed her, briefly, on the top of her head. He patted her on the shoulder. "Thank you," he whispered.

As he pulled away and stumbled back into the cargo bay, Molly's face and ears burned. She could hear Cole and Walter introducing themselves over the pounding of her pulse, but just barely. She tried to imagine how the two of them were going to get along on the flight to Earth, and it made her feel as though she should be remembering something important, something she needed to tell Walter or ask him. *Did it have to do with the food cart, or a key?* Her stomach interrupted her, the thought of Palan prison food making it erupt in protest. She gathered her voice and threw a request over her shoulder. "When you guys get done talking sports, could you bring me something to eat?"

On the vid screen, she saw Walter bolt into action, hopefully rustling up better fare than he'd served yesterday. Meanwhile, she busied herself with the systems checks she *should've* performed before takeoff—the routine tasks that seem to get in the way of prison breaks. She checked the astral charts first, and the news there wasn't good. Drummond was supposed to have updated them, but the charts were almost as old as she was. At least a hundred planets had been discovered since these things were made, and a few stars were no longer around. Dozens of safe jump zones had moved and better ones located.

Jump zones. *Drenards!* Molly looked at the small fusion fuel readout and felt sick. It showed 20 percent and falling! She'd forgotten the aluminum rig and the wires, assuming she could just turn off the drive and it'd be safe.

"Cole?" she yelled over her shoulder.

"Yeah?"

"I need you to take the stick for a minute."

Molly turned as he entered the cockpit, chewing on something. He slurped on a small bag of juice. "Some of Drummond's stuff," he explained, his mouth full. "Walter's bringing you some."

"In a minute," she said, taking in Cole's appearance. His face was bruised, and blood was caked below his nostrils. Molly felt an urge to tend to him, but she needed to worry about the hyperdrive first. "Keep us heading away from Palan, and don't turn on the hyperdrive."

Cole worked himself into the pilot's seat. "You don't want to jump out of here?" he called after her. But Molly was already crossing the cargo bay, heading toward the engine room.

Passing the workbench, she grabbed a welding glove and a scrap of aluminum pipe left over from her "craft time." She tugged the glove on and clutched the pipe as she entered the engine room—where she discovered what she'd feared she might. The hyperdrive indicator was flashing green; the thing was running, even though the cockpit controls were locked off!

Molly surveyed the main hyperdrive housing. The device was as big as a refrigerator lying on its side. Most of the interior was a firing chamber for the fusion fuel. There wasn't much else to the device: its principles of operation were closely guarded secrets. Hyperdrive Mechanics had been a weekend Lab tacked onto their semester of Advanced Thruster Repair. All cadets had to know was how to ensure coordinates were fed properly from the nav computer and to make sure the four drive wires were grounded to the ship's chassis.

It was the drive wires that Molly had rerouted in order to spring Cole. And all four of the posts she had soldered them to were sparking slightly. They hadn't been before.

There must be a short somewhere, she thought, *probably in the cargo door.* Luckily it had happened *after* Cole's crazy stunt, or else he wouldn't be here anymore. He would've moved thirty meters up, bumped into the rock in his way, and winked out of existence.

Molly stepped forward, raising the pipe with one arm. She swung it as hard as she could at the nearest post, hoping to break the wire off. Time slowed to a crawl. She flashed back to the day before, to the brutality of hitting that Navy man in the head. At the time, she thought she'd killed him. . .

Molly was jarred back to the present as she struck the post and knocked the wire free. The hyperdrive light went red. And most of the aluminum pipe disappeared right out of her hand!

Only a few inches of the metal tube were left, the rest probably warped thirty meters straight up. The cleanly severed tip stuck out of her gloved fist, the polished metal interior gleaming in a way that no mechanical cut ever could. Molly loosened her grip on the bit that remained and wondered what would've happened if the hyperdrive had been turned up a little more. *Would she be looking inside her wrist?* And what did she think the welding glove would have protected her against?

She left the piece of pipe in the engine room and decided, right there, that this little episode would never leave the engine room.

Returning the glove to the workbench, she accepted the rations Walter held out to her. He seemed extremely pleased with himself and with all the goodies he had strewn around the cargo bay. Molly took a sip of juice and squeezed his arm. "Thanks for getting us out of there," she told him.

"My pleassure," he said.

"There are four cabins past the engine room. You can have either one on the Starboard side, okay?" She gestured back toward the rear of the ship. "Right side," she added, pointing for emphasis.

Walter nodded.

"And since you seem to be good with merchandise and gear, I would love to have you as my Cargo Officer. At least until we get to Earth."

Walter beamed; it was nothing like his sneer at all. He rubbed the shoulder Molly had squeezed. "Officser," he repeated.

"Yeah, Cargo Officer." Molly opened a few drawers and cabinets, looking for the ship manifest. Every compartment appeared to have been rummaged through, not at all like her father normally kept things. She eventually found the clipboard under a stack of manuals for the ship's mechanical and electrical systems.

"This is a manifest," she told Walter. "You keep up with everything on a ship with this. How much, what it is, what you paid for it, what you hope to sell it for, who owns it, where you got it, where it's stored. . ." She ran her finger along the top row, reading the header and wondering if the Palan was able to follow along.

oooo

Walter watched, mesmerized. The way most Palans did things was *much* different. Nothing stayed in one place long enough to bother writing anything down. This was more like the way *he* did things. The way he would lay out team duties for his band of junior pirates when they went on market raids, or the way he'd organized his food cart after his uncle punished him with prison duty after that last heist.

His uncle. Walter figured his uncle would have a bounty out on his head by now. Stealing a spaceship and two prisoners in a single morning probably meant he could never go home again. The thought didn't make him sad. Not at all. It made him think of the differences between him and his uncle, and of all his great ideas the old bastard had waved away.

"You *can* read and write, can't you?" Molly asked him.

The insinuation hurt. He nodded vigorously then followed Molly's gaze as she glanced around at the messy cargo bay. Nothing had been stowed properly before they took off; boxes of supplies had toppled, their contents strewn across the cargo bay.

"Until we get the Navy to reward you for helping me, I can't offer anything more than room and board. Understand?"

"Of coursse," he said. "It iss enough. I took a few thingss from my uncle anyway. Iss no problem."

Molly shook her head as if she didn't want to know. "All you have to do is keep up with all the items in the ship, put them in sensible places and write it down so we can find them. So, have fun with it or go get some rest. I need to tend to Cole and do some pilot stuff." She smiled at him and turned to the cockpit.

He watched her go. Forlorn, like a puppy tied to a park bench studying its departing master.

○ ○ ○ ○

"Hey, pal. You're in my chair."

Cole looked over his shoulder at her. He had some of the meal bar on his chin, ruining Molly's mock anger. She laughed and pointed to her own face. He wiped it off, stepping dutifully over the control console and into the nav chair.

"*This* is going to take some getting used to," he said, adjusting the harness on the back of the seat. "Where'd you rush off to?"

"Bathroom," Molly lied. "Nothing on SADAR?"

"A little glitch a few minutes ago, some hyperdrive discharge and a very small contact. Probably just ice peeling off or a problem with the SADAR. Other than that, geez, it's too quiet up here. This orbit is completely dead."

Molly agreed. "Especially for a pirate haven," she said. "The only thing I can think is they're fighting over some spoils somewhere. Or the recent shift in power has everyone locking down their hatches." She looked at Cole, studied his furrowed brow. "You aren't going to add this to your conspiracy theory, are you? You think our escape is being allowed, don't you? 'Cause I can tell you, buddy, it's been some damn hard work."

Cole held up both hands in mock surrender. "Easy, I'm not saying that at all. You just keep on pointing out the obvious, and I'll look for the difficult clues, okay?"

Oooh. She wanted to punch Cole in the arm, but he was smiling at her. And the bruises on his face made her want to hug him rather than hit him.

"You look terrible," she said.

His smile widened. Molly would never understand why boys were so proud of their scrapes and scars. Whatever their heroics proved, the pride they had in their nicks undid it.

Cole turned back to the nav screen in front of him. The large square monitor displayed their astral charts—currently centered on Palan and her three moons. Another planet was also in view, circling the same star on a tighter orbit. "Where to, Captain?" he asked her.

"Earth, if we could, but our hyperdrive's low; it's gonna have to be someplace closer. Do you think the Orbital Station here is safe?"

Cole looked at her as if she were crazy. "Are you crazy?" he asked, confirming the look. "The last time we went to the Navy, we nearly got ourselves killed. *Twice.*"

"Okay, fine. So we need to go someplace with very little Naval presence that also has fusion fuel. How do you propose we pull that off?"

Cole looked at the charts again. "Here's one that fits. And I hear Palan is nice after the rains."

"Funny." Molly sipped from her juice pouch. It tasted like nectar after that prison muck. "I say, for now, we just pick a safe entry zone for a small jump. We get showered and changed and get some sleep. I'm not thinking clearly enough to make a rational decision."

Cole nodded his agreement. She watched him scroll to a spot in the vacuum of space perpendicular to Earth's vector, a place nobody would think to follow. She could've done the calculations in her head, but she watched him hammer them out on the nav computer. He wielded the equations in his own way, and she bit her tongue; there were probably a dozen things he'd be doing differently if he were sitting over here. They were both going to have to be patient with each other as they learned their new roles.

"Locked in and confirmed," he told her.

Molly checked the numbers. The hyperdrive was turned back to its normal settings, locked for the ship's current mass via the SADAR unit. She raised the glass shield over the jump button and thumbed it.

The stars shifted.

15

They spent the next two days in the middle of nowhere and full of bliss. Molly had been so busy using *Parsona* to flee Palan, she missed her chance to fully appreciate the reunion. As they drifted out along the edge of the Milky Way's Frontier Arm, she finally had an opportunity to look over the ship.

Her ship.

A lot of the tools she remembered watching her father use were still here. Some of them looked worse for wear: the fuel cell in every power tool was bone dry; a few manual screwdrivers were missing; one of the large hammers she'd barely been able to lift as a child had a large spot of strange rust on it that needed to be filed off. Despite the abuse, most of it was still there—including her father's old ratchet set, the sight of which flooded Molly with nostalgia.

It was the closest thing to a toy box she'd ever had. She would spend hours playing with the shiny cylinders, stacking them like blocks, building precarious things that quaked as her father stomped by. She used to hold her open hands to either side of her little metal castles as they threatened to fall, holding them upright by the force of her will alone.

That came to an end after she spilled the entire set in the engine room and had to spend the rest of the day digging greasy bits out of the bilge, cleaning them and re-sorting them. It was the last time she'd opened the large metal box.

Molly ran her fingers across its silver hasps; she flipped them up, paused a moment, then hinged back the lid. Every piece was still there, each one in its proper place. She grazed a row of metrics and picked one at random, held it up close, then put it back. That was what she loved about the ratchet set. Everything had a slot that it went into. Everything *fit*. You could mess it up, but it would go back together again, just as it had been.

She wished it were a metaphor for life, but it wasn't. She knew.

It seemed odd that an old set of tools would stir such emotions, when the staterooms elicited hardly a response. Her own room had been rummaged through; nothing remained from her last time aboard. And the captain's quarters, which she entered hesitantly, no longer smelled like her father.

Molly recalled sneaking into his room whenever the strange noises in the ship gave her bad dreams. He would sit up and hold her, softly explaining which pump or motor was turning on and what it was doing to create each sound. The next morning, she would wake up in her own bed.

Moving into his room, rather than sleep in her old one, may have appeared to the others a natural result of her rank, but Molly knew it was something different. It was a scared child once again looking for respite from her bad dreams. And it worked. The nightmare that'd been haunting her for ten years didn't make its customary appearance that first night. Nor the next one. No longer terrified of being left behind, Molly had become a part of what she'd been chasing.

Another wonderful discovery was the ship's original logs. They went all the way back to *Parsona's* maiden voyage. Molly pulled up the waypoints her parents must've used on their first flight to Lok. She traced her finger across the nav screen, thinking about the planet where she'd been born, imagining her mother alive and happy, her parents in love.

She read the log entries that went with the routes, knowing they would've been typed in by her mother or father. The words glowed phosphorous green on the readout—her parents talking to her across time and beyond the grave. As a pilot now, in charge of their old ship, she felt connected to them both in a way she never had before. Eighteen years ago, her father had left the Navy and moved with his new bride to a frontier planet. They would've been crossing the galaxy just as Molly was about to, trying to start a new life.

While she spent her time reminiscing, Cole launched into a whirlwind of productivity. Nobody appreciated the hot shower as much as he did. The swelling on his face and the purple around his ribs faded with rest, medical cream, and clean bandages. And surprisingly—to Molly at least—it was Cole who busied about the utility room, washing the mildew out of the sheets, trying to salvage their Palan clothes, and organizing their supply of soaps and cleaners. Molly couldn't remember him being this fastidious at the Academy; then again, the only way to recognize an overly neat person in the military was to note the few people who *weren't* complaining about mandatory hygiene and strict dress codes.

Walter also kept himself busy. He took his new duties as "Cargo Officer" more seriously than Molly had expected. It turned out the kid could do more than just read and write, he was a whiz with computers.

Probably from a childhood of hacking into banks or stealing holovids—Molly didn't dare ask. He wasted no time retiring the manifest sheets and writing his own inventory program into a small computer. Molly had no idea where it had come from, but it seemed suspiciously newer than anything else on the ship. He carried the device with him at all times, hissing with delight when he found something new in a hidden cubby.

Between Cole's cleaning and Walter's organizing, the wreck of *Parsona's* interior quickly transformed into a model of perplexing orderliness. This is *not* what living with two males should be like. Especially when one of them was a citizen of Palan, after she had seen what passes muster on that planet. Then again, perhaps this was the way Walter had chosen to rebel. Or maybe it was his attempt to impose order on the universe. It was no longer a mystery to Molly that her offer to get the boy off-planet had succeeded where other deals had fallen short. He must've been miserable there.

The only bad news, besides the hyperdrive reading eighteen percent, was the lack of some common spares for the thrusters and the state of a few mechanical systems. Numerous lights were out and needed replacing, the air conditioning unit in one of the crew rooms was broken, some paint needed to be chipped off and re-applied, and various other tasks started filling the to-do tab in the ship's computer.

The only deal-breaker was the hyperdrive. They had no way of charging it up themselves.

In fact, filling up the hyperdrive and avoiding the Navy were going to be difficult to do at the same time. Supposedly, only a few people in the entire Galactic Union knew how hyperdrive engines worked. Fusion coil technology was a closely guarded secret, and refills were overseen at Orbital Stations under the watchful eyes of Navy personnel.

There were dozens of rumors about who had actually discovered the technology and owned the rights. Conspiracy theorists maintained an alien race had sold the technology to Humans ages ago, but Molly didn't buy it. Every race Humans encountered in the galaxy had received hyperdrive technology from *them*, not the other way around. The only exception was the Drenards, who had made the same technological breakthrough at some point, and the only technology *they* seemed eager to give humans were missiles. Lots of them. Pointy ends first.

Filling up with enough fuel to reach Earth seemed an intractable problem, one Molly struggled to solve while everyone cleaned and recharged their spirits.

It was Cole who came up with an idea. It happened as he was poring over the astral charts in *Parsona's* nav computer, logging in potential jump routes to Earth.

o o o o

"This makes no sense," Cole said, his voice tinny and subdued by the bilge. Molly had her head under a floor panel in the cockpit, tightening some hydraulic lines. It made communicating difficult, so naturally Cole was being unusually chatty. "Hey, Molly, you ever heard of Glemots?"

"Glemots," she repeated. "Why does that sound familiar?" She raised her head to hear him better and banged it on a floor truss. She nearly dropped her wrench.

"Be careful," Cole cautioned. "And Glemots aren't a *that*, they're a *them*. Remember the race that left the Galactic Union all those years ago? They completely shut out the rest of the universe. You can't even get near their home planet."

Rubbing her head, Molly pulled herself out of the bilge. She could see grease on her own cheeks, black smudges in the edge of her peripheral. She had her hair tied back under a triangle of white cloth and figured Cole had already seen her at her worst after the Palan rains. "Are they the ones Unity Now tried to help out after a supernova irradiated their corner of the galaxy?"

"Bingo. The UN sent a few supply and refugee ships, and not a one of them was ever heard from again."

"And what makes you want to go and say 'hello'? Was that dinner you cooked last night some attempt to fatten me up for the savages?"

"They aren't savages. Or weren't, anyway. Look, there's a log in the nav computer about them. The Navy first encountered these guys back in the frontier expansion, so it must've been over two hundred years ago. Smart race, roughly humanoid—"

"That is *such* an offensive term, Cole. You're supposed to say *bilaterally symmetric quadruped*." Molly sang the term with the cadence of something memorized but not completely understood.

"Gimme a break, I'm just skimming what it says here." Cole gestured to the nav screen. "As I was saying, let's see here. . . oh, so the Glemots had no technology when the Navy found them, so they put the Meln Imperative in place."

"Watch, but don't interfere," Molly recited. She felt as if they were back in classes at the Academy.

"Right. But get this: the Glemots were flying ships out of orbit just four years later."

"So the Navy had it wrong. They had technology."

"Not according to this. Supposedly they worked out the principles of space flight from their limited contact with the Navy."

"From nothing?" Molly got up from the floor and gaped in disbelief over Cole's shoulder. "That's impossible. Someone made a mistake, or the Navy broke the Meln Imperative or something."

Walter poked his head into the cockpit. "What are you guyss getting sso loud about? Can I look?"

"Pilot stuff." Cole and Molly said in unison. They smirked at each other.

"Well, I'm going to go do more *Officser* sstuff," Walter said haughtily. "The sstorage lockerss in the bilge are almosst done," he added with pride.

While she waited for Walter to pad away, Molly noticed how close her face was to Cole's. The nav screens were hard to see clearly from an angle. She could've pulled up the display on her own computer, but she'd just leaned over to read his. She hadn't noted their proximity to each other while they were talking, but now, in silence, she could feel the heat from his cheek radiating out to hers. The warmth made her want to pull away sharply, or douse it with a kiss.

She did neither.

Instead, she reached over him and pointed to the monitor, trying to focus on something else. "An observation satellite?"

Cole nodded. "That's the theory the Navy settled on. They lost a planetary probe during the reconnaissance phase. A faulty thruster sent it crashing to the surface. They probably decided a recovery would risk direct contact. Must've figured nothing useful could survive atmospheric entry and an impact like that."

Molly moved to the Captain's chair and pulled up the same star chart on her screen. She just couldn't concentrate while hovering so close to him. It felt like flying next to a canyon wall in a stiff breeze.

Cole continued talking, seemingly unaware of Molly's struggles. "And once the cat was out of the bag," he said, "the Meln Imperative no longer applied. In fact, according to this, the Glemots made first contact *themselves*. And they had a rough grasp of English . . . oh, wait. You are so *not* going to believe this."

"What is it?" she asked, trying to scan down the report to find it for herself.

"This is how the Navy figured out the satellite may have caused the sudden spike in technology. The English spoken by the first Glemot astronauts was heavy in engineering jargon. They had pulled their vocabulary straight from the satellite computers."

"You're right," Molly agreed. "I don't believe it. For once I'm thinking one of your conspiracy theories would make more sense. And what's the point of this lesson?"

Cole glared at her. "The reason this star system matters to us is that the Navy built a small Orbital Station there before the Glemots kicked them out. The station's *still there*. If the Navy left in a hurry, there might be some stuff we could use. Maybe some fusion fuel or a Bell radio that still works."

Molly shook her head. Bell radios were the key to instantaneous communication across long distances, but they wouldn't find one operational. The devices employed Bell's Theorem, a bizarre twentieth-century discovery in quantum mechanics. The theorem hypothesized the ability to entangle two particles so a change in one resulted in a change in the other, no matter how far apart they were. Molly knew her quantum mechanics. Entangled particles are kept in magnetic storage units; they'd decay without anyone around to keep them up.

But the fusion fuel? That was a real possibility. Worth checking out. "It *is* close by," Molly noted. She traced a finger across her pilot screen. "Twenty thousand light years, and in the right direction. Let's call it six percent from the hyperdrive. We would still have enough for another small jump or two if nothing panned out. We could make the Navy station at Cephus as a bailout."

Cole agreed. "I can't think of anything else to try. Unless you want to go turn ourselves in to the Navy straightaway. Hope the Palan office was an anomaly."

"What do *you* think?"

"I think the behavior there was part of a larger pattern. The simulator sabotage, the early graduations, the way you were run out of the school. Nothing makes sense to me right now except the Navy acting screwy—"

"*More* screwy," Molly corrected him.

"Yeah, more screwy." Cole laughed. "Or *screwier*. Anyway, I'd feel safer with you and some backwoods savages than I would with the authorities right now."

"Okay, but if we're gonna do this, it has to be stealth-like. Jump in behind this moon, here, and use the thrusters to head to the Orbital Station. No spooking the natives."

"I don't think they'll be a problem. The reason they left the GU is because they started to distrust technology just a few years after they mastered it. After they incapacitated the Navy, they got rid of or stored away everything they'd built. Several groups thought this made the system safe again, Navy included. But nobody has visited them since and returned to talk about it. Nothing but a few system scans by the Bel Tra, from the looks of things."

Molly felt wistful at the mention of the Bel Tra, the best cartographers in the galaxy. "I wish we had *their* latest charts instead of these old things," she said.

"Hey, if we're quiet, they won't even know we're there."

"Like the UN ships?" she countered.

"That's different; they were going down to the planet. Probably trying to hand out potatoes in a hailstorm of arrows and rocks."

"Yeah, probably so," she said, hoping he was right.

Walter bounced excitedly into the cockpit's short hallway. "The cargo bilge iss ssorted!" he announced. Molly turned to see him fiddling with his little inventory computer before looking up at her.

She smiled at him and pointed up at *Parsona's* ceiling. "Have you looked in the overhead bins yet?"

His eyes lit up, his cheeks pulling back into a sneer. "Overhead binsss?" he hissed.

○ ○ ○ ○

The three crew members spent another full day doing prep work and checking over the ship and its gear. Walter uncovered four space suits in the airlock room, complete with helmets. One was in questionable shape, but the other three would keep any of them alive if they needed to work outside the ship or if the hull lost structural integrity.

Just as important was the collection of flightsuits he'd gathered from the crew quarters. These thinner outfits would be crucial if they needed to do any strenuous maneuvering on their way back to Earth. The anti-gravity modules in them were much simpler (and weaker) than the Navy's suits, but they provided at least a modicum of protection against heavy Gs.

Cole proved himself quite handy with a needle. He made adjustments to the flightsuits to make sure they fit snugly, augmenting the effect of the anti-G fluid. Each suit also had name patches above the left breast reading "Parsona" or "Mortimor." Cole told Molly he felt uncomfortable wearing an outfit with her father's name on it, but she insisted he leave it.

She also asked him to take a patch off an extra suit of her father's and add it to her own. Molly tried on the outfit after another round of alterations. Standing in front of the mirror, both of her parent's names emblazoned across her chest, she felt a mixture of nostalgia, sadness, and joy that made her feel hollow inside. Not depressed—just empty. And kinda cold.

Walter shared none of Molly and Cole's uneasiness with the suits. He was absolutely ecstatic to have one of his own. When he found out they had no way of embroidering a patch with his name on it, he just printed it with a black marker, as neatly as he could. He took to wearing the thing all the time, even as Molly kept reminding him it was only useful when they were accelerating.

The helmets that locked into these flightsuits were looser than the Navy variety, but Molly and Cole were both growing out their hair, which should eventually pad the space. For Walter's close-cropped pate, there was nothing to be done, but he didn't seem to mind. He would shake his head vigorously and fill the helmet with muffled laughter as it continued to bobble around.

Overall, their safety gear was in far better shape than it deserved to be. If the Orbital Station didn't have any atmosphere—which they fully expected after hundreds of years of disuse—they would be able to carry their own in with them.

As the plan solidified in Molly's mind, she started forming various lists of the things she wanted to salvage, ranked by likelihood. A long-range communicator was on top on her Implausible List. Even without entangled particles, it would be nice to grab one. An operating fusion coil full of fuel headed up her Dream List, along with a functioning manual pump to move the precious stuff to *Parsona*. On her Necessities List was all the food and spares they could get their flight gloves on. Even if they didn't need the stuff, they could sell or barter it down the road. Salvage laws applied to Navy property after fifty years of abandonment. If nothing else, grabbing as much as they could would keep Walter occupied; they had enough room in the cargo bunkers to keep him out of their hair for the rest of their passage to Earth.

As she compiled these lists and contemplated the wealth of supplies that likely awaited them, Molly became more and more confident with the plan. Almost as much as Walter, who had gone bonkers when he learned what they were preparing for. He ran around the cargo bay in tight circles, hissing excitedly. *"Loot a GU Orbital Station?"* He practically tackled Molly, throwing his arms around her and thanking her endlessly.

They eventually settled him down and explained the mission, how they needed to go about this very quietly. Not a hiss. Walter nodded violently while his helmet, visor open, stood perfectly still. "I undersstand," he said. "An eassy 'in and out' job."

He got half of it right.

○ ○ ○ ○

Parsona winked out of hyperspace in the middle of an L2, the Lagrange point on the other side of Glemot's largest moon. "Largest" being a relative term; the rock was small enough to keep its odd shape rather than crush into a rough sphere with the force of its own gravity. Still, a few hundred kilometers wide, it was more than enough to conceal their arrival. It wasn't as if a primitive race was going to be scanning the sky with telescopes, but Naval training was strong in two thirds of the crew. And the remaining third consisted of a born-and-bred *sneaky bastard*.

They swept the far side of the potato-shaped moon with SADAR, revealing the Orbital Station just beyond. Everything was still out of sight as they crept up behind their lumpy, cratered shield. Cole scanned for any electrical or mechanical activity from the station, but they were on the extreme edge of their sensor's range for those functions. Meanwhile, the Glemot planet dominated the SADAR display with its quiet bulk.

"All clear?" Molly thumbed through the post-jump systems checks. Seeing the hyperdrive down to twelve percent made her stomach knot up.

"All clear," Cole confirmed.

Molly checked the cargo cam. Four crew chairs with life-support hookups were arranged across the bulkhead outside the cockpit. They faced backward, two to either side. Walter had been strapped into one of them after much cajoling and a bit of force, unable to contain his anticipation of the heist ahead. His head was bent forward as he toyed with something in his lap, probably working on the game he'd begun programming into his computer. He'd been trying to show it to her for the past two days, but Molly never really had the time.

Satisfied that they were prepared for pretty much anything, Molly pushed *Parsona's* nose around the small moon. The first glimpse of the Glemot planet rose over its dark surface like a green sun. It was a spectacular contrast to the sight of the last planet they'd left. Where Palan was almost entirely blue, with just a single high continent of eroded brown rock, Glemot was the vibrant hue of photosynthesizing life, a verdant color that triggered something emotional in the primitive parts of Molly's and Cole's brains.

They both gasped at the sight of the large planet as it rose into view, almost as if their lungs could suck in all that oxygen from across the vacuum of space. No clouds obscured the land, an oddity neither of them noticed at first. Instead of vast oceans, thousands—possibly millions—of tiny lakes dotted the orb. It was one thing to read the dry Naval reports during the planning of this operation and something else entirely to see it with their own eyes.

This was why at least one poet should be assigned to every survey vessel, Molly thought, *just to do images like this justice.*

"So pretty," she said aloud.

"Stay focused," Cole told her, but it sounded as if it could've been a reminder to himself. He couldn't keep his eyes off of the green world, either, or the thin halo of pale-blue atmosphere clinging to it.

A red indicator popped up on one of Cole's readouts, breaking the spell.

"Mechanical activity on the Orbital Station. Looks like thruster signatures."

Molly pulled it up as well.

"It's just maintaining its orbit. That's not a good Lagrange point. Moon's too small, so it's gonna have to boost itself periodically."

"After all these years?" he shook his head. "Something's not right. I've never known the Navy to build anything that didn't need a weekly greasing. Wait. Thruster's off now. Okay, maybe you're right. That orbit can't be stable, anyway. Too much mass in the OS and not enough in the moon. And yet, all these years later it's orbiting the planet in lockstep—"

"And at a lower orbit," Molly added.

"You think this is good news or bad news, Cap?"

"I'd say good. There's no ship activity in the area. The thing's probably just functioning on its own. That means we have a good chance of fueling up the hyperdrive." Molly looked over at Cole and noted his furrowed brow. "You thinking we should pull back?"

"No. You're probably right. But can you get us around the moonlet and behind the station? That planet is so pretty I might ask you to take us down for a look."

"Absolutely," Molly said, gripping the flight controls and nudging them forward.

But she wasn't the only one trying to control the ship.

16

The first sign of trouble was the flickering of the nav screen. Cole rapped the top of the dash with his fist in the primitive problem-solving reflex common to males. The screen returned to normal.

"Better," he said.

Molly rolled her eyes at the unfortunate result this would have at strengthening a silly habit. She didn't think any more of the glitch as they approached the station.

When they closed to within a thousand meters, Molly prepped for docking maneuvers. The universal coupling on the outside of *Parsona's* hull needed to be lined up with the one on the Orbital Station's maintenance bay. The airlock on the GN-290 was high up the starboard side to prevent the wings from getting in the way, so Molly rolled *Parsona* over and began her approach. Hopefully, they'd be able to open the hangar doors manually from inside the station to make loading salvaged goods even easier.

Molly focused the external camera on the Orbital Station. Distances were displayed on a nearby readout, but she felt uncomfortable doing this for the first time without a spotter.

"Would you mind going to the airlock and calling out distances?" she asked Cole.

He nodded and moved to unbuckle himself from the nav seat—but the ship lurched forward, pressing him back into his chair. "Hey!" he complained.

"I'm not doing that!" Molly hammered the emergency stop, attempting to kill the thrusters. "Uh, we might have a problem here." She watched the main thrusters ramp up to full RPMs, while the accelerator between the flight chairs remained in neutral.

Parsona was going haywire.

"I'm going to the engine room," she said. "You take over here."

Cole nodded as she unbuckled herself. Only then did she realize how tricky this was going to be. *Parsona's* forward thrust was pushing her toward the back of the ship. That was where she wanted to go, but not quite so fast. She glanced at the handholds recessed into the ceiling and floor. They were too small, meant for emergencies that resulted in zero gravity, not *excess* gravity.

The longer she hesitated, the worse it would get. Molly turned sideways in her chair, her right shoulder pressing back into the seat. She glanced at Cole and then around to the rear of the ship. No way could she survive a fall that far. Her flightsuit would protect her up to a few dozen Gs as long as it was plugged in, but as soon as she left—she'd be on her own. And what would she do even *if* she made it to the engine room? If the secondary emergency stop didn't respond, could she shut down the fuel lines running back to the thrusters?

Molly placed one hand on the control pedestal and started pressing herself out of the chair. A glance at the controls sparked an old memory. *The remote docking panel.* Her father had rarely used it around her—they lived on a frontier planet where starships just landed in fields—but she could remember one tricky locking maneuver where he'd stood by the airlock, using the panel as he guided the ship in visually. She looked around to see if she could even recognize it.

One of the rectangular panels next to her seat had a small set of maneuvering controls with two metal handles curving out on either side. Molly pulled on them, and the entire unit popped out of its housing. Just to be sure, she tried thumbing its own emergency kill switch. Nothing happened.

She wrestled the panel, already heavy from the excess Gs, across her body. A thick trunk of electrical and hydraulic lines spooled out after. The device was frowned upon by veteran pilots as a psychological crutch, but Molly hoped it could serve her as a literal lifeline to the engine room far below.

She tried to let the unit fall back through the cargo bay slowly, but her gloves didn't have enough grip. The trunk slid through her hands; she squeezed as hard as she could. Walter made a loud hissing noise as the object flew by his chair, matching the sound of the rubber zipping through her flight gloves.

When it reached the end, the cord lashed harshly across Molly's chest, pinning her back into the chair. *That was dumb*, she thought, wriggling out from underneath the taut cable. She popped off her flight gloves and flexed her hands a bit.

"What are you *doing*?" asked Cole.

Molly didn't have time to explain. "Keep trying the kill switch while I'm gone. Radio me if something changes." She crouched on the back of her seat. "Down" was toward the rear of the ship, the floor a vertical wall. She teetered, perched on a cushioned ledge, and peered over the thirty-meter drop. At the end of that fall the closed metal door leading to the lazarette looked tiny, yet menacing. This was starting to feel like a very bad idea.

Molly swung her feet out and gripped the bundled cords. She had to act *now*. The longer she waited, the heavier she'd get.

Wrapping her knees around the trunk of lines, she estimated they were pulling around three Gs already. Her body felt as if it weighed over 150 kilos. Her muscles, unfortunately, were the same ones acclimated to working out in a single gravity. She was asking a lot of them.

She slid down the first meter before locking in a solid grip. When she looked up to secure her hands better, she saw Cole gaping at her from above. Beyond him she could see the green planet dappled with blue spots. It was getting bigger.

Molly turned away from the sight and began working her way down, out of the cockpit and into the cargo bay below. When she became level with Walter, the boy let out another hiss of alarm. It looked as if he was trying to say something, but Molly's visor was down and her head throbbed from the effort. Her arms screamed as well, already quivering, and she'd gone only a fraction of the distance.

Her knees were doing very little work, their grip on the trunk of cables too feeble. Molly let one of them go, pressing the toe of her boot into the series of zero-G handholds on the floor.

Much better.

She twisted her right arm around the cable, already growing more taut under the extra gravities, and found a toehold with her other foot. Now she was rappelling down a pockmarked cliff instead of trying to slide down a slick rope. Molly locked her legs into the weight of her torso and let her boots do a lot of the work.

She could do this.

By the time she reached the bottom of the cargo bay, *Parsona* had to be doing 5 Gs. The engine room was another six meters away, and her ankles felt as if they might snap under the strain. She balanced swiftness and safety—for every second she delayed, the task became that much more brutal. Looking up to secure her arm a bit better, Molly could see up the shaft of the ship, through the cockpit, and out to the green planet beyond. It completely filled the windshield.

She needed to focus.

Working her way down a few more steps, she entered the hallway leading back to the engine room and crew quarters. She was about two meters from the end of the cable when one of her boots slipped out of its hold. The arm she had wrapped around the cable was wrenched violently before coming loose. Her other hand remained around the cord, sliding painfully as she crashed into the remote docking panel.

She landed with a grunt, straddling the device like a rope swing. Catching her breath, her heart racing, she clutched the cables with both hands and pressed her head to the wire. *That could've been bad,* she thought. But she was level with the engine room door, at least.

Struggling to her feet, Molly felt as if she had a hundred kilos of extra weight strapped to her body. She wasn't sure how much the cord could take; she peered down at the twelve meters of space between her and the metal door below.

Not wasting time, Molly kicked off from the airlock door beside her to see how much play there was left in the cable. It barely moved. She kicked harder and swung slightly toward the engine room. Catching the jamb and stepping off, she pulled herself into the thick doorway and was immediately pressed back against it. The forces on her body were incredible, but at least she was on her back, standing sideways in the engine room passage.

Her arms and feet felt numb; she wasn't sure if she'd be able to reach the fuel lines. There were more objects to grasp in the engine room, but much of it was scalding hot. She wasn't even sure she had the strength to leave the doorjamb. She contemplated her next move, and then saw that it wouldn't matter. Nothing would. The thruster relays across the mechanical room were firing. On and off. Just as they would be if someone were piloting the ship.

Parsona wasn't out of control or in a runaway state.

Activating the helmet's radio, Molly shouted for Cole.

"Molly? Are you okay? Where are you? We're pulling seven Gs right now. You need to get that flight suit plugged in!"

"I'm by the engine room. You're not touching the controls, are you?" She took some deep breaths, her chest feeling as if three men were standing on it.

"No, I'm trying to shut down all subsystems from here. Now get that suit plugged in. We're gonna hit atmosphere in a few minutes!"

Oh, no. If the ship went into turns at this speed, she'd be thrown all over the place. Then she thought of something and would've kicked herself if her leg didn't weigh a ton. She thumbed the mic again. "Do you have life-support controls?"

There was a pause. "Yeah. I think I do."

"Route everything you can to the grav panels forward of the engine room and turn off the panels aft of here."

"Doing it now. But we're closing in on eight Gs. I don't know if the panels will take away half that. You need to get your suit plugged in!"

Across the hall from Molly, the door to the airlock slid open. She grimaced a smile at Cole's thoughtfulness.

Grunting, she pulled herself up as the effects of the grav systems kicked in. She hoped Cole's and

Walter's flightsuits were absorbing the extra weight; it was unpleasant to think of them suffering just to give her a little boost, and not even one that made her feel stronger—just *less weak*. She didn't have much time before the Gs crept back up or they hit atmosphere. She looked to the hallway; the panel was still swinging slightly. The strain on the cable made it more like a steel cable under tension and less like a dangling rope.

Unable to reach it, Molly took a chance by kicking a foot at the hanging remote panel. It struck, but the weight of her leg out in the void nearly sent her over the edge and down to the lazarette, twelve meters below. She pulled herself back into the jamb, her knuckles white, and watched the panel swing away from her on a slow arc. She would only have one shot at this.

The panel was little more than half a meter square, its hydraulic cables never meant for such stress. It swung toward Molly—she crouched in the intense pull of acceleration, her muscles tense. It was impossible to know how hard to jump. Her vision told her body to exert a certain amount of effort, but under these gravities, it would've barely gotten her feet off the doorjamb. She decided to give it everything, even though the distance would be less than a meter.

Just before the panel got as close as it would, Molly leapt, her legs uncoiling like springs. Heavy arms came up and scrambled for the cord. One foot landed on the small target. But she had jumped too far, her weight carrying past the small platform as it began swinging toward the airlock. She was over a meter from the door when she lost her grip. Her hands came free, one foot still on the slow swing. She pushed off, hoping the momentum would get her to the thick jamb of the airlock door.

Again: too much. Molly grabbed for the doorway as she sailed through, her feet tripping over the edge as she hurtled through the passage and crashed into the rear wall of the airlock. Reflexively, she brought her right arm up to protect her body, and heard it snap. Heard it before she even felt the pain, like the sound of a thick branch being popped into two pieces. Her torso crunched down on top of it, grinding the fragmented bones together.

Molly gargled with pain and nearly blacked out.

Pressing down with her left hand, she forced her body up and over to her back. She was lying on the wall beside two of the space suits—her arm at her side, her wrist at a funny angle. Molly felt sick seeing it like that. The limb must belong to someone else. Her brain couldn't process this new shape—it made her stomach churn.

Lifting her head, she could see the airlock life support panel not far away. She used her feet and good arm to kick and drag herself across the wall, every centimeter a minor victory.

Pulling the panel open, she grabbed the cord inside and plugged it into the receptacle near her armpit. The relief was immediate. Pockets of anti-grav fluid raced around the chambers of her flight suit, countering the Gs as if she were still buckled into her seat.

Molly fumbled with the mounting straps on one of the spacesuits and dragged it out of the way. She buckled herself in its place, wrapping the webbing across her chest and thighs while she fought back the waves of pain emanating from her useless arm. She wasn't satisfied with her one-handed knots, but she couldn't take any more.

She lay her head back on the wall, her helmet forming a cushion for her skull, and smiled, reflecting on how odd she must look strapped between two empty suits, her arm twisted like one of their folded sleeves.

Parsona shuddered, probably entering the green planet's atmosphere. Molly gasped as the vibrations sent shivers of agony though her arm. It jounced into a new shape, and blackness pressed in around her vision, a sensation she was beginning to recognize. Molly summoned the last of her energy, using it to scold herself for passing out in moments of crisis.

Just in time to do it once more.

17

Molly flinched, startled from a bad dream as something large blotted out the pale light filtering through her eyelids. She lifted her head and blinked in confusion as the form came into focus. The sight sent her head crashing back down onto the hard surface beneath her; a massive, bear-like creature hovered close, its face a row of hungry teeth. Molly thrashed against the restraints across her body, the pain in her arm nearly knocking her out again.

The bear lurched out of her vision and made a growling noise. The ground shook as the creature moved. Molly's brain struggled to make sense of where she was. She was tied to a rock ledge. Palan? No.

What was the last thing she remembered? She'd taken a shower and gotten in bed—no, something past that. They'd made the jump, the potato moon, the Orbital Station. . .

Her arm crushing in the airlock.

Molly tried to move her right arm beneath the restraints, the pain confirming her hazy memories and driving back the grogginess with needles. They were on the green planet.

Her pulse quickened, her breath trapped in her throat. It was a *Glemot* that woke her. Had to be. She wondered if Cole and Walter were still alive and okay, and then she realized: whatever happened to the UN volunteers was now happening to *them*. An alien race capable of running off the Navy had her strapped to some hard surface—and possessed the ability to control her ship!

Parsona. Had they crashed? How hard had it been? What would be left of her?

Molly felt a soft breeze and heard the whispering of fabric. She raised her head as far as she could to scan the room. The walls and ceiling were both made of cloth, some kind of tent. Basic first aid material lay scattered on one table: gauze, bowls of leaves, and some kind of paste.

She lowered her head back to the hard surface and tried to focus on her breathing exercises, calming her mind and body. She almost had her pulse back to normal when small tremors and padded thuds signaled the return of her captor. This time, two bear heads leaned into view. One of them opened its mouth—wide teeth flashed like a row of blades. From this angle, seen across the edge, they appeared sharp and menacing.

The Glemot threatened her in a deep growl. "Minimal movement should be attained," it said, the words rumbling like distant thunder. Molly could barely hear the first half of "movement," it was grumbled in such a low register. Its hands went to her chest and did something to her restraints.

Molly ignored the advice and lifted her head to scream for help, and then saw that the large paws were *untying* her restraints. They came free, and she tried to sit up but couldn't find the strength. Another paw, as wide as her back, helped her. The Glemot that had spoken produced a sling made of tightly woven grasses.

It all felt like a waking dream. The fear receded; she wasn't going to be eaten. Still leaning against the large, soft paw behind her, she studied the other Glemot. The wide teeth looked square and friendly viewed straight on. The massive face, three times the size of a human's, divided itself with a mammoth smile.

"My reference label is Watt," the Glemot said. "Uttering that sound will guide my attention to the speaker."

"Molly," she muttered, watching the other Glemot secure the sling to her shoulder. Her arm was swollen and multi-colored. Two smooth sticks were tied alongside her lower bones, secured with braided, straw-like threads. There was some kind of paste on her skin—she touched it with her other hand, expecting it to come away sticky, but the stuff was stiff and dry. She looked down her body at the long white robe, the same material as the tent, and the twined grass that secured it around her.

Cole.

"My friends—" she blurted out.

"A unit of your companions is ambulating within five hundred meters of your location. Do you desire for this range of proximity to decrease?"

Molly had to repeat the sentence in her head several times. She felt like a drunk being taught quantum mechanics. She shook her head to clear it and then realized this gesture may be taken for an answer.

"Yes," she said. "Absolutely. Increase proximity, or decrease the range. I'm sorry, can I just see them? Does that make any sense?"

"Extreme accuracy, low precision. Come."

The Glemot behind Molly helped her down from what she saw now to be a chiseled stone table in the center of the tent. This Glemot was smaller than the other.

"Whitney," it said, holding its hand to its furry chest. Its voice wasn't quite as low and Molly automatically thought of Whitney as a female, but she wouldn't be surprised if it proved to be the other way around.

"Molly," she repeated as she accepted the help down. It was a good two-meter drop. She looked back and found her head level with Whitney's abdomen. Molly felt like a child. The surface of the stone table was higher than her head. The restraints hanging from the rock surface took on a positively humane aspect from this perspective, meant to keep her from falling.

Whitney moved to a slit in the fabric. She held back one side, creating a wedge of bright light, and waved Molly through. She complied and stepped, blinking, into a vista that made it difficult to breathe.

The tent stood on the crest of a gradual rise. Several varieties of green grasses covered the hill in a lush carpet sweeping down to the forest below. Molly could see a thin blue ribbon of water sparkling in the sunlight. It curved around the base of the hill and fed into a calm lake. She scanned its shore, thick with trees, all of the same species: tall, straight, and thrusting proudly into the blue sky.

Dotted across the green were little spots of color from wildflowers. Molly could see small creatures bobbing on the breeze, diving in and out of the grasses. The sunlight shimmered everywhere, reflecting off the lake in a plane of sparks—it even flashed off the waxy grass.

It was quite simply the most beautiful setting she'd ever seen. The haze in her head vanished, replaced with an overwhelming but pleasurable sensation. Every one of her senses popped from the overload. Fighting her awed lack of breath, Molly sucked in a huge lungful of fresh air, a gift from an atmosphere filtered thousands of times a day. The extra oxygen sent pinpricks of light dancing in her vision, filling her weary bones with a powerful energy.

On either side of her, similar tents spread out along the rise. Dozens of Glemots bounded about on powerful legs the size of small trees. Two smaller ones wrestled, rolling down the hill in a furry ball. Pots hung over cooking fires, the smoke wafting up into the cloudless blue. Molly, her cheeks sore from smiling so wide, turned to Whitney. The Glemot nodded back, seeming to understand what she was thinking. Somehow, these incredible beings were not completely inured to the gift that surrounded them daily.

Shielding his eyes with one paw, Watt peered up at them from further down the hill. He waved, beckoning them along. Whitney set off and Molly followed eagerly, all hints of danger dissolving. She had to skip and bound and let gravity suck her along to match the pace of the two casually strolling giants. Nearly tripping on her white robe, she hitched it above her knees with her good arm and labored to keep up. She felt like a pixie from a children's book, frolicking in a land where everything was too big.

Near the stream below, Molly saw a clump of Glemots huddled together. It took her a moment to spot Cole, lost as he was among their larger forms.

"Cole!"

He turned and smiled. She rushed down the hill as he leaped to his feet and ran up to meet her.

They were both out of breath as he swept her up in a tight embrace.

Molly leaned into him, her cheek on his chest as tears welled up in her eyes. She fought them back and squeezed him as hard as she could with her good arm, ignoring the pain in the other as it was pressed between their bodies.

Cole kissed the top of her head. She thought she could get used to this feeling. Broken arm and all.

When they pulled out of the hug, Cole grasped Molly's shoulders and gave her a stern glare. "Now stop trying to impress me, doofus. Every time you do something brave, you just end up passing out like a sissy."

Molly slapped one of his arms away with her free hand as choice insults piled on top of questions. She longed to know what had happened, what she'd missed, but Whitney and Watt were continuing down to the stream, and Cole pulled her after them.

"We're interrupting a Council meeting," he whispered. "They've been letting me hang out and listen in."

"Where's *Parsona*?" Molly asked.

"There's good news and bad news, I'm afraid. We'll talk about it later. For now I want to hear what they're going to do about the Leef Tribe."

"The what?" But they were almost on top of the group now, and Molly had to file the question away for later.

One of the largest Glemots continued to talk as she settled herself on the grass. Parts of his brown fur were turning black in wide ridges along his arms and legs. The language was English, but the jargon was so technical and obtuse, she could hardly follow. It sounded like politics and planning, so her brain turned off and she soaked in her surroundings instead.

Beside her, Cole leaned forward and seemed to hang on every word. Molly rested on her good elbow, her hand idly stroking the long, wide blades of grass. Insects the size of her thumb flitted about in the lush carpet, an unseen world going about its day right beneath her.

The two wrestling youths tumbled down to the stream and splashed each other. At one point a Council member grunted something in their direction, and they chased each other away. Molly thought one of them had been studying her and Cole with some degree of curiosity.

She looked around for signs of Walter, wondering where he and *Parsona* were. Not knowing was torturous, but she could tell from Cole's posture that he couldn't be interrupted. He was rapt. Molly tried listening in again and could only catch a few words here and there.

Then, something flashed in her peripheral, breaking the surface of the lake. Molly turned just in time to see a giant splash, a plume of white shooting up from the rippling water. She didn't see what it was, but it must have been *big*.

She left her gaze on the sparkling water. Searching the shore, she could easily imagine building a little fort up in those straight trees with a long dock reaching out into the water. She and Cole would live and play here for the rest of their lives.

Molly lay back on the soft grass and looked up into the cloudless blue sky, dreaming.

oooo

Her imaginings were interrupted by the quaking ground. The meeting was over. Molly sat up and saw worry on Cole's face as he stared at the grass, dragging a stick through the blades as if tracing various possibilities.

The large Glemot with the black fur approached them; Molly scrambled to her feet, but it hardly made a difference. The friendly-looking creature sank to his knees in front of her, which helped.

"Fair union, Molly Fyde. My designation is Franklin." Molly could feel the words in her sternum. This guy could give her a back massage just by talking about it.

"Greetings." Molly felt pressure to watch her vocabulary around these guys. After hearing some of the Council-talk, she knew they were already dumbing it down for her. Unfortunately, the middle ground with these guys was still a stretch.

"The Campton Tribe of the Glemots accepts you both. Integration complete. The mechanical advantage of your positioning will be determined, and you will facilitate the engineering of Campton Tribe as it incorporates all of Glemot via rapid expansion and population controls. We highly anticipate determining your optimal positioning as a cog, which will gain purchase for the whole."

He looked solemnly at her wounded arm. "Unfortunate. It will decrease your worth significantly in the short run, but the Council will recalculate as operation of that limb approaches normalcy. The pleasure achieved from this communication has been extreme from the perspective of this speaker. Between mastications we will resume in three point two Earth hours. Joyous afternoon, Molly Fyde."

Franklin rumbled off after the rest, his back almost completely covered with ebony fur that seemed shiny to the point of wetness. She looked at Cole, expecting to find him laughing at the ridiculousness of the setting and speech.

But he just looked extremely upset, his eyes locked on something beyond the horizon.

"What's wrong with you? Isn't this wonderful?" she asked.

Cole shook his head, his eyes focusing back on her face. "This is some crazy stuff, Molly." He glanced at her sling. "It's a damn good thing you didn't break both your arms."

"Well, no nebula! It's even better that I didn't break both of my legs and have my head lopped off. Thanks for putting things into a cheery perspective."

Cole didn't laugh.

Molly knew all of his looks just from the shape of his lips. She'd spent hundreds of hours with him in the simulator as they went through every set of emotional states humanly possible. But she'd never seen this one. The closest she could remember was when she'd looked at him during the start of the Tchung Affair and they both realized, with absolute certainty, that they were about to die.

She asked him, her voice flat and full of trepidation, "Why am I lucky I didn't break my other arm, Cole?"

The lips broke from a frozen purse. "Because they would've killed you."

Molly suppressed a laugh. "These guys? They seem perfectly gentle! My gods, look at this place! It's too fantastic for nonsense like that."

"Keep your voice down." He scanned their surroundings. "Let's walk along the stream and talk. I've picked up quite a bit and filled in most of the blanks between. We've a little over three hours until we won't have another chance to talk like this."

Molly looked over her shoulder at the giant mounds of fur loping effortlessly up the hill. Activity was spreading out among the tents, the smoke from the cooking of various foods rising—solid white pillars holding up a windless sky. She was having a hard time feeling afraid.

"Walter may already be dead." Cole said.

"What?"

"Keep walking. I'm sorry to be abrupt, but I understand your euphoria; I felt it yesterday. Gods, I felt it as soon as I found you alive in the airlock. So I'm sorry to shatter your expectations, but I need to do it fast."

"How'd he die?"

"I said he's *probably* dead. It's been determined by the council that he's 'without proper function.' Also, the ship's being dismantled as we speak. You already wouldn't recognize it. These guys are big, but their claws are prehensile. It's as if each of them has a complete tool rig in both paws."

"Without proper function?"

"Listen, this beautiful land is at war. Constant war. They have formulas for how to preserve the natural state of this planet, but tribes keep breaking off and establishing new ones as they argue over which formula is right and which is wrong. I can barely understand most of it, but they have genetics reduced to mathematics. They can tell what the average age in each population should be, and they maintain it."

"Maintain it how?"

Cole steered her away from the edge of the woods, more in the open. "How do you think?" he whispered. "If the average gets too high, they kill a few of the elders. If it jumps up too fast, they kill their own young. There's no hesitation, either. What they consider to be the 'natural' order must be maintained. That pursuit is so much higher than all else—it makes lesser ethical problems vanish in their eyes."

"I don't understand. I think I'm missing something, or you skipped a step." She reached down to pick up a stone and then tossed it into the stream in frustration.

"Okay. Quick history lesson. And keep in mind, some of this is from them and some is from the Navy reports we read; no telling how much I'm missing or getting wrong." He cleared his throat and glanced around before beginning. "The Glemots were a race of warring tribes for thousands and thousands of years. Evolution, of course, rewarded some of the same nasty traits in *their* genome that we find everywhere else. But instead of civilizing and overcoming these traits, they created a culture around them.

"Despite intellects that—well, I'll just say that what they did to control *Parsona* doesn't amaze me in the least anymore. Despite this, they never got into technology. Not because their brains weren't capable of seizing it, but because their lives were too brutal to invest in it. There was no foundation there. It was like us prior to organized agriculture, before some of us got bored and started tinkering."

"And then the satellite," Molly offered.

"Exactly. The satellite. The problem was, the Glemots thought they found another natural discovery. They saw this tech as something handed down from the gods. Or maybe something bubbling up from within the planet, who knows? So the tribe that found it, the Leefs, they went from smelting ore to seven-dimensional calculus in less than a year."

"No way."

"Way. I'm serious, the intellect here is off the freakin' charts. And they age more slowly than we do, so the amount they retain over an average lifetime is just crazy."

She opened her mouth to ask a question, but Cole headed her off. "Don't interrupt, I'm getting to the important part. So they had incredibly advanced tech within three years. The Leefs gained an advantage—and they guarded it closely. Nearby tribes were hunted nearly to extinction with their new weapons. I imagine the tribes on the other side of Glemot still have *legends* about what happened over here.

"Of course, they didn't just build weapons. They also built the first complex devices common to all tech-savvy races. Radios, micro/telescopes, the sensors that augment our senses. That's when they spotted the 'gods' in the sky."

"The Navy."

"Right, the Navy. So they tried to communicate with them using means that were actually beyond our ability, or maybe we weren't listening. Either way, the legend is that they tried everything to hail our boys in black, but no response. So guess what they did—they built their first ship and flew up to say hello! Needless to say, they were pretty disappointed. They learned about the GU and the GN, and they came back and had a Council meeting, a famous one. They still talk about it all the time."

"What was it about?"

"What to do next. There were two main lines of thought. The leaders of the original Leef Tribe, a tribe that now lives in the forests beyond here, they wanted to expand out and exterminate what they saw as a danger to the natural order. Namely, our entire race."

Molly's eyes widened at this.

"Yeah, I had the same reaction. Luckily for us, one of the Glemots, another male named Campton, saw the Leef response as the *ultimate* disruption of the natural order. His thinking was that whatever aliens did with their creations was *also* part of the natural way of things."

"What, like beehives and anthills?"

"Exactly. Which was heresy to those that hated the new technology, especially once they learned about its 'impure source.' These guys wanted to use *some* technology to destroy *all* technology. The Glemots following Campton wanted to use as little technology as possible to restore the balance they had *before*."

"So the tribe that just 'accepted' me, they're the good guys?"

"There aren't any good guys here. Not in my view. Granted, I'm glad the Campton Tribe formed and kicked some Leef butt or the war with the Drenards would look like a cakewalk in comparison. Look at what they did with our ship, what they must have done with the UN ships. The fact the Navy was ousted from the OS and never won it back must be a mere *hint* of what they can do. Now imagine ground warfare with those things."

Cole's voice trailed off as a Glemot thundered by, rushing from the woods and back up the hill. Molly's gaze followed the lumbering beast. She tried her hardest to imagine a brutal side to these creatures. She couldn't. But mainly because she was still resisting the idea that they could do harm. "But this place is paradise," she complained.

"Paradise at a *cost*. I was talking to one of the younger Glemots last night, a kid named Edison—"

"What's up with the names?" she interrupted.

"Hah. I picked up on it, too, and one of the adults confirmed it. The Camptons name themselves after famous human engineers. The ones they think did more good than harm. They know all about our history, more than you and I combined. They got all kinds of data files from the Orbital Station, but getting back to the point—I was talking to Edison last night, and he's a cool kid. Well, I say *kid*, but the guy is smarter than any human I've ever met, even though he's still considered a pup. I have no idea how old he is in Earth years, but he comes across as a complete prodigy when he talks.

"Anyway, Edison was talking about today's Council and comparing it to one several years ago. The Camptons—the tribe you and I belong to—found out the tribes on the other side of the planet were reproducing too quickly. They were warring less and finding new resources for food. This was deemed so serious that a truce was called between the Leefs and the Camptons. They came together and devised a solution."

"Which was?"

"A new disease. Genetically targeting a specific strain common to two of the largest tribes on the other side of the planet. Like I said, the Camptons won the civil war, and they have the tech they need to keep things in balance. So they released this disease and killed the tribes."

"All of them?" Molly looked horrified.

"Millions of them." Cole stopped walking and looked out over the lake.

Molly felt her stomach churn. They stood in silence for a while. Finally, Molly said, "But it's so beautiful here."

"Depends on where you look."

They had wandered close to the forest again and turned to follow the stream back toward the tents. Molly wasn't sure what to say, or even what she believed at the moment.

"We have a name for what the Glemots live by, you know."

"Crazy?" Molly suggested, even though she grudgingly admired the results of their actions.

"No, Molly, these guys aren't crazy, they're just driven by an extreme form of something you and I fall for all the time."

"What?"

"The naturalistic fallacy. It's when our aesthetic sense of beauty in nature confuses us into thinking that if it exists there, it must be good. Or maybe 'right' is a better word than good."

"I'm not following you. It's obvious to me that if I think that lake is beautiful then it *is* beautiful; that's all our emotions are." She really didn't want to get into a philosophical discussion. She barely passed that class and hated every subjective minute of it.

"No, *deeper* than that. It's when we think that whatever state we happen to find our world in when we become philosophically aware *must* be the state we keep it in. Even though the world changed naturally leading up to this understanding, we think we shouldn't allow it to progress any further."

"I really don't want to talk about this, Cole."

"It's important if we're going to get out of here."

"Why *leave*?" She threw her one good arm up. "Where could we go that's better than this? Let's say I clear things up with the Navy, run a shuttle or courier service for the next forty years. You know what I'd want to do with the money I saved? I'd want to come build a house right over there and live the rest of my days strolling through these forests and swimming in that lake and collecting bugs."

Cole frowned at her; she'd never seen him look so sad. "That sounds great. Really, it does. But they wouldn't let you *build* that house 'cause it'd destroy the look of the shore. They wouldn't let you walk the same path every day because you'd trample the soil. And if you deviated from whatever they calculated the 'norm' was, they'd kill you with a *vote*. I'm sorry—and trust me, I've gone through the same emotions over the last day, and I hate that you have to do it with less time—but we need to finish this conversation."

Molly shook her head. "This talk is worse and more confusing than being in prison on Palan was."

"*That's* an exaggeration."

"Yeah, a little," she admitted, but not smiling. "Okay, forget the philosophy stuff. Even if we assume that our survival depends on getting away from this paradise, how do we fly away from them if my ship is being dismantled and they can control it from orbit anyway?"

"Simple," said Cole. "We start a war."

"We do *what*?"

"Hear me out: not every Glemot agrees on what balance to fight for. Hell, not every Campton agrees with one another. Just like with humans, it takes a strong leader to keep order here. Franklin is getting old, even by their standards, I think, and the Leefs have been making some progress with getting their technology going again."

"How did they ever lose their technology in the first place?"

"Campton's rebels. They created all kinds of anti-tech technology. EMPs that fry electronics. Little micro-bots that eat away specific metals. But their guiding principles meant every victory against the Leef technology required them to ratchet down their own. They try to control the spread of tech using the simplest tools required. As long as they stay one step ahead, they can remain there. They've almost progressed back to the Stone Age from a starting point that was beyond our own technology. That's why you woke up in a tent with a balm on your arm instead of a high-rise hospital full of beeping things."

"It's hard to argue with the result," Molly said, sweeping her arm at the vista around them.

"Now *you're* the one bringing up the 'philosophy crap' you hate so much. Yes, this is beautiful. We have parks on Earth that look like this. But we also have Mozart and Dali and Spengle and T'chuyn and even the Drenard sculptor Tadi Rooo. We can admire the cosmos and the atom. We have a *diversity* of beauty that's just as natural as *this*." He also waved his hand at the scenery." He paused. "I'm sorry to be so strident here. I honestly hope we can discuss this in detail one day, and we can both see neither extreme is tenable. Right now, though, I want to devise a plan that *wins* us that day."

Molly nodded. She turned her head away from the beauty of the lake and looked up the hill. But there was no escaping the sensual pleasure of being here.

She listened as Cole got into the meat of his plan. Molly felt detached from it all but was able to point out some tactical flaws. She agreed it would work as long as the dozen or so various "ifs" they foresaw were the only ones that existed. And of course, a lot depended on the Glemots.

Maybe too much.

oooo

Molly had hoped she'd be able to chew on the tragedy of this place over dinner, but the event turned out to be too much of a distraction. Without exaggeration, the meal she had that night was one of the highlights of her life thus far.

Most of the food varieties on Glemot were the common forms of energy storage found all over the universe, the biological shortcuts nature was fond of taking. But each example was full of a rich vitality that knew no Earth equal. There were analogies to familiar foods, but no comparing the quality.

The main course, a species of large fish, had been roasting all day over a low fire. Encrusted with a thick layer of spices, it made Molly think of cinnamon, sage, and some sort of tangy pepper. The powerful combination was offset by a sweet cream slathered over top, much like Earth honey. Small shapes of cut fruit were arranged to the side, and little berries dotted the plate. The berries looked hard, but they dissolved in her mouth, bursting with a fresh sweetness so unusual, it tasted like a primary color. Molly couldn't believe *her* taste buds could be tickled in such an alien way.

Also on the side were large vegetables boiled creamy-soft and infused with something woody and citrus, like hickory and lime, only *different*. The combination, strange and intoxicating, delighted her. She followed these nibbles with bites from a large salad, each of its dozen constituent parts a unique meal on its own. A bowl of nuts passed by; the Glemots picked through these choosily, hunting for their favorites.

The Glemot distaste for furniture meant Molly and Cole were not uncomfortable around the dinner "table." The entire tribe gathered around dozens of cloth mats, the pups getting up and rushing about to serve the adults each course in turn.

Every murmur of delight from Molly brought appreciative smiles from the Glemots, especially those who had helped prepare the meal. Then she noticed the look on Cole's face and realized her joy just made this harder on him. She tried to contain herself. This became easier when a female across from Cole, out of nowhere and with a calm voice, let him know that Walter would be "naturalized" in the morning. She watched him fight any change in his behavior. He continued to smile and converse and chew his food thoughtfully, but she had felt it since their walk: Cole was wearing a thin veneer of compliance over a core of rage.

Thinking about Walter soured the meal for Molly as well. She picked at her food distractedly, still ended up eating too much, and retired as soon as the first Glemot rose. She and Cole carried their stone plates down to a brook to rinse them off.

"Cole?"

He looked around to see if any of the Glemots could hear them. Several were heading their way and would be within earshot in moments. "Yeah?"

"What if we went to the other side of the planet? Just got away from the war between these two tribes?"

Cole gave her a sad look, one he'd successfully concealed for most of the day. But Molly could see it vividly—even in the pale starlight.

"They're all at war," he said. He looked out over the lake, its calm surface reflecting the stars perfectly. It was like a hole in the planet through which the cosmos could be seen. "War is *natural*," he added, with disgust.

Then he turned and walked past the approaching Glemots, back to the tent they'd assigned him to. Molly wanted to rush up to him and hold him tight and make him happy. But right now she couldn't even make herself happy. Even in this place, she couldn't be the perfect thing she wanted to be.

Sitting alone by the bubbling brook, she sniffed quietly while nearby Glemots debated death.

18

The chirping of morning creatures pierced Molly's tent, rescuing her from the return of bad dreams. One of the Glemot youth sat up beside her, rubbing his eyes.

"Edison?"

The pup turned to Molly, blinking. "You have me confused for my approximation." He yawned, stretching his arms wide and flashing a dangerous mouth. "Pardon my reflexive inhalation. My designation is Orville."

"I'm sorry."

"Apology accepted. Do you desire assisting in relocating the temporary structure?"

"We do what?" Molly shook her head. These guys were exhausting—especially first thing in the morning.

"Relocate the temporary structure. Our daily hibernation flattens grasses, occludes the sunlight from their photoreceptors. We relocate temporary structures every Glemot rotation to preserve the natural."

"What's natural about a tent?" Molly asked.

Orville frowned. "That statement reflects my approximation's thoughts." He rose, gathered his blanket, and stormed out without another word.

Molly sighed and adjusted her garment around her. It was a lovely way to dress if only it would stay put. Every movement shifted the fabric and threatened to bare her to the world. She wondered what Cole thought of her dressed up like this. He looked like a Roman statue in his, of course, but he treated the get-up like an annoying necessity, an "undercover prop," as he would have put it.

Outside, Molly saw the tents being shifted in a carefully orchestrated pattern. She was the last sleeper out, which seemed to create a sense of relief from some of the adult Glemots. They hurried over and started carefully extracting stakes from the ground.

Molly tried to stay out of the way, peering around for some sign of Cole, but his tent was no longer where it had been the night before.

"Molly." It was Watt, her doctor. He approached bearing a leaf slathered with his medicinal cream.

Molly shrugged the sling off her head and presented her arm. He removed the splint first, carefully scraped the old salve off, then reassembled his handiwork. Molly flexed her wrist a little, amazed at the reduction in pain. She wondered if perhaps she had just fractured the bone, and then remembered the odd angle it had been in before she passed out.

"Thank you very much." She patted his arm as he tied up the sling.

"It is my function. I recommend minimal exertion for two rotations." He smiled down at her and scratched her head with an uncanny gentleness. Molly smiled back and tried to picture Watt killing children in order to restore a sense of "balance." Even with her brain bent into odd shapes, it still couldn't wrap around the idea. She watched him lumber off and felt overwhelmed with how complex life was. If she and her friends got off Glemot alive, something new would be carried with her. She would never think of right and wrong, good and evil, beautiful and ugly the same way ever again.

Her thoughts were interrupted by Cole's voice leaking out of the woods behind the camp. She turned as he and the other Glemot youth emerged, the latter standing a good meter taller. Molly learned last night, as she noted who served the food, that a lot of the Glemots here were considered youths. Orville and Edison were mere babies as far as the adults were concerned. In thirty years, a short time for Glemots, Edison would be as big as the others. And then it would be time for a proper female to be selected for him, if he was designated a "procreator."

Molly walked over to meet them. Cole nodded at her as she approached, as if to say, "all systems are go."

"Greetings for the third occurrence, Molly."

"Hello, Edison. You boys been busy this morning?"

"Delightfully disturbing the balance all evening," Edison said, his voice sonorous and soothing.

Cole put a hand on her shoulder. "Let's go for a walk," he said.

Edison nodded to both Humans and bounded off to help move a tent.

Molly walked with Cole to the woods and let him take the lead. She was worried about the dark circles under his eyes. His shoulders also sagged with fatigue. He looked a lot like he'd been acting lately. Glum.

But even beat down and exhausted, she couldn't help but admire the shape of his body. His Portuguese ancestry had blessed him with a bronze complexion that required no sunlight for upkeep. His back was a broad V tapering down to a thin waist. Wide shoulders, even stooped as they were, rounded down into well-defined arms. She watched them swing easily in the revealing robe as they walked along in silence. He possessed a rare combination of strength and litheness that comforted her when they were in danger—but made her worry for her sanity when they were alone together.

Cole slowed so she could catch up, prematurely ending her anatomical inventory and making her blush as if she had been caught thinking aloud.

"We're going to see the *Parsona*. I just want you to be prepared."

Molly bit her lip and nodded. "How's Walter?" she asked.

"Edison and I broke him out just in time." Cole smiled at her. "'Even sssteven,' he told me."

Molly managed a chuckle at Cole's impersonation. Another cultural awareness lesson was probably in order, but it comforted her to see his mood lifting.

"Our very own Campton tribe has sent out a search party to look for their missing prisoner." Cole pointed through the woods off to their right. "The warrior village and training grounds are just through there. Edison left behind a patch of his fur, so the Leefs will be suspected for nabbing Walter."

Molly nodded. Little could go wrong with the first parts of their plan. Many "ifs" were to follow, though.

"Have you found the EMP yet?"

"No, but Edison thinks his twin brother Orville knows where it is. Orville's tutor for the Council is the head of the Technology Prevention Subcommittee."

"I can't believe there *is* such a thing," Molly mused aloud.

"Are you kidding? There're several of them on every planet. Earth included. They usually go by something else, of course. I just wish we could get Orville in on this, but I don't think he's quite as open to change as his brother."

"Don't be greedy. I'm shocked you found a Glemot who would turn on his own tribe. I feel guilty using him this way."

"Who's using whom? Did you know that when your America was being overrun by my European ancestors, the natives thought they were using these pale men in their schemes to wipe out neighboring tribes?"

Molly shook her head. "That's not what I learned."

"Trust me. This planet's history is a detail of groups splintering apart. Hell, I'm not sure if I talked him into this plan, or if he talked *me* into it. The kid—gods, the guy is bigger than me, smarter than me, and older than me, and I refer to him as 'the kid'—he's been jockeying for something like this for a long time. I think he sees us as a sign or something."

"Okay, I get it. Now I feel *used* instead of guilty."

"Funny. Now listen, the timing on this will be intense. We're about to meet with members of the Leef council, and we need to have our story straight."

"I know my part," Molly insisted. After a pause, "But let's go over it one more time."

They conferred as they walked. A few minutes later, the couple ascended a rise, the trees thinned, and they could see *Parsona* below. Molly fell silent, save for a pained intake of air. Her good hand came up to her chin, resting her fingers there, trying to prevent her jaw from dropping any further.

The ship stood alone in the clearing below, its profile recognizable, but just barely. Molly and Cole could see straight through the once-mighty machine in many places. Parts, panels, equipment, gear—it was all spread out across the grass. A checkerboard of dirt scratches marked off a grid of some sort. Cole explained that every piece was set for repurposing in the Campton's anti-tech cause or designated for complete destruction.

Behind the ship, Molly could see patches of grass charred black from the landing. The thrusters above the dark spots were in a state of mid-disassembly. She was sure the ship would never fly again. She had owned it for less than a week.

Cole put an arm across Molly's shoulders, pulling her close and trying to console her. "Hey, keep in mind that a small group took this apart in just a day. They've been pulled off for the battle, but a large group of Glemots just as skilled can put her back together in no time." Cole paused. "At least Edison seems to think so."

"She's dead." It was all Molly could say.

Cole kept his arm around her, guiding her back through woods and on to their meeting spot. "She's *close* to dead. You and I have been there. Look at us now."

Molly did. She noted the light bruises on Cole's face from his beating by the Palan guards. She glanced down at her shattered arm. She didn't answer at first. Instead, she walked along, her head tilted into Cole's chest as she sought a rhythm to match his—something to keep their wounds from smarting.

"Yeah," she eventually said. "Look at us now."

oooo

They walked in silence to their meeting spot with the Leefs. At one point they crouched down to sneak along quietly as the sounds of the Camptons drilling for war thundered nearby. Eventually, they reached the clearing where Cole said they'd handed a freed Walter over to the Leefs. They stepped into a pool of daylight, and three Glemots left the concealment of the trees and greeted them.

"Your presence is recognized, humans," the largest one said, his fur just starting to show the faintest signs of black. Molly was beginning to associate the coloring with age, or rank, but she still didn't have a clue how old these people were.

"Detail the coordinates of the tactical fusion warhead—" blurted a smaller Glemot standing to one side. The middle figure held up his paw, cutting the words off.

Tension formed; Cole prodded it. "First, we'll tell you where our ship is. When it's fully repaired, you guys receive the nuke. It needs to be no later than tomorrow morning, before the battle."

"Extreme confidence for a diminutive one," the smaller Glemot joked. All three Leefs chuckled—it sounded like semi-flat tires rolling on pavement.

The larger Glemot spoke again. "Our accomplishments will be swift and precise while your limitations are apparent. The fusion device will be transferred prior to the local horizon's occlusion of the nearest star by the rotation of Glemot."

Molly and Cole looked to one another. "Before nightfall?" she suggested.

There were nods and grunts of assent from the aliens.

"Fine," Cole said. "We'll meet here with the nuke. Oh, and just so you know, there's some Camptons drilling nearby—"

The large Glemot waved him off. "Previously known." They turned to go.

"Wait," Molly said. They stopped and turned. "How's Walter?" she asked.

The darkest Glemot shifted uncomfortably. "The metal one is . . . adequately secured," he said. With that, they thundered into the trees.

Molly and Cole were left in the clearing with their troubled thoughts. Molly felt awful for Walter but glad that he was alive. Her stomach knotted with worry. And guilt. She had betrayed the people who had patched her arm, housed her, and fed her. She tried to focus on the millions of Glemots the Camptons had killed, but weighing impersonal facts—a million souls extinguished—against her own experiences produced sickening results. *Shouldn't the former outweigh the latter?*

In silence they walked back to the camp, their thoughts out of character. Molly philosophized, dwelling on the nature of relative harms, while Cole focused on the practical and pressing matter: how were they going to find their "nuke" in time?

○○○○

Something felt different as soon as they emerged on the Campton's hill. Hundreds of Glemots milled about down by the stream, several of them arguing loudly, their voices rumbling. The entire hill shuddered from heavy feet stomping this way and that. Two Glemots rushed over to her and Cole.

"Detail recent coordinates!" one of them demanded with a growl.

Molly was unable to speak, her stomach crawling up her throat and attempting to flee.

"Uh, reporting back from the training camp," Cole said.

The two Glemots bristled with anger, the fur along their shoulders waving in the windless air. One of them held a stick as thick as Molly's thighs; even his casual gestures with it seemed life threatening.

Another Glemot down the rise yelled, "Nikola! Leo!"

The duo turned and waved, then spun back to Cole and Molly. "Report to Doctor Watt," one of them commanded before they bounded off.

Molly spotted Watt by one of the tents; he waved at them frantically. She and Cole rushed down, marveling at the level of activity on what yesterday had been such a quiet sylvan glade. Like the Navy's satellite, *Parsona* had arrived and disrupted the order of things. Now they needed to do the impossible: piece her together and return to orbit. Molly felt overwhelmed by their plan as she hurried down to Watt.

The doctor checked Molly's arm before surveying their faces. "Your acquaintance Walter, and Edison, my offspring, have simultaneously been apprehended by the Leefs."

Molly had no problem feigning worry. Confusion looks similar enough. *Why would Edison be missing? This wasn't part of the plan.*

Watt also informed them that some from the council saw the arrival of their ship into the Glemot system as a bit of a coincidence. So much had happened, and happened fast, since it was brought to the surface. There was talk of recalculating risk/reward formulas that involved Cole and Molly. So far, it was just a few Glemots, but the growling would spread.

"How do you know Edison's missing?" Molly asked. She hoped the pup was off looking for the Campton's EMP device, the one they were going to pass off to the Leefs as a nuke.

"Moderate fur samples matching Edison's were discovered near Walter's containment area," said Watt. "Querying observers resulted in counter-claims. Several noted Edison in the vicinity of camp late morning, approximately. The antitheses is suggested by group two: the subject in question was in fact his littermate Orville. No sample saw both simultaneously."

Molly couldn't believe it. The fur Edison and Cole had used to frame the Leefs was backfiring. There would still be a war, and a trap, but events were moving too quickly . . . emotions amplifying equations.

"Where's Orville?" Cole asked.

"Whittling war sticks alongside the young."

"Can we talk to him? See how he's doing?"

This seemed to please Watt immensely. He pointed down to the woods beyond the stream.

Molly patted Watt on the arm before she hurried off. "Your boys will be okay," she told him.

"Everything will," Watt said, his thick jargon missing from the simple phrase.

○ ○ ○ ○

Cole led Molly into the forest, following the sounds of young Glemot chatter. "Let me do the talking," he told her.

"Glad to," she replied.

As they approached, the circle of pups fell silent and turned to glare at them. Cole had a bad feeling this wasn't going to go well. Orville shot up from the ground and strode toward them, a sharpened stick in hand.

"Follow," he said as he rumbled past.

Cole grabbed Molly's hand, and they followed the pup deeper into the woods, out of sight from the rest of the youth. He spun on both of them, his swiftness startling.

"Inciting hostilities? Brainwashing my littermate? Enunciate!"

Cole held up both hands, palms out. If this came to blows, it would go badly for them. Somehow Orville had sniffed out his brother, so lying was probably not the best option. But neither was the whole truth.

"Whoa, pal. Your brother came to *us*. Said he had a plan to disrupt the balance or something. That he'd kill us if we didn't go along."

Orville's face flashed as some part of this registered. "Disrupt the balance?" Orville repeated.

Cole seized on this. "He said he had a way of wiping out the Leefs. He wanted to use our friend, Walter, as bait. We agreed if it meant sparing his life."

"This ruse I am previously cognizant of. My suspicions were great when he queried me on the electromagnetic pulse device."

Cole wanted to groan out loud, but contained himself. *Everything* hinged on that device, and on Edison being able to deliver it.

"Where's your brother?" Molly asked.

Orville shifted his gaze over to her. "Detained." It was all they were going to get.

Cole squeezed her hand; he tried a different route. It didn't look as if Orville was going to kill them or turn them in. And if they were from the same litter, perhaps their goals were different, but their basic needs were the same. "Did Edison also tell you how he was going to get onto the council?" he asked.

Orville bent his knees and lowered his face down to Cole's level. The hair on his shoulders waved back and forth. "Talk," he said.

Cole did. And he hoped it wouldn't trouble Molly to see how good he was at stretching the truth. . .

○ ○ ○ ○

". . .and after the last Leef was killed in the trap, Edison would reveal to the adults that it had been *his* plan. He'd show the detailed calculations, the numbers of increased Campton procreation, how an overall balance could be restored while breaking the local one. Your brother thought the Council would honor him with a seat, that he'd be on a fast track to leading this tribe, long before his fur darkened."

Molly tried to keep her composure as Cole wrapped up his fictionalized account of the past day. She could tell Orville was riveted—she had been as well. It fascinated her how Cole weaved truth with lie, understanding which emotions to trigger and reeling his prey right in. She wondered if his imagination for conspiracy theories tapped into this ability or if the skill was just finely honed, thanks to his paranoia.

She chewed on this possibility while Orville seemed to be considering something else.

"Edison," Orville finally said, shaking his head. "That deceptive brigand." He looked down at Cole and waved his stick back and forth through the air between them. "Enormous wisdom to divulge completely, young human. My sibling attempted many untruths, a crazed speech of tactical warheads and double-crosses. Your account contains accuracy. Come. Together we confront the upstart, and his plan transfers to *me*. Afterward, my littermate's rumored demise becomes *reality*."

Orville thumped the ground with his stick and slapped Cole on the shoulder. It nearly drove him off his feet. "Come," he said cheerily, and bounded through the forest.

Molly and Cole looked at one another. The plan was falling apart, but they had no choice. They hurried off after Orville, struggling to keep up.

19

The brutal pace quickly exhausted them both, their lungs burning while Orville loped along with an effortless gait. He weaved through the trees, sensitive to accidentally creating a path, while his long, youthful fur whisked up and down like miniature whips as he bounded along. Molly lost herself in the sight of them as she fought to steady her breath. Her broken arm jounced in its sling, thrumming with pain.

Orville came to a sudden stop in a section of the forest no different from the rest. He looked around in every direction while Molly and Cole bent over, huffing. He reached down into the leaves and pulled up a patch of the forest floor, hinging it away neatly. A dim light floated up from the square hole; Orville waved them down first.

It was a simple ladder, but the descent felt as dangerous for Molly as the one that had broken her arm. The rungs were spaced over a meter apart, their diameter too big for her to properly grasp. With one arm strapped and useless, she was forced to employ her chin, pressing a knee against the side rail as she adjusted her grip. Cole tried to descend beside her, steadying her back with one hand and giving her encouragement as Orville shouted at them to increase the pace. It seemed to take forever to get to the metal floor below.

Metal. It was jarring to see something modern on Glemot. The ladder, the lights, the floor—they didn't prepare her for what awaited as she turned around.

They were inside a long rectangular chamber carved out of the dirt and lined with metal panels. Along one entire wall stood a massive row of consoles with readouts that reminded Molly of SADAR units, and stations that resembled cockpit controls. A large tactical table dominated the center of the room, and a solitary male Glemot hunched over one of the stations. He turned to appraise this intrusion, pulling a wire from one of his ears.

When he saw Orville step off the ladder behind them, he nodded, replaced the wire, and turned back to his work. Molly glanced at Orville and saw fury in his eyes; she followed his gaze across the room. Edison huddled in the far corner, bound and gagged. The poor pup's eyes were wild with fear, his fur bunched around the restraints.

"Your nefarious plan is uncovered, brother." Orville marched toward him and twirled his sharp stick. Primal fear surged through Molly, the weight of the jungle floor pressing down from above. They were a couple of puny humans in a lair full of monsters. *Could the plan work with Orville rather than Edison? Would she even want it to?* She couldn't imagine allowing Edison to be harmed just so they could get off this planet.

She turned to Cole, who practically vibrated with nervous energy. The only thing going for them was the adult's distraction. The important activity on the screen ahead seemed to require more attention than the squabbling of cubs behind.

Orville was halfway across the room, walking by the tactical table. He spoke to the screen operator. "The plot is far simpler than we thought, Mentor, but the cunning exponentially greater than my brother's falsehoods. A mere maneuvering for stature, nothing beyond."

Oh, gods, thought Molly, *this was Orville's mentor, the anti-tech council member!* The only way out of this room was going to be with Edison dead and their plan ruined.

It would be a mad dash deep into the woods as their promises to both tribes met on tomorrow's battlefield and were destroyed.

Orville's mentor turned away from his screen for a moment to look back at his protégé. "End him." He stated it like the solution to some playful riddle.

Molly took a step back, reaching for Cole to pull him toward the ladder.

But Cole was no longer there.

She watched in horror as her friend rushed off to his death.

oooo

Time slowed as Cole raced to the tactical table and threw himself up to the top. He ran by Orville, who stopped and turned, seemingly confused. Cole scooped up one of the battle pieces off the table; it looked like a painted metal figurine of a tent. He figured it would be useless against Glemot hides, but maybe it would help him unlock the only weapon in here they could use.

He leaped to the ground on the other side of the table, still moving at full speed. Ahead of him, Edison cringed back into the steel wall. He seemed unsure of which of these approaching figures meant him more harm: his brother with his large stick or the strange alien rushing him with an improvised dagger.

Orville roared from behind, obviously realizing what Cole had planned. The Glemot pup lurched after him, bringing his stick up high. Cole dove, crashing into Edison and hacking at the rope around his arms, not concerned at all about harming the pup. Edison's arms strained against the fibers; a few vicious slashes and they parted. His freed paw struck out at Cole, knocking him roughly to one side. He slammed into one of the consoles, drawing the attention of the adult. Orville's stick swished the air where his head had just been, barely missing Edison's face.

The room filled with a confused silence as each combatant sized up the others. Cole noticed Molly rushing toward the brothers, her one arm still trapped in a sling and useless. Orville was readying another blow with his massive stick while the adult attempted to untangle himself from his station, yelling at both pups to stay where they were.

The adult was the biggest problem. Literally. Cole knew he'd be ripped in half by the monster, so he pushed off the console and charged into Orville, choosing a foe closer to his size. Tackling a bear would've been easier. Cole tried to hang on as the enraged child thrashed, clawing at his back to tear him to shreds.

Molly arrived at full speed around the clear side of the tactical table. Cole tried to shout her down as she threw herself into the air, bringing her heels into the back of Orville's knee. The pup crashed down under Cole's weight, the stick pinned beneath him.

Edison pressed off the wall and rushed past to meet the charging adult. They crashed into each other with a boom, the rage in the youth enough to match the elder's size. Molly wrestled with one of Orville's arms, trying to keep it pinned back, as Cole launched a series of blows at the cub's skull. The strikes stung his fists, but he wasn't sure the angered youth even felt them. He looked up to see Edison gouging at the elder's eyes, the two locked in a fight to the death.

Orville howled beneath him and lifted his shoulder, sending Molly flying back toward the table. With a thud, Cole drove a knee into the bundle of fur. Orville just pushed his bulk from the ground with Cole still on top of him, wearing him like a cape. His massive stick whizzed through the air, narrowly missing Molly's head.

Cole screamed and reached around for Orville's eyes, but the pup shrugged him off his back like an afterthought. Cole felt a massive paw wrap around his knee before he was tossed into the metal wall. He collapsed in a heap and fought for his senses. Molly yelled something; he looked up to see the sharpened stick, like a battering ram, hurtling toward his abdomen. He fell flat, and the deadly log exploded against the steel in a bloom of splinters.

Orville howled with rage.

Cole pushed himself up and wrapped his hands around a fragment of wood the size of a baton and sharp as a dagger. Orville looked down for what remained of his weapon, and Cole obliged by shoving the shard right into the pup's eye.

The room rumbled with the sound of pure fury. The other two Glemots stopped clawing each other to see what had happened. At the sight of his wounded protégé, the adult let out a roar of his own. He tossed Edison aside with a shiver of rage and took a step toward Cole.

○ ○ ○ ○

Molly was already backing away from the terrifying creature when Cole turned to her. "*Run!*" he commanded.

She stumbled toward the ladder, the sound of thunder echoing off the steel around her. Cole caught up, steadying her as they rushed past the tactical table. Molly glanced over her shoulder to see the adult thrashing toward them, striking the wall with his fists as he went, mad with fury.

Running to the ladder filled Molly with the dread of a living nightmare. She was trying to climb a fence and feeling the bad thing at her back. She knew it would get her, but she had to scramble anyway, her arms not working.

Fear traveled up her spine; she jerked her arm out of the sling and grabbed rungs, one after the other. She kicked and fought her way up. Every time her right arm took its share of weight, Molly had to bite down on her body's urge to pass out. Each rung brought pure torture.

The ladder was wide enough for Cole to come alongside her, just as they had descended. They were over two meters up, scrambling as fast as they could, when the adult reached them. He yanked Cole down first, his arm banging on a rung at her feet. The Glemot raised both paws to pulverize him into the ground. Molly didn't hesitate. She launched off the ladder and wrapped both arms around the creature's neck. The adult peeled her off and cast her aside, tossing her violently into the wall. A wall of fur flashed before her and Molly tensed for death, but it was Edison joining the action, a large fragment of splintered wood in hand.

Molly flinched as he crashed into the larger alien, driving the shard deep into the Glemot's side. The adult's howls deepened and strengthened. Edison stabbed again. And again. The injured beast swung his arms and stumbled back against a console, looking at the blood on his fur, pawing at it confusedly.

The fear on the adult's face knotted Molly's stomach. They were not battling a trained warrior—this was a *politician*. Pity stirred and then recoiled from her rising wrath. This was the sort of beast that killed with calculations, concocting war and disease and wiping out millions from the safety of a council meeting. She wanted to launch herself at the wounded thing and peel its flesh.

But Edison beat her to it. . .

oooo

The aftermath made her want to vomit. Molly had been trained to kill, but from a distance. A puff of fire and a cloud of silent debris was as close to death as she was ever meant to be. The hand-to-hand courses at the Academy were a formality, designed to instill confidence and build muscle.

They'd never prepared her for *this*.

The council member was dead—his blood everywhere. The tangy scent of it filled the air; Molly could taste it like the metal of a dry spoon. At the other end of the room, Edison and Cole subdued the injured Orville, tying him up in Edison's old restraints.

Molly tore herself from the gruesome sight of the dead Glemot and made her way toward the others, drawn by Orville's howling. At the tactical table she paused, reaching up for a metal figure, the one resembling a pointed tree. It looked to be the sharpest.

She gripped the painted metal in her left hand, her right arm out of its sling and limp with pain. She remained unaware of it and paid no heed to the disarray of her robe as it barely clung to her shoulders. She approached Orville and lowered herself to her heels, clutching the tree with white knuckles.

"I'm sorry," she told him. She reached down and raked the metal point across the fabric of her robe, cutting off a wide strip from the hem. The hunk of wood had already been removed from his eye, and blood matted down the fur on half his face, dripping with the universal red of life in contact with oxygen. Molly folded the fabric up into a pad, making sure a clean portion was left on the outside. She pressed it to Orville's eye and looked to Cole for help, hoping he'd understand why she needed to do this.

Cole nodded and tore a long strip from his own robe. "For you," he told her. "Not for him."

Orville's face displayed no gratitude, but his angry panting subsided. The youth seemed resigned to his fate, whatever it would be.

Edison.

Molly turned to see how he was taking all of this. After flaying the elder and rushing to secure his brother, the pup had collapsed into one of the station chairs.

His eyes were focused on a blank spot on the opposite wall. He could have been catatonic or calmly planning for world domination—it was impossible to tell.

Orville began testing his restraints for a weakness while Cole stood over him warily. Molly rose and walked over to Edison, placing a hand on his shoulder, the fur sticky with sweat and much else. There was a lot of blood on him.

On all of them.

"The plan is still viable," he said calmly. He broke his gaze away from the steel plating and looked into Molly's eyes. "The great imbalance remains a possibility."

Molly couldn't think about it clearly. There was too much horror down here. She needed to get out and breathe some fresh air, to think about what had just happened and what it meant for their immediate future.

"I have to get out of here," she said.

Neither Cole nor Edison tried to stop her. They just looked at each other: breathing hard, sweating, unknowingly forging the bond that only battle welds. They sat like this as Molly made the slow and painful climb.

Up and out.

oooo

Cole spoke first. "What do we do with your brother?"

"He remains incarcerated here. We secure the hatch mechanism from without."

"Where's the EMP?"

Edison shrugged and looked side to side. "Here, somewhere." It seemed like a guess.

They began pulling panels off the cabinets and below the consoles; they rapped the walls. Orville seethed with anger but they didn't waste time questioning him; Edison assured Cole that they could only expect delaying lies.

Edison shoved the tactics table to slide it out of the way and get to the consoles on the other side of it. The top hinged up instead.

"Located," he said.

Cole had to hoist himself up and rest his stomach on the lip of the open chest to look inside. There were two large EMPs nestled in individually padded compartments. Each looked extremely impressive, complex enough to pass for a much more dangerous device when presented to the Leefs.

"Are you sure they won't know the difference between an EMP and a nuclear bomb?" Cole asked Edison.

The pup smiled at this. "Trust me completely, Cole. Ascertaining the difference will be impossible for them."

Cole smiled back. There was still a chance this could work.

○ ○ ○ ○

In the corner of the room, Orville groaned to himself. He thought back to the plan his brother had spilled and realized the horrific truth of it all. He wanted to scream, but he knew it would serve no purpose. He was better off down there, anyway.

Of *that*, he was sure.

20

Cole crawled out of the bunker and found Molly collapsed against a tree. She looked horrible, but at least her arm was back in the sling and her robe refastened. He knelt beside her and checked her splints—saw she'd already secured them. Her chin was down, her hair matted to her forehead. Cole placed his fingers below her jaw and lifted her gaze to his.

"You okay?"

She didn't say anything. She just pulled him down to her by his neck and pressed her cheek to his. Cole slipped an arm around her back and helped her stand up. It was getting late, and they needed to keep pressing forward.

Edison walked up with the device cradled in front of him, leaning back with the weight of the thing.

Cole had sudden doubts about the device's reach. EMPs were great at knocking out electronics over a wide distance, but what kind of range would they need in order to fly out of here? Edison had said there were several hidden bunkers like this, each capable of locating *Parsona* and taking control of it, but he wasn't privy to all of their locations. And all it would take was not reaching one of them, and their escape would be short-lived. The other problem was making sure they were beyond the EMP's range before it went off. Otherwise, *Parsona's* electronics would be hit, she'd go lifeless, and they'd all come crashing back down to the planet.

Timing would be everything.

The trio set off through the woods on a long, circuitous hike that would bypass the activity around the Campton hill. It would be an excruciating hike for Edison. Cole felt horrible, but he was useless for helping with the load. He had tried to assist in removing it from the case, but he was unable to budge the thing. It certainly was an impressive device, able to pass for a nuke even to his Naval eye.

He thought about the trap the Leefs would set with it, their fury when the weapon proved to be nothing more than an electromagnetic pulse, scouring the hidden bunkers as *Parsona* broke through the atmosphere.

Cole's eyes drifted from the device to Edison's tense frame. He couldn't work out what the Glemot youth was getting out of this. Sure, if the Leef trap ended up a Campton rout, he could take credit for the plan and assure his fame and fortune. But was that really enough to explain the brutality they'd witnessed below the forest floor? What about Orville? Why keep him alive?

Could Glemots really be this calculating over what they thought was right or wrong? Maybe they had some evolutionary advantage that prevented emotion from usurping their decision making. Cole considered this possibility and wondered about his own habit of using people to achieve his own goals. Did it excuse him that he felt bad about it later? His brief time on Glemot had been punctuated by little lies to every side. What made him any different? He glanced at Molly and cringed from other lies he'd told, despite his powerful reasons for telling them.

The guilt served to distract him from his plan's worst-case scenario: disturbing the balance on Glemot. If they set this force loose on the galaxy—this trinity of wrath, genius, and power—it could mean the end of *everything* else. Perhaps in the universe.

No, that was not something Cole could afford to dwell on. Thoughts like that made action impossible.

o o o o

By the time they arrived at the meeting spot, Edison was visibly worn out. They hid the EMP nearby, and Molly paced nervously, looking back to where the sun had disappeared over the horizon. She fretted over whether or not they'd been too late.

Out of the darkness, a dozen forms emerged. The Leef warriors. They surrounded them noiselessly and pressed in. One warrior spoke quietly to Edison, noting the matted blood in the pup's fur. Several other warriors approached the youth and patted him, speaking softly. Molly could make no sense of this other than some sort of alien cultural tradition.

The plan had been to get Molly and Cole to their ship to oversee the repairs. Only *then* would the "nuke" be handed over. But time had grown short; exhaustion within both parties moved them along the shorter path of faith and trust. They agreed to exchange the device right there and rush the repairs.

Edison, Molly, and Cole huddled for a brief moment to touch and speak, sharing the electricity that courses through those who have been willing to die for one another.

Molly wished Edison the best of luck as Cole pulled her away, allowing their guide to lead them toward their ship. By the time her thoughts had returned to the task at hand, she realized they were going the wrong way. She tugged on Cole's arm and gave him a questioning look.

"They probably moved it," he said, shrugging.

A pan-galactic starship? Through a forest? With no mechanical advantage? Molly assumed the ship would be repaired in place, the Camptons too busy war planning to guard it adequately. If her ship was safer, she couldn't complain, but something in the demeanor of their new allies told her that all was not honest with them. She wished Walter were here with his olfactory lie detector.

Her growing mistrust melted when she heard the rattle and clang of construction filtering through the trees. A shifting light could be seen ahead, dancing like a hundred fairies. It sounded and looked like a party of sprites celebrating by banging pots and pans.

They followed their guide through a line of trees and popped into a massive clearing. Molly gasped aloud. Hundreds of Glemots crawled over the frame of her ship, many of them wearing straps on their wrists that glowed with enough light to work by. They worked furiously and efficiently. Lines of smaller Glemots passed parts along, communicating softly.

Ahead of them stood one large adult who surveyed the progress, his paws on his hips. Their escort approached this figure and tapped him on the shoulder. The adult whirled to take in Molly and Cole. She thought she recognized his posture but couldn't make out his face, silhouetted as it was by the floating lights beyond.

Their escort returned. "Follow," he said. The other Glemot spun to face the work before him.

Molly led Cole down to the ship, hope rising in her chest. Fifty meters away from *Parsona*, they were spotted, and Walter came bolting out of the cargo bay, his face almost nothing but teeth. He rushed straight for Molly and practically tackled her with a hug.

"Molly," he said, his silver face pressing against her shoulder.

She could feel the coolness of his skin warming with joy. She hugged him with one arm and fought to keep the other from being broken again.

After a moment she had to push away, confident Walter would have remained like this forever. "It's good to see my Cargo Officer is still on duty."

"Molly, thesse animalss are putting everything in the wrong placsse." He swept his hands around the scene and seemed absolutely anguished at the ruining of his organizational system.

She squeezed his shoulder firmly, as a good Captain might a real crew member, and said with seriousness, "We'll have plenty of time to fix it when we get out of here, okay?"

Walter sniffed and nodded. Molly watched Cole rush over to offer some advice and realized she could be useful here as well. "Get back to work, Officer."

Walter grinned. If he knew how to salute properly, she felt certain he would have done it right then. He spun back into the cargo bay, shouting orders to Glemots several times his size.

It was going to be a long night, Molly realized.

21

Molly stood in the cockpit doorway and watched as one of the smallest Leefs installed the last panel. The first rays of morning sunlight sliced through the tall trees and sparkled against the carboglass. All night she'd been mesmerized by the way the Glemots worked individually and in groups, and she finally had a chance to see what their prehensile claws could do, twisting into various shapes for driving screws or shaping metal. They were not above digging into *Parsona's* well-stocked tool chests but rarely needed to.

The Glemot took a step back from his work, and indicator lights lit up the dash. Molly threw her arms around the pup and squeezed him. She leaned over the dash and pulled up the nav computer and the SADAR—it felt like a miracle. She turned and looked up at this young member of the Leef tribe; he beamed with pride. Molly smiled back, but the closer they got to leaving, and the more she'd worked with these people, the worse she felt about betraying them. She patted him on the shoulder and hurried out to find Cole.

In the cargo bay, Walter was conducting an orchestra of organizational activity. Most of the repair crew had already departed to join the warriors, leaving just the children to help clean up. Walter had pulled them off those duties and was using them to sort and arrange *Parsona's* gear. Most were smaller than Edison, but this still meant a crowded cargo bay and a lot of noisy stomping. Molly weaved through the activity, shaking her head.

Outside, Cole was conferring with the few remaining adults. Molly walked up behind him and placed her hand on his shoulder. "We have basic systems running right now," she told him. "The ship is going through its diagnostics, and I'm cycling the hyperdrive."

Cole nodded, thanked the Glemots, and pulled Molly back toward the ship. "Our timetable still looks pretty good, but we need to think about getting out of here soon. These guys are very anxious to use the *device*," he stressed the word and Molly heard both meanings, "and the ship's systems are not going to be happy if they get caught in the *blast*."

"How much time do you think we have?" Molly sorely missed the steady days on Earth, where donning a watch made some sort of sense. Here, on various star systems and in the void of space, when you can circle a planet in a few minutes, you were left just counting arbitrary ticks between two events.

"Probably not even an hour. I say we do a basic flight check and see if the thrusters fire up. Worst case, we fly to another clearing halfway around this green rock and do more repairs there."

"Sounds great to me." Molly nodded to the Glemots and walked back up the cargo ramp. Walter stood just inside the bay, ordering the placement of more gear. "I'm gonna need you to get your crew out of here, buddy. We're taking off as soon as the engines are warm."

"Yess, Captain!"

"And Walter? Make sure we don't have any stowaways. Check every compartment big enough for a toddler."

"Yess, Captain!"

He hurried off, and Molly smiled as Cole strode in to join her. It was good to have the group together again. Strange how they'd already created such a bond that a day apart felt like a week. Molly turned to close the cargo ramp and paused at the sight beyond. If all went well, it would be the last time she ever set foot on this planet. She pulled in a deep breath of the fresh air—rich with oxygen—and held it in. She admired the way the sunlight filtered through layers of leaves, turning the very air green. The grass that wasn't trampled from the night's work popped with leaping and flying things. Massive trees stood erect all around the ship like duty-bound sentinels.

It felt *wrong* to flee this place, to *want* to leave it. Molly hoped beyond all hope that they'd have a chance to return. She longed for an opportunity to see this place cloaked in peace rather than war. She sighed and keyed the cargo hatch, watching the cold steel rise up and choke away the view. As beautiful as Glemot was, Molly was happy to be back in her temporary home of metal and electricity.

She made her way to the cockpit and settled into the captain's chair, her flightsuit itchy and uncomfortable after she had gotten used to the soft robe. She pulled up the chase camera to make sure no Glemots were near the rear of the ship. Every device she touched clicked right into operation, filling her with wonder. The Glemots had done an incredible job putting everything back together; the thrusters fired without a hitch. If anything, they sounded healthier than before. They whined up to their working speeds without the accustomed stutter around 1,500 RPMs. Strong and vibrant sounds hummed up from the back of *Parsona*.

"Better than new is right," she muttered.

As tired as she was from being up all night, Molly forced herself to do an engine room check before they pulled away. As she crossed the cargo bay, she saw a few Glemots through the portholes lingering by the edge of the forest, as if to watch their handiwork take flight. Molly gave the engine room a visual inspection and opened the door to the lazarette. The thrusters purred with precision, the fluid and temperature gauges reading normal.

She headed back to the cockpit, pausing to ensure Walter was buckled in tight. The boy seemed immensely appreciative of her attention.

"Looks good back there," she told Cole as she settled into her seat.

He nodded, checking the angle of the thrusters to make sure they were ready for lift and gave her a gloved thumbs-up. Molly pointed to her sling. "You have the honors," she reminded him.

"Oh—of course," he stammered.

Molly watched him grip the flight controls with his left hand and felt a mixture of nervousness and humor. "You wanna switch seats with me?" she asked.

He gave her a hurt look. "I'm fine. It's just been a while . . . and this baby was a bucket of bolts, literally, like a day ago."

Molly raised her eyebrows.

"Okay, I'm nervous," Cole admitted. "Does that make you happy?"

Molly laughed. "Hell no, man, it just makes me nervous, too." As much as her broken arm annoyed her, watching hours and hours of simulator banter play back in reverse nearly made it all worthwhile. She settled back in her seat while Cole gripped the throttle.

"Liftoff," he whispered, giving the ship thrust.

Unsteadily at first, then balancing with the increase in height and speed, the GN-290 Starship *Parsona* suspended itself in the heavens once more. Walter whooped from the cargo bay. Molly checked the chase camera and watched the trees recede into forest and then into a carpet of green. After a series of wild escapes, such a banal exit seemed foreign and strange to her. She braced for the ship to be taken over, wondering how long it would be before the EMP cleared the ground of electronics. They'd be out of the atmosphere before long, but she knew from experience that the range of those bunkers extended out to the largest moon.

Every second that nothing bad happened got them closer to the Orbital Station. Molly felt as if their luck was finally changing for the better.

The thing hiding in *Parsona's* escape pod #2 would have agreed with her completely.

22

Mekhar huddled with a few other Leefs in the small clearing, disbelieving his good fortune. Many years of precise calculations had led up to this moment. That he had been picked with the flip of a stick symbolized much: The Great Ambush embodied Glemot planning, yet it would be topped off with a flourish of randomization.

He could see the fear and envy in the eyes of his tribemates. Their fur shivered anxiously, along with his own. One of his paws rested on the impressive device in the center of the group. He glanced expectantly from it to his great leader, waiting for the signal.

The sounds of heavy marching filtered through the trees, likely from the Campton forward guard. The legions of great Campton warriors would follow, armed with their sharpened sticks and more sinister devices. Mekhar thought of the battles he'd been lucky to survive. He looked down at his scars, like white worms trampling his fur, and recalled how badly things had gone in the past.

This time, though, things would be different.

He leaned forward to shield the shiny device with his wide back. One glint through the woods would give them away. He glanced up at the great leader, but the old Glemot still looked to the sky, waiting on just the right moment. Mekhar could now make out the footsteps of individual Camptons and grew nervous. They could have sprung this trap from anywhere. *Why here?* he wondered.

The ground vibrated as the main column of Camptons drew near. Mekhar imagined it was the old planet shivering in anticipation. He took it as a mystical sign to begin his assignment, but fought the urge. The great leader would tell him when. His paw moved closer to the first of two buttons.

At first, the roar of thrusters burning in the atmosphere sounded like another column of warriors. When the marching stopped, however, the sound of last night's hard work became clear. With a great roar, the machine he'd helped reconstruct lifted into space. Mekhar wished he could see the look on those Campton faces as they realized they'd become mere variables in a Leef calculation. He rested his finger on the first red button; the great leader turned to him and held a paw up. Mekhar felt the first chill of hesitation as the enormity of this moment vibrated through him. He met the gaze of this great Leef, who had chosen to live as a Campton, and tried to borrow some of his strength.

The paw closed, leaving a single digit out. Mekhar looked down at his own hand. The claw on his first finger twitched; he forced it into a dull shape. The button went down with a loud click and the device whined up like a turbine, humming with great power. Mekhar thought about what this mechanism was alleged to do and had a moment of doubt. Deep inside, down where calculation gave way to intuition, something told him that the device would not go off as planned. Surely this moment was too big for the likes of him. He looked up, certain he should voice his concerns, when a second digit flicked out of his leader's paw.

All eyes were on him, and he hesitated. His first bout of weakness had come at the worst time. He scanned the faces around him and felt their surety, found power in their conviction. He moved his finger to the second button and closed his eyes, summoning the courage to do something great. Something terrible.

He pressed down. The button clicked, but no ear would ever hear it. Rushing ahead of that sound was a wave of heat and light, consuming all.

The Camptons, retreating back to their camp in worry, confused by the sight of *Parsona* rising, never saw it coming.

oooo

A dozen alarm lights went from green to red, bypassing amber entirely. Molly's first thought was another hijack. She turned to Cole, who seemed to understand that pounding the dash was not going to fix this. Then she noticed one of the blips was a munitions warning. There was nothing out the windshield ahead of them.

The chase cam, still selected on the vid screen, held the answer.

"Cole. Oh my gods!" She pointed at the screen. Cole tore himself away from the confusing indicators and leaned over to look.

"What in the galaxy—?"

A bloom of white expanding out from the forest. A circle of smoke ringed a cap of puffy cotton, pushing its way up into the cloudless atmosphere. It grew and grew to an incredible size. Part of Molly's brain knew what she was seeing, but it was unable to communicate with the rest of her.

"That's not an EMP," Cole said.

Molly could sense her chest sinking in. It felt hollow. Her vision swam, and she reached for her wrist with her left hand, trying to cover and protect the broken parts of herself.

"What have we done, Cole? What have we *done*?"

The explosion explained the warning lights, but nothing could explain the *explosion*. How had the Camptons turned an EMP device into a fusion bomb? One had nothing to do with the other. If you could do that, you may as well build your own from scratch.

"It was always a nuke," Molly said out loud. She could not piece together what had happened over the last day, but she knew this: *it was always a nuke*.

Below, the ring of smoke was replaced by a hoop of fire. Eerily concentric, it spread out at a furious rate. Beyond the billows of peaceful cotton, orange tendrils of fire and plasma danced and grew. Paradise was ablaze.

"Uhh, I think we have another problem," Cole said.

How could this get worse? Molly thought. She could feel herself sinking into a depression, but she couldn't tear her eyes from the carnage below.

"I don't think I'm in control of the ship," Cole said.

That got her attention. She reached across her body with her left hand and confirmed it for herself; the thrusters were no longer responding. And suddenly, she didn't care. She cinched her harness down and made sure her flight suit was plugged in. "Don't fight it, Cole." Her wet eyes went back to the vid screen, watching the orange-and-red circle expand faster than the planet could shrink in their wake.

"We're vectoring toward the Orbital Station. Six Gs and steady. You sure we shouldn't be fighting this?"

Molly looked at him, her cheek pressed back into her helmet, her helmet resting on the headrest. She didn't have a response—she just wanted to look at him—at something that made sense. She could feel her entire body relaxing its grip on the world, sinking back into her suit in the steady single gravity it fought to maintain.

oooo

An hour later, Cole was still wrestling to resume control of the ship. He'd given up on communicating with Molly, who seemed nearly catatonic. All he felt was pure vehemence. She might want to lie there and allow some beast to shred her, but he'd die first, just to delay it.

Parsona lined up to dock with the Orbital Station. Cole unbuckled his harness and fumed in his seat, building up his rage for whatever came next.

A metallic thud rang through the hull as their tiny craft mated with the vast station. Cole sprang out of his chair, closed the lower half of his helmet, and rushed toward the airlock, ready to die or kill.

But something was already inside the ship, squeezing itself out of the escape hatch in the floor beyond the airlock. Cole skidded on the metal decking and fell down in fright and confusion. Behind him, Walter hissed in alarm.

The large beast rose to its full height, its head nearly brushing the ceiling. It lumbered in Cole's direction.

"Minimal alarm, Cole." Edison had his hands up, his claws as blunt as possible. "Minimal alarm," he repeated.

Pushing with his feet, Cole scampered back and yelled for Molly. His world felt upside down. Edison should *not* be on the ship with them. And yet, there he stood. Right beside the airlock. He watched his friend thumb the inner hatch open.

"Follow," he told Cole before stepping through. The outer door made a sound as it rushed open—the air pressure inside *Parsona* remained constant. He stumbled back to the cockpit, working his helmet loose.

"Molly, you aren't going to believe this—"

She pointed to the vid screen, the cargo cam active. "I saw," she told him.

Cole reached over to see if control of the ship had returned. It hadn't. "Stay here," he said. "I'm going to find out what's going on. If you get control of the ship back—get the hell out of here and keep the chase cam off. I mean it."

She thumbed the latches on her helmet and popped it off. "I'm coming with you."

"No, you're *not*," he said firmly. He startled as Walter squeezed in beside him.

"I'm sssorry, Molly. I forgot about the esscape podss. Ssso ssorry, Molly. Ssso ssorry." Walter's head was against the small cockpit hallway, metal on metal. He looked absolutely dejected.

"It's fine," Molly said quietly. "It's a very minor thing. Don't worry about it." The words leaked out of her, but to Cole it sounded like someone else.

"I'm coming with you," she told him again.

"Me, too," added Walter.

Cole moved closer to her, reaching a hand to her shoulder. "Molly, you're exhausted and confused. I want you to stay here and get to safety. If you can—"

"I DON'T WANT SAFETY!" she screamed from the captain's chair. Both of her hands clenched up into fists, her broken wrist popping out of her sling. Her feet lifted from the cockpit floor, and her knees pulled into a fetal position. Molly's head bent forward, completing the impulse.

"I WANT ANSWERS!" she yelled into her lap. Her left hand slammed into the arm of the chair, legs springing out in anger and protest. She shot up, nearly ripping her suit cord out of its socket.

Cole had never seen her like this. He and Walter flattened against the wall as she stormed by. After the initial shock drained away, he chased after her, yelling, "Molly! Wait!"

oooo

She ducked through the airlock and into the Orbital Station. The dock led directly into a long hallway. Cole and Walter caught up with her as she started down it. None of them spoke; the sight at the end of the passage drowned out even their thoughts. Edison stood by a massive expanse of glass, an observation window. It faced his old world beyond, which glowed in the wrath of fire. Beside him stood another Glemot, tall and as black as the space that framed him.

Neither alien turned as Molly and her crew approached. They stood, transfixed by the sight of utter destruction below. The ring of burning trees was halfway to the horizon already, and night had fallen over a portion of the devastated land. Before long, the fire would be wider than a Glemot day.

There was no rain to stop it. No oceans or cleared fields for buffer. The lakes were skirted as easily as a child hopping a puddle. The most beautiful thing Molly had ever beheld slowly turned to fire and ash. And *she* was the cause of it.

Her rage melted at the sight of the horror. She could feel the urge to sleep overcoming her again. Her stomach, her entire body, felt hollow. She was overwhelmed by a lack of appetite—for food, air, even *life*.

"Why?" The pathetic question trailed out of her in a feeble voice. Directed at no one in particular, she wasn't sure if it ranged beyond her own ears.

Edison turned away from the view and met Molly's wet eyes with his own. "Inevitable," he said quietly.

She looked beyond the pup to the large black Glemot, who had turned to face them. Water streaked down the fur on his cheeks and his dark lips were pressed tight, his small ears folded flat to his head. He addressed them all in perfect and jargon-free English. "Go get some rest. I will answer your 'why' soon enough."

oooo

Cole had to physically drag Molly away from the depressing vista. Rooms were offered on the Station, but Cole ignored the black beast, his anger defused by the obvious sadness resonating between the Glemots. Nothing made sense, but they weren't going to kill them. Yet. Rest and then some answers sounded good. In that order.

Back in Molly's quarters, he helped his friend out of her flightsuit, but left her jumper on. He held the sheets back as she curled into the bed, a thing with no will. To Cole, the sight of her suffering was even sadder than the horror below, the blackness growing in her more blinding than the firestorm on Glemot. It was the destruction of something even more beautiful in his eyes. He wiped moisture off his cheeks and turned to his own quarters.

Walter passed by, heading out the cargo door with his computer in hand and a bounce in his step. His joyful energy twisted Cole's last nerve into a knot.

"Officser Walter out to sscout," he announced to nobody and everyone.

Cole moved to throttle the kid, unadulterated wrath coursing through every fiber in his body. He wanted to harm the boy, to hurt *something*. He moved behind Walter, but stopped himself just in time. He leaned against the bulkhead and watched the kid bound through the airlock.

Walter had *no clue* about the nightmare below. The amount of destruction unfolding, the number of creatures dying, he probably didn't understand the danger his own life had been in, or what Molly and Cole had gone through to get them all off the planet. To Walter, his time on Glemot had been just another dandy adventure, and now he was off to loot a Naval complex.

Cole's anger faded into irritation, and then envy. He could imagine how nice it would be to not understand. To see one's microcosm as the macrocosm. To focus a meter beyond one's own nose. *Who was Walter harming by remaining ignorant?* Cole wondered. *Who was Molly harming by regressing?* Curling up in a ball and having something else keep you warm—it was an ugly, yet seductive, coping strategy. Cole went to his room and stripped down to his bare skin before sliding between sheets that smelled of forest floor, of moss and bark.

He shut his eyes and dreamed of not knowing or caring. The hideous and alluring thoughts danced in front of him, beckoning and repelling at once.

PART 4
BETRAYALS

"The mind rejects the very things worth knowing."

~ The Bern Seer ~

23

Molly had no idea how long she'd slept. The urge was to stay there forever. To waste away between the sheets, carried off by invisible critters one dead cell at a time. But her brain hummed with questions, urging her up and out. Part of her needed to see the damage she had wrought, to see if the ring of destruction had fizzled out or finished its task.

She rolled over and extended her numb legs out of the covers. Her jumpsuit was on; she couldn't remember getting into bed. Lowering her bare feet to the cool steel decking, she wiggled her toes. Her mind still felt hazy—disconnected from the rest of her body.

Her sling lay folded on the dresser. She donned her flightsuit first and then secured her arm with the woven Glemot grasses. *Perhaps this was all that remained of their planet.* Molly fingered the reeds, brown and dry—she couldn't help but think how readily they would burn.

Soft sounds from far away trickled into her ship, warning her that a door was open—an outer world attached. She followed the sounds of distant pumps and circulating fans through the airlock. Down the long corridor and out the carboglass observation window she could see Glemot, like a beacon of cruelty. There was no one by the window—or so she thought. As she got closer, she recognized the black silhouette. Against the pitch-black of space, his ebony fur made him almost invisible. Molly could only distinguish the fringe of the massive beast, so dark it verged on purple, as it sheened in the light of distant stars.

"Good morning, Molly," he said without turning.

Molly met his reflected gaze high in the glass. "Is it morning?"

"Up here, it's morning when you get up. It's evening when you become tired." He turned to look at her. "Maybe, for me, it will be evening forever."

"Who are you? And do you know what happened down there?"

"My real name would sound funny to you," he interrupted, his voice a sonorous bass. "Call me by my Earth-language name."

"Which is?"

"Campton."

So many of Molly's recent memories were still bubbling to the surface, it took her a moment. "Like the tribe?" she asked.

"Just like the tribe. And yes, I know what happened down there. I caused it, not you."

Molly stared at him, her teeth clenched. She envisioned climbing up his back, her fists full of fur and fighting to the death, but his imposing bulk, his calm stillness, the sadness in his eyes—they confused and paralyzed her.

"I know you have many questions, I see the obvious ones on your face, but first I would like to give you some answers you don't even know to ask for. Will you listen?"

Molly turned away and squinted at the fiery orb. She touched the glass hesitantly, as if the planet could burn her, but the thick pane was cold from the vacuum of space. Outside, a fiery new star existed where a green planet had once been.

"I'll listen," she said, "but I can't promise you I'll understand, or my anger will lessen. I'm pretty kinetic right now, but you probably don't know what that—"

"I know what it means. You're upset. Angry. I understand that. If I don't sound like my brethren, it's because I've lived up here with Earth's archives for so many of your years. And I'm old. My wisdom has grown far beyond the juvenile stage that most Glemots. . . Well, imagine a human that learned so much about language, it could babble back and forth with a child. That should help you grasp—"

"So now I'm a *baby* to you? I said my anger wouldn't *lessen*, I never promised it would remain where it was." She turned around and sank to the decking, her back against the glass. Not wanting to look out the window, or at Campton, anymore, she stared down the hall into the small mouth of her ship.

"No, Molly. You are not a baby to me. I have come to respect you greatly. Edison is quite taken with you and your friends. I just. . . don't think my kind can empathize enough to talk for *another's* ears. They talk for their own." His voice trailed off. Molly wrapped her arms around her knees.

"I use the present tense, but if the fire has met itself on the far side, Edison and I may be the only two Glemots left in this universe."

Molly had been thinking it. Spoken, the horror became real. "Why?" she whispered.

"Other answers come first. You need to know something about our kind. I do not think you'll be able to carry this with you otherwise."

Campton paused, as if considering where to begin. "Glemots do not die from natural causes. Barring accidents, properly nourished, we live forever. It's a poor design, even though most other species yearn for it." He paused for a moment.

"I don't understand the point."

"Sorry. The problem is that we continue having children. Our population grows. Our solution is warfare and murder. Almost all Glemots die at the hands of another. If we did not, there would never be room for new Glemots. This is why our species thirsts for a balance."

Molly swung her arm to the side, slamming the glass beside her. The sharp slap echoed down the corridor. "What kind of balance is THAT?" she yelled, not willing to face it.

"The *ultimate* kind," Campton said. "You need to understand, the Glemots were a threat to the universe. I did not see this until a friend explained it to me: that once we realized the surface of our planet was not the limit of our niche, we would begin an expansion outward. We would fill every crevasse, every nook, and all else would perish. Eventually, we would run out of even that much space and begin to kill one another anew. We would be right here, right where we started, but there would be nothing besides us.

"When we discovered technology, most of us were eager to begin this expansion. Some cautioned against it. A Council decision was made that we hold off on development while we worked out the balance calculations, which were more complex than any we had attempted before. But a small group, led by a good friend of mine with the Earth name of Leefs, built a starship and went off to learn more. They had defied Council decree and were to be executed."

"They went to see the gods," Molly said.

"Ah, you know the legends. But probably not the facts that spawned them. Leefs returned a changed Glemot. He had learned about the universe beyond. Hunted by the Council, his band of rebels tried to get the message to the rest of us. Meanwhile, we were waging a new war on imbalance with our technology. We flushed the Navy out of our system with EMPs—"

"They were NUCLEAR BOMBS!" Molly slapped the floor in protest.

"That is what they were to *you*. When you built them on *your* planet they were designed for *this*." Campton swept a paw above her and toward the planet below. "A side-effect of your device is a pulse that wipes out electronics. It's a by-product. But they are the same thing, Molly. Camptons built them for the pulse, and *our* by-product is what you saw yesterday."

"Why build something like that? Are you all *insane*?"

"Are you?" he asked. "The EMPs are what drove the Navy away. Incapacitated their ships, scrambled their communications, and made this station a lifeless hulk for some time. The balls of fire they created in space were as meaningless to us as the pulse was to your Japan and your Israel. While my tribe grew in power in order to restore the balance decreed by the Council, Leefs was trying to explain the great threat our race posed. Of course, none of us would listen, even when they kidnapped me and tried to. . ."

Campton fell silent. Molly turned to him, but the large creature looked away.

"It wasn't until Leefs died by my own hands that I understood. That was when I felt the truth of his last words in my own claws. Like a fool, I went to the Council. I wasn't calculating anything. I should have just taken one of the orbital EMPs and activated it without a word to anyone. Instead, the council found me insane, which is un-useful. I was *designated for termination*, as they would say. But the doctor couldn't do it. Watt couldn't kill his own father—"

"You're Watt's *father*?" Molly asked.

"Yes, and Edison's grandfather." He gestured toward Molly's splint. "And I recognize his work. I am glad you met him."

"Are you glad I KILLED HIM?" she demanded.

"No. Not glad. Satisfied, maybe. Resigned. But so was he. I imagine he was there when they activated the device."

The thought made Molly feel sick. She remembered the familiar form overseeing the repairs and a knot crept up into her throat. Again, thinking on the *one* who died was about to make her cry, where the billions just left her numb.

"He would be happy you mourn him."

"SHUT UP! JUST—SHUT UP!" She smacked the floor again and bent over, her forehead nearly touching the metal plating. Tears dripped down from the pull of artificial gravity and broke up on impact.

Campton remained still, looking out into space. After a few minutes, he spoke softly, "I am sorry for using you like this. I really am. I am sorry the one had to be someone like you, someone who really cares. It would have been better if those UN ships—"

"Why was Watt helping you if he was a Campton?" She wasn't sure why she wanted to know, but she did. She couldn't fathom why Edison would help do *this*.

"Leefs was Edison's other grandfather. Watt's marriage was a forbidden one. Whitney did not just bring her father's blood into that union, she brought his ideas. Watt understood better than I what needed to be done. If he could have gotten his paws on the device, or persuaded Orville to join us—"

"I've heard enough," Molly said. She tried to get her legs beneath her, but Campton sank to the floor, a gentle paw resting on her shoulder.

"I do not think I have said what you really need to hear. It is very important."

She looked away, but settled back to the ground.

"Things *change*, Molly. And we must let them."

"Let them? Or *force* them?" she asked.

"It is hard to explain this to someone who lives such a short life, so let me try to give you some tools you can take with you, some thoughts you can explore as time closes your wounds. Please, just hear me out."

"Talk."

"Let me ask you a question." He turned to the side and nodded at the burning ball beyond the glass. "Why was Glemot beautiful?"

The past tense choked her up again, but she wanted him to know. This was getting to her own questions. "Because I *felt* it. We all did. There doesn't need to be a *why*, it just *was*. It made me feel better than I ever had in my whole life, if just for a moment!"

"Ah, so the beauty was in *you* and not out *there*?"

"You're getting ready to start sounding like my . . . like my navigator. And I hate those talks."

"I understand, but tell me, would Glemot be beautiful if no brain ever beheld it? If it was the only thing in space?"

"I would know it was beautiful."

"And there you are again. Creating a 'you' in order to create the beauty. Do you not see? The beauty is in *us*, our senses, our experience of Glemot. Glemot is just a ball of rock covered with mold."

Molly shot him a look.

"Which universe would contain more beauty: a space with Glemot and no one to ever know it, not even us making up the example, or a universe of billions of people, like you and me, who were shown a mere *photograph* of Glemot? Which one would contain more beauty?"

Molly weighed the two and didn't answer. She couldn't.

"The sad truth is this: the way to create more beauty in the world is to create more organs that can sense it. The wrong solution is to selfishly limit those organs so the few, already alive, can hog the beauty for themselves."

"How can you talk about creating when you just helped me commit *genocide*?"

"Because neither extreme is correct. My old tribe was right to worship balance, but wrong to think they could control it. Glemots would have destroyed the universe, or filled it to capacity before warring with one another on a scale beyond even my ability to calculate. Nothing would have remained, not even a picture.

"Leefs was right when he came to me and explained the threat we posed. Balance has been restored, and our planet will come back, as beautiful as ever. If I choose, I can sit here and watch it happen. For me it will not take much time at all."

"It will never be the same."

"You are correct. And it shouldn't be."

They both fell silent for a moment. Molly digested this.

Then Campton continued, "When I was a pup, our species lived huddled near the equator. Ice covered most of Glemot as our sun went into its usual period of hibernation. Only a thin band of green ringed the planet. When the ice retreated, our desire for balance and stasis sent us into a fury. At the same time, the expanding zones of lushness created a rush to reproduce and gather resources. It was a bounty, and we cursed it for being foreign.

"Glemot, of course, did not care. It had been doing this long before we were around. It will do it long after we are gone. Only our star will finish the cycle when it expands and consumes the four planets nearest it."

They both sat in silence again, thinking.

"I wish you could live a long life, Molly. That you could come back here thousands of years from now. You might pick me up in your spaceship and take me down to the planet. The ash will be good for the soil. And all of Glemot's water percolates up through the unbroken plate, feeding the entire surface from beneath. We could explore the new planet together, meeting creatures and eating fruits that do not yet exist anywhere in the universe. And *that* is the thrill of change. The diversity of beauty that occurs when we do not cling too hard to what we love. Maybe none of this will ever make sense to you. Perhaps your span of living is much too short. But I have come to know these things. My friend and I made a very tough decision based on this knowledge, one that hurts me more than you will ever know."

Wiping tears from her eyes, Molly looked at him. Campton's chest heaved as he pulled in a breath and let it out slowly.

"I will sit here and cry for longer than you will live," he said. "I will question myself and balance cold calculation with the surety of my heart, and I will never know why one is stronger while the other is right."

Molly stood up. Her brain was full, and she'd heard enough. She turned back to the ship, her bare feet sticking to cold steel. She could hear Campton's deep voice following her down the corridor. "I will never forget you, Molly Fyde," he whispered. "For the rest of my years, I will remember and think of you. . ."

But the rest never reached her. Like Campton's thoughts, they would live with him in orbit. Alone and forever.

24

Cole woke to the sound of the hyperdrive spinning up and almost rushed out of his room without getting dressed first. He emerged from his quarters hopping on one leg, tugging at his pants and cinching them off.

"Molly?" he hollered.

"Sshe iss in the Captain chair," Walter said, popping his head out of the engine room. It nearly scared Cole to death.

"What in the world is she doing?"

"We've been topping off the hyperdrive coil, *Navigator*." Walter spit the last word out with a sneer, obviously thinking he outranked Cole with plenty of room for several crew members between.

"*What?* How long have I been asleep?" Cole reached into his room for his only shirt and pulled it over his stiff back.

"Long time. I have sstored much while you do nothing."

Cole shot him a look and hurried to the cockpit, where he found Molly going through the pre-flight routine. He leaned over the control console so she would notice him before he spoke. He didn't want to startle her. "Feeling better?" he asked.

She looked at him. "A little. Not much. And good morning."

"Is it morning?"

"For you it is. Walter hasn't slept a wink. I've no clue what keeps him going. Well, the loot, I suppose." She finished booting the nav computer and swiveled in her seat to face him. "Sit down," she said.

"I'd rather go talk to our hosts, figure out what in hyperspace is going on around here."

"It might be better to hear it from me." She gestured toward the nav chair again.

Cole sat and studied her closely. "What? You talked to them?"

Molly nodded. She told him what she'd learned from Campton—who he was, why he had fought to extinguish his own race. Cole listened, his own anger turning to confusion, then disgust. He controlled the urge to interrupt until Edison's name came up.

"He's Edison's grandfather?"

"Yeah. And it gets weirder. Turns out he's descended from the Leefs as well. We can diagram it later if you like, but can we please work on getting out of here and talk about this between jumps? I can feel that place burning from here, like it's on my skin. I'd jump into space if that'd make the feeling go away." Cole saw her lips purse into the slimmest of smiles. "I'd even be willing to endure a few of your horrid jokes, see if that'd help."

Cole relaxed. "My jokes are nebular," he said.

Molly rolled her eyes at him. "Well . . . go tell them to Walter. The drive is warming up and showing eighty-five percent. Stand by the coupling, and I'll let you know when you can release it."

"Aye, aye, *Captain*." He gave her a salute.

She made a rude gesture.

○ ○ ○ ○

The fusion feed snaked across the hallway in the rear of the ship, leading through the airlock and into a mechanical hatch. Walter fussed with some crates, trying to shove them into one of the cargo pods.

"How'd you make out, there, pal?"

Walter flinched, and Cole felt some revenge for the scare earlier.

"Lotss of goodiess. The Navy can keep their reward!"

After another shove on the crate he turned back to Cole and said, "Forget you heard that. Very little ssleep for the Cargo Officser."

Cole slapped him on the back and ducked into the mechanical room. He couldn't believe most of this ship's parts had been scattered in the dirt a few days ago. It looked even cleaner than before. *Parsona* was probably *more* reliable having passed though Glemot hands.

The Glemots.

He forgot about the fusion feed and rushed down the corridor to the observation glass. The planet was half-lit up by the planet's sun, the terminator between night and day splitting the planet in two. But you couldn't tell. Both sides were lit up. They were just slightly different shades of orange and red. However long he'd been asleep, it wasn't longer than it took a planet to burn.

There was no sign of the two Glemots. Cole considered going off in search of them, Edison at least, but the branching hallways going off in all directions left him not knowing where to start. Peering up through the glass, he could see entire wings of the Orbital Station jutting out into space. There was a lot of potential for scavenging here, but the empty expansiveness of it all just left him feeling overwhelmed and lonely. He trusted that Walter had stocked up on enough valuables, stuff they could trade later for actual necessities.

Feeling far removed from the *Parsona*—and Molly—Cole left the planet behind and jogged back toward the ship. He could hear her yelling "One hundred percent!" just as he ducked through the inner airlock door.

"Gotcha!" he hollered back, trying not to sound out-of-breath.

He unplugged the fusion cord and stowed it back in its locker. The only thing tethering them to the station now was the airlock. He stepped through it to return the Station's section of the fusion feed and opened the filling hatch, releasing the putrid odor of dried fusion fuel—the smell of something rotting or dying. He averted his head from the familiar scent, an odor that permeated ship hangars and OS fueling stations, and coiled the cord into the hatch.

Securing the locker, Cole looked around a final time to make sure everything was in its place. The usual procedure of cleaning up for the next ship jarred him into a realization: there was nothing keeping people away from this Station or the planet anymore. The Navy would be very interested in hearing about what had happened on Glemot and sending a recovery team to secure their property. He considered this as Edison and his grandfather strolled into view. Cole corrected himself, recalling the way their ship had been commandeered. It would *never* be safe here.

The two Glemots conferred, their low grumbling rolling down the hallway, indecipherable. Cole fought the urge to go and talk to Edison, to wish him farewell. There weren't any ships on the station, but he could imagine the two beasts eventually whipping one up and going down to survey the damage below. When the larger alien wrapped Edison in an embrace, Cole realized the pup had different plans. Edison turned away from his grandfather and started lumbering down the corridor toward the *Parsona*. He had a bundle over his shoulder.

Cole's heart ached with conflicting emotions.

Deep down, he felt connected to Edison on a primal level. Their all-night adventure to rescue Walter and engineer *Parsona's* escape, no matter what horrors it had led to, had sealed their fates to each other. They had also risked their lives under the forest floor, saving each other from certain death. There was something in their male makeup that would never let them forget this. If Edison came and asked to join their crew, Cole would not hesitate. But then—he had Molly to consider. He couldn't imagine her wanting a constant reminder of this tragedy around. He wondered if she could ever again see his coat without remembering the matted blood and the stench of death on it. And no matter what he felt for Edison, Molly came first. Her feelings came first. Especially now.

He steeled himself to turn Edison away—when Molly brushed past. She walked down the corridor to greet him, throwing her good arm around the large youth and leaning into his fur.

Edison dropped his bundle and returned the embrace. Molly's face was buried in his robe, but Cole could still hear her muffled sobs. He respected the moment and ducked back through the airlock hatch.

Behind him, down the corridor that pointed out to Glemot, another orphan officially joined their unlikely crew.

oooo

They never saw the fires on Glemot again. Molly pulled the airlock door closed while Walter secured the last of his loot. For two hours they did a full preflight check, going over all of the ship's systems; it was the first chance they'd had to observe proper ship procedures since acquiring *Parsona*. There was no doubt they were running away from something once more, but they could do it at their own pace this time.

While Cole went over the engine room and checked the thrusters in the lazarette, Edison made some changes to the crew seating. In less time than it took to prep the ship, he was able to modify the two jump seats on the starboard side to better accommodate his bulk. Unfortunately, they didn't have a flightsuit that would fit him, but he assured Molly and Cole he'd be fine, just as long as they didn't lose cabin pressure.

Walter stuck his head in the laz. "Edisson keepss moving toolss!" he complained.

Cole replaced the dipstick back in the thruster and wiped sweat off his brow. "You two need to get along, okay buddy?"

"I like Glemotss better when they're on Glemot," he told Cole.

"Well, he helped me save your butt," Cole reminded him. "You guys need to get along. Hey, why don't you show him your video game?"

Walter huffed out with a hiss, and Cole finished his check of the thrusters. He secured the rear door before heading up the hall to the cockpit. *Parsona is full*, he realized. Unless they wanted to start bunking together, they needed to stop collecting runaways. At the rate they were going, they'd look like a bus of refugees by the time they got back to Earth.

He nodded to Walter as he crossed the cargo bay and gave Edison a playful slap on the shoulder. They were bent over Walter's little computer, grumbling and hissing, while it emitted sounds like exploding fireworks.

Cole joined Molly in the cockpit and marveled at how natural all this felt, like a home. He even considered the "girlie" chair his, so long as Molly didn't rub it in.

"Everything good back there?" Molly asked.

"Pristine. The thrusters are purring better than before. You ready?"

"Absolutely. Popping the outer seal now."

Cole grabbed the flightstick with his left hand and nudged *Parsona* away from the station. He peeled away for a long run on thrusters. No matter where they went next, they didn't want anyone tracing them back to the Glemot system from their hyperspace signature. Besides, the entire crew had agreed: a few days of burning thruster fuel would be good for them. It would allow Molly's arm to heal, along with her other, *internal*, injuries.

oooo

After a few minutes of steady thrust, Molly turned down the music in the cockpit. Hearing her parents' old collection of tunes was just making her sad, anyway.

"I vote Navy," she said. "Avoiding them hasn't seemed any safer than trusting them."

"I agree," Cole said. "Both have been *equally* dumb so far, which is why we need a third or a fourth option."

"It is an either/or scenario, genius." Molly immediately felt bad for her tone of voice. It was an old habit that was starting to feel silly: calling Cole names instead of telling him how she felt. She'd been doing this for two years in the simulator, and Cole had always returned the jousting. Molly wasn't sure what was different, if it had been the Academy, if she was growing up, or if she had just grown weary of the ruse.

The worst part was, she didn't know how to stop this routine once she'd started it. A thousand times, even before this adventure, she'd wanted to tell Cole she was attracted to him. But she'd built a wall around her, erected with a million tiny insults, and she didn't know how to start taking them back. She just couldn't get the first word of that sentence out of her mouth.

Molly wondered if boys felt as stupid as girls sometimes do.

"Not necessarily, *sweetheart*," Cole responded. And two of Molly's questions were answered.

"There are different ways of running *to* the Navy," he continued, "and different ways of *avoiding* them."

"Do tell, *snookums*." Gods, she couldn't stop herself!

"Before I do, you want the chase camera up to watch our six?"

She didn't need to be reminded what was back there. "I'd prefer not," she said, "if you don't mind skimping on protocol."

"No problem. So, as I was saying, we have new options now."

"Well, yeah. For one thing, we have a full hyperdrive. Two jumps and we're home."

Cole nodded. "We also have a Glemot. And loot."

"A Glemot. Sure. But what does Edison have to do with anything?"

"Well, I'm starting to think we keep flying into deep trouble with an unarmed aircraft, and it's none too wise, so what we could—"

"You want to militarize *Parsona*? After what we just went through?"

"*Especially* after what we just went through. I'm not saying I ever want to see a nuke again, just that we need some chaff pods, at least one laser, and maybe a missile rack or two. I'm starting to feel naked without them."

"That's because you're a delusional paranoid who thinks everyone is after us."

"Haven't they been?"

"Maybe," she admitted. "So what's your plan?"

"Darrin, one of the systems we considered before we settled on Glemot. We couldn't reach it before, but we can now."

"Remind me why we were considering Darrin?"

"It's on the way to Canopus—and Earth. It was settled by humans, which is a plus. And it's another spot the Navy doesn't like to go. But for *known* reasons, this time." Cole leaned forward and consulted the report on his nav screen. "Darrin is dominated by its arms trade. It's a pretty hot place, as in illegal. It would've been good cover before, but now it's even better. I saw some of what Walter managed to scrounge together, and there's some quality parts and computer supplies in the holds. I have no doubt we could get a lot for them. I say we jump to one of the two Darrin planets, trade some of our goods for arms, and have Edison hook it all up. At least then, whatever we decide to do next, we'd have a few options. Hell, if *Parsona* or the UN ships had military-grade jammers, the last week wouldn't have *happened*."

"Nonsense. We have no idea what kind of jammers it would've taken to stop what they did. I agree with your premise, don't get me wrong, but not your conclusion."

He opened his mouth to argue another point, but Molly cut him off. "Do they allow strangers to come in—especially Academy cadets—and just take their weapons?"

"According to the Navy, their only motivation is money."

"How old are those reports?"

"Twenty years. But c'mon, how much could change in twenty years? We'll bounce back and forth and have the two planets begging us to *take* their goods!"

o o o o

Jumping into a star system for the first time posed some tough navigational decisions. Safe entry points were rare, the few good Lagrange areas were normally cluttered with satellites and commercial traffic. With the Darrin system, the conundrum was reversed: it had two habitable planets and so many good Lagrange points, it was hard to settle on just one. The luxury of choice caused a paralysis just as real as the fear of jumping into a system full of debris. Partly because if something went wrong after a careful selection, it was the *navigator's* fault, not fate's.

Without an Orbital Station's Bell radio, there was no perfectly safe method for jumping anywhere. But—as navigators loved pointing out to shaky pilots—the ridiculously long odds of two ships jumping in-system at the same time and place were mathematically implausible.

Pilots loved pointing out, in response, that it happens now and then anyway—math be damned.

Ships went missing all the time, and superstitious pilots loved jumping the gun and blaming a hyperspace collision. It didn't matter that in most cases these ships showed up later with a valid excuse (or were busted for doing something illegal). Every pilot remembered that initial scare plastered on the front page of their reader's daily, and then they ignored any good news buried on the fifth tab two days later.

Molly was forever accusing Cole of this sort of reasoning; the calculating navigator in her had not yet given way to the paranoid pilot. She still marveled at his ability to remember the hits and forget the misses, leading to all sorts of paranoid conclusions. Take the Navy, for instance. Molly felt sure they could jump their way to a major Navy station, perhaps at Canopus, and everything could be explained. The death of the men on Palan—their whereabouts since—everything.

But Cole had some good arguments for being cautious, and Molly was willing to be tactical. They'd had some close scrapes, she told herself. And then, there was the other reason to go to Darrin. One Molly was just becoming aware of. It was an irrational excuse, but she knew the moment they returned to Earth with *Parsona*, Cole would be off to the front lines and she'd be back in class at Avalon. The investigation into her father's death would mothball her ship for months, if not years. It would be two more semesters to graduation before she could go off to make it as a ship's captain, even if she could win some jobs as a young female pilot.

Their adventure had gotten off to a rough start, to say the least, but who'd want to go from flying around the galaxy to pretending to be a kid again? It was hard enough to go from being trained by the Navy to save the universe to hearing Gretchen Harris rave about how nebular her new sneakers were.

The more that happened to her, the quicker she grew up—making the idea of going back seem impossible.

Then again, if she was right and Cole was wrong, what would the Navy say when they showed up with *Parsona* armed to the teeth? Calling this the *prudent* option was stretching it. Cole, of course, insisted the additions would be defensive in nature, but Molly knew how the Navy would see it.

Cole continued to debate entry points and jump offsets while Molly thought about the overall direction they were heading and how far they were from reaching their goal. What *was* their goal? To get home? Was home still Earth? Or was it becoming this ship?

"Cole." She interrupted his argument for Darrin I, which was just as well since she wasn't listening to a word of it, "How long ago did we leave Earth?"

Cole looked up to the ceiling as if the answer was on one of the readouts there. "Let's see, how many twenty-four-hour cycles did we spend between Palan and Glemot?"

"Four," Molly offered.

"Okay. Fourteen days, total. Counting today. Oh, *man*. Really? Has it only been *two weeks*?"

"I was just thinking the same thing. And about our final destination. Beyond arming the ship and challenging the Navy to a fight, what's our ultimate plan, here?"

"What? I don't want to fight the Navy, I'm *in* the Navy. I just don't trust whoever is screwing with us. And that's *my* final destination. Standing in front of the person who toasted our simulator and watching his nose bleed."

"So this is all about the Tchung simulation for you?"

"Yeah. What else is there? We've had some crazy stuff go down in the last two weeks, but it isn't *that* strange when you consider we landed in a pirate zone the day of the rains with our Navy contact shut out, and then we jumped into a civil war on a planet nobody has ever returned from. In all likelihood, you and I have used up our Crazy Quota for the rest of our lives. Hey, we can't go into every situation expecting to plan a prison break or to pick up another runaway."

"Says the guy who thinks the Navy is after us."

"Would you rather jump to Canopus, Menkar, and then Earth? You really think we'd get past Canopus?"

"I think I'm with you on feeling naked without any way to defend ourselves. And Edison's toga is no good if we have to press some Gs." Molly sighed. "Okay. Let's hit Darrin, get some jump suits, add a few discrete defensive options, and then see about Canopus."

"Excellent. Glad we agreed on this. *Again.*" Cole gave her a lopsided grin. "Now, are we settled on Darrin I over Darrin II?"

"Fine. But if they brag about how their 'new houses are older than Darrin II's *old* houses,' I'm leaving."

Cole laughed at his own Euro/American joke and started keying in the jump coordinates.

Molly couldn't help herself, she began double-checking him, fighting the rise of nausea in her stomach ahead of the jump. Her intestinal tract could anticipate them just from her thinking about it. The simulators were great at inducing the nausea that was supposedly common to hyperflight, but after a few jumps in *Parsona*, Molly was starting to think the Navy had the volume too high. Her stomach hurt far more in training than it had during the flight to Palan or Glemot. In fact, she couldn't remember getting sick when her father brought her to Earth from Lok. It seemed like one more thing the Navy thought best to overdo.

Still, as Cole punched in the arrival coordinates to the spooled-up hyperdrive, Molly could feel something gnawing at her. Maybe this time her stomach knew something she didn't? Cole counted down out loud and placed his finger over the jump switch. Molly gazed through the porthole on her side in anticipation, expecting the familiar sight the Navy had gotten right: stars shifting a little in space.

Instead of this, however, Molly was treated to the jarring horror of all those pinpricks of light simply disappearing.

A Darkness took their place. Poised to strike.

25

"What the hell?" Cole asked.

Molly assumed he was referring to the new void they'd entered, but she turned and found him fixated on the SADAR. She looked at her own screen—the normally black-and-green display was slathered in red warning lights. She'd never seen anything like it. She leaned forward and peered through the canopy—into the impossible blackness beyond. Where in the galaxy had they ended up? How could it be devoid of stars?

The emptiness had bits of detail: a fuzzy line of lighter gray, a jagged string of deepest black. It looked like a wall of charcoal shifting before her.

And then it hit the carboglass, right in front of her nose, with a jarring *thunk*.

Molly nearly flew out of her skin, yelping like a girl in a horror holo. She instinctively threw her right hand up to shield herself from the thing coming at them, her elbow catching in the grass sling. Cole shifted the flight-stick back, moving the ship away from whatever it was.

They crunched into something behind them. A sickening thud, and the screech of twisting metal tore through the hull, setting Molly's nerves on fire. The familiar shiver of a bad docking maneuver overcame her, but this time it wasn't a simulator. She glanced at the SADAR; red flashes filled the entire screen. *Parsona* crept forward again, toward the mysterious darkness that had left a mar on the carboglass.

Molly peered through her side porthole and caught a glimpse of a star—it was quickly obscured by something black, and then it flashed out again. When it disappeared once more, she realized where they were. Her chest filled with the dull terror that overtakes people when they realize, only too late, what sort of danger they've just avoided. It was the same feeling she'd had a week ago when the hyperdrive nearly zapped her arm off. Only this could have been worse. Much worse.

"Don't move the ship, Cole." She reached across with her left hand and rested it on his. "We're in an asteroid field."

"Bad noisse in the back!"

Molly turned to see Walter behind their seats, one hand on her headrest, the other pointing toward the rear of the ship. Edison was twisting around in his crew seat and looking forward, a quizzical furrow in his brow.

"Oh my gods—" Cole squinted through his own porthole, watching black shapes twist by, the occasional star poking through. "It's *dense!*" he said.

Molly tasted adrenaline in her mouth. That they were alive wasn't accessible to the part of her brain that knew they'd very nearly disappeared forever. She tried to plan the next move, but she was still admonishing herself for what a stupid thing they'd already done. She watched Cole zoom the SADAR all the way out, but it just turned the display solid red, unable to distinguish individual contacts. He shook his head. "We should totally not be here."

"You're right, we should be in the L3 off Darrin I."

"No, I mean we shouldn't be *here* here. In the cockpit. Talking about this. *Existing*. I'm looking at, say ten meters to the rock behind us and about twelve to the one that bumped the nose. There's a biggie to my right and a cluster of junk on your side. WHOA!"

Molly flinched. "What?"

"Man, something just moved across the edge of my range *fast*. Not all of these are just milling about. We need to get out of here, and quick-like."

Walter hovered between and behind them, hissing at the bad news.

"Go strap in, buddy," Cole advised.

He put his hand on Molly's shoulder. She could feel the cold through her flightsuit.

"It's okay, Walter, I need you to go buckle up. I don't want anything happening to you."

He nodded vigorously and backed away, his eyes fixed on the shapes beyond the glass.

"How's your wrist feeling?" Cole asked.

"Better. Why? Do you want me to take this?"

"Either that, or we need to switch sides. I'm not comfortable over here at all."

"I'll take it, then. It's been feeling better; I'm just getting in the habit of letting you drive. Do me a favor and call out distances if I get too close."

"You're too close right now."

"Hilarious. Now . . . watch me get closer." She pulled the sling over her helmet, the brown Glemot grasses stabbing her with memories. She dropped it in her lap and rubbed her wrist before gripping the flight controls. They felt strange and familiar at the same time; Molly nudged *Parsona* forward with the smallest of thrusts.

"Uh, you want to fill me in with your plan?" Cole pressed his helmet back into the chair, turning it away from the looming mass as it drew near.

"Making some room. How close are we?"

The nose of the ship banged softly into the meteor, answering her question. She gave a twitch of extra thrust to keep the hulk from bouncing away, a ship-to-ship docking trick that prevented multiple impacts.

"We're pinned," she said. "Increasing thrust. Let's hope there isn't anything bigger on the other side."

Ramping up the throttle, Molly pressed *Parsona* forward. She was a porpoise pushing a black ball through water. Out of balance, the part of the meteor jutting toward the windshield got closer. Molly gave one more burst of thrust before pulling back. Plumes of forward thruster kicked up dust from the rock ahead, but there was no impact as the massive wall rotated and receded, clearing out the space beyond.

As Cole had said, it was dense. Dangerous boulders and wannabe moonlets drifted lazily on every side, like primordial monsters grazing on vacuum. Molly held her breath, as if a noise could spook them and create a deadly stampede. A small, skittish lump of rock smashed into one of the larger ones, sending it twisting amid a cloud of quiet debris.

Molly flipped on every exterior floodlight and set the external cameras to cycle at one-second intervals. She needed three more brains to process it all. Cole, at least, gave her another. "Incoming, starboard side," he said.

Molly twisted the ship down and away, like a bullfighter sucking his cape into his side. It wasn't a big one, she noted as it slid past, but it would've made a dent. "Any idea which way is out?"

"Not from the SADAR." Cole whipped his head around, looking at each portal. "There!" he said. "I just saw a cluster of stars at ten o'clock."

Molly turned to port a few degrees. She saw the flash of lights beyond the weaving shapes of black. She moved forward with as much trust as skill, feeling as if any second could be the beginning of something bad.

"Should we have the boys on lookout?" she asked.

"Good idea. Walter, Edison," he shouted over his shoulder, "get to some windows in the airlock or the staterooms, holler if anything gets too close!"

"Definition of 'too close'?" Edison asked.

"Uh, fifty meters, pal." To Molly: "Two o'clock."

"I see it." She flicked the flightstick around with ease. Her wrist was stiff, but it didn't hurt as bad as it had just two days ago; she needed to remember to ask Edison what had been in that balm. She was starting to suspect it wasn't just topical.

She dodged another small rock; it felt good to be flying again. Every now and then the moving shapes dictated a new "up," and Molly rotated *Parsona*, providing width for the wings and readjusting her sense of top and bottom. After a few close calls she started to feel the thrill of being in the simulator, running down canyons in atmospheric flight, banking around sudden turns with a blue ribbon of water below. And Lucin thought those games were a waste of time.

"Is it thinning?" she asked.

"I can't tell yet. I think we're in a bit of a pocket here. Yeah, I can see the edge on SADAR now. Keep going this direction."

More stars were visible, but the motion of the asteroids became more violent as they neared the periphery. A small chunk the size of one of their escape pods crashed into a monster in front of them, calving the latter in two and turning the former into dust.

"*Damn.*"

"As soon as I see nothing but stars, I'm making a run for it," Molly said. "Some of these puppies are blazing out on the edge."

Edison roared from the airlock. Molly saw it and dodged out of the way, pulling between two large, slow-moving moonlets. They were coming together, about to pincer *Parsona,* when suddenly the path ahead looked mostly clear.

"I'm going for it," she said, thrusting forward and out into clear space, free of immediate danger.

They both breathed a sigh of relief while Cole dialed out the SADAR, adding some range to the display. They could now make out the edge of the massive asteroid belt.

The location indicator—a device that took the arrangement of the stars outside and compared them with known charts—beeped. It had reacquired their position.

"Where are we?" she asked. She was dying to know, desperate to determine what had happened with the hyperdrive. She hoped it wasn't something the Glemots had reinstalled improperly.

"This doesn't make any sense," Cole said.

Molly looked away from her flight path long enough to check for herself. They were right where they had intended to be. Just outside of Darrin I's third Lagrange point. The problem: Darrin I was no longer where *it* was supposed to be.

"Flanking Drenards," Cole said. "I think I know what we were just flying through."

"Educate me."

"That, back *there*—*that* was Darrin I."

Molly glanced at the SADAR overlapped with her star charts and she saw what he was getting at. "Wait," she said. "What are those?" She pointed to the large contacts ahead of them, well beyond the wall of dangerous rock they were leaving behind.

"I don't know, but are those *ships* coming out of them?"

"My gods. I think they're heading this way."

oooo

There must have been a hundred of them. Possibly more. They streaked directly for *Parsona* from every direction, having pulled out of what Molly assumed were small space docks of some sort. It was hard to tell at this distance.

"BUCKLE UP!" she yelled over her shoulder. She could hear Edison banging his way back toward them and hoped Walter was doing the same. She turned perpendicular to the oncoming ships and gave her crew time to strap themselves in.

"I have over two hundred contacts. You think we should get back in the rock? Because there's *way* too much mass here to jump away."

"I'm never jumping blind again. Are the boys strapped in?"

Cole pulled up the cargo cam and used the control stick to twist the view toward the crew station. "Yeah, buckling up now."

Molly hit the thrusters with a sharp burn, zooming along the wall of rock and looking for any strays. They were really being squeezed here. Luckily none of the attackers had launched any missiles yet. She wouldn't consider diving back into the asteroids until they did.

That's a weird formation, she thought. The SADAR showed bizarre flight patterns: the ships were blazing toward them, but they continuously crossed each other's flight planes, jostling against one another rather than fanning out to prevent various escape vectors.

"Geez, girl, do you have a bounty on your head? Because those guys are coming at us like the first one wins a prize."

"I was just thinking the same thing. It's like junior cadets playing Galaxy Ball, each kid running after the orb and nobody running to space for a pass."

"Yeah. And now we know how the orb feels."

Molly pulled a few Gs and flew closer to the field of debris. She placed a large straggler the size of a small moon between her and the herd of eager pursuers. The *Parsona* was fast for a civilian craft, but every single one of the ships coming after them was reeling her in as if she were sitting still.

"I'm starting to agree with you on feeling a bit naked without some defenses."

"Some consolation. Hey, no two of those ships are the same. SADAR doesn't even register the designs."

They were already halfway upon them. "And?"

"I don't know," Cole said. "It just reinforces that these guys aren't together. That and their tactics."

"You want me to pull over and roll out the welcome mat?"

"Yeah, when hyperspace freezes over. I'm just sayin' that they don't seem happy with us, but we're not under a coordinated attack."

"Oh, great. So all I have to do is defeat each ship, one at a time, without weapons? Remind you of something?" She had the long trail of ships in a tight clump now, slanting down from their distant docking stations and toward the meteor field. Now that their angle of attack had been herded into a single vector, she pulled the stick up hard, hoping it wouldn't be too many Gs for Edison.

"Good idea," Cole said. The flat trajectory along the rocks had everyone lined up. Instead of running from two hundred ships, Molly could now act as if she were running from one. If they could get clear of the mass from the asteroid belt, maybe they could jump back to the coordinates they'd just left, the one known landing zone they could be comfortable with.

"Some of them are wising up," she said. Dozens of the pursuers were branching out in various directions, while the bulk of the pack just altered course straight toward them. They still weren't acting coordinated, it's just that a few were willing to take a gamble. Molly looked at how far they'd need to get to make a safe jump, and it didn't look good.

She altered course again as swiftly as she dared. The vid screen still showed the two boys, and Edison seemed fine. With the new vector, *Parsona* was heading slightly toward the mysterious, dark stations. The herd shifted, adjusting course and jostling around one another for position. Again, their selfish tactics were hurting each individual, slowing them down and giving her an advantage. As soon as the pack had itself arranged, she went back to her last vector and watched them jockey once more.

Three of the gamblers had gotten lucky and were clear favorites. They would reach *Parsona* well ahead of the others, who were too busy fighting among themselves. Molly could almost sense the frustration of the herd as their vectors fluctuated. The uncoordinated insanity made her more nervous than a textbook attack would have.

"Not enough space," Cole said. He'd completed the mass equations on the computer that Molly had performed in her head.

"I know. I'm just culling a few from the herd. I want to see what they're up to on a small scale. Didn't want all the pack getting to us at once."

"You thinking piracy?"

"Yeah. Scavengers or pirates. They want us alive, and they want us bad. Hell, I haven't felt this desirable since my first day at the Academy."

"Ha. Until the boys realized you were better than them."

"Yeah, I guess the romance didn't last too long. Hold on."

Two more maneuvers widened the lead for the three closest ships. *Parsona* felt a little sluggish to Molly. Maybe they'd done some real damage backing down on that asteroid.

When the trio behind them got within a hundred kilometers, Molly knew for sure they weren't out for a quick kill. She was being evasive, with random spirals and some standard low-G stuff, but they still could have tested her with laser fire. One thing she could see was that these guys were *good*, one of them especially. He was flying as the leader, with the other two only keeping up by mimicking his every move. And some of those moves reminded Molly of the Tchung AI, but with more creativity.

Cole whistled at one point, obviously admiring the same thing.

"How are you guys doing back there?" Molly called over her shoulder. She really needed to get a suit and helmet for Edison; it seemed they couldn't go anywhere in this galaxy without needing to pull serious Gs.

"Edisson won't give me my game back!" Walter hollered.

Molly smiled and shot the vid screen a look. She was going too easy on them. She moved the G-warning up to twenty, giving her more room to play. Now she *really* started toying with the guys behind her. She'd set up some obvious habits earlier, like a boxer who would always lower one glove before a hook. She quickly switched to the same tell for jabs. It was a feinting process that worked well on experts, the pilots who memorized patterns during dogfights. It almost made two of the ships careen into each other. The third seemed to anticipate it—or he was just getting lucky again and again.

"I think they just want to play tag," Cole said.

He had a point. Mr. Lucky was within a few hundred meters now, and there was no other reason to get so close at these velocities. She could hit the brakes or turn the wrong way, and they'd both be in a galaxy of trouble. In fact, the closer the ship got, the less she could try to do in order to shake him. Any bold move would spell suicide, and the two stragglers were making up ground. *Parsona* was pinned.

The lead ship rolled around her and presented its belly; Molly recognized the maneuver, even if she didn't understand it. She eased back on the throttle and held a steady course. "Turn on the outer airlock lights and prepare for boarders. Whoever this 'troid is just won the rare honor of meeting a Glemot."

Cole laughed nervously and flipped the docking switches. He unplugged his suit and gave her shoulder a squeeze before heading aft.

Her suitor made his move, darting in with such suddenness and skill that the maneuver was over before she realized it'd started. The airlock collar clicked, confirming the union. The rest of the blips on SADAR reacted at once, breaking off the chase and vectoring back to their lairs. In a way, the response was even eerier than the manner with which the hunt had begun.

Molly didn't waste time pondering the strange behavior; she launched herself away from the helm and headed after her crew, ready to kill with her bare hands if needed.

Edison had already set up for an ambush; he stood aft of the airlock passage, just inside Walter's room. Molly took up a position with Cole and Walter at the end of the cargo bay to serve as a distraction. Cole handed her a wrench, his eyebrows arched with worry.

The airlock door hissed open. Their *own* door. Not blasted down, but sliding aside as if welcoming company. Molly tried to stay focused, expecting a flood of boarders with weapons drawn.

In strolled a man wearing a business suit and swinging a briefcase.

○ ○ ○ ○

"Wai—" She nearly got it out before Edison lunged. The Glemot pup swung a set of claws at the man's head. But instead of decapitating the man, Edison's fist snapped back and he howled in pain. Molly reached out to grab Cole and Walter, but they were both too stunned to make a move anyway.

The businessman seemed untouched. He turned his back on Edison and approached Cole, a pale, meaty hand outstretched. Fine wisps of hair were combed from one ear to the other over a bald pate, and his fat cheeks were held apart by a small, smiling mouth. His suit sang as it rubbed on itself, shiny in the way expensive things were when they begged to be admired.

"Excellent choice, my good sir," he told Cole. "You'll not be disappointed. Albert Gaines at your service. I look forward to doing business with you." His jabbering filled the cargo bay full with naught else but shocked silence.

Molly watched Cole accept the hand and allow it to be pumped. Edison, still holding his arm, looked to her for orders to try again. She raised her hand slightly, palm down. Edison nodded and examined his hand, brushing aside fur as if some mystery lay beneath.

Albert dropped Cole's hand and looked appreciably around the cargo bay, sizing it up like someone looking for an apartment to rent. "Excellent. Wonderful bones. Obviously in need of some improvements, am I right?" He met each of their eyes with a glow that suggested they were all his favorite. "I'm right," he confirmed. He held out his briefcase level with the ground, his bushy eyebrows raised as if to say, "There should be a table here for this, but there isn't—what gives?"

Molly broke the spell that had fallen over her crew. "Just what in *hyperspace* do you think you're doing here?" She stepped forward and pulled Cole back at the same time, a maneuver he seemed more than happy to go along with. "I'm the Captain of this ship, and I want to know who you are and what you were *thinking* out there. You nearly got us all killed!"

Albert dropped the briefcase to his side and let out an exasperated sigh. He reached into his coat, creating a clichéd sense of panic in the entire crew. Out came his pudgy hand, holding a business card. The expensive-looking suit made more noise as he extended it to Molly. "Albert Gaines, Ships Armaments and Defense Procurement. And I assure you that I was *not* trying to get you killed out there. The opposite is true, my dear lady. I was merely protecting you from those . . . *vultures*." He spat out the last with clear contempt.

Raising the briefcase up with both hands flat underneath, like a babe being offered to the gods, Albert asked, "Now, where should we put this so we can go over the contracts?"

Molly and Cole locked eyes, each probably hoping the other was going to take over. The stalemate left Molly in charge. "Contracts?" she asked.

Albert pulled in a breath and looked her up and down. There was nothing sexual about the leer, but it gave her the creeps nonetheless. She felt as if he were sizing her up for a coffin, or figuring out the best way to shear her. He smiled, brushed past Walter, and plopped into one of the crew chairs with the briefcase placed across the perfect creases along his thighs. Two gold-colored locks flicked open with a loud click. The lid swung up, and out came several pieces of paper. He tapped their edges on top of the briefcase to line them up.

"This is obviously your first time in the Darrin system for business. Not many regulars jump into the middle of old Darrin the First, you see. Crazy business, that. Trying to sneak up behind us or get yourselves killed. But hey, I like your style, and the customer is always right!

"As you can see, if you look outside, my ship is taking us back to Albert's Arms. There we will be able to set you right up with whatever you need. Provided you can pay for it, of course. But before we go over that, I need you to sign these sales representation agreements. I've already worked hard to win you over as a client, and I sure don't want you to make the mistake of working with my competition. Not a one of them would look after you the way that I will. I give you my guarantee."

The smile returned. Molly looked from it to the view out the cockpit windows and saw that they were turning slowly back to that string of distant lairs.

Albert cleared his throat. "Now then, the contracts. . ." He held them out to Molly.

26

Even a decade of military jargon and naval technical manuals did not prepare Molly for the convoluted abuse of the English language she held in her hands. She gave Edison's immeasurable IQ a chance, but it was even worse for him. His need for absolutes in communication recoiled from the lawyerly phrasings. Each sentence could mean three or four things when read individually; taken together, they had all the potential of a chess game prior to the first move. His advice was to burn them, not sign them.

She considered giving Walter a chance, as he hailed from a planet of devious barterers, but the boy was too distracted by their new guest. He kept sizing

Albert up like a direct competitor, but he also wore something of a leer, an expression Molly often saw him direct toward her. Other than his video game and loot, she'd never known anything to fascinate him so.

Albert must've noticed the way Molly was staring off into space. "You seem confused by the contracts," he said, "but I assure you they're standard fare. We use them all the time. It just means you and I will do all of our business together. If you need something I don't have, I'll ask around—no need for you to go elsewhere. It's all about making this process easy on the customer."

Molly laid the contracts in her lap and leaned back against the bulkhead. "Easy on the customer? Are we even *customers*? I'll tell you what's confusing me, and it isn't these contracts: it's you. And this place. What in hyperspace just happened? We jumped into an L3, found a ring of rock instead, got pounced on by a fleet of suitors, and then you practically mated with my ship without even buying her flowers." She picked up the contracts and waved them at Albert. "And now you wanna get married?"

Cole covered his mouth and stifled a laugh.

Albert beamed. "Well *that* explains your odd behavior! And quite nicely, as well. Your charts are a tad out of date, I must say. Not very safe, as you've just learned. No worries, I also have the latest star charts—several versions in fact, from the survey efforts of three major races. For a special price, we can load the trio into your ship's computer! My goodness, you sure are lucky to have found me. One of the first things you'll learn about Darrin from the Bel Tra charts and reports—and I'm giving this information to you at no charge, even without those contracts signed, just to show you what sort of man I am—is that the war between Darrin the First and Darrin the Second in the year 2402, a very somber year for us, did not go well for either side. The belt you flew into is all that remains of Darrin the First, and they didn't get the worst of it. Darrin the Second is in smaller pieces. Not to brag, but *much* smaller. They lie scattered beyond our far more sensible orbit." He wrapped his arms around his chest and shivered for effect.

"I kid, of course. We've set those differences aside, and now all the people of Darrin get along famously. We've had peace for seven years straight! Not a shot fired. Well, pretty much. Besides, the few of us who deserve to make a profit have found it more lucrative if we compete on an individual level, rather than banding together and squeezing as a unit. Things get out of control that other way. It's really a shame we didn't think of it earlier, but what's done is done and business is finally getting back to some of the prewar levels." He frowned and then added in a somber voice, "After accounting for changes in population and per-capita GDP."

"You people blew each other's planets to *bits*?" Cole had gone from covering his mirth to controlling his outrage.

Albert recoiled from the outburst and looked sad, but only for a moment. He beamed once again and boasted to all four of them, "You want the best starship armaments in the galaxy? You obviously came to the right place!" He gestured toward the contracts, still smiling. "Now, please sign away before we arrive at my store. We must do these things properly, or my impeccable reputation for fair dealing could suffer. Nothing you sign there mandates a minimum purchase amount, and frankly, if your budget is reflected by the ship's condition—well, please understand that I'm used to dealing with a more demanding clientele and will consider our transactions over the next several days as a favor to you in the hopes you'll always return to me when you need a good deal."

Albert spread his arms and gazed hungrily at the papers. "But of course you will. It's all there in the contracts, after all." He smiled at each of them as if they were the only people in the universe.

oooo

Signing the contracts put Molly in a bad mood. She despised being forced to do anything. Even if it was something she'd been planning on doing already. They'd come to Darrin to make illicit improvements on a starship, so they expected to put up with shady arms dealers on back-moon shipyards. But having someone *force* her to do the exact same thing made her want to resist. The urge was as infuriating as it was nonsensical. She would've been happier if the escape from the asteroid belt had been met with laser fire. At least then she'd be dealing with a threat she understood.

Albert pitched products while the two mated ships cruised back to his shop, seemingly on autopilot. These "feeding frenzies" were reserved for new clients, he assured them. Brutal markets meant each customer had to be "won over." The little scuffle between Darrin I and Darrin II had decreased supply somewhat, but the demand had shot down even faster. The word was not completely out that the system had returned to business as usual, and *Parsona's* unwise entry demonstrated another unfortunate reality: the buyers of their astral charts were probably disappearing from the market altogether. Literally.

"Once we get my charts installed and register your ship as one of my exclusive clients, you'll be able to come and go as you please," Albert told Molly. She forced a smile and considered telling him how unlikely a return to Darrin would be.

A beeping sound interrupted the discussion, and Albert pulled something from his belt, a small black device with a single-line LCD display. He held the gadget up and squinted intently at the readout. "We're about to land," he announced to the room. He flapped back one side of his suit jacket and struggled to thrust his pelvis away from the seat before securing the device back to his belt. With a satisfied grunt, he pushed himself up, collected the contracts with a grin and a wink, and busied himself arranging them in his briefcase.

"Not many of these old GN-290s around, are there?" He smiled at Molly, his face completely innocent.

A chill spread through her limbs, and her palms moistened and began to cool. *What in the galaxy did he mean by that? Did he know who they were? Was there a bounty out on the ship?* She shot Cole a glance. His arms were folded across his wide chest, his face frozen in a glower.

"It was a few design flaws that did this model in," he said. "Putting the cargo bay on the starboard side with the airlock, for instance. Horrible idea. Can't open both at once. We'll leave the ships docked so you don't have to land her, but that means you'll have to pass through my baby to enter the shop. Do me a favor? Don't touch anything as you go through. And do *not* feed the Drenard." He laughed out loud.

Molly tried to soothe the tension out of her body, but she couldn't tear her eyes away from his briefcase. It felt as though a chunk of her soul rattled around within.

As they entered his hangar bay, a soft light filtered through *Parsona's* portholes and moved from front to back, popping through each window in turn. Every head swayed in unison as the landing gear scraped on metal decking, signaling their arrival. Molly was furious at the gear for lowering at another's behest. For the second time, someone else had assumed command of her ship, and she hated it as much as people controlling *her*.

"Ladies and gentlemen," Albert began with a flourish, "welcome to Albert's Arms. Please follow me for a quick tour. Again, mind the mess as we pass through *Lady Liberty*. I was not expecting company today." He winked at Molly as if this were a private joke between the two of them and strolled back into the airlock as calmly as he had exited it. Molly felt another stab of betrayal when she heard her outer airlock door slide open for Albert. Walter rushed after him like a puppy while Cole gave her a vicious look. Edison was still absently rubbing his injured paw.

"I don't like this any more than you guys do," she said.

"We aren't the ones who signed those contracts, though, are we?" Cole replied.

"Flank you, Cole." Molly shot out of the crew seat and stormed across the cargo bay. "As soon as we arm *my* ship so you feel less 'naked,' we're out of here. And straight to the Navy this time. I'm sick and tired of doing whatever other people want." She trailed the rant behind her and spun into the airlock, slapping the doorjamb with her palm as she ducked through.

Yeah, it was a design flaw, she thought. She squeezed through the outer door and marched across the mating tube to *Lady Liberty*. She had pointed out the airlock problem to Cole while they were on Glemot, but hearing it from someone else made her angry. Or maybe her disgust with having signed those contracts had her lashing out.

She stepped through the coupling into Albert's airlock and nearly choked on the smell. Something sticky and formerly edible mixed with the odor of plastic upholstery; the combination assaulted her olfactory senses. She could hear Walter and Albert in an animated discussion beyond and hoped the boy's bartering skills were being put to good use. She also hoped Albert's shop didn't smell anything like his airlock. She stepped through the inner hatch and joined them in a room lined with spacesuits and padlocked storage compartments. It looked like a Navy MP locker room. She could only imagine what an arms dealer would keep in those bins.

Albert smiled at her. "Right this way," he said jovially, stepping into *Lady Liberty's* cargo bay. Walter followed, and Molly hurried after them before Cole and Edison could catch up. She already regretted lashing out at them but fought the urge to be contrite.

The cargo bay was a wreck, but at least the open ramp allowed fresh air in from beyond. Albert and Walter clanged down and out to the hangar. Molly took two steps and glanced to one side, down the hallway of Albert's ship. She felt the urge to snoop, looked the other way, and saw something move in her peripheral.

She froze.

The shape. The color. Years of training triggered synapses wired for fear. Molly reached for a stunner that wasn't there. She pawed behind her for Cole. She looked for a stick or a weapon of some sort.

Albert had not been joking about having a Drenard onboard.

27

The Drenard's presence triggered a primal kill response in Molly. Her nerves, already frayed, sent jittery commands to adrenaline-soaked muscles. Her knees went numb and she would've collapsed, but Cole arrived in time to steady her.

She looked back to mumble her thanks and saw the mask of pure terror on his face as well. She spun back around, expecting to be attacked at any moment, but the creature hadn't moved. Huddled on the floor, not five meters from her, was a living Drenard. The race they and the rest of the GU had been at war with for longer than she'd been alive. This was what they were programmed for at the Academy: hunt down and kill

Drenards. Pictures of them graced their gun-range targets, their punching bags, the Navy's recruitment posters. Training holos incorporated front-line video from soldiers lucky enough to encounter and mow them down. A generic-looking representation of a Drenard popped up on the scoreboard after simulated battles to tally victorious kills.

This creature looked similar enough to startle her, but as most of her fear and rage drained away, she saw that it wasn't *exactly* like the aliens from the videos and posters. The biggest difference was how small and emaciated it looked. The hairless body was a lighter shade of blue, almost translucent. And instead of wearing the white flight suits and combat armor of the Drenard Navy, this one had on nothing but dirty, tattered rags. Shackles on both of its slim ankles completed the pathetic getup; a chain snaked from them around the corner and into the cockpit. The miserable thing had its knees bent up to its chin—long, thin arms wrapped around its narrow shins. With large, wet eyes it peered directly at Molly, and the last of her fear and anger fell uselessly to the metal decking. Pity and shame started to rise up in their place.

"A real beaut, eh?" Albert called up from the cargo ramp, his voice full of pride. "One hundred percent real Drenard. Not another like her this side of the Milky Way. Priceless, as you can imagine, but I'd never sell her. No sir-ree." He marched back into the ship, smiling at Molly and Cole as if their reaction pleased him. He crossed to the poor creature and patted its head.

Molly watched the captive flinch slightly, the chain rattling like a spooked snake. But the Drenard's eyes never left her own.

"Anlyn here sure brings in the customers, let me tell ya. Just a gem. And it's true, you know. They can go forever without food. All you have to do is water them. Damnedest thing. She's learning English too. Pretty good at it, but she doesn't choose to say much. Still a little frightened, but coming around. Come this way and I'll give you a full tour of the shop and introduce you to my family." He went back to the ramp and waved them along. "I'll give you a sense of what I have in stock, and you can show me what sort of price range you're looking at. Then I'll let you get some rest and talk over your needs with your weapons officer. I'm assuming that was the clever fellow who tested my private shields?" He whirled on Molly and held his hand to one side of his mouth, but said, loud enough for everyone to hear, "Doesn't say much, does he?"

Molly didn't respond, and it didn't feel as if Albert expected her to. He strolled out into the open hangar, a constant flow of jabber following him. The habit reminded Molly of his contracts: a heap of words designed to hinder communication rather than facilitate it. She cast one last look at the Drenard and followed him out into the cavernous hangar.

The walls of his shop were rough stone, the entire facility chewed out of a massive asteroid. Cabinets and shelves lined one wall, a flat workbench another. Above the latter hung a wide board with hundreds of hooks. Every tool she knew—and some she didn't—was suspended there. She turned to the others; Edison's fur bristled at the sight of it all; Cole had disappeared.

Molly spotted him wandering toward the rear of the ships, mesmerized by the door they'd flown through. Primarily because it wasn't there! She rushed over to join him, stopping in the pocket of heat near *Lady Liberty*'s thrusters. Ahead of them a plane of light shimmered where the hangar ended and the vacuum of space began. An invisible wall somehow kept the two separate. A force field.

"Look, but don't touch!" Albert called out gaily.

Molly and Cole half-spun toward the warning and ended up locking eyes with each other. His were green and wide, his brows raised. Molly knew what he was thinking.

"You want one," she guessed.

"Oh, *yeah*, I want one. Are you kidding? This stuff is still science fiction on Earth. Crap we read about in the pulp that circulates through the Academy." Cole lowered his voice. "And this creep uses it for his garage door."

"Don't forget, he's wearing one as well. Talk about not feeling naked, he could *be* naked and still be invincible." Molly looked away from the force field and down at her feet. "Speaking of feeling naked, I'm sorry about what I—"

Cole reached over and squeezed her hand. "Forget it. I'm sorry too. Hey, you think his field comes from that black device on his belt?"

Molly turned to one side. In her peripheral she could see Albert by the workbench, explaining something to Edison. She supposed all was well between the two, the attack forgotten. "I don't think so. More of a silent communicator. Maybe just a readout from his ship. Look, we need to play this like a simple shopping trip. The guy just wants to trade and make a buck, and we want what he has. We're as powerless here as we were on Glemot, maybe more so. So don't make any moves we might regret."

He nodded and dropped her hand. "What do you make of that Drenard? I almost rushed the poor thing to take its head off. Could you believe we were seeing one in person like that?"

Molly looked away. "Let's talk about it later. I'm . . . I'm not sure what I felt. No, that's a lie. I . . . I felt the same thing you did, but I'm not sure what I feel right now. Sick, I guess. I don't like seeing anything chained up like that."

"Oh, gimmee a break. I remember you checking Orville's restraints with care. And that was a *Drenard* in there."

"I said I don't wanna talk about it right now. Later. Just stay focused on what we came here for."

Cole scrunched up his face and turned back to the force field. "Sure thing, *Captain*."

"Hello, guys?" Albert called across the hangar. "I'd like to introduce you to my wife." A large woman stood beside him, wiping her hands on her apron, prepping them for a polite shaking.

Molly led Cole over to the rest of the group. Her eyes flickered over to the distasteful sight of *Parsona* and *Lady Liberty*, still conjoined. The sense of violation would not go away, and it left a bad taste in her mouth.

"Gladys Gaines." Her outstretched hand still had some white cooking residue on it.

Molly accepted it and found her grip warm, inviting. She reciprocated the gentle shake. "Molly Fyde," she said.

Albert lifted a hand to the side of his mouth for another loud aside. "The ship's *captain*," he said, obviously impressed with Molly's age or gender. She wasn't sure which irked her more. Actually, that's not right. She definitely knew which one.

Cole repeated the ritual with Mrs. Gaines, introducing himself.

"What can I get you kids to drink? Tea? Coffee? You'll be joining us for dinner, I hope?"

Molly lost herself in the surreal scene as her crew put in beverage orders with a gunrunner's wife. They were understandably eager to drink a beverage that wasn't in a bag, but their excitement stabbed at her chest. This wasn't supposed to be *fun*.

Edison's joy hurt her the most. She recalled that glorious meal on Glemot and realized, for the first time, that the poor pup was used to eating like that regularly. It had been a unique and glorious one-time event for her, but for his taste buds, it was the accepted standard. Eating would probably never be the same for him.

Albert snuck up behind Molly and put an arm across her shoulders, causing her to flinch like the chained-up Drenard. "Is the furry one your Weapons Officer?" he asked her.

They didn't *have* a weapons officer, she nearly told him. They'd never had any *weapons* before; they'd only been a crew for two weeks. Fortunately, she stopped herself, understanding the need to tell Albert as little as possible. She already felt as if he knew too much.

"Actually, that would be Cole," she finally said. "He also does navigation duties."

"Ah, excellent! Then I can deal with one person for both armaments *and* the star charts we discussed. I'm assuming you're still interested in that triple package?

It really can't be beat, you know. And I'll provide free updates for the next fifty years, just stop back by anytime. Now, Walter and I have been talking payment. The chap is very sharp, thinks highly of some of the goods you guys have to offer. But I have to tell you, the Navy tech he's bartering with isn't quite as rare as he's making out. I'll be doing you a favor, honestly, to take it off your hands. But don't you worry about any of that nonsense just yet. Let's eat some dinner and get some rest. We'll have plenty of time for business tomorrow."

But Molly couldn't relax on command, even if she wanted to.

oooo

Later, in her bunk, her belly stuffed with a home-cooked meal, Molly still couldn't make herself relax. Despite her exhaustion, there was no way she'd be able to sleep. And it wasn't just seeing the Drenard for a second time—curled up in a ball on the cockpit floor as they returned from dinner. Nor was it the pressure of the business to conduct the following day. These didn't help, to be sure, but Molly's torment came from other thoughts.

First, she couldn't help but second-guess her decision to avoid the Navy. Cole was persuasive with his theories, but she trusted Lucin completely, which made running feel *wrong*. Was she really betraying the closest thing she had to a family just because some dreamy boy batted his eyes at her? Lucin would feel betrayed when *Parsona* returned with chaff pods and laser canons. It seemed logical to her when she agreed to this mess, but now she was hearing her crazy explanation from Lucin's perspective, and it sounded like pure gibberish.

Then there were the deaths she'd been responsible for. Glemot was almost too big a mistake to fully comprehend. Even though she had been used, she felt the full weight of a race's genocide on her shoulders. The depression she'd dipped into briefly wouldn't leave her, as hard as she tried to fake it for Cole's sake. She could feel how edgy and dangerous she'd become, able to snap without provocation. It worried her.

And the more personal, up-close deaths haunted her with a more vivid ferocity. The sight of Edison flaying that council member. The numbness in her elbow when she struck that Navy man. The look on his face as the rains of Palan smeared him against that windshield.

Her big adventure and romance in space had turned into a mess larger than herself. Other people were getting hurt. She had watched everything she'd hoped for and dreamed of dissipate into the cosmos or get crushed into small pieces.

Molly wondered what the other kids at Avalon High would be up to right then. How great it must feel to be developmentally stunted. They could be physical adults, but gloriously brain-dead from years of rote memorization and regurgitation. Numb to the world from playing with toys well into adulthood rather than being honed for the ugly reality of a dangerous life. Molly had always felt so superior to those kids: beyond them in wisdom, power and ability. But that solid view was developing cracks. Which of them was happier right now? Which of them continued to hurt the universe?

Molly tossed her body to its other side, trying to find a comfortable pose, as if the conundrum were physical. She had no idea how long she'd been doing this, or what time it was, when she thought she heard a noise echo back from the front of her ship. She sat upright, already developing the unnatural skill that all pilots and captains possess: the attenuation to any change in the direction of their ship's heading and a sensitivity to any foreign sound, however slight.

She slid out of bed and pulled on her jumpsuit, eager to be awake and *doing* something rather than in bed and dwelling on her sadness. As she slipped her shoes on, she found herself hoping it was Cole, unable to sleep himself. Hopefully he'd be willing to talk some. Because if it was Walter reorganizing the cargo bay at this hour, she was going to have a hard time being nice.

Unfortunately, Molly had no plan for what to do if it was Albert Gaines nosing into their ship's computer.

28

"What in hyperspace are you *doing*?"

Albert was leaning over the flight controls, fiddling with something on her dash. Molly felt an intense burning sensation creep along the surface of her scalp. Her entire being wanted to reach out and see if that damn shield of his was active.

"Molly!" he turned and beamed. He held a small device up for her to see. "Just checking your nav computer, seeing which adapter I would need to get those star charts installed. Didn't want to wake you."

"Well you *should* have," she spat.

"Of course, of course. Hey, this is a strange collection of gear you have here. Some really nice stuff mixed in with some obsolete—I hate to use the word 'junk, but let's not beat around the bush, okay? Maybe after we get you set up with defenses and charts we can talk about swapping this SADAR out for something, let's say—more 'appropriate' for the type of work this ship was designed for. I could probably work out a discount on the chaff pods if we did that trade."

"The SADAR unit stays," she said. "It was my father's."

She immediately regretted saying this. Her anger and lack of sleep made this conversation potentially dangerous. She took a deep breath. "Look, just . . . please get off my ship. I'm tired, and we can do our business later, okay?"

"Sure. Absolutely. No offense meant. I'm a full-service kind of guy. You get your rest and don't worry about a thing. I'll check back in with you in a few hours."

Molly waited for him to leave. She listened to the traitorous swish of her own airlock obeying his commands and then crawled into Cole's navigation seat and tried to get some sleep.

When a hand squeezed her shoulder hours later, Molly incorporated it into a bad dream featuring Albert and Drenards. She nearly snapped the arm connected to the hand, but it shot back in fear.

"Wow. Easy, tiger. Just checking in on you."

It was Cole.

"*Gods,*" Molly groaned. "You scared the hell out of me. Don't do that."

"Do what? I touched you. And you're in my chair."

Molly rubbed her eyes and tried to twist the cramp out of her back. "Technically, Cole, every chair in this ship is *mine.*"

"Man. I was just checking in on you. I got scared when you weren't in your room, and the door was open and I couldn't get through the airlock to go find you. Sorry for being worried." He turned and stalked out to the cargo bay.

"I'm sorry," Molly called after him. "Cole, wait. I was having bad dreams, you just scared me, okay? I didn't mean to snap at you."

She leaned around the seat to see if he'd heard. He paused near the crew seats, his back to her. "It's fine," he said. "Don't sweat it. It's my fault, I guess. I . . . I keep forgetting that I'm just along for the ride."

"That's not true," said Molly. "We're in this together."

Cole looked back over his shoulder. "Are we? 'Cause I thought you were running to the Navy when we got outta here. That you felt like I was controlling you—"

"I didn't mean that. My head's been screwy since Glemot. . ." She glanced at the other chair. "If you wanna talk. . ."

"Nah, I'm fine. Gonna get dressed and hail our jailor." He marched off toward the rear of the ship.

Molly grabbed his helmet from its bin above her and flopped back into the chair. She checked her reflection in the visor, forcing a smile that seemed wooden and unnatural to her. "Well, I'm *not* fine," she told herself.

Cole's voice rumbled through the hull from the loud hailer. Molly put the helmet back and scurried toward the airlock. The boys emerged from their rooms, weary-eyed and confused.

"Morning," Molly said as she joined them by the airlock.

"Morning, Captain," Walter hissed.

"Pleasant awakenings," grumbled Edison.

Molly squeezed Walter's shoulder and patted Edison on the arm. *I'm fine*, she lied to herself.

Cole's voice boomed in the distance, muffled by *Parsona's* steel shell. She stuck her head in the airlock as he repeated his request in the loud-hailer. She could see the volume cranked all the way up, a setting used more for atmospheric flight than hangar bays.

The outer door whisked open, causing Cole to jump back.

"Ah, good morning!" said Albert. Without even needing to look, he reached in and turned the volume all the way down. "We can scratch off looking at hailer catalogs this morning, can't we?" He said it with a friendly smile and no trace of sarcasm. His hand remained on the knob, touching it like he owned it.

"Come, let's get down to business, shall we?" He turned and made his way through the mating tube toward his own ship.

"Be right there," Molly called after him. "Leave the door open for us so we don't have to ring you, okay?"

He turned, the smile returning to his lips a hair too late. "My pleasure, Captain. Just trying to give you kids your privacy. Come to the lobby when you get freshened up. I'll be taking care of some paperwork." He strolled off, calling out as he went, "Just because I treat every customer like they're my only concern doesn't mean they're my only customers!"

"The friendlier he gets, the more I want to strangle him," Cole remarked, watching him disappear.

"Tell me about it."

Molly stuck her head into the cargo bay, looking for Walter. He was fiddling with his computer and telling Edison which things to pull out and where they were located. He seemed giddy with anticipation, probably eager to get bartering.

"Walter, I need to speak with you."

"Of courssse, Captain. You know I love our talkss." He holstered the computer and smoothed his gray jumpsuit. It was still too big for him, the wrinkles and folds just moved down to his waist, making his thin frame seem pudgy.

"What's your sense of Albert? Smelling sense, I mean. Does the guy reek to you?"

Walter's face scrunched up in concentration, the dull sheen of metal flesh glowing slightly. "Not one bit. I meant to ssay ssomething lasst night after dinner, but I wasss too sstuffed to remember. Ssomething Palan insside is sscreaming 'a lie!', but no ssmell. Nothing."

"Really?"

"Yess, but I musst tell you a ssecret." He glanced at Edison, paused, then continued. "Palanss can rarely ssmell a lie on each other. We're sso good at it, sso many generationss of—bargainerss. It'ss only useful for . . . tourisstss." He had a hard time spitting it out. "Of coursse, I'm telling you what otherss tell me. I know little of thesse thingss. I would never lie to you, Molly." His face flattened into a shield of sincerity.

"I know you wouldn't." She turned to Edison, glanced at his paw. "How're you holding up?"

"Adequately improved." He flashed his wide teeth. "Unless your preference is otherwise, I would appreciate the opportunity to conduct repairs on the aft section of *Parsona* with the day's initial hours."

"That would be great, Edison, thanks. Are you sure you don't mind helping us install whatever we trade for today?"

"Few actions could increase my pleasure more."

She patted his fur. "Thanks. Cole and I are going to meet with Albert. Keep an eye on Walter for me."

Edison nodded and Molly returned to the airlock, where Cole was waiting for her.

"After you," he said.

Molly ducked through the airlock hatch and crossed once more to *Lady Liberty*. Albert had clever excuses for the arrangement, but she had finally figured out the real reason for keeping the ships together: he just wanted to keep them locked up at night.

She felt another tinge of trepidation as she stepped out into the ship's cargo bay. Knowing that a live Drenard lived aboard was unsettling. She glanced to the creature's corner of the bay—it was empty. The thick chain, one end bolted to the bulkhead, snaked across the decking and curled up into the navigator's seat. Something moved. Molly saw the Drenard's head, small, bald and translucent blue, peeking around the corner. Those sad, wide eyes once again locked onto Molly's.

She froze, then raised one hand toward her sworn enemy. Her fingers bent slightly in a small wave.

The head sucked back around the corner, and the chain jangled softly.

Molly felt Cole's hand on her back, guiding her toward the ramp.

"Hey, do you—"

"Yeah, I saw it," he said. They clanged down the ramp together and he headed straight for the store entrance. Molly pulled him to a stop.

"That wasn't what I was gonna ask." She paused. "Do you think Albert was flying *Lady Liberty* yesterday?"

Cole's eyes widened and darted up to the ship's cockpit. "The Drenard? Gods, I bet you're right! If so, *man. . .*" Cole shook his head. "The simulator doesn't do them justice, does it? Wow. That would totally explain the Battle of Eckers, eh? And how they keep holding us off with inferior numbers."

He glanced back up at the cockpit and chuckled. "That Drenard is better than *you*, you know."

"Hey, I was working with a fractured wrist and a busted thruster." Molly couldn't believe his boy brain—making everything a competition—or the fact she fell right in with him. "Wanna tell me who wrecked my thruster?" she asked.

"Hey, I had nothing to do with your wrist, *Ms. Sensitive*." He dodged back as he said it, obviously expecting a slap to the shoulder.

Molly considered it, but the return to their usual banter didn't feel normal yet. They'd have to fake it a while longer before she could hit him in play. She forced a smile, hoping it didn't look as bad as it had in the visor, and crossed to the store lobby.

She entered, and Albert rose from behind his desk. "Welcome, welcome!" he said, as if a customer had just strolled in from the street. "And here's our Weapons Officer. Good morning, Cole!"

"I just saw you five minutes ago," he complained, a thumb pointing over his shoulder.

"Of course, of course. I'm just excited to be doing business with you two. I've been updating my price sheets, and I really think we'll be able to cut you a fantastic deal. Nothing top of the line, not for what you have to trade with, but something better than what you have now, right? I mean, anything is better than nothing!"

He moved around the desk and handed Molly a tablet. It displayed defense and arms modules with specs and pricing. He pointed at a number in the corner. "Here's your total. I'll let you know when you exceed the value of the goods that your wonderful little Cargo Officer has set aside." He smiled and said it again. "Wonderful title, that. Cargo Officer." He laughed again at some private joke.

Cole ticked items off his fingers. "Chaff pods, ECM, two lasers, a missile pod, suits for the crew, hand-stunners, a better first-aid kit—"

"Whoa, slow down," Molly said.

Albert's chuckling stopped; he looked at them gravely. "Are you kids planning a little war?" The serious facade cracked with more laughter. "Just kidding, of course. That sounds great, I'll get right on it. The suits, of course, will take some time. I have a friend a few shops down the row who has the material we'll need, and my wife is a wizard with alterations. Let me get started on that while you two take your time with the catalogs. Just mark here," he indicated a box, "with anything you're interested in. Add as much as you like, we'll compare the packages when I get back.

"Oh, and make yourselves comfortable." He gestured toward a leather sofa crouching behind a glass table on the other side of the lobby. While Molly and Cole followed his gaze, Albert snuck away to his living quarters, his fancy suit singing as it rubbed together.

They plopped down with the tablet between them and started hammering out the details. Without knowing what they could or couldn't afford, they had to set up multiple packages in a wide range of prices. When they came to pages of Navy regulation products they recognized, and a few pieces of forbidden technology from other races—Drenard included—the tactical debate turned into an ethical argument.

Molly felt relieved that her father wasn't there, that he couldn't see her in this seedy joint, contemplating the purchase of contraband. The guilty feelings that had kept her awake the night before came flooding back, making her feel tired and depressed. Gradually, Cole assumed command of the conversation, and Molly's doubts wilted under the glare of his cold rationality.

The Weapons Officer ruse had become reality without her noticing.

oooo

They had been at it for over an hour when Walter came in, looking sheepish. "Where'ss Albert?" he asked them.

Cole nodded toward the living quarters. Walter didn't hesitate, rushing after their host as if he were welcome anywhere in the asteroid. As the door swung open, domestic sounds flooded the lobby: cabinet doors slamming, children screaming after one another, Mrs. Gaines admonishing someone, and Albert, his voice an echo, backing up his wife.

Molly shook her head at the normalcy. This combination of arms dealer, captor, slaveholder, family man, and business tycoon made pegging Albert impossible. She could dwell on one aspect of the man, depending on whether she wanted to vilify him or attempt to trust him, but neither answer felt right. She needed him to sit in his lair, rubbing his hands together as his henchmen gathered around and he planned his domination of the galaxy. Anything redeemable—if he oozed all that slime simply to help his family slide through life—made him harder to loathe.

What Molly needed was a reminder. "Are you good here?" she asked Cole.

He looked surprised. "You going in there as well?"

"No way. I just . . . I wanted to check on Edison. See how the thruster repairs are going."

"Yeah, sure. I think I know what sort of balance we're settling on here. Go ahead. And hey, if the crazy bear has added two more thrusters and upgraded the landing gear, don't be surprised."

"I won't," she grinned.

Because I'm not checking in on Edison, she added to herself.

29

Molly entered the hangar to the sounds of Edison hammering on *Parsona's* aft section, performing repairs. She used the cover of the two ships and the loud noises to sneak up *Lady Liberty's* gangway. Entering the cargo bay, she noticed the chain still led around the corner of the cockpit.

Molly hesitated for a moment.

Then she took a few steps toward the front of the ship, approaching from the side to get a clear view around the doorjamb while keeping her distance. When the chain rattled slightly, Molly nearly turned and fled out to the hangar, but somehow she kept her nerves in check.

The small, blue head peeked out at her. Molly raised both hands, showing her palms to the alien. The eyes withdrew, but she could still see the crown of its bald scalp, the light from the hangar filtering into the carboglass and then through its clear skin. It looked like a mere child, half the mass of an adult Drenard. Molly's size.

So frail, she thought.

Molly took a few more steps forward, and the rest of the head withdrew. She called out softly, "It's okay. I'm not here to hurt you. I'm a friend, okay? My name's Molly." She continued to reassure the Drenard, and herself, as she crept into the rear portion of the cockpit. When she could see its shoulder over the edge of the nav chair, she stopped. Fighting to keep her voice steady, she asked, "Your name is Anlyn, right? That's a very pretty name, Anlyn. Very pretty. My name's Molly. Can you say my name?"

"Molly." It came out less than a whisper but more than a sigh. The pronunciation was flawless. It seemed the act of communicating at all was what the creature needed practice with.

"That's right. My name's Molly. I'm a ship captain. A pilot. Do you like to fly?"

Molly saw an immediate reaction. The alien's smooth head turned to her, its pale eyes locking with her own. The sight of this poor thing gazing up at her filled Molly with the anguish of conflicting emotions. Part of her wanted to sweep the girl into her arms. Part of her just wanted to bash those chains. And years of training lashed out at both ideas.

Anlyn parted her thin, blue lips. "I can fly," she said. "But I don't like to."

Molly wanted to ask her why, but the Drenard cut her off.

"You're not supposed to be here, and I'm not supposed to talk to you. Albert will hurt me if he finds us. Go, please," she whispered.

Her head pressed back to her knees, her eyes fixed on her toes.

Molly thought of a dozen things to say but remained silent. She imagined herself walking a little farther and touching that clear shoulder, but she didn't. Instead, she became overcome with sadness. A new kind. Directed at someone besides herself.

She turned and followed the chain back to the cargo bay.

○ ○ ○ ○

Molly found Edison at one of the workbenches, working a rag over some contraption. He turned to face her as she approached, a massive smile dominating his face. "Technology is spectacular," he said. "I'm extremely appreciative of the opportunity to manipulate it."

She scratched his arm and pressed her lips into a flat line. "Have you seen the girl in Albert's ship?"

"The Drenard? Absolutely. Extremely fragile, in my estimation."

"She's a slave, Edison."

"I concur. Liberated organisms do not decorate themselves with chains."

Molly thought about some of her classmates at Avalon and wondered if arguing Edison's point would serve any purpose. *Probably not*, she thought.

"You desire assisting her, correct?" Edison asked. "Emancipation? The similarities to Cole's plan in liberating Walter immediately returns to my attention."

"No, buddy. I mean, yeah, I wanna do something for her, but we're not in any shape to help out. Nothing Albert's about to sell us is gonna dent the stuff he keeps for himself." She thought about this—about the obvious need for such an imbalance. You can't sell arms that you don't have your own defenses for. She glanced at the invisible hangar door. And you could never release defense technology *like that* into the wild; it would put an end to your arms trade. The irony of it all—the way the market worked here in Darrin—it hurt Molly's brain the more she examined it.

"Hey, I need you to do me a favor. I'm not sure if it'll help, but there's an hour-long back-scratching just for trying, okay?"

Edison nodded vigorously, agreeing before she even got to the details.

Behind them, a pale blue head rose in the cockpit's porthole, and two small eyes watched the scene below.

The wetness on them could've been mistaken for the glare of hangar lights on carboglass.

oooo

Molly re-entered the lobby and found Cole, Walter, and Albert crowded around the store computer. Walter nodded gravely as Albert summed up the list Cole had picked out. Molly joined them on the other side of the desk to see for herself.

The list contained more than she felt comfortable getting, and more than she figured they could afford. Cole seemed satisfied, however, and she'd resigned herself to leaving him in charge of this. The more she could distance herself from this decision, the better off she'd be. If Lucin wanted to blow a gasket later, she'd blame the mods on Navy-boy.

"Excellent choices," Albert said, slapping Cole on his back. "You guys sure are lucky to have come to me, and that I like you so much. You couldn't get a deal like this anywhere else in the galaxy. Of course, my wife won't be happy to see how well old Walter here talked me down. Haha!"

Walter, Molly noted, did not have the carriage of a victorious Palan. It was hard to think of their little Cargo Officer as a bastion of humility, but here he was, showered with compliments and shrinking from them as if they stung. Molly also noticed that he couldn't stop sniffing the air around him. She tried to hurry things along. "Can Edison begin installing the gear soon?"

"Installing? My goodness, dear, we don't have the facilities for that! My garage is for the upkeep of my own ship. Highly illegal and improper to have you cobbling your war plans together here in my shop."

His look of feigned moral outrage almost seemed sincere. "No, no, these things are best left to the less scrupulous monsters over at Darrin the Second's line of shady establishments. Of course, I would never recommend your going over there. Frightful place, naturally. Vicious people. It's better to go somewhere else in the galaxy that does that sort of thing."

"Are you kidding?" Molly frowned. "You're gonna dump this gear in our cargo bay and send us somewhere else to have it installed? And where else can we go besides Darrin?"

"Dear, dear. I'm sorry for any confusion, but it's all in the contract. We can't be in the business of modifying starships for combat, no sirree. Wouldn't do. We'd have the Navy around here asking too many questions. Those unscrupulous jerks over around Darrin the Second's asteroid field, now *those* guys will do anything for the right price. Good thing they don't sell gear, I tell you. They'd pull shady deals that might put us right out of business over here.

"Now, I say those rats can't be trusted, but if you do decide to go over there—again I recommend against it—there *is* one guy I'd suggest you see. Not too bad as far as Darrin the Second folk go. I've had some dealings with him in the past. As straight-shooting as that lot gets. You tell him I sent you and he'll cut you a deal, no doubt. I'll even call and tell him you're coming."

"Great," Molly muttered. Now she understood how they could afford all this gear. The next question was: Did they have enough left to install it?

oooo

It took another day to procure the new flight suits, which provided plenty of time for finishing the physical side of the trade. The first order of business was to finally separate the two ships. To Molly, it felt like removing restraints from a dear friend. She and Cole had decided that this was the intended purpose: to keep their crew guarded until a deal was settled.

Albert boarded his ship and made airs of performing the complicated maneuver himself, but Molly knew he wasn't flying. She watched as *Lady Liberty* decoupled and slid to the side, nearly brushing up against the hangar wall. *Parsona's* cargo ramp could now be lowered, and the swapping of goods could begin.

The computer technology that Walter had stowed all over her ship was crated up and carted off. Albert's children joined in the fun, carrying off some of the lighter bits, oohing and ahhing at various spoils while their father chastised them to keep it down. Walter stood by the door, checking every item with a hiss, and making entries in his computer.

When Albert indicated all was square, they started moving the wooden crates of contraband aboard, the sight of which made Molly's gut sink. The illegality of these actions crashed into her upbringing and her training. It could've been justified in a Navy hangar, or as part of a sting operation, but the truth was, she was a civilian. No, a *criminal*—on the run and dealing arms.

It filled her with shame.

"Excellent doing business with you, my dear. As soon as the suits arrive, you can be off. Please tell Frankie I said hello and that he really should move shop over here. Nasty blokes he deals with over there."

Molly nodded absently. She wished the suits were already here so they could just leave. Somehow she doubted Darrin II could be as bad as this inhospitable and soulless wasteland.

That night they dined again with the entire family. With no business to tend to anymore, there was an eager gaiety surrounding the meal, but Molly still couldn't partake in it. So far, in what she'd seen of the galaxy, the fairy tale she'd concocted in her brain didn't exist except in her imagination. The gorgeous scenery on Glemot had been marred by the nasty brutality of its people. The cliffs of Palan were pockmarked with prison cell windows. She had no idea what Darrin I or II even looked like. War had turned them both into rubble.

Molly played with her food. She felt envious when Edison excused himself early, but sat with her own thoughts until the end of the meal, as was expected of a ship's captain.

Albert shook hands with the entire crew; Mrs. Gaines pecked each of them on the cheek. It felt too bizarre for Molly. She went through the motions numbly, smiled weakly at the exhausted children, and followed Cole and Walter back to their ship.

Strange, but she felt a little sad that they didn't have to cross through *Lady Liberty* to get there. She yearned for a chance to say goodbye to the Drenard. And to point out the changes that Edison had made to *Lady Liberty*.

Namely, to its chains.

○ ○ ○ ○

Molly slept horribly for the second night in a row. She left her flightsuit on and lay on top of her sheets, waiting. When Albert knocked on the cargo door, she leaped up to open the ramp and help him load the parcels. The sound of the hydraulic arms gearing down the hatch stirred the rest of the crew. They appeared just in time to not have to do their share of the work.

Everyone exchanged a final set of goodbyes while Molly checked the engine room. As she crossed the cargo bay to the cockpit, Albert told her that the shield would go down as soon as he retreated to the store lobby. Walter shook his hand a final time, pumping it madly and hissing something to the big man privately.

Molly closed the ramp and hurried forward to fire up the thrusters. She waited while Cole checked the restraints on the weapon crates and Edison put away a few scattered tools. Walter pawed through one of the crates and pulled out his brand-new space suit.

"You won't need that today," Molly told him. "It's gonna be a long, slow burn across to those other thieves."

Walter seemed annoyed at this, but he put the suit back in the box and patted it proudly.

"Let's get buckled up," she told everyone as she performed the last of the pre-flight checks.

Cole joined her in the cockpit and booted the nav computer. "Brand new charts!" he said.

"Yeah, but you know what they say: those things are out of date the second you install them."

"True. Hey, can I delete our old charts from the system? They've been nothing but trouble, anyway."

"*Absolutely*," Molly said.

Cole typed in a few commands and hovered his finger over the enter key. Molly shot a hand out and grabbed his wrist. "Wait," she said. "The nav tracks from the trip with my father. Gods, I know it sounds stupid and we really don't have the space to spare, but . . . will you hold off on deleting those charts?"

"Sure thing," Cole said, smiling. "And that doesn't sound stupid to me at all. When we get some time, I'll copy the tracks and waypoints over to the new charts and clear up the space."

"Thanks. I appreciate it. Are the boys strapped in?"

Cole checked his vid screen and gave her a thumbs-up. Molly had the chase cam up to watch for a change in the force field. When the shimmer of light disappeared, she pushed the thruster throttles forward, gently lifting the ship. She retracted the landing gear immediately, keeping them from scraping on the decking as the *Parsona* slid backward into space.

She spun the craft around just outside the door and faced the long line of asteroid-based shops strung out in the distance. The sight of them gave Molly a sudden impulse to do a full burn, charring the far wall of Albert's hangar with black soot, but she resisted the temptation. Instead, she nudged forward—expecting resistance at any moment—but finding none.

30

Molly had hoped leaving the crooked line of shops in Darrin I would bring relief. Instead, she found herself heading out to their mirror image. SADAR showed the line of asteroids marking Darrin II in the distance. Beyond them, drifting and colliding, another ring of planetary debris loomed.

They could have chosen to jump across through hyperspace, arriving at Frankie's shop in less than an hour, but Molly had lied to Albert about being low on fusion fuel. She looked forward to the respite of another slow burn, beginning to appreciate the time between waypoints that she had once found painfully dull.

She locked in two Gs of acceleration, the most *Parsona's* grav plates could balance out and allow movement about the ship. When they reached the halfway point, she'd spin them around and decelerate at two Gs until they reached Frankie's. She left Cole on watch and went to take a hot shower, her second of the day. Walking past the crates of illegal arms in the cargo bay, she had a feeling that another mere rinse would not make her feel much cleaner.

At the workbench, Edison tinkered with yet another project. The sight of him in his Glemot robe, fresh and white, deepened her funk. Otherwise, she would have stopped and given him encouragement and inquired about his latest invention.

Molly paused by Walter's room before turning into her own. Through the closed door, she could hear him mumbling to himself in his own language. The sounds of water bubbling over stone were interspersed with hissing English words for which his language had no substitute. "Navy" and "video game" caught her ear, creating the illusion that she understood a bit of the Palan tongue.

Molly had completely forgotten about her promise of a reward. What would Lucin say when he found out the Navy owed money to this strange kid? And surely the boy wasn't thinking about blowing his reward on those silly games of his.

After her shower, Molly yanked her jumpsuit out of the washer/dryer. It was still slightly damp, but she pulled it on anyway. The uncomfortable coolness matched her mood. She strolled out to the cargo bay and froze at the sight of an open crate. Edison leaned over the contraband, fiddling with something.

Molly didn't want to dissuade her friend from showing initiative, but those crates represented something bad about herself—she didn't care to see them toyed with. She also didn't want to take out more of her frustrations on her friends, so she walked to the other side of the crate and gently asked him what he was finding.

"Plasma inducer in excellent condition," he told her. "Impeccable. And fully charged, no less. Simple mounting procedure required, is all." He looked up at her with a wide smile. "Installing these units would be highly enjoyable."

Molly scratched his head. "I know you'd enjoy it, pal. And if Albert would've let us use his garage and tools, you'd be doing just that. Heck, if there was a safe place we could go right now that had a pile of scrap metal and something bigger than our ship's welder, I'd take you there."

She looked down into the open crate at the long gleaming shaft of the laser canon. "Imagine having to scratch my back before I scratched yours. Like in a Council meeting when you have to give someone a vote to get a vote in return. That's why we have to go to Frankie's."

Edison nodded. "My understanding of the situation is complete. Just expressing my imagined pleasure."

She patted him again and set off to relieve Cole when something Edison had said made her stop in her tracks. She whirled on him. "Did you say those things were already *charged*?"

He nodded. "Fully. A simple depression of this mechanical device discharges a stream of modulated plasma with an amplitude of—"

She held up both hands. "I understand. Do me a favor? Please put the lid back on and go check the chaff pods. Or try on your space suit and make sure it fits and breathes all right, okay?"

"Absolutely, captain. With haste."

She exhaled, turned to the cockpit and nodded at Walter. The boy had returned to his computer, programming away. Despite her annoyance with him wasting time with that game, she couldn't imagine life on *Parsona* without that thing to babysit him.

"Bored?" she asked Cole as she wiggled into her chair.

"Yeah, and loving it. You missed a new arrival while you were in the shower." He pointed to the SADAR display.

Molly looked. Back at Darrin I, the entire fleet of pushy salesmen raced out of their shops to greet a new customer. Except, unlike her, this buyer had jumped in safely and knew to sit and wait. Molly felt sorry for the poor guy, then caught herself. Anyone doing business here did *not* deserve her pity. Herself included.

One of the red blips rushing out had a clear lead. Molly imagined it was Anlyn, chained to her chair and out-flying everything in the system. She hoped the poor girl found Edison's alterations before Albert did. And as much as she'd love to watch the starved slave bust free, Molly hoped there'd be a lot of distance between *Parsona* and that fight before it broke out.

"There *has* to be a better way of conducting business," Cole said, studying the chase on SADAR.

"Well, whatever they were doing *before* worked none too well." She traced her finger across the SADAR image of all that debris, wondering what had happened, who had fired the first shot, and how many people had died. Her brain flashed back to Glemot, but she didn't allow it to linger there.

"Hey, Cole, what was it like where you were born?"

"It was like Portugal."

"I'm serious. Your village, what was it like?"

"Small and dirty." He paused a moment. "But I loved it there. No, actually I was bored out of my mind back then, but I love to remember myself as happy there. Maybe it's because I know I'd be happy there *now*."

"You wouldn't be bored after a while?"

"Possibly, yeah. After a few weeks of doing nothing, I'm sure I'd be yearning for the rainy season on Palan." He chuckled and turned to face her. "Why do you ask?"

"I don't know . . . I just feel sometimes like you and I don't really know each other as well as we should. All those hours in the simulator together, and we spent most of our time talking about *previous* hours in the simulator. There's times when I feel like you weren't born until you got to the Academy."

"Well, don't you feel that way about yourself sometimes?"

"Me? No. Not really. I think my upbringing, my father especially, had a lot to do with who I am. It made me into something that wanted to join the Academy in the first place."

"Hmm. I suppose the same is true for me. But it was my friends that made the difference."

"What do you mean?" Molly knew nothing of Cole's old friends.

"I just stayed in trouble a lot. Made some mistakes. When I got in one bad fix, my only way out was either to run from the authorities or join them. I chose the latter. Went to a recruiter and signed up for the Navy. The aptitude tests said 'pilot,' so here I am."

"Yeah, in the *navigator's* chair." Molly laughed at her own joke, and Cole joined her. It felt good.

"You know what isn't funny?" she asked after they settled down.

"You."

"No, the fact that you're in the same spot now that you were back then."

"I don't see what you're getting at."

"Well, we're in a jam, and the choice has been to run from the police or run toward them. Only this time you are making the *opposite* decision."

"Hmm. Hadn't thought about it like that." They both fell silent for a moment. "It's gonna suck like a hull breach when I wake up one day and realize I was wrong both times."

Molly hoped he meant that to be funny—but neither of them laughed.

oooo

Albert had marked Frankie's shop on their charts. They were several thousand meters from the nondescript asteroid when Molly thumbed the short-distance radio and tried to hail him.

"Frankie's Mods, *Parsona*, channel sixteen, come in." She released the mic key and glanced over at Cole. He was watching the SADAR intently.

"This is Frankie's Mods on sixteen, over."

"Frankie, this is Molly, the captain of the GN Class starship *Parsona*, requesting permission to land."

"Permission granted. The door's open. We look forward to doing business with you."

Molly looked to Cole again. "See? Now *this* is how you're supposed to do it. None of that scaring-people-half-to-death and chasing-them-all-over-the-star-system nonsense."

Cole nodded and turned back to the dash. But as paranoid as he was being—as intently as he studied the SADAR—there was no way he could've known that one of the bumps on the back of Frankie's asteroid was a Navy Firehawk, lying in ambush.

Molly moved cautiously into Frankie's hangar, a carbon copy of the one they'd left earlier that day. She braced for an impact as *Parsona* broke the plane, wondering if the locals ever got used to the fear of hitting one of these glass doors.

"I wonder where Frankie's ship is?" she asked.

"Wife's probably out shopping for milk and eggs, or taking the kids out to Galaxy Ball practice," said Cole.

Molly shook her head at the image, another strange glimpse of domestic normalcy in the middle of an arms-dealing village. She felt extremely sad for the kids growing up here. Once again, she made a promise with herself: never return to Darrin, ever again.

After clearing the entry, Molly spun *Parsona* around and docked Navy-style, with an eye for leaving suddenly. The invisible door shimmered to life in front of them, and atmosphere poured visibly from large vents in the ceiling. Their landing gear settled, rocking slightly, as they came to rest.

Molly thumbed the cargo ramp, and she and Cole joined the boys by the crates, everyone rested up and expecting a long day of hard work as *Parsona* had some fangs installed. Molly was torn about the method but resigned to the outcome. She hurried down the ramp ahead of the others, eager to get this over with.

She rounded the rear of the ship as the door to Frankie's shop opened. An old man in a blue mechanic's suit strolled out; Molly started to introduce herself and her crew when a second man entered the hangar.

The strangest sensation overcame her. She recognized the guy, but some other part of her brain knew: *the person she thought it was could not possibly be here*. The two pieces of logic collided over and over, both trying to find purchase but grasping for the same sliver of her attention. Molly stood there dumbly, waiting for the thoughts to sort themselves out.

Cole helped her by providing a name, cementing the impossible thought in her head. "Jakobs?" he asked. It sounded like a question to Molly, but it wasn't. It was the lilt of confusion.

The boy nodded gravely. He looked more like a man now. He and Frankie both had weapons in their hands—and they were leveled at the four of them. Molly's brain revolted against what she was seeing.

Cole started to say something else, but Jakobs interrupted. "On your knees, Cole. Hands behind your back."

"Flank you," he replied.

Jakobs moved the gun slightly and fired a shot into Edison's chest. The pup released a deep howl and collapsed forward, right on his face. The floor shook with the impact, and Molly heard herself scream. She ran to her friend, threw herself on her knees, her chest across his back, protecting him.

"On your knees, Cole." Jakobs moved the laser pistol back.

"Do it!" Molly yelled, feeling for any sign of life in Edison.

Cole sank to the ground, his hands on top of his head, and spat obscenities.

"Don't worry, the Glemot will be fine," Jakobs told Molly. "Heard you were traveling with one, but personally, I never believed it. I'm gonna owe Dinks a beer now."

Molly felt Edison's back rising and falling, but just barely. She glared at Jakobs. "Dinks?" she asked.

"Yeah, he should be bringing the ship around soon. We read the few reports the Navy system had on these brutes," he pointed the pistol to indicate Edison, "and

I never really bought it. Now that I see how small they really are, I guess I was right to doubt the intel, just wrong to think you weren't flying with one. Can't wait to hear the story there."

"Where did you hear this?"

Frankie pulled plastic strips out of his coveralls and cuffed Cole; he gave Walter a careful appraisal.

"Plenty of time to talk about that later," Jakobs said. "First, we need to get you back to Lucin and turn this traitor in."

Molly's thoughts were still on Edison when she realized that Jakobs meant Cole.

"*Traitor?*" She repeated the word. Surely she'd misheard.

Frankie guided Molly away from Edison's body and secured the Glemot with multiple strips of strong plastic. Molly couldn't speak; Cole alternated between cursing Jakobs and pleading with her to listen.

Jakobs holstered his weapon and asked Molly to come and sit so he could explain some things to her. She walked through the door leading out of Frankie's hangar, the confusion behind her closing like a fog in her wake.

31

"Don't feel bad. He had us fooled for a long time as well."

Now that they were standing close to each other, Molly could see the faint marks on Jakobs's face from Cole's handiwork. Those medical reports were flashing back to her, each entry corresponding to a white line on his young skin.

"You have to be wrong," she said. "Whatever you think Cole's doing, he's not. I can explain why we're avoiding the Navy. When we got to Palan—"

"We know about Palan," he interrupted. "We found the three office workers who died in the rain. We found Simmons—you probably knew him as Drummond—and we're pretty sure Saunders and Cole were behind it all."

"*What?*" Molly had no idea "traitor" implied all this. "No," she said. "They were trying to *kill* Cole. *He's* working to uncover the whole thing. You have this backward."

"I understand what you think, I just need you to look at something with an open mind, okay? Just watch this video. It's a lot simpler than trying to convince you that the way you remember things was not how they happened."

He held a small video device out for her. She took it.

"Watch," he repeated.

She did.

The still image displayed on the screen made her throat constrict with nostalgia: the simulator room. A long line of white pods and a wall of bare block. Someone walked on-screen. It wasn't a still image; it was a security video. A cadet, walking away from the camera, went straight to her old pod, fourth on the left. He did something by the rear of the simulator. He looked around once.

Molly knew.

When he finished, he returned the plate and fastened it. He turned back the way he'd come, facing the camera. But she didn't need to see his face to recognize the way Cole walked. Her world shattered.

"Why?" she asked, the question directed more at the boy in the video.

Jakobs took the player back and tucked it away. He motioned to the sofa, but she couldn't move. "Listen," Jakobs said, moving closer. "Your father's ship was discovered almost a year ago, long before you heard about it. The Navy wasn't too eager to get it back at first; the guys holding it were asking far too much for a civilian craft. Lucin pushed as hard as he could, but there was a lot of resistance. He just didn't want to get your hopes up before he had the craft in hand. He asked me to tell you that.

"When Saunders realized what was going on, he blew his top. He thought Lucin's past was destroying his focus, his ability to do his job. He wanted you gone, and he . . . he promised Cole a major promotion to Special Assignments if he helped him out. After the Tchung simulation, he had you expelled, and he thought that'd be the end of it."

Jakobs shook his head. "But Lucin thinks the world of you. He kept fighting for the *Parsona* and doting on you during weekends and breaks. When he went over the replays from the Tchung simulation, he suspected Saunders was up to something. The problem was, he went to *Cole* to help uncover it. He was trusting Saunders's own agent to uncover his plans. Since then, Cole has been doing everything he could to keep you away from the Navy while he tried to get in touch with his boss. We don't know what his next move would've been. Fortunately for us, when an arms dealer called to report someone traveling with a Glemot, he gave us the name of the ship, and someone high up recognized the name *Parsona*, called the Academy, and luckily, Lucin heard about it first. We've been trying to keep all this in-house, of course. Cadets who know you and whom Lucin can trust.

"So here we are. And everything's gonna be fine, now. We'll get the prisoners secured aboard *Parsona*—in your staterooms or the escape pods—and then you and I will follow the Firehawk to Canopus. There, the Navy can take over."

Molly understood the words, but it didn't feel as if she heard them. They had just appeared, like mysterious wounds after a long battle.

"I know it's a lot to absorb, but think about this: Lucin will be able to get you back in the Academy once Saunders has been exposed and put on trial. You might even get to fly again. And I know me and some of the cadets were hard on you, but we were all hard on *each other*. It's part of the toughening-up process. . ."

Molly locked her eyes on his. Jakobs paused, but seemed to take the look the wrong way. He moved closer. "And I don't know about you, but I always thought there was something between us. Something physical that we never—"

She slapped the next words out of Jakobs's head. As hard as she could. Pain lanced out of her tender wrist and shot up to her shoulder. It felt like electricity. It felt *great*.

She turned away from him and marched back to the hangar, ready to go wherever they were taking her. As long as it was away from *here*.

When she entered the hangar, Molly saw Dinks hovering in his Firehawk outside the force field. He waved at her through the carboglass; she ignored him and stomped into the cargo bay. Walter sat at the workbench; he looked up from his game.

"Cole iss a bad guy?"

"I don't know, pal. And I don't wanna talk about it." She glanced around. "Where's Edison?"

"They took him into hiss room. He iss chained up. Awake and very angry."

"Angry is better than dead." She hesitated. "And Cole?"

"Locked up too. But I am not in trouble, they ssaid. Navy reward."

"I'm sure they'll give you a big reward. Now don't worry about this Navy stuff, okay?"

"Okay, Molly." He bent back over his game.

Molly wanted to go and talk to Cole, but she knew her voice wouldn't work, even to ask him to explain himself. The raw hurt and sense of betrayal she felt at that moment—the ability to be completely crushed by another human being—made her realize something. She had, indeed, been in love with Cole.

And now she hated him for it.

oooo

"You sure you don't want to fly us out of here? It *is* your ship."

Molly looked over from Cole's seat where she was nestled in the depression he'd made. She shook her head, her helmet twisting with the momentum.

"Okay," Jakobs said as the shimmer of light ahead of them vanished. *Parsona* lifted unevenly from the floor, one of her landing struts scraping loudly across the deck for a few meters, and then they punched through the boundary of the hangar and into space.

Dinks took the lead in the Firehawk while Jakobs followed. When both vessels were clear of the asteroid, they turned and started out to a safe hyperjump point.

Molly turned to Jakobs. "Are Cole and Edison going to be okay in the staterooms?"

He glanced over and then jerked his head back forward, concentrating on flying. "They'll be fine. I told Dinks to take it nice and easy out to the jump point. From there it'll be two short hops to the Orbital Station at Canopus."

"And then to Earth, right?"

Jakobs looked at her again, longer this time. "Eventually, yeah. But you do realize they're gonna court-martial Cole, right? The Navy should be able to put a panel together at Canopus in a few days. We'll probably be there a week or more. You'll have to testify, of course."

Testify? Against Cole? The thought had never occurred to her. And testify to what? Sabotaging their simulator, playing dead, and then kidnapping her? Or for saving her life several times since?

Jakobs kept turning to study her face through their open visors. She noticed *Parsona's* nose drift down and to the right whenever he did this. The fact that this clown had graduated early and been put on Special Assignments irked her.

"If he was a civilian, he might get life in prison," said Jakobs. "But he's Navy. Ship theft and going AWOL are capital crimes. Hell, even if the murders of the Navy men don't stick, he just purchased illegal arms. This is just the stuff we *know* about. There's no telling what will come to light once we get you and your crew on the stand."

Her crew. Walter. The nuke on Glemot. Molly felt sick to her stomach. And Jakobs wasn't through.

"They'll airlock him for this, Molly. I hope you realize how serious this is."

She spun on him. "*Airlock* him? *Kill* him? Those guys on Palan died in the *rains*. They were trying to kill *us*! The jail we broke out of? They were going to kill Cole that very day without a trial! And we bought guns because everywhere we go, the boys in black seem eager to do us harm. Your little *ambush* is what we've been running from."

Jakobs's face turned red. "Ambush? This is a *rescue* mission. The Navy said I could shoot Cole on sight if I needed to. It turns out your *hero* has a shady past, and now he has a service record to match. So stop *defending* the guy. *He's* the one that screwed you during the Tchung simulation and got you kicked out of school." Jakobs pointed to the scars on his face. "Look what he did to me!" He took a deep breath and looked ahead, correcting his course.

"You saw the video yourself," he went on. "And when the Navy Panel sees that and the evidence brought in from Palan, your *friend* is gonna get what's coming to him. Now get on the right side of the law before I consider cuffing you up in your stateroom."

Molly looked down at her palms, resting in her lap. "I need to use the bathroom before we jump," she said meekly.

What she really needed was to get away from Jakobs and that conversation. But also, a small part of her hoped that just being *nearer* to Cole would provide some answers. She had so many questions welling up. If she could be wrong about him, she didn't think her brain could ever again be trusted to draw a correct conclusion.

Walter hissed at her as she entered the cargo bay, trying once more to show her his video game. It had become a little contest between them: him eager to show off his work and her hunting for an excuse. Right now she didn't have the energy to play, so she leaned over and pretended to be interested in his computer.

Even in her funk, she had to admit: the game was impressive. She'd seen enough of them around the Academy to appreciate the graphics. Surely he hadn't programmed the whole thing. "You made this?" she asked.

"Yesss," Walter hissed, his voice dripping with pride.

"It's amazing," she told him. And it was. Running across the surface of a detailed planet, a space cadet waved blasters in both hands. There were all kinds of things to shoot and kill—typical boy stuff—but done realistically enough that even she might get into it. She handed it back to Walter, who beamed at her.

"Keep it up," she said, patting his head. Walter resumed control of the figure, destroying things for points, while Molly retreated to her stateroom. She closed the door and hoped that small ounce of attention would keep him satisfied all the way to Canopus. She didn't have enough energy to take care of herself, much less someone else.

She sat in the bathroom for a few minutes, pretending to use it, then got up and flushed the air chamber, capping the pointless ruse. After another pause, waiting for answers that should've been forming, she gave up and walked out of her room.

Instead of going to the cockpit, though, she snuck back to Cole's quarters. His door was locked—sealed with her Captain's codes. She could key it open and demand answers, but how would Jakobs and the Navy see that?

She took off her helmet and pressed her cheek to the door. The thrumming of the thrusters vibrated through the metal, singing along the length of the ship. Molly could hear her pulse racing through her ear.

She pulled herself away and went to Edison's door, pressing a hand to the cool metal. She wondered what the Navy would do with him. Especially when they found out he was one of the last of his kind. The pain of what happened on Glemot piled on top of her new miseries, crushing her. She didn't know what would come out in a trial, but it would be difficult to explain the things she didn't understand herself.

She headed toward the cockpit and noticed that Walter's door was open. She stepped inside, looking for any excuse to stay close to the two prisoners. Surveying herself in the mirror over Walter's dresser, she hardly recognized the person looking back. The girl's brown hair was too long—matted and unkempt. Her eyes appeared too old for the rest of her. Her mouth was sad. The poor thing's shoulders drooped like someone who had worked for years under a heavy burden.

Molly took a deep breath and tried to hold it in. Her eyes wandered to a few of the pictures Walter had taken and printed out with the ship's computer. They were tucked in the frame of the mirror, their edges curling.

One showed a group of Glemots working on *Parsona*. She didn't even know he'd snapped any photos back then. The lush greenness in the background didn't do the planet justice, but Molly reached up to brush her fingers across the image—the image of a land she'd helped destroy.

Another photo he had on display must have been pulled from one of the security feeds. It showed her patting Walter on the head. She didn't even remember when it had taken place, and before she could be upset at him for hacking into the ship's computers, she saw another picture behind it. Hidden. She pulled it out. It didn't make any sense. She stared at it, as if it eventually would.

The picture showed the simulator room at the Academy, taken from eye level. A few cadets milled about that she didn't recognize. Rows of simulator pods faced the familiar block wall.

Why in the galaxy would Walter have a picture of this? She turned the photo over and looked at the back. Nothing was written there, but it wasn't the photo paper the ship used. Where had he found this?

She put it back in its place and reminded herself to ask him about *both* pictures. The one he hacked from the computer upset her, almost as much as the hidden one confused. Molly put her helmet back on and stepped back into the cargo bay. Walter looked up at her, sneering. He was playing his game and obviously having the time of his life.

She thought about the video game.

And the picture of the simulators.

Her vision squeezed in from the edges until only the center was visible, like looking through a straw. She nearly fainted to the ground, staggered forward, steadied herself on one of the large crates, and then sank to her knees.

Molly looked up to the cockpit and spotted Jakobs's video player on the panel by his seat. Past Jakobs, and through the carboglass, she could see the Firehawk ahead of them. Dinks was slowly pulling away for the jump through hyperspace. Beyond that, glints of a fleet winked in the starlight, dashing about in a cluster. The ships of Darrin I were chasing down another customer.

Molly took all of it in—and none of it. Her brain raced and reeled, assembling pieces like a planet coalescing out of dust, all of them orbiting Walter's video game. How *realistic* it looked. The little cadet running around with his pistols—she recognized that figure. Knew his artificial gait from somewhere. She realized how easily that alien world could be substituted for a room full of simulator pods.

For a Navy *reward*, of course.

oooo

Jakobs turned to look back at her, his visor up. He must've been yelling at her to return to her chair so they could prep for the jump. Molly knew this, but she couldn't hear him—her head pounded with depression and rage. She pulled the lower half of her helmet closed, sealing it tight. If anything, the pounding just got louder.

She dug her gloves under one side of the crate, tossed the lid off, and peered down at the gleaming metal contraption inside.

Molly thought about them killing Cole. For what? For protecting her? And they would do it with bad information. *Dirty* information. It reminded her of that day in Saunders's office. Of being berated after having done everything right. And now an innocent man, a *good* man, was going to be killed by liars and cheats.

Over her dead body.

Over *all* of their dead bodies.

She sighted down the length of the crated laser cannon, eyeing Jakobs. He froze in the act of unbuckling his harness, his mouth and eyes wide open. Molly allowed herself to sink down—down into the well of dark thoughts rising up within her. Part of her, some sliver of sanity, yelled. It pleaded for a return to her senses. But it was a small girl—lost in a nightmare—unable to find her voice. The rest of Molly flared with anger. Betrayal after betrayal had finally worn her down. Eaten to her core. Her thin crust of hope had been ablated off by a galaxy of cruelness.

She peered into the crate. Her head roared. She ignored the consequences and hit the lever Edison had shown her.

Hit it and held it.

32

Dinks died never knowing he was in danger. One moment he was spooling up the hyperdrive, the next moment a bolt of laser bored a tunnel through his defenseless Firehawk. The vessel combined explosion and implosion in a confused cloud of debris with a hint of gore.

Molly, Jakobs, and Walter flew through the new hole in *Parsona's* carboglass. The vacuum outside sucked at them greedily, pulling out every ounce of pressurized air within. Molly didn't even try to catch herself on the edge of the windshield as she went past. She concentrated on reaching Jakobs ahead of her.

She collided with the boy's legs and held fast. They both glided ahead of *Parsona* through a slightly warmer patch of space: the cloud where Dink's Firehawk had been. Molly pulled herself up Jakobs's body, which felt rigid with shock. His visor had snapped shut with the loss of cabin pressure, but there was always a delay. Molly could see it in his eyes; they were bloodshot and full of fear. Blood trickled from his nose.

Molly considered saying something through the suit's radio, but decided he didn't merit the trouble. She fumbled for the latches on his helmet, her gloves thick and unwieldy. Even in his haze, Jakobs seemed to grasp her plan. He pawed at her arms, trying to wrestle them down. They struggled for a moment, twisting in space. Molly's fingers found the snaps, there was a satisfying click felt through her gloves, but silent in the vacuum.

The helmet shot off from the internal pressure of his suit, and Jakobs's face swelled immediately. The look of fear drained out of his face, replaced not with pain or anger, but incredulity. His eyes pleaded with her, begging to know how she'd uncovered the lie.

No part of her cared to satisfy him.

Molly heard the speaker in her helmet keyed as a radio made contact. The sound startled her at first, then a voice crackled through. There was no mistaking its owner.

"Sssorry." It sounded like the air leaking from Jakobs's suit, as if it could make itself audible.

Molly turned away from the lifeless body to look behind her. Walter floated alone between her and her damaged ship. She could see blood coming out of his nose and down his lips through the lower half of his helmet. She shoved off Jakobs's body as hard as she could, gliding toward the one that had betrayed her.

"Sssorry," he said again, as she reached to him, the force of her arrival sending them into a slow spin. She held him, their helmets almost touching. He mouthed an apology over and over again. Molly thought for a moment about groping for the latches on his helmet as well, but she stopped herself from considering it.

They were both dead, anyway. Their suits held mere hours of atmosphere. With no way to maneuver back to *Parsona*, Molly resigned herself to holding the Palan boy until one of them breathed their last. Perhaps, by then, she would understand why he'd done it. Could it have really been for a stupid reward? Was it Albert who conned him? She wanted to know, but uncovering a justification as petty as money would just make the betrayal worse.

And did it really matter?

Molly made a rough calculation of the volume of air in the staterooms, wondering how much longer her two friends would last. Would a slow asphyxiation here be better or worse than the airlocking the Navy had planned? She didn't know.

And she didn't notice the action taking place in the distance. A fight had broken out near Darrin I, and it headed their way.

Molly snapped out of the trance when a ship exploded just a few thousand kilometers away. The arms dealers from Darrin I closed in on another ship; only *this* time they were attacking it.

As the group neared, crossing the vacuum between the two planetary orbits, Molly finally recognized the ship being chased. *Lady Liberty*. The vessel ran and fought at the same time, taking out two pursers with a series of feints and attacks that roused the pilot within her.

At least she and Walter would go out with a good show. As they spun around, facing *Parsona* and then the fight, they both craned their necks to keep up with the action. One ship with incredible power fought a dozen others with matching defenses—and the solitary one was winning. The only imbalance in this fight lay in their unequal skills.

Several remaining Darrin I ships peeled away—whatever they sought was not worth dying for. Molly couldn't imagine what warranted such deadly fervor and then noticed the lead ship had vectored straight for her and *Parsona*. During her next lazy revolution, she scanned the space behind her, but nothing lay there save the rubble of Darrin II. Her brain, still hazy, wrestled with the coincidence. Molly remembered: she didn't believe in coincidences. The melee had something to do with *Parsona*. Albert was coming back for his gear. Or rushing to Frankie's defense. In Molly's state, the alternative never occurred to her, despite the fact that she and Edison had engineered it.

She turned her focus on Walter. There wasn't enough sunlight out here to blind them, so she hit the lever that raised the mirrored visor and took in his entire face.

He looked horrible, his metallic-looking skin webbed with red lines. Capillaries full of blood strained to the surface as crimson rivulets trickled from his ears and streaked around his silver cheeks. His nose dripped globules of blood that floated around his helmet in the absence of gravity. His eyes were red, like Jakobs's. The only difference was the way they locked onto hers. They wavered between pain and adoration.

"Sssorryy."

He didn't know, Molly realized. He had no clue how this betrayal would make her feel. He didn't understand the bond that existed between her and Cole. Maybe a Palan couldn't know. What would a world that washed itself clean each month teach you about building for the future? About creating anything that *lasts*? What if Molly had known she only had a few weeks with Cole? Would she be just as detached as

Walter? Caring about just herself and her own wants? She couldn't honestly say. She had bonded with Cole in the way that people planning a *forever* could: with an eye to spending the rest of eternity with each other. Something that Walter couldn't possibly envision.

Realizing this, Molly thought of something she needed to say to him while she still could. She keyed the mic switch inside her glove and answered his pleas.

"I forgive you," she said.

She whispered it again, holding his little body in her arms, their visors pressed together. "I forgive you, Walter."

His eyes squinted with pain. Physical, emotional, or both—it was impossible to tell. Walter parted his lips and hissed another "ssorry" as if the last of his life leaked through his teeth. Small spheres of blood and salty water collided in a chamber of dwindling air. They stuck to one another but did not mix, like the helmets pressed together beyond them.

○ ○ ○ ○

Lady Liberty approached, and Molly held Walter's body tight and waited for laser fire to consume them both. She didn't look up until the gleaming hull blocked out all else. The cargo ramp opened up—the ship slid sideways to swallow them!

Molly instinctively reached out a hand to clutch a zero-G hold as they skidded across the ship's decking. The cargo door hinged shut, and air and gravity were both pumped into the room. Molly lay on her back, unwilling to move. Ever again, if need be. A broken length of chain rattled as gravity snaked it back into a heap.

The cockpit door slid open, and a figure emerged. With silent steps, it crept up to Molly and Walter. She should've known. Should've recognized the maneuvers. Albert wasn't on this ship at all. His prisoner had returned the favor of a rescue.

Molly stirred and fiddled for the release catches on her helmet. Anlyn rushed to help her. The alien seemed to understand what she wanted and delicately reached for the clasps. The helmet came off with a pop.

Tears rushed from both sets of eyes. The young Drenard leaned over to hold her.

"Molly," she whispered, in a soft, clear voice. "I don't want to fly ever again." The poor creature's eyes were wide, unblinking, coated with tears. "Please don't make me fly, Molly. I don't ever want to fly again."

Molly was speechless and numb. She wrapped her bulky space suit around the fragile creature, swallowing her up and wishing she could pull her inside.

"I promise," she told Anlyn. "I promise you'll never have to fly again if you don't want to."

The Drenard sank into her chest, taking in deep breaths of freedom.

oooo

This time, when *Lady Liberty* and *Parsona* joined together, it was consensual. Walter had been cleaned up and locked in one of *Lady Liberty's* staterooms. He seemed to be more emotionally drained from his treachery than physically harmed from its consequences. Molly left him to suffer alone as she rushed to the airlock of her ship.

When she opened the inner door, the air in the lock puffed out toward the cockpit and then into open space. She breathed through her suit, back at the scene of her deadly outrage. The crate lid floated by, a sign that no gravity awaited her—the panel must've been destroyed in the blast.

She worked her way forward, toward the hole in *Parsona's* nose. There should still be air in the staterooms, but she needed to work fast. She pulled out an emergency patch kit from one of Walter's well-organized emergency bins and began inflating the flat disk. She adhered it in place, the two epoxies mixing and turning the pliable material into hardened steel. In the middle of the expansive carboglass windshield, there would be a massive disk of blue plasteel, but at least she could try to return atmosphere to the rest of the ship.

As she suspected, the gravity panels were shot. Luckily, the life-support systems rebooted to full operation. Molly pumped air back into the ship, enabling her to open the airlock between the two hulls.

She opened the outer door from inside the airlock, watching the air between the two crafts mix. Anlyn pushed away from the comfort of gravity to join her. One of her small, translucent hands worked into Molly's padded flight gloves. Together, they floated toward the staterooms, pulling along at the recessed holds in the floor.

Molly opened Edison's door first, and Anlyn helped her remove the restraints from the frightened and confused Glemot. He asked them a confusing stream of questions and fumbled in the odd state of atmosphere and weightlessness. Molly left Anlyn to try to soothe the bristling bear with her soft, angelic voice. Two aliens, polar opposites and each rarely seen by any other race, tried to comfort each other. They were already at the back of Molly's mind as she pushed off toward the room across the hall.

She punched in the code to unlock Cole's room. Tears of worry were already floating out of her eyes and through the weightless air. It seemed to take forever for the thing to hiss open. When it did, their eyes met, and Cole mouthed her name. She pushed off the jamb, rushing toward him and wrapping him in her arms, his own still tied behind his back.

"I'm so sorry, Cole. I'm so sorry." She held each side of his face with her hands and kissed his forehead. She apologized again and again through her tears and the wetness she left on his skin.

"It's okay," he told her. "It's okay." He tilted his head back to look up at her. "Gods, I'm glad you're all right. Stop apologizing, okay? I forgive you. You didn't do anything wrong."

"I'm doing *everything* wrong," she sputtered. "Everything I try to fix, I make it worse. It makes me not want to try anymore."

"Untie my hands, Molly."

"See?" she blubbered, wiping the tears off her face. "I can't even rescue you right." She tried to laugh, but it came out as sobs.

As soon as Cole's hands came free, he reached up and held her face, one hand cupping each cheek. Molly released her hold of the ship and she floated in space, held only by his embrace.

They looked at each other for what seemed an eternity. Cole's face had a blank serenity Molly had never seen before. The tension that lived eternally in his brow, either from worry or deep thought, had disappeared. His mouth exuded happiness without smiling. Molly thought he'd never looked so gorgeous, so desirable, and so much like what she always pictured was beneath his mirrored visor.

"You make everything *better*, Molly Fyde."

She started crying and tried to shake her head. In the absence of gravity, it just set the couple spinning.

"You do. You just don't see it. You're like that damn simulator, taking points from yourself whenever you do something brave. Look at how many times you've rescued me. On Palan. Here. You're the bravest, most incredible person I know."

Molly parted her lips to argue—and he kissed her. Pressed his lips to hers. They held each other like that for a moment. Molly felt her worry and pain drifting out, sliding through every tingling pore of her being.

Cole pulled back and flashed her a mesmerizing grin. "I'm sorry, were you about to say something?"

Molly glanced up. She had been on the verge of correcting him about something. What was it?

"Oh, yeah," she said. "Technically . . . I saved your ass *twice* on Palan."

Cole tried to laugh.

But Molly interrupted him.

Outside, two ships drifted. Locked together and sharing an atmosphere. They orbited each other around a common center, spinning in the absence of gravity.

PART 5
FINALS

"Cruelty is foiled by compassion."

~ *The Bern Seer* ~

33

The Navy Inspection shuttle broke away from another ship as a ring of crystallized atmosphere puffed from its airlock coupling. The vessel floated down the line of crafts awaiting clearance and locked up with the cargo ship directly ahead of them. Molly and Cole fidgeted in *Lady Liberty*'s cockpit while they waited their turn. In the distance, ships alternated between disappearing and reappearing in Canopus's L1, a major hub for hyperspace travel. An old Orbital Station loomed nearby with several large Navy frigates and two cruisers attached to its military wharf. Commercial and private yachts intermingled while the frame of a new Orbital Station took shape not far away.

After the ship ahead of them cleared, their forged documents would receive their first test.

"What's the plan if the IDs don't work?" Cole asked.

Molly focused on the Inspection shuttle ahead of them. "We'll find out soon enough," she said.

"You're too trusting."

Molly assumed he referred to Earnie, the Darrin I scoundrel they'd worked with to secure IDs for themselves and Albert's ship. "I'm sure he did his best work," she said. "I sure would've, what with a Glemot and a Drenard around."

Cole jerked his head to the cargo cam. "I meant *him*."

Molly looked at her own screen, which showed Walter bent over his video game. "We both agreed it was my call," she said.

"Yeah, I agreed it was your call, but I never agreed to *agree* with it. I'd airlock him right now, but it'd probably create paperwork with the inspectors."

"That's not funny."

"Yes, it is."

Molly giggled. "Okay, it's a tad humorous. But give me some time to prove you wrong. You didn't see him afterward, once he saw the consequences."

"Whatever. All I know is having him double-check Earnie's work on the documents is like trying to put out a fire with some plasma. I don't trust either of them."

"I don't either. But Earnie doesn't know that, so having Walter sweat him out served the same purpose."

"Forget it. We're up." Cole leaned forward to turn on the docking lights and unlock the outer hatch. Molly looked up and saw the Inspection shuttle maneuvering their way.

"I hope ours goes that fast," she said.

A thump vibrated through the hull, followed by the clicking of collar locks. Molly wondered what this experience would've been like if their trip to Palan had gone as planned. She probably would've been nervous with the inspection process, but with normal first-time jitters steadied by the surety of innocence. Instead, she had the pure unadulterated terror of guilt working up and down her spine. She followed Cole through the cargo bay, a sudden surge of adrenaline weakening her knees.

The inner door of the airlock hissed open, and stern Navy boots stomped out. Molly stopped by the workbench as Cole moved to greet the inspectors.

"Welcome aboard," he said, his voice much calmer than Molly felt. He shook hands with each of the two men as they popped off their helmets. Molly gathered them politely as if they were having guests for tea. She laid them on *Lady Liberty*'s workbench and hoped the tension she felt was a normal part of this process, something exuded by the guilty and innocent alike.

The two inspectors surveyed the cargo bay intently; one of them cleared his throat. The other man, brandishing a thick mustache, took the ship's registry from Cole. He held it in one hand and rubbed his whiskers with the other. The questions came without looking up, but his partner kept a keen eye on everyone's face as they responded. Now and then he cleared his throat, which made Molly want to unzip her skin and launch herself into space.

"Just three crew?" He injected as much doubt into his voice as possible, making the innocuous seem ludicrous. Earnie had warned Molly it would go like this, every question meant to make bad people lie over stupid stuff, trapping them in a corner they weren't prepared to fib their way out of.

Cole wasn't fazed. "Just?" he asked. "We left Earth with two and picked up a deck hand in New Caledonia. Hell, either of us could do this run by ourselves, but you know how insurance companies are these days."

The mustached man looked up and smiled knowingly. Molly wondered if anyone was immune to Cole's charm. Besides Walter, of course.

"What's in the cargo holds?"

Cole loaded his voice with disgust. "Not enough, that's what. Some computer parts, mostly. Our major trade was outbound. We're bringing back credits for the company and some software updates. Which means not much of a bonus for the crew."

Mustache used one of the documents to gesture toward Walter. "And you picked up the Palan on Farar?"

Walter looked up at this. Molly hoped he wouldn't hiss a sound.

"That's right," said Cole. "He was getting off another ship. It's all in there, the captain's name and whatnot. I never met the guy. I'm sure he ditched the kid for slacking, but we've been working him hard, no problems. Isn't that right, Rudy?"

Walter didn't move. He'd already forgotten his new name.

Cole turned to look at him. "Isn't that right?" he asked again.

Walter sat there for a second. Molly thought she could hear his brain whirling into motion.

"That'ss right," he finally said.

Cole looked back at the inspectors and pointed to one of his own ears. "A little hard of hearing. Probably spent a lot of time in loud engine rooms growing up. You know, degreasing anything the color of his mama's face."

The three humans laughed at the alien's expense. Molly tried her best to join in.

The two Navy men stared at the three young crew members, one after the other. Molly expected them to start poking around, do a full systems scan, check their retinas against the Navy computers. The galaxy had given her a three-week course in cruelty. She tensed for the next lesson.

"Well. Everything here seems to be in order. You enjoy your jump to Menkar. It'll be outbound lane three, and you'll probably have a half-hour wait." They each tipped a nonexistent hat toward Molly, who waved back in mock salute. She had to force her arm to do it lazily, years of habit threatening to give her away with a militarily precise snap of her wrist.

She gave them their helmets back, and the airlock shuffled the duo through with a sigh.

Cole turned to Molly. "Well, now. *That* was easy."

She gave him a stern look while unspent adrenaline worked its way through her body. She felt nauseous, on the verge of throwing up.

Walter had already gone back to his video game.

oooo

The jump out and into Menkar went just as easily. Molly's nervousness shifted to a dull realization: *this* was commercial space travel. In a trade of instantaneous movement from point A to point B, it was the inspections and the loading/unloading that ship crews got paid for. The long hours of moving by thruster remained a Navy-only affair as they searched for the unscrupulous jumpers who sneaked into busy systems. Legal trade coursed along known paths between peaceful worlds, shuttling goods and bodies back and forth along queues of ennui.

After a few weeks of nonstop excitement, Molly couldn't tell whether she'd enjoy that life or not.

She pulled forward in the outbound lane at Menkar. They'd passed another round of inspections; the next jump led to Earth's orbit. While they waited, she examined how differently this trip had gone compared to the one she'd expected. They should be flying back aboard the *Parsona*. With a chaperone. Instead, their chaperone was dead, and in his place they had an illegal alien who had nearly gotten them killed. The craft they would arrive in belonged to an arms dealer, while her father's ship, not even flight worthy at the moment, underwent extensive repairs by a sworn enemy and the last of a mysterious race.

Molly thought back to that conversation with Lucin under the pink blossoms of the cherry tree. Back then, she'd concocted a fairy tale out of this trip's potential. So far, it had all gone the opposite direction.

With uncanny timing, Cole reached over and rubbed her forearm as she brought *Lady Liberty* into Menkar's L1. The gravity sensors went to zero, the Orbital Station ahead cancelling out the mass of ships behind. She interlocked her fingers with Cole's and smiled at him. At least *one part* of her fantasy had come true.

Cole engaged the hyperdrive, and the sprinkle of stars disappeared, replaced with the familiar sight of Earth. Molly felt a pang of regret. Part of her wished she could finish school at Avalon and maybe find work with her father's old ship. She hadn't even ruled out the option of selling it and starting a terrestrial business. The dream of reconnecting with her parents had been another massive failure—all she'd found was danger and betrayal. Part of her wondered if digging into her past any further would be a bad idea, just piling up the disappointments.

Fortunately, these doubts composed a very small part of her. Too much else had changed for her to regress and pine for a lost childhood. She'd become a woman, somehow. She had responsibilities and others to think about—an entire crew of lost youth that relied on her, one of whom she was madly in love with.

Thrusting toward Earth, Molly felt an odd trepidation. Instead of feeling ecstatic to arrive home, she saw the ball of swirling blue and white as just another trap. A gravity well she could fall into and not be able to escape. She glanced at Cole and wondered what he thought about this mission of theirs, if the answers could possibly prove worth the risks. Or . . . would they have been wiser to run and just keep running?

oooo

They cleared into a private space pad in New Mexico, just a few hours from the Academy. Molly had one more talk with Walter, making it as clear as possible that he wasn't to touch anything while they were gone. *Anything.*

"Yesss," he said over and over. Molly told him to just keep playing that video game of his. Not to stop, even if he got thirsty.

Walter seemed to like this plan a lot. She closed the cockpit door and locked it, just in case.

Cole pounded up the boarding ladder and into the cargo bay. "I've got a rental waiting for us with a full charge. We should get going."

Molly agreed. They both changed into clothes that Earnie had procured for them. Molly wore plain canvas pants and a loose white top probably meant for boys. Cole had on similar pants, but baggy with large pockets, and a tight T-shirt. They both appeared to be wearing their siblings' clothes rather than their own.

Molly gathered her things. Her assignment on this mission couldn't be simpler or more rewarding: ask questions and demand answers. The only weapon she needed was the small recording device to transfer everything back to Cole.

Cole's job was to talk their way in. And, if things went sour, fight their way back out. Molly watched him dig something out of *Lady Liberty*'s smuggling compartment that she hoped would not be needed, even if his secondary task became their primary concern. She'd tried everything to talk him out of purchasing it, but Cole's paranoia made compromise impossible.

oooo

As they drove down the interstate, they went over the plan for the umpteenth time. Cole spent most of the time talking while Molly craned her neck at the scenery speeding past.

Her own planet looked alien.

Glemot green lined the steel highway, fading to dry earth that could use a Palan rain. An incredibly blue sky hung overhead. The sun and the air were crisp and strange after so much time spent inside one ship or another. Molly's fears about returning to Earth transformed into a dread of leaving. Her thoughts drifted to Edison and Anlyn and how impossibly far away they were. It required three hyperjumps just to get *back* to them. They weren't even in this arm of the Milky Way.

The distance made Molly sick. When they formed this plan at Earnie's, each event was as near as the next word uttered—as close as points on a paper chart. The unfathomable distance that would divide her crew couldn't be appreciated while they huddled together in *Parsona's* cargo bay.

Molly felt an enormous doubt envelop her, followed by a certainty: she would never see her friends again.

"Right?" Cole asked her.

"Yeah. Of course," she responded.

Cole glanced over from the driver's seat. "Were you even listening?"

She couldn't lie to him. "Actually, I was thinking about Edison and Anlyn. How we just left them at Earnie's and whether we'll ever see them again."

He didn't respond at first, just peered forward while the road slid under the rental. "We will. In a few days, max. We just need to find out if anyone outside of the Academy cares where we are. We'll never be free until we know."

"How'd we get like this? I mean, with you devising a plan that takes us to the Navy and me wishing we could just fly away?"

"I think we both went from curious to angry, and you and I react oppositely to each. Now stop dwelling on our friends; we'll see them soon enough." He looked at her. "I promise you."

She really wanted to believe him.

34

Getting into the Academy contained as many risks as jumping through to Earth. They had to rely on the guard at the gate not recognizing Cole as he filled out a visitor's pass. It wasn't as if they were ever passing through here while they were cadets, but they couldn't know how guards rotated out with the rest of campus security.

Cole used one of the underclassmen he knew as an excuse, pretending to be his older brother. The credentials they had purchased from Earnie had last names that matched, and Cole turned on his charm. After a few minutes with a clipboard, a new pass was programmed and their rental was waved through.

He handed Molly the visitor's pass, and she tucked it under her seat. It wouldn't open the one set of doors she needed to get into—but Cole's badge would. She checked that she had it in her front pocket and adjusted the recording device under her collar.

They circled the parking lot several times to find a suitable parking space. Cole backed the rental up so his window faced the Academy. They both peered at the wall that housed the administrative offices, and Cole's finger jabbed out as he counted the windows from right to left.

"That's Saunders's office," he said, pointing. "The one with the lights off."

Molly leaned forward to look through his window, but she didn't need to know which office belonged to the Captain. She just wanted him to be there when she came calling. "How long before the cadets are in the simulators?" she asked.

Cole already had the small heat scope up to one eye, scanning through the windows for signs of life. He pulled it away and looked down at his watch. "Another half hour. Hopefully Saunders is back by then."

"If not, I wouldn't mind talking to Lucin first. Once we clear him, we could probably use his help in confronting Saunders."

Cole turned and frowned at her. "You need to keep in mind how badly Lucin is gonna take this, even if he *is* innocent. Dropping out of Avalon and taking to the stars is not going to be a fun conversation to have with the old man. And if he isn't involved, he's gonna want the authorities so wrapped up in it that your fear of never seeing our friends will become a reality—"

"Okay. Gods, I get it. This isn't going to be easy no matter what we find out."

"Darn right it's not." Cole squinted back through the scope while Molly watched the clock. Once again, she appreciated the Navy's precision. Right then, for the brief respite it offered.

oooo

At 1430, Saunders's lights still had not come on. Molly looked to Cole for permission to move, and he nodded. They both got out of the car, Molly heading for a side entrance and Cole stepping back to the trunk. They both had serious military faces in contrast to their civilian disguises.

Molly strolled swiftly to the administrative entrance by the corner of the building. She felt exposed in front of all those windows, but anyone who might recognize her would soon get a personal visit, anyway. She felt better concealed as she sank into the pocket by the door, visible now only to the security gate across the lawn.

With the first pass of Cole's badge, Molly watched the red light blink off—and then back to red. Her heart skipped a beat. She waved it again, and it had the same effect. She looked around at the empty lawn and parking lot, sure that someone would be watching her and growing suspicious.

After the third pass, the light went green. A pleasant beep rang out, followed by a mechanical click as the internal lock released. Molly blew out her held breath and pressed the door open, entering air-conditioned halls with checkerboard floors that smelled of industrial cleansers. The familiarity of the scene rocked her. She approached Saunders's office, compelled to reach out and rub her fingers along the walls, greeting, if not a friend, at least an old acquaintance.

The Captain's lights had been off as she rounded the building, but her anger drove her there first. She hoped Cole was already in position as she banged on the thick oak.

Nothing.

She waited a few moments in frustration, her body eager to wash away its memories of their last confrontation. She couldn't wait to be the one performing the dressing-down.

The silent door denied her that satisfaction, and the worn bench mocked her. She gave up and walked down the hall toward Lucin, trying to push aside the adrenaline coursing through her from just being near Saunders's office. She worked to replace her anger with the hope of seeing an old friend.

She rapped her knuckles on the old wooden door as if her being here were the most normal thing in the galaxy. She heard the squeak of an old chair emanate from within, followed by the quick steps of Lucin's lithe gait. The doorknob started to twist, and Molly felt a surge of excitement rise as she prepared to surprise the Admiral. The door opened swiftly; she stepped forward to wrap Lucin up in a hug.

"Molly?"

One of his hands froze on the doorknob, but the other arm came up around her. Molly squeezed him tight while Lucin leaned back to see her face, obviously needing a second, confirming glance.

She obliged him by stepping back, smiling.

"Molly!" he repeated. Lucin poked his head out the door and looked up and down the hallway, and then pulled her inside and shut it.

"I thought you were dead!" he exclaimed.

She tried to point out otherwise, but he continued talking.

"When you never jumped back, we tried not to assume the worst, a hyperdrive malfunction or something, but—oh, my goodness! I'm so glad you're alive." He clasped both of her shoulders with his hands, studying her. "I've been blaming myself. I thought I sent you . . . I thought I got you killed."

He turned and glanced out the window, walked over and peered through the slits of the blinds. "How's the ship?" It was as if he'd expected to see *Parsona* in the parking lot.

"It's safe," Molly said. "And I'm sorry to worry you. We've had nothing but problems since we landed on Palan."

Lucin turned and half-sat on the far edge of his desk. He gestured to the chair by Molly, and she gladly plopped down. "Safe?" he asked. "But where is it?" His forehead bunched up with worry.

Molly ignored the question; she had too many of her own to consider. "Where's Captain Saunders?"

Lucin cocked his head. "Why do you ask?"

"We think he's been trying to get us killed." She leaned forward, her elbows on her knees, and lowered her voice to a whisper. "Simmons was killed on Palan. The Navy there didn't have us in their system. There were problems with the pirates—"

Lucin waved her off. His look of relief had become impatient agitation. "I'm well aware of what happened on Palan. There's still an investigation open, and a lot of questions. But I can assure you that Saunders had nothing to do with it. Now where is that ship? We really can't let it fall into the wrong hands—"

"Wrong hands? I'm talking about people trying to kill me and Cole. Someone sabotaged our simulator, and two cadets—" Molly stopped. "Wait. What's so important about *Parsona*?"

Lucin blew out his breath, looked up at the ceiling for a moment, and locked eyes with Molly. "What I'm about to tell you cannot leave this office. Ever. Do you understand?"

The hairs on the back of Molly's neck stood at attention. She nodded.

Lucin swiveled to look out the window, as if at a distant memory. "Your father did not retire from the Navy to settle on Lok. He and your mother were both in Naval Special Assignments." He turned, his face full of sadness. "They weren't supposed to have you. I think some people in the Navy still blame your birth for what happened on that planet. Not that *I* do, of course. But some."

Molly hadn't prepared herself for this. These weren't the answers she'd expected. She could feel her brain throbbing against her skull, forgetting why she was even there, or what had happened over the last several weeks. "What are you saying—that they didn't *want* me?" Molly pressed one hand flat to her chest. "That I was some kind of *accident*?"

Lucin shook his head. "Gods, no. Not at all. They had you *in spite* of Navy orders. Your parents were on a very important mission, they knew they had some pull. But your father couldn't know what would happen . . . years later." Lucin's voice trailed off and he looked down at his desk. "But I . . . I can't get into that. What matters is that the results from their mission were thought to have been abandoned forever. Later, we realized your father had only brought you to Earth so he could set out to *complete* the mission. When Special Assignments figured this out, it restored some hope in their offices."

Lucin looked up from his desk. "That hope disappeared with him and the ship. When *Parsona* was discovered, it was thought that a botched mission could be salvaged."

It took a moment for any of this to settle into Molly's brain. Then a dozen questions flinched up within her. "If it was so important, why send ME?" As soon as she said this, she realized: Lucin had come to Avalon *knowing* she'd want to go. That she would volunteer. He must've already had Cole lined up to assist, and Simmons in place on Palan.

"Yes, I used you to go get the ship back," he said, as if he could read her face. "I'm sorry. There was no other way. Very few people in the Navy know what your father was up to, or that he was even *in* the Navy anymore. It was supposed to be a simple mission. From what I can tell, the Palan Naval Offices had a radio out and problems with their computers. I've seen the video of you and Cole in the office, and it was just a misunderstanding. You guys raised their suspicions, they reacted, you reacted to that, and next thing you know, Cole is zapping a Navy officer—"

"That man was trying to *kill* us. They were firing guns and trying to run us down in the streets."

Lucin wiped his brow, looking up at the ceiling. "Was this before or after you guys ran and stunned one of them?"

Molly shook her head. There was no way that could've been a misunderstanding. "They killed Simmons," she reminded Lucin.

"*Who* killed Simmons?"

She couldn't say. She left that line of questioning and pounced on a known lie. "Why were Jakobs and Dinks trying to frame Cole for messing with the simulator?" she asked.

Lucin's eyes grew wide with this sudden change in topics. He looked confused or shocked. "Jakobs and Dinks found you guys? Where are they? And Molly, please stop for a second and tell me where *Parsona* is."

"Jakobs and Dinks were waiting for us in the Darrin system. They tried to convince me that Cole was a bad guy, working for Saunders. They said they were working for you, but we uncovered a mess of lies. Who sent them there, Lucin?"

He didn't answer at first. Instead he got off the desk and sank to his chair. He opened one of his drawers and looked inside, confirming something.

"I sent them," he admitted. "I told them to get you guys to Canopus and send me a message, whatever it took. Now, where are they? And where's that damned ship?"

"Is the ship the only thing you care about?"

"Of course not. But what's on it could be very important. Something that could change this galaxy. A promise of—"

"There's nothing like that on *Parsona*. We've taken her apart and put her back together again. Literally. It's just a ship. Now tell me what in hyperspace is going on, and I'll tell you where she is."

This made Lucin look around suspiciously, as if an invisible person had joined them in the room. "Where's Cole?" he asked.

"He's with the ship, in another system a few jumps from here. I came back on a passenger liner with a fake ID. Now can we please stop exchanging questions? I don't have much more time here, and I need to know if we're safe or if we need to keep running."

"Keep running? What—?"

"I'm not here to stay, Lucin. There's nothing for me here. I'm going back to the *Parsona* so I can help a few friends out."

He shook his head. "No. You are *not*. That ship is coming *here,* and we're going to figure out what your father found. I don't know what's gotten into you or who you think you are, young lady, but you're dealing with forces you do not understand." He glanced back in the drawer, but both hands moved to interlock on his desk, as if they needed to restrain each other.

Molly felt Cole speaking through her, his doubts and paranoia eroding her defenses. "Have you been trying to get me killed?" she asked.

Tears immediately welled up in his eyes. "Never, Molly. *Never*. I told Jakobs that the *Parsona* and you were to be protected at all—"

"In that order?"

Lucin let out his breath. "You cannot possibly conceive the importance of your father's work. We need to determine how far along his mission got and what we need to do to continue it. What he found could *end* the war with the Drenards, Molly. End the potential for *all* future wars in our galaxy . . . in the universe!"

Molly glanced at the clock on the wall. "I have to leave in fifteen minutes, max. So answer my questions before I get out of here. I want to know who sabotaged our simulator before the Tchung mission. I want to know why this ship is so important. And I want to know where Saunders is so I can demand whatever answers you don't have."

Lucin's head sank; he looked defeated. It may have been the last mention of Saunders, but Molly couldn't be sure. He reached into the desk drawer and drew out the gun she'd already assumed was there.

She didn't flinch or try to cover herself. She had already played out this scene in her head a dozen times. Only it was always Saunders with the gun.

"Please don't move," he said. "I really don't want to hurt you, you have to believe me. But if Cole kicks that door down while I tell you this next part, I *will* kill him. I'll shoot him as calmly as I would if he were a Drenard."

Silence fell over them; the clock on the wall sounded out a few ticks. Molly absorbed this promise while Lucin seemed to steel himself for another admission.

"*I'm* the person who sabotaged your simulator, Molly. *I* set you up to get expelled."

Her brain recoiled from the thought, unable to accept it. Not even with the gun backing up his claim.

"Your father's ship was discovered months earlier. *Before* the Tchung battle. I tried everything to get it back myself, but without involving the rest of the Navy, it proved impossible. I even pulled Simmons, a former student of mine, out of Special Assignments and had him attached to me, personally. When he proved ineffectual, unable to secure the ship on Palan himself, I started trying to figure out who had the requisite skills, who I could trust with this secret. Nobody in the service fit.

"Then, one day, Saunders was complaining about having a girl at the Academy for the hundredth time—and it hit me. You. You were the best pilot I knew, you were unhappy here, and you were the legal owner of the ship. I just had to get you expelled so you could claim ownership as a civilian. Once you were in the Navy, you would've started a mandatory five-year tour before you had the freedom to go to Palan. I couldn't wait that long."

"You—?" Molly still couldn't grasp it. Cole had tried to prepare her, but she wouldn't allow it. She stared at the gun in disbelief.

"Yes. I set you up so Saunders would expel you. Hell, I tried a dozen other things before that. It was almost impossible to get him to pull the trigger." Lucin nodded at the gun. "Pardon the expression.

"You know, as hard as he was on you, I actually think the fat fool wanted you to succeed here. Me? I would've been crushed to see you in a career as a navigator. I was doing you a *favor*, Molly."

"That's a *LIE!*" She leaned forward, her voice shrill. The gun stiffened in Lucin's hand, and Molly fought to control herself. She still needed to know what was so important about *Parsona*. Everything else she could piece together, given time. The best news was that Lucin had acted alone. If Cole could hear the transmission clearly, she imagined he was breathing a huge sigh of relief. All she could personally feel was the crushing sensation of being betrayed by a good friend. For the third time? Or fourth? Was friendship a bond or some sort of *tool*?

"That's a lie," she said again, sadly.

Lucin wiped the water out of his eyes with his free hand. "It's the truth. You would've been better off graduating from Avalon. If the damn rains on Palan hadn't screwed things up, you would've brought *Parsona* back here weeks ago, I'd have picked up the trail your father left, and you would've graduated and claimed your inheritance. Things would've even sorted themselves out if Jakobs had done his damn job. But maybe this is all my fault for trying to get what I needed while keeping you safe at the same time. Maybe I've been wrong to put your welfare ahead of my quest to end this war." He narrowed his eyes. "Maybe it's time to get serious."

Molly watched the knuckles poking out from the gun whiten.

"I'll ask you one more time," Lucin said. "If you do not answer me, I'm going to put a bullet in your chest. I will *not* hesitate. And I *will* find that ship by other means if I have to. So. Final chance. Where is the *Parsona*?"

His hand came off the desk, extending the gun toward her chest. Molly felt real fear creep up in her throat. She started to speak into the recording device when someone knocked on the door.

Lucin's eyes swiveled toward the sound, but the pistol stayed put. "I'm counting to three, and then I'll be putting a bullet into you before I put one through the door and your boyfriend out there."

"Lucin, don't do this—"

"ONE!"

The doorknob was just a meter from Molly. It started twisting, rattling in protest of being locked.

"TWO!" Lucin lowered the gun and aimed it at Molly's knees.

"PLEASE, LUCIN—!"

The banging on the door became insistent. The small office reverberated with too much noise.

"THREE!" Lucin's arm started to flinch in anticipation of the first shot.

"*DON'T SHOOT!*" Molly yelled, but not at Lucin.

The banging on the door grew furious. The old oak slab rattled in its hinges.

Shots were fired. Lucin and Molly couldn't hear them, just the crinkle of glass they made, like three coins dropped into a pile of change. Lucin's face twisted up as if he smelled something familiar—wondering what it reminded him of. He collapsed across his old desk, his arm locked straight, the gun still pointing at Molly.

Three spider webs in the office window let in tight pools of bright light. Molly bolted out of her chair and pressed both hands across the three corresponding holes in Lucin's back. But nothing was going to stop them from leaking out puddles of life.

Molly wanted to scream at Cole, tell him how stupid he was, that Lucin would never have shot her—but she needed to convince herself first.

The banging at the door became mixed with worried shouts.

Molly felt like cradling her old friend, her adoptive father, but she could imagine Cole's voice telling her he had been right and she had been wrong—and they both needed to get the hell out of there.

Molly grabbed Lucin's gun. It felt nice to have it pointing it away from her. She turned to the door, worried about the fact that someone wanted in as badly as she wanted out. With no time for pleasantries, she turned the knob and stood back, allowing the pounding to do the rest.

When her eyes locked with Saunders's, she found her own confusion mirrored on his face. Molly still had not yet sorted this man's innocence. Years of anger welled up within her. And he stood in her way.

She saw him glance at Lucin's body. Before he could turn back, Molly took one step forward and brought her other leg up after. Her knee was a ball of bone, swinging up between Saunders's Navy blacks. The blow landed with a dull thud. Molly had to stop the forward momentum of her attack by placing one hand to the fat man's chest. It became a guide, helping the poor seaman splash down to the blue carpet at his feet.

She didn't say a word to him, just vaulted over his curling body and rushed down the hallway. If the Navy hadn't been looking for them before, they would now. But at least she'd know *why* and what they were up against.

She ran down the checkerboard tile, the smell of industrial cleaning agent stinging her nostrils. For the second time in the past six months, she found herself fleeing the Academy with an unknown future ahead. And once again, she left behind two men with tears of agony on their faces.

This time, Molly Fyde had none.

EPILOGUE
THE PARSONA RESCUE

"If it's worth finding, don't ever stop looking."

~ *The Bern Seer* ~

A buzzing erupted by Molly's head. The unique blend of tone, frequency, and duration created a magical brand of annoyance unimproved in almost half a millennia. Molly swatted at the alarm, groaned, and pulled the sheets up against the chill. The muscles in her back writhed in agony from three days of crawling through *Parsona*'s holds and bilges looking for the supposed salvation of mankind. The longer she searched, the more she suspected Lucin had lied to her a final time, or perhaps he'd just been wrong. Either possibility made his death more tragic and pointless.

It had been a week, and the tension between her and Cole over Lucin's death had grown worse. She'd been incredibly hard on him, perhaps insisting too much that Lucin would never have shot her, but Cole remained just as stubborn. He insisted that he'd saved her life, and he refused to apologize.

This unwillingness to bend, to apologize, hurt like a fourth bullet. The first three, nicely grouped, had already done enough damage by killing an Admiral, a rare friend, and severing a thread leading back to her past. Now, just when she needed Cole the most, she found herself pushing him away.

The clock ticked. Another minute slid by. A minute she should've used to get up and don her flightsuit. She rolled on her side and faced the door, wondering which section of the ship to search next. She needed to know what her father had been up to. She needed to uncover *Parsona's* mystery. Her conversation with Lucin stirred old fantasies, bringing them to the surface. Every cadet dreamed of ending the war with the Drenards. She'd eventually outgrown that delusion, but now it loomed again, tantalizingly real and completely unfathomable. *What in the galaxy could a stupid ship contain to end an entire war?*

Another minute flicked by on the clock.

Molly imagined the Navy was just as thrilled with Lucin's death as she. Until they found a news outlet, she assumed the reports went something like: *Disgruntled Female Cadet Returns and Shoots Admiral, Attacks Captain.*

School Records Show Unwillingness to Follow Orders and Inaptitude for Flight.

Unbelievably, even Walter seemed upset with her. As she and Edison rummaged through the ship yanking off wall panels, he followed along, hissing obscenities and attempting to reorganize. He kept asking Molly what she hoped to find and sniffed, annoyed at her lies.

He'd become surly with the only crew member willing to forgive his treachery! Cole wanted to drop Walter off on the next moon they passed. Edison's calculations came up with a similar recommendation. Even gentle Anlyn couldn't stand to be around him.

So many problems . . . Molly's clock ticked up to 5:56, as if counting them.

She felt like staying in bed for another shift and flopped over to the other side, pressing her face close to her small porthole. She sighed, frosting the glass. Through the moisture, something large and bright glimmered. She wiped her breath away with a corner of her bedsheet and marveled at the sight beyond.

A black hole. She couldn't see it, of course, but she could see the star orbiting it—could see its effects. A single plume of plasma streaked out of the yellow orb and spiraled around the pinprick of dense mass. As they orbited each other, a curve of flame millions of kilometers across formed. It reminded Molly of a pinwheel firecracker at a Lokian fair.

Parsona hovered directly over the center of the spiral, lying over on her port side. It provided Molly with the best view possible of one of nature's largest and most spectacular wonders. She forgot her worries for a moment and snuggled up in a contented ball to enjoy the sight.

It took her morning brain a few minutes to work it out: that such an amazing vista lining up on *her* porthole could not be a coincidence.

Cole.

Wow.

A romantic gesture or an apology for Lucin, it didn't matter. She appreciated it. Growing up in the military, Molly never dreamed of a healthy relationship with a caring man. Ending a major war seemed more likely. And yet, someone had just laid a flower the size of a small solar system on her pillow.

Molly wept. After mourning Lucin—after suffering a month of wild emotional swings—she had resolved to go a week without crying. She decided these didn't count; they were good tears. And through her blurred vision, the spectacle outside looked even more surreal.

The clock ticked up a minute, and the alarm went off. Molly slapped the snooze button and decided she could take another ten minutes to wallow in how good this felt.

Something told her Cole wouldn't mind.

○ ○ ○ ○

Molly woke up to her alarm once more, newly energized. *Today* would be the day that she uncovered *Parsona's* secret. She'd said the same thing the last two mornings, but this time she *felt* it. She wiggled into her flightsuit and keyed open her door.

She wanted to head straight for the cockpit to kiss her navigator and thank him for the gift, but the low rumble of a snoring Glemot caught her attention. Molly snuck aft to check in on Edison and Anlyn.

With almost a week together repairing *Parsona*, a fascinating bond had formed between the two. Anlyn had become smitten with Edison; she absolutely refused to sleep alone or in the dark. It was difficult to know what Edison thought of this; the rational and obtuse way he talked about Anlyn seemed anything but romantic. As far as Molly could tell, the two were having a positive effect on each other, so she gladly gave them some space.

Peeking into their room, she could see Edison's head propped up on the wall behind his bunk, his knees poking up in the air, the space much too short for him. He snored contentedly through his open mouth while Anlyn, curled up on his chest, seemed tiny and serene by comparison. Both of her arms draped over one of the Edison's massive paws. It made Molly's heart hurt to take in the scene. She could understand why Anlyn hardly left his side; his embrace looked like the safest place in the universe.

Padding away quietly, Molly walked through her dark and sleeping ship. She passed Walter's room, the door closed. She hoped he was asleep and not up to anything they would all regret later. Keeping him out of the computer systems had proved difficult; Molly constantly reminded him that very little trust had been restored with the rest of the crew—and that would soon include her. Walter, however, visualized his penance as something to barter over rather than pay wordlessly.

Molly stole through the cargo bay and noticed that Edison had yet another project strewn across the workbench. Seeing the things he came up with made her long for the resurrection of Glemot. Other things he built, however, demonstrated the reality of Campton's fears: a race so dangerously powerful could only be kept in check by others of equal strength and cunning. The tragedy of their planet haunted her, and it probably would forever. It remained one of the few hurts that Cole couldn't soothe away.

He possessed a talent for that, she'd realized. His soft voice and engaging face were *good* things. They weren't a mask with which to fool people, nor were they a tool he used to adjust others. It was just who he was—his wonderful self—and she didn't need the nose of a Palan to sense it.

Cole turned and smiled at her as she entered the cockpit. "Morning," he said, trying to act as normal as possible. As if a flower made of plasma didn't linger off to port.

Molly grinned. And then it occurred to her that she could kiss him *right now* if she wanted. He wouldn't stop her. He'd *welcome* it.

The sensation had been with her for a week, but she still hadn't got used to it. She hoped it would take millions of kisses to remove that thrilling awareness.

"What're you smiling—?" Cole started to ask. Molly bent down and kissed him on the lips.

Just because she could.

"Thanks for the flower," she said, squeezing into her seat.

"You're welcome." He paused. "It's our anniversary today."

"What anniversary?" Molly asked. "Our *one week*?"

"Our one *month*, knucklehead." He gave her a stern look. "You and I have been together since the first day we faked it."

Molly's laughter filled the cockpit and drifted out through her sleeping ship. The release felt wonderful. "Wow," she said. "I can't believe it's only been a month."

"Yeah, we've been busy little beavers. Speaking of which, Edison got the last of the mods done before he hit the sack. That one crate back there is just full of scraps, so we can jet it into a star the next time we get close to one."

"Excellent."

"Oh, and as your navigator, I'd like to point out that we're down to twenty-four percent on fusion fuel."

"It'll be enough, right?"

"According to Anlyn."

"Then it will be."

"Well, I'm glad *you* have complete faith in the offspring of mankind's enemy, 'cause I'm not there yet."

"Walter can smell a lie. He says we can trust her."

"And you trust *Walter*?" Cole shot back.

After a moment he followed up with another source of contention. "You know, we could get more rest and shave some time off the trip if she'd take a shift or two. No flying, of course, just sit and watch the instruments while the hyperdrive cycles."

She turned to Cole, dead serious. "She does not set foot in a cockpit until she chooses to, okay?"

"Okay, okay. I'm just worried we aren't getting enough sleep. Between thrusting along looking for good jump points, respooling the hyperdrive, and tearing the ship apart . . . I just think everyone needs to be helping out. Spread the load."

"I know, Cole." Molly rubbed her hands up her face and through her hair. "I'm sorry to snap. I just have some of Edison in me, I guess. Something makes me want to wrap that poor girl up and keep her safe."

"She certainly elicits that reaction."

"Please try to trust her. For me."

"I trust *you*," he said, turning to gaze through the porthole on his side.

She smiled at that and looked back to the pinwheel of fire.

"It is beautiful out here." After a pause, she added, "With you."

Their hands found each other without having to look, a dominant hand healing from its wounds and a clumsy one groping and trembling to do its best.

They intertwined. Indistinguishable.

"I'm sorry," Cole said.

○ ○ ○ ○

They sat like that for a long while, allowing everyone, the ship included, to enjoy the rare state of rest. Cole broke the spell, leaning forward to the nav computer and the work that had been keeping him occupied for the last two days.

"Why don't you go take a nap?" Molly asked. "It's my shift."

"I can't sleep right now."

"Why? What're you working on?"

"I'm still trying to integrate these four different star charts. The three new ones differ in places, and our old copy is the absolute pits."

"What makes you say that?"

"Uh, you mean besides flying into Darrin the way we did?"

"They're just *old*, Cole. And they are my parent's charts, so you need to talk nice to them." She pouted, which drew a chuckle. "Besides, I just wanted them for the nostalgia; you shouldn't be using them for navigational purposes."

"I know, but look at this." He pulled up an area around Menkar. "You see these stars here?"

Molly nodded and Cole continued, "This is from your parents' charts, the ones that've been getting us in trouble."

Molly shot him a look.

"Watch," he said.

He clicked away at the keyboard as Molly turned back to her screen. The stars disappeared. "Hey, don't delete them."

"I didn't. All I did was pull up the GN charts we bought from Albert." He tapped his screen. "*These* stars aren't in his charts at all. Any of them. I wouldn't have noticed the difference, but this is the chart that leads back to Earth. I know it by heart, even at a glance."

"What do you think it means?" Molly studied the chart on her own screen. "Could it be really old data? Could all three have gone nova since this chart was created?"

"Statistically unlikely, as Edison would say. And lemme zoom in, the stars have really weird names. Listen to this: *Horton Hears a Who*, *The Cat in the Hat*, *Green Eggs and Ham*. I know astrologers are a loopy crowd, but c'mon, have you ever heard star names that bizarre?"

Molly's jaw dropped. She stared at the nav screen. "Actually, I *have*."

"Yeah. Right."

"I'm serious. Those are books my parents used to read to me, back before we left Lok and came to Earth."

"Your parents read you books about these three stars?"

"No, genius, these stars must've been named after the books. In fact, I doubt the stars are *real*." She looked back at the screen. "My parents must've inserted them on purpose."

"Well that might explain the weirdest part. Watch this."

Cole clicked on the triple star system and tried to open them up for inspection. Normally this would zoom in to another level of detail with orbiting planets, survey data, and cultural history. A standard text input box popped up instead:

NAME (FIRST/LAST):_

Molly backed her hands away from the computer. She'd never seen a dialog box on a star chart.

"I just found this a few hours ago," Cole said. "I tried your name and each of your parents' names. I was hopin' to crack it before Walter got a chance and did it in, like, two seconds."

"Did you put in Mortimor or Mortimus for my father's name?"

"Both. I *do* pay attention to your stories, you know."

Molly leaned forward and gave it a shot.

NAME (FIRST/LAST):WADE/LUCIN_

She hit enter, but nothing happened. Molly racked her brain, unable to think of anyone else this might've been meant for. Then it occurred to her. A name she'd long forgotten. "I know what it is," she told Cole.

NAME (FIRST/LAST):DR/SEUSS_

She pressed the enter key. Again, nothing happened. She tried spelling out "Doctor" with the same result. She searched her memory but couldn't remember the author's first name, if he even had one.

"And you tried my name?" she asked.

"Yup."

"Have you tried the names both ways?"

"Nope. It clearly says first then last. I tried with and without the slash, though."

Molly nodded, then froze. Her own question had jarred loose an old fact: the Lokian spelling of her name, the one she'd been given at birth, changed later to conceal her planet of origin. This was her *parents'* ship. If they put this in here for her to find, they would've used a spelling only the three of them knew.

Molly felt a tingle of excitement shiver through her. *This* was the secret she'd been hunting for, it had to be. And no wonder she couldn't find it! The secret was just a bunch of 1's and 0's locked away in a computer.

She felt dizzy as she typed in the answer. In mere moments she would receive a message from her father. Something that would help the Navy end the Drenard War. Maybe enough to go to the Navy, explain Lucin's death, and stop running. All this and more flashed through her head as she finished typing the answer:

NAME (FIRST/LAST):MOLLIE/FYDE_

She hit the enter key and waited for something to happen.

The nav screen went blank. The star charts disappeared. In their place sat a green phosphorous cursor. Flashing. Letters spilled forth, one at a time, as if someone were typing them.

MOLLIE?_

She glanced at Cole, expecting to find his fingers at the keys. He stared back at her, his brows coming together. "Someone must be connected to us through a nearby relay station," he said, but not with conviction. "Or Walter is playing with us." He unplugged his flightsuit and cast off his harness.

Molly put a hand on his chest, holding him in place. She typed a response.

THIS IS MOLLIE_

She hesitated to press the enter key this time. None of this made sense; the secret had to be something else. She hit the button.

MOLLIE. THIS IS PARSONA. YOUR MOTHER_

The words flowed out from left to right in a steady stream. The impossible nature of them punched her in the gut. The screen went a little out of focus.

"I'm going to kill him," Cole said, pushing up from his chair.

Molly turned to him, trying to convince herself by convincing him. "Cole, there's only two people besides me that spelled my name that way. And both of them are dead. Do you think—?"

"Not even Lucin?"

"No, my parents would've taken that to the grave. And who would even care to know? It was just to avoid the xenophobia wild in those days."

"Maybe—" Cole began, but the computer interrupted.

WHERE WERE YOU BORN, MOLLIE?_

Both of them looked at each other again. "Shouldn't she know?" Cole asked.

Molly wasn't listening. She was inputting the answer.

LOK_

As soon as she hit the enter key, the next question coursed across the screen.

SPECIFICALLY_

She typed, absorbed in the conversation as if it were real.

IN THE COMMONS OF A SMALL VILLAGE_

A few heartbeats elapsed . . . then:

WHAT WAS THE NAME OF THE VILLAGE?_

"Molly? What's going on?"

"I don't know. Hold on a sec."

IT DIDN'T HAVE A NAME_

Their screen went blank. Then:

MOLLIE_

The typing paused for a second, the curser flashing as if it needed to think. Then it continued:

I NEED TO ASK YOU FOR A FAVOR. A LARGE ONE. IT WILL REQUIRE A LOT OF TRUST. THERE WILL BE MANY DANGERS INVOLVED_

Molly reached over and gripped Cole's hand in hers. She squeezed it and pecked at the keyboard with one finger, blinking away the hope that this may actually, somehow, be her mother she was conversing with.

ANYTHING_ she typed.

She pressed the enter key once more. And when the response came—Molly sobbed once and then caught her breath. She read the message over and over again, her right hand crushing Cole's.

The words stood there in green phosphor. Impossible and promising:

I NEED YOU TO HELP ME RESCUE YOUR FATHER_

Printed in Great Britain
by Amazon.co.uk, Ltd.,
Marston Gate.